OVERWHELMING FORCE

OVERWHELMING FORCE

THE BAD COMPANY™ BOOK SEVEN

CRAIG MARTELLE

MICHAEL ANDERLE

DISRUPTIVE IMAGINATION

THE OVERWHELMING FORCE TEAM

Thanks to our Beta Readers

Micky Cocker, Dr. Jim Caplan, Kelly O'Donnell, and John Ashmore, Maria Stanley, Leo Roars

Thanks to the JIT Readers
Kerry Mortimer
Rachel Beckford
Micky Cocker
Dorothy Lloyd
Dave Hicks
Misty Roa
John Ashmore
Daniel Weigert
Diane L. Smith
Peter Manis
Jackey Hankard-Brodie
Jeff Goode
Veronica Stephan-Miller

If I've missed anyone, please let me know!

Editor
Lynne Stiegler

LMBPN Publishing
PMB 196, 2540 South Maryland Pkwy
Las Vegas, NV 89109

First US edition, June 2020
ebook ISBN: 978-1-64202-970-3
Print ISBN: 978-1-64202-971-0

We can't write without those who support us
On the home front, we thank you for being there for us

We wouldn't be able to do this for a living if it weren't for our readers
We thank you for reading our books

CHARACTERS & TIMELINE

World's Worst Day Ever (WWDE)

WWDE + 20 years, Terry Henry returns from self-imposed exile. *The Terry Henry Walton Chronicles* detail his adventures from that time to WWDE+150

WWDE + 150 years—Michael returns to Earth. BA returns to Earth. TH & Char go to space

Key Players

• Terry Henry Walton (was forty-five on the WWDE)—called TH by his friends. Enhanced with nanocytes by Bethany Anne (Queen of High Tortuga after Federation is formed and the Empire is dissolved), wears the rank of colonel, lead the Force de Guerre (FDG), a military unit he established on WWDE+20 years, and now leads the Bad Company's Direct Action Branch.

• Charumati (was sixty-five on the WWDE)—A were-wolf, married to Terry, carries the rank of major but is his equal partner

• Kimber (born WWDE+15 years, adopted approximately WWDE+25 years by TH & Char, enhanced on WWDE+65 years)—a major

• Her husband Auburn Weathers (enhanced on WWDE+82 years)—provides logistics support

• Kaeden (born WWDE+16 years, adopted approximately WWDE+24 years by TH & Char, enhanced on WWDE+65 years)—a major

• His wife Marcie Spires (born on WWDE+22 years, naturally enhanced)—a colonel

• Cory (born WWDE+25 years, naturally enhanced, gifted with the power to heal)

• Her husband Ramses—a major, died on Benitus Seven, WWDE+153 years

• Kailin, Auburn's and Kimber's son (born on WWDE+78 years)

Vampires
• Joseph (born three hundred years before WWDE)
• Petricia (born WWDE+30 years)

Pricolici (Werewolves that walk upright)
• Nathan Lowell (President of the Bad Company and Bethany Anne's Chief of Intelligence)
• Ecaterina (Nathan's spouse)
• Christina (Nathan & Ecaterina's daughter)

Werewolves
• Sue and Timmons (long-term members of Char's pack)
• Shonna and Merrit (long-term members of Char's pack)

• Ted (married to Felicity, an enhanced human)

Weretigers born before the WWDE:
• Aaron and Yanmei

Humans (enhanced)
• Micky San Marino, Captain of the *War Axe*
• Commander Suresha, *War Axe* Department Head —Engines
• Commander MacEachthighearna (Mac), *War Axe* Department Head—Environmental
• Commander Blagun Lagunov, *War Axe* Department Head—Structure
• Commander Oscar Wirth, *War Axe* Department Head —Stores
• Lieutenant Clodagh Shortall, *War Axe* engine technician
• Sergeant Fitzroy, a martial arts expert and platoon sergeant
• Kelly, Capples, Fleeter, Praeter, and Duncan—mech drivers

Other Key Characters
• Dokken (a sentient and enhanced German Shepherd)
• Floyd (a sentient and sweet wombat who gives gifts of poop cubes when she loves you)
• The Good King Wenceslaus (an orange tabby domestic cat who thinks he's a weretiger, all fifteen pounds of him)
• K'Thrall—a four-legged Yollin, used to be systems

analyst on the *War Axe,* now a warrior with the Bad Company

- Ruzfell—new systems specialist on the *War Axe*
- Clifton—human pilot of the *War Axe*
- Bundin—a four-legged shell-backed blue stalk-headed alien from Poddern
- Ankh'Po'Turn—a small bald humanoid from Crenellia. Erasmus, one of Plato's stepchildren, is his AI
- General Smedley Butler—EI/AI on the *War Axe*, who they call the General
- Plato—Ted's AI from R&D
- Dionysus—the AI tasked to assist with running Keeg Station
- Iracitus—the AI assisting Shonna and Merrit in the asteroid mining effort
- Paithoon—A Belzonian, escort for Kaeden and Marcie
- Bon Tap—a teal-skinned, silver-haired Malatian, a warrior in the Bad Company
- Slikira—an Ixtali, four legs, a spider race, called "Slicker," a warrior in the Bad Company

Other Bad Company warriors: Tim, "Skates" Mardigan, Chris Bo Runner (Harborian), Jones, Einar, Gefelton, Eldis (wife is Xianna, a green-skinned Torregidoran female), B'Ichi Aharche (Keome)

Background From Bad Company 4—Onyx Station

"I always negotiate from a position of power." Nathan smiled easily and made his friends feel welcome. They took seats on a couch and overstuffed chairs in what otherwise was a nondescript office. "We have a few minutes before your destroyer leaves for Belzimus."

Marcie and Kaeden looked at each other. "We thought we'd be based out of here." Marcie stood and started to pace.

Terry appreciated her style; it reminded him of someone he knew.

"You will be, but like me, you probably won't spend much time here. What you'll be doing will be more hands-on until you have a feel for your front-line leadership team."

"Are we going to have to earn their respect?" Kae asked. Everything stopped within the room—the fidgets, the pacing, even the breathing.

"There has to be more to your question," Nathan said.

"I don't want to have to beat anyone senseless, but is some ass-munching Klingon going to challenge me to a duel?"

Terry bit his lip. Char elbowed him to keep quiet.

"The army you'll be building is made up of people who look and act human, but they most assuredly are not. I think you won't be surprised by the broad range of person-alities you'll find on Belzimus."

"What do we call them?" Marcie wondered.

"Belzonians. There's a big difference between them and humans. They're hermaphrodites. You can't tell them apart, because there is no apart to tell." Nathan checked his monitor to make sure it was off and he wasn't broadcast-ing. "They like to spread their DNA as wide as possible in order to ensure their species remains strong."

"What the butt-hugging nut-roll does that even look like?" Terry wondered.

"An orgy, or so I've been told," Nathan explained, quickly looking away.

"Why does that matter?" Kae asked.

"You'll find there's no jealousy on the planet, not because of sex. They are still envious of position and rank and stuff like that, but not about what tends to distract humans the most."

"I'm starting to like the Belzonians," Marcie offered. "We transmitted our recommended organization chart based on what we'd seen. What do we need to change?"

"The only thing I saw was the reliance on existing Belzonian command structures. I believe you'll be better off if you move the leadership laterally and make them uncomfortable enough to learn the new way. If they stay in positions they think they know, they'll do it how they think they know it, if that makes any sense."

Kae and Marcie both nodded. "It does," Kae replied. Nathan stood and held out his hand.

"That's it, huh?" Kae asked.

"That's it. Time to go." They shook hands while Terry and Char waited by the door. After the hugs, Marcie and Kaeden strolled out. The door closed behind them.

Kaeden and Marcie returned to the hangar bay. They spotted a number of sleek ships as well as a wheeled vehicle. "Space-fighters and cars? I wonder who those are for." Kae pointed at a cordoned area of the deck.

"It doesn't matter. Our ride is this way." Marcie motioned in the opposite direction.

"Clearly not one of Ted's shuttles," Kae lamented.

"He's had the technology up and running for a whole *week* now," Marcie replied. "It's going to take a long time to get out here, so no. Nothing for us, not yet anyway."

"But we know people. Maybe we can get the FDG moved up the priority list?"

"Is that what we're going to call this group?"

"Do we get to name it?" Kae's lip twitched upward to form a half-smile. "I'll have to think on that one."

"Don't hurt yourself," Marcie quipped. "Maybe the Etheric Federation Peacekeeping Force."

"We need something intimidating but supportive, like Bad Guy Ass-Kicking Army."

Marcie stopped walking so she could more effectively roll her eyes.

"How about the Power Rangers?"

"Big nope." Marcie started walking again. Kae stayed by her side as he continued to generate names in his mind.

"Army of the Etheric Federation, or Federation Peace-keeping Etheric Army."

"That's more like it. We'll see what the General has to say. I suspect he has something in mind."

"You're probably right. He'll have a good reason for what he chooses, based on other factors within the Empire, and later, the Federation."

"It might have once been the Queen's Army. You never know," Marcie said when they reached the shuttle. A uniformed guard stood at the hatch.

"Colonel. Major. I'll be your escort during your transit to Belzimus. My name is Paithoon. If you need anything, tell me, and I will acquire it for you." The man saluted by thumping his chest and dropping his hand back to his side.

"We'll need to learn your customs, so that'll start as soon as we reach the destroyer."

"The *Candied Moon* awaits."

Marcie and Kae both stopped dead in their tracks. "Our destroyer is named the *Candied Moon*?" Kae stated the obvious.

"It is an honorable name."

"Does it terrify you to hear it?"

"Of course not," Paithoon replied.

"How about *Vengeance*? We need ships that people can rally around, not throw parties on."

"We love a good party," Paithoon said as his gaze drifted away.

"There seems to be a lot for us to talk about, Paithoon. The change starts right here, right now. The next party we throw will be when we're planting a flag where our enemy used to be."

"Sounds wonderful. Would you like me to start organizing that?"

"*No!* I don't want you to organize that. It'll be a while before this group goes into combat. When that happens, we'll know what we need to do. Are you a fighter?"

"Oh, no. I'm in the protocol office. The fighters? Those Belzonians are wired differently. Weird bunch."

"Now you're speaking my language. Let's head over to the *Vengeance* and get this show on the road."

"I'm sorry?"

"You haven't spent much time with Earthers, have you?"

"None, sir."

"You'll learn." Marcie jousted with the man briefly, trying to encourage him to go first, but gave up and entered the shuttle.

"Somebody will learn," Kae whispered out the side of his mouth. "The *Candied Moon*? What in the big bone jobs did we sign up for?"

CHAPTER ONE

War Axe, **Interstellar Space**

"You want us to do what?" Colonel Terry Henry Walton wondered. The bridge of the *War Axe* was bustling with activity since Captain Micky San Marino was training supplemental bridge officers. Despite the extra staff filling the space, it was business as usual. Terry and his wife Charumati stood in the middle, staring at the main viewscreen.

"Relax, TH. I wouldn't send you on anything too dangerous." Nathan Lowell, appearing as his usual executive self, stared back.

"That's all you send us on, Nathan! We're going back to the planet of the Grays to check on the interdimensional rift to verify that the Skrima have not returned? Can't you just ask them?" Terry didn't want to say the planet's name, which was Benitus Seven. That was where their son-in-law Ramses had died.

"No, because they won't be able to also check out the space station. We need a second set of eyes to double-extra-verify it's structurally sound. We think we can tow it back to Federation space."

"Did you say double-extra-verify? Are you making shit up? Don't you have engineers who do this kind of thing?"

"Kind of, but not really. I know you do, though. Char, rally your pack and head out soonest." Nathan cut the link before either could respond.

"Rally the pack..." Char mumbled, slowly shaking her head.

"Won't they be surprised!" Terry scowled as he pulled Char close for a one-arm hug. He turned to the captain. "You heard the man. We have some *volunteers* to hunt down and drag aboard."

"I'll talk to Cory," Char said softly.

The *Vengeance*, Belzonian Destroyer Assuming Orbit over Belzimus

Colonel Marcie Walton and her husband Major Kaeden Walton stood next to the command chair on the bridge, which was located in the center of the ship behind multiple bulkheads, armor, and defensive systems. A side screen showed a serene blue and green planet, but all eyes were on the main screen's tactical display.

The Belzonian fleet had formed up for a flyby before the *Vengeance* sent a shuttle with the very important people, the VIPs, to the planet's surface to meet the ground forces they would soon command. Paithoon, their escort, directed the show.

"First up, the picket line of destroyers and cruisers clearing the way." The smaller ships transformed from two rows of six ships each into a spear point with two up front and four more ships trailing each wing. The last two cruisers formed the shaft of the spear, ready to exploit any success in battle. The ships accelerated past the *Vengeance*, increasing the distance between them to make themselves harder targets for an enemy.

"Next, the cream of the Belzonian crop: our state-of-the-art troop transport system." He waved his arm toward the screen and swept it as if revealing something behind a curtain.

Kae and Marcie didn't care about his presentation, but they didn't want to crush his soul by telling him to stay out of the way. They glanced at each other, silently confirming their commitment to remaining polite to their protocol officer.

Six massive ships lumbered through space before them. With launch ports for the landing shuttles, these beasts weren't designed for intra-atmospheric flight. They delivered the troops to the system, and the shuttles dropped to the planet. The transports maneuvered into a formation that looked like the cylinders of a revolver. They presented a minimal target with the most protection for each other unless the enemy was directly in front or behind.

"Only twelve pickets for a six-ship transport fleet?" Marcie asked. The simulations she was running in her mind suggested a determined enemy would cause the formation a great deal of pain, reducing the Belzonian power-projection capability.

"This is the entirety of the Belzonian fleet. Additional warships would have to be requested from the Federation." Paithoon sounded less confident.

"What is the capacity of each transport?"

"Four thousand!" Paithoon answered proudly in his best show announcer's voice. The softball question renewed the vigor that had briefly waned. "We can move the entire army using only three ships."

"Or we can split the army onto all six and increase survivability to deliver a combat-capable force even with some resistance to landing," Marcie suggested. Paithoon started to stammer. He was a protocol officer, not one of the combat arms branches. She waved her question away. "That's for the army commander. My apologies."

Be polite, she reminded herself. Kae turned the snicker behind his hand into a forced cough.

"Belzimus has never lost a transport." Paithoon tried valiantly to recover his announcer's voice.

Kaeden couldn't let it go. "Have they ever been under fire?"

Paithoon deflated as if a body blow had been delivered. "Once, from a pirate ship."

"No matter," Marcie remarked, cutting the conversation short. "Kae, make a note to get a list of available assets from the Federation. Visit the transports to see what we have, take a shuttle on a joyride to see what we're going to put the troops through, and then... Well, I'll think of more."

Kaeden spoke softly into a small recording device. Marcie had one with her, too, but she intently watched the formation, thinking through the strategy and tactics of employing such ships in support of the ground forces. If she was going to take command of the entire operation, she needed to see it from the widest view. Kae was good with his role as her executive, and when needed, commander of the armored forces.

Paithoon flicked his hand at the screen. "Also, our support ships," he said without conviction.

"Amateurs talk tactics. Professionals talk logistics," Marcie repeated the phrase she had heard Terry Henry Walton say time and again. "I'll want to know the lift capacity and supporting functions of each ship, along with redundancies in case of combat losses and impact to support assets."

Marcie was talking to herself and Kae far more than she was talking to Paithoon. Kae repeated the key points into his recorder as he expanded their to-do list to an obscene length.

"When are we going to meet Colonel Braithwen?" Marcie asked, referring to the Belzonian ground force commander who had cross-trained with Yollin peace-keeping forces while also studying human strategy and tactics.

"Immediately after the final support ship passes." Paithoon spoke evenly and administratively as he refer-enced the schedule on his datapad. He read an entry. "He is a big fan of Colonel Terry Henry Walton."

"You have that in the schedule?"

Paithoon stuttered his response. "I-I had written it down as a topic for conversation since he's your father and father-in-law, respectively, respectfully."

"Relax," Kae told the protocol officer, guiding him to the side to leave Marcie to focus on the shipping. He knew she was cataloging the Belzonian approach to supporting the ground troops. Their fleet had not been built for space combat, but to support a land force occupying the planet surface once a modicum of air and space superiority had been achieved.

"We wanted you to be pleased with the aerial display," Paithoon pleaded.

"We are!" Kae exclaimed. "Immensely so. I'm sorry we didn't seem more appreciative. We've been given a mountain to move, and we have to do it one shovelful at a time. You'll have to forgive us for being a little short. We have a lot of work to do."

Paithoon nodded, his coifed electrum mane tossing with each movement of his head, then brightened. "There, the last ship."

The final supply vessel, an ore hauler, drifted past. Kaeden wondered what units required raw ore, but he put it out of his mind. They'd repurpose the vessel unless they retired it and removed it from inventory.

Paithoon clapped dramatically. "Take us in," he requested of the captain, who had remained silent throughout. "A landing area has been prepared just beyond Training Area Zoranitus' command post."

The *Vengeance* was of modern design, capable of interstellar travel using the Gate system while also providing lift to and from the surface of a planet. They accelerated into the upper atmosphere, heading toward the horizon to lessen their angle of entry. That would reduce the friction against their hull.

"Combat suit?" Kaeden asked.

Marcie shook her head. "The exercise will kick off the second we arrive. It's best we observe only at this point and get to know Shaky Jake Braithwen." Marcie turned to the captain. "Please keep the ship on the landing pad in case we need access to our equipment."

Once the captain had confirmed, they headed for their quarters, and Paithoon ran after them.

"Oh, Colonel!" he called.

Marcie clenched her jaw but didn't snap at the protocol officer. "Yes, Paithoon?"

"Where are you going? The airlock is this way." He pointed in the other direction, but they didn't see because they hadn't bothered to turn around and look.

"We're getting our ballistic vests and helmets."

"But we'll be in the command post," Paithoon explained. "There will be pastries and fruit drinks."

Marcie stopped in her tracks, then turned and fixed him with a cold stare. "And we'll enjoy them while wearing our ballistic vests and carrying our gear. I'm sorry, Paithoon, but as of an hour ago, we're training for war, and that means always being prepared. War is a mindset. I want it to be second nature to all our people because with it, they will have a better chance of survival. I want our army to have minimal casualties. There's nothing that will crush spirits faster than watching people die needlessly."

Paithoon dropped his eyes to stare at the floor. "I understand. It's what we do, but not what we do. We win the peace. My job is not war, but diplomatic relations." The protocol officer's voice sounded whiny and pleading.

"We're going to need help with that since I don't know anything about that bullshit." Marcie spun on her heel and hurried to their small quarters with Kaeden. She wanted to step off the ship as soon as it arrived.

"You just called Paithoon's job bullshit," Kae noted.

"The diplomacy side *is* bullshit. I like pastries and fruit drinks. Paithoon serves a purpose. I haven't figured out what yet, but he wears a uniform. Everyone fights first."

"Do they have to? Did the FDG or Bad Company make your mom fight?" Kae tightened his vest, checked his railgun, and fastened his helmet. He knew the answer. They had been side by side for the past hundred and fifty years.

"Your point?" Marcie was ready to go but hesitated.

"Treat him as non-combat support, which he is. We have a full army—regiments and battalions with the structure to support them when in combat. Not everyone has to fight. Do you want Paithoon carrying a gun?" Kae waved his railgun for emphasis.

Marcie chuckled. "Maybe he should put on a different uniform. I can't have him walking among the warriors and them deferring to him on anything related to discipline and tactics."

"As the boss, you can make it whatever you want." Kae kissed his wife before opening the door. "After you, Colonel."

"Why, thank you, Major. Let's go kick the tires and see how well this baby runs."

Kae and Marcie watched slack-jawed as the attack kicked off. A battalion of armor raced into the center of the training area. Four regiments of infantry in a line-abreast formation followed. Artillery thundered, sending round after round into the distance.

Colonel Braithwen trod heavily down the stairs from

the small tower above the building and strode into the main observation room. The look on his face suggested he was displeased with something, or maybe that was his usual look. He wore a helmet, so his choice of exotic hairstyles wasn't immediately obvious.

"You must be Colonel Walton. I'm Colonel Jacobus Braithwen. Welcome to Belzimus," he said. His voice was gravelly but smooth, the product of too much yelling. He offered his hand, and Marcie took it.

"My XO, Major Kaeden Walton." The two shook hands as well. "I hear they call you 'Shaky Jake.' What do you wish to be called? Not everyone can be called 'Colonel.'"

"Jake is fine, ma'am," he replied, keeping his voice low so the others in the command post couldn't hear. One table held a cornucopia of pastries and the other fruit drinks, with two uniformed soldiers standing ready to serve. Five other Belzonians operated computer and communications equipment as they managed the exercise. None of them wore helmets or body armor. One individual wore gym shoes. Marcie tried not to stare.

"Could you brief me on what we have, starting with the training parameters?"

The colonel looked past her to the windows. "A simple fortress assault. The exercise ends with the breach of the fortress' perimeter. A small-unit building-clearing exercise is scheduled for tomorrow. As you requested, I've had nothing to do with the operational planning for this exercise. My executive, Lieutenant Colonel Chantai, is handling everything." The look on his face suggested he wasn't pleased with his exec's plan.

"It starts with training the front line troops until they

can execute without hesitation." They turned to the formations struggling across the field. They were starting to lose integrity, not because they were increasing spacing, but from leaving stragglers behind. Live artillery started falling among the armored vehicles at the front of the attack and the impacts crept toward the advancing troops, at least the few hard-chargers racing ahead of the rest.

Kae made eye contact with Marcie, a pained look on his face. His eyes darted to the formation, then he quickly looked back at Marcie. She nodded slightly.

"Give me the comm," he ordered without further hesitation. One of the technicians at the console handed him a cordless headset.

Marcie looked sideways at the technology the Belzonians were using. Just because the style of warfare was old-fashioned, it didn't mean the technology needed to be. "Missile launchers and integrated comm," she whispered to Kae before turning her attention back to the colonel.

"Echo, Echo, Echo. I say again, this is the CO. Echo, Echo, Echo." Artillery continued to fall for another ten seconds. The armor rolled on for twenty more seconds, and the infantry didn't stop until they reached the armor and someone leaned out of a turret and yelled. Jake bowed his head. "This is beyond embarrassing, Colonel. The failure of this exercise is mine alone. I'll accept whatever punishment you deem appropriate."

Marcie put her hand on the Belzonian's shoulder and looked him in the eye. "Bullshit. There are technical limitations, and then there are training and discipline issues. Have you ever conducted large-scale operations before?"

"I have, with the Yollin Empire, before it fell to the

Queen. Only one other Belzonian spent time with the Yollin military, Sergeant Major Monsoon. He's with my XO." Jake pointed to a small, wheeled combat vehicle slowly meandering across the battlefield.

His tone said everything Marcie needed to hear. "Get the sergeant major on the hook and put it on speaker."

The colonel nodded to the comm chief. Marcie didn't appreciate that the troops didn't respond to Kae's direct order, but this wasn't the time to get into a power struggle. There were other issues to settle.

Colonel Braithwen gestured for everyone to leave the command post except for the communications operator. Paithoon tried to remain, but the colonel glared holes through the protocol officer's skull. He followed the others out.

"Sergeant Major Monsoon," the rough voice answered. He too had had a long life of yelling.

"Colonel Braithwen here with our new commander and XO, Colonel Walton and Major Walton."

Marcie quickly jumped in. "I look forward to meeting you in person, Sergeant Major. Can you tell me what happened that the formation fell apart so quickly?"

"Don't you want to talk to Colonel Chantai?"

"No, Sergeant Major. I know you're used to boots on the ground, and you can give me the perspective of what the front lines saw and what they were reacting to."

"I would rather deliver that report in person, Ma'am," Monsoon replied.

"Return to the CP ASAP, Sergeant Major." Marcie drew a line across her throat, and the comm operator killed the link.

"Why didn't you talk to the XO? It was his plan," Kae wondered.

"Because I'm going to fire him. I wanted to hear from the only one out there who knew beyond a shadow of a doubt how fucked up this thing was, the sergeant major. Because we," she made a circle with her hand to include those standing there, "are responsible for fixing it. The only four combat veterans here are going to take these troops for a long drive so they can learn what it means to have proper spacing based on enemy weapons' blast radii, about employment of armor based on the objective, how to use artillery to pin down an enemy, how to effectively employ our infantry, and most importantly, how to keep from killing our own people!"

Marcie got more animated as she spoke. She wasn't furious, but she was not looking forward to managing her list of things that needed to be accomplished. She needed Braithwen as an ally, but some of the issues they had just seen went to basic training and discipline. Those fell squarely on the commanding officer's shoulders.

Marcie remembered her initial training in North Chicago. Discipline and physical fitness were established before anything else could happen. It was the same thing she had done with the new recruits in the Bad Company.

It was what she was going to do with the Belzonian Army.

The combat vehicle bounced across the boundary of the training area and sped to the command post. The lieutenant colonel climbed out first and straightened his uniform while looking around, then threw his head back and strolled toward the door. The sergeant major stepped out of the back without any wasted movements. His eyes focused on the window through which Jake, Marcie, and Kae watched. He removed his helmet, showing his bald head and wiping it with his sleeve before replacing his lid and joining the XO.

Chantai threw the door open and walked through, not bothering to hold it for the sergeant major. Marcie willed herself to not jump down his throat, her cheeks twitching as she tried to control herself. The sergeant major shut the door behind him and pointed at the comm operator, who jumped up and ran for the exit.

The lieutenant colonel smiled broadly as he removed his helmet to unleash a rainbow shock of hair that tumbled onto his shoulders and down his back. "I'm Lieutenant Colonel Chantai." He strode forward with his hand out.

Marcie crossed her arms, feet planted shoulder-width apart.

"I'm not sure of human customs. My apologies, ma'am." He executed a sweeping bow.

"Lieutenant Colonel, I'm going to be straight up with you because there's no time to beat around the bush. We have a military force to prepare for action sooner rather than later, and my plan doesn't include you. You're fired."

"But..." The Belzonian collected himself before trying a second time. "I request a higher-level review. This doesn't seem right."

"No. It's fine. The Belzimus government has delivered these troops to Federation control in return for a rather substantial investment in your planet. As of two weeks ago, I was designated as the Federation's highest authority regarding the Belzonian component of the combined Federation military assets."

Kae stepped close. "You're done, and we have work to do, so if you don't mind, we need to move on."

The former XO stood there, dumbfounded.

Kae clarified, "Get out," and physically turned the Belzonian toward the door. He even opened it for him. "Paithoon, make sure the newly retired lieutenant colonel gets a ride home after turning in his gear. Console him for us, would you?"

Kae hastened the former officer's departure with a firm push through the door.

The sergeant major leaned close to Colonel Braithwen. "The troops are still in the field, sir. With your permission, I'll order the recall and return to garrison."

He nodded. "Good call, Crantis. Thanks for looking out for the troops."

"They weren't happy. Too many conflicting orders. No focus."

"It's called a lack of leadership, and I'm not talking yours," Marcie nodded at the two Belzonians, then headed for the pastries and a chair. "Let's talk about what we need to do to get this army ready for deployment with the Federation."

CHAPTER TWO

War Axe, Terry and Char's Quarters

Cory stared blankly at the wall. Dokken nuzzled her hand until she absentmindedly petted his head and scratched behind his ears. The intelligent German Shepherd had become Cory's constant companion, following Ramses' death a couple years prior.

Terry and Char waited, letting their daughter process the mission orders.

"You can stay at Keeg Station if you want. This is supposed to be a non-combat mission."

Cory shook her head slowly before lifting her chin. "It's okay. I need access to R2D2 and Ted before we go. How much time do we have?"

"We'll take as long as we need," Char replied. They'd been given two days to get underway and she knew that, but she wasn't about to let the Federation timeline interfere with her and her family. Terry agreed. He would beg the Federation's forgiveness before putting extra pressure on Cory.

"What do you have in mind?" Terry asked, finally relaxing enough to take a seat.

"A mobile critical care system. Cryofreeze on small platforms deployed with all ground forces. In case anyone gets hit, we freeze whatever's left of them to bring back and put in the Pod-doc. I've been thinking about this for a while because I keep asking the question, 'What would have saved Ramses?' The cryopods should be simple to deploy. Send two or four on each transport Pod. They follow the landing force members around at a discrete distance. We use the internal comm chips to summon them or make it automatic if someone's life signs drop to zero."

"Doesn't sound too hard." Terry paced in a small circle, hands clasped behind his back. Char watched him for a moment before turning her attention back to Cory.

"We'll get the wheels turning as soon as we return to Keeg Station. We'll need to conduct a quick resupply, but we're bringing the whole pack for this op."

Cory turned to her mother. "The whole pack? Are they going to be good with that?"

"Always worried about others," Char said softly. "That makes you special."

"No more than you." Cory stood to go. Dokken sneezed.

"Bless you," three people said in unison.

Thank you, the dog replied. *Are you hiding any bistok in here? I smell something.*

"You don't smell anything," Terry shot back.

Ah-ha! Dokken ran for the closet. Terry dove, grabbing a handful of tail to hold Dokken back. The dog twisted one hundred and eighty degrees to bite Terry's wrist. With a wince and a cry, he let go. Dokken shot toward the open closet door.

TH massaged his wrist. Dokken emerged chewing on a plastic-wrapped package. Cory hurried to get between her father and her friend and held out her hand. Dokken didn't question it, just dropped the package into it. Corry removed the wrapper and handed the bistok jerky to Dokken.

I know who my friends are, he told the Walton family.

Char brightened, relieved by Cory's recovery. Ramses' death had hit them all hard. They hadn't thought Cory would ever return to the normal world, but here she was, finally, and the prospect of going back to Benitus Seven refreshed her in a new way. "We'll make sure you have everything you need to build the cryopods," Char stated.

Terry agreed. "Everything." Cory gestured for him to hold out his hand. When he did so, she slapped the dog-saliva-covered plastic into it. She waved at Dokken, who was still chewing, and he joined her on the way out.

"I'm watching you, Dokken. We're going back to your favorite space station."

The dog turned and angled his head, one ear flopped sideways. *You will not tape me to your face. Repeat after me: I will not tape Dokken to my face.*

"What I will *not* do is let you die. How about next time, you don't lick my mouth?"

How about we don't have a next time? Dokken snarked and disappeared into the hallway.

"Did you hear the thanks I got for saving his life?" Terry pleaded with Char.

"Yes, dear," she replied casually. "Smedley, can you

connect me with Ted, please? I'm calling as his Alpha, so make sure he knows that and will take my call."

Belzimus, Command Post and Training Area Zoranitus

"Get your asses over here!" the sergeant major bellowed over the loudspeaker. The troops were taking their sweet time recovering from the field. Many were lollygagging to the extent that it would take the rest of the day to get them back to the barracks for an exercise that had taken a grand total of twenty minutes.

Sergeant Major Monsoon was having none of it. Colonel Braithwen unleashed his senior enlisted to put the fear of Belz into them.

"Double-time, you sorry sacks of shit!" Some of the troops chuckled at the latest pronouncement. "What are you laughing at?"

When the eye of the dragon settled on their heads, their mirth disappeared. The sergeant major held up one hand and counted down on his fingers. When he closed the last one to show zero, he took a new tack. "STOP!" The troops meandered to a halt, remaining where they were. Some picked at their faces. Others put their rifles down and leaned on them.

Crantis Monsoon had not spent the time he wanted with these troops. He'd been deployed for two years. When he and the colonel had returned, they'd found that nearly the entire army had turned over. Belzimus had sent their best to the Federation to save face. It was also how they got on the radar: the contribution of a complete army. The

Federation had signed an agreement based on what they'd seen from Braithwen and Monsoon.

It was time to pay the debt.

"On your faces and push until I get tired!" The sergeant major bellowed the order, the loudspeakers threatening to melt with the increased volume. Ten thousand troops were packed into a few hundred square meters. Monsoon jumped down and stormed through the ranks, stepping on the backs of those making light of the effort and "encouraging" others with a growl and an ear flick. From one area to another, he seemed to float over the writhing mass of bodies. Marcie, Kae, and Jake watched the sergeant major get the troops' attention.

When Monsoon was satisfied that the majority of the army was making a decent effort, he stopped and saluted. Marcie used the cue to take the stage, which was the top of the wheeled combat vehicle. She held the microphone in one hand, ready to speak, but stopped and waved for Colonel Braithwen to join her. She handed the microphone to him once he was standing beside her on the vehicle's roof. The troops were in the front leaning rest or the pushup position. He left them that way.

"Soldiers of Belzimus. I would love to say that we impressed our new leadership, but we did not. When we give the order, you'll return to the barracks and clean up to prepare for inspection at seventeen hundred hours. Tomorrow, your day starts at oh three hundred to prepare for the troops' PT, which starts an hour later. Junior officers will join us at the command post immediately following this formation. Let me introduce your new commanding officer, Colonel Walton."

CRAIG MARTELLE & MICHAEL ANDERLE

He handed Marcie the microphone. "Get on your feet," she ordered, giving them a brief respite from the pain that would fill their lives for the foreseeable future. "We are tasked by the Federation to create an occupation force to guarantee the peace on member planets suffering from a leadership upheaval."

"You mean, civil war?" someone said above the sounds of heavy breathing and shifting feet.

"Yes, I mean civil war. We're bringing the peace, and we're going to enforce it. Many of these worlds will have standing armies still fighting. We will see combat, and I don't want any of you to die. To reduce your risk, we need to do a great deal of training so you can operate better as individual soldiers and as cohesive units. That is going to take time and repetition. Over the next month, you're going to grow tired of Training Area Zoranitus. At the end of it all, you will feel better about yourself and better about our mission. You won't just survive a war, you will thrive. Sergeant Major, they're all yours."

"Roger, ma'am!" Monsoon shouted loud enough for all ten thousand to hear. "On my command, you will double-time to the barracks. Once there, you'll clean your shit up and prepare for a full locker and bunk inspection. Fall out!"

One of the junior officers intercepted the sergeant major on his way to the command post. "Sergeant Major, why did you find it necessary to swear and call names?"

"Who in the holy jump the fuck up and down are you?" Kaeden called from behind. He made a beeline to the two, glaring at the lieutenant without blinking. "Did I hear bull-shit dribble out of your cakehole?"

"Why you gotta say such hurtful things?" the lieutenant wondered.

Kae wanted to choke the Belzonian, not because he didn't get it, but because this lieutenant represented an attitude he and Marcie would have to change. "Because if they don't get their shit under control, people will die. By 'they,' I mean 'you.' These embarrassments are your fault, lieutenant. Substandard performance means we'll lose soldiers. Those troops are going to die if they don't have discipline and training. Right now, they have neither. That's *your* fault since they are your troops, so fix your shit and get it done yesterday!"

"I get it, sir, but gosh! You guys are kind of mean," the lieutenant persisted.

"You need to get over that. No one is being mean since if you all die, I die. I don't want to die, so I'm going to do something about it right now. That means creating a harsh environment within which a force learns to operate. If you want to be the baddest motherfucker on the battlefield, you have a high bar to reach. You aren't always going to have a soft bed and a congenial enemy."

"I understand, motherfucker," the lieutenant said proudly, snapping to attention.

Kae fought to keep from laughing. "Is that you trying to swear?"

"Yes!" He beamed.

"Don't. You're bad at it, and it'll get your ass kicked." The lieutenant deflated, and Kae clapped him on the back. "You made my day, Lieutenant. Now get your dumb ass to the briefing."

Kae walked away from the youngster and stood by himself, watching the junior officers file into the area. Each glanced at him as he passed. Many looked ragtag, even though their equipment was mostly new. They were a well-outfitted army, benefitting from lessons learned by those who had fought elsewhere, equipped with weaponry that had been effective decades earlier.

"You have to play the hand you're dealt," as his father would say. He would add, *"Sometimes you get to draw cards, too, and that's where you make your own luck."*

When all was said and done, a thousand officers of various ranks filled the space between the command post and the *Vengeance.*

Join us on the ramp, Kae, Marcie requested, using their internal comm. He expected they'd be using it more each day as they coordinated their efforts without letting the army know what those were. He wondered if the colonel and the sergeant major had been fitted with comm chips since they had been insiders with the Federation's small military. He let his thoughts drift as he worked his way through the mass of bodies. There was complaining and far too much whining.

"Fucking party is over," he snapped at one of the seemingly endless field of tassel-headed youth. In his experience, complaining warriors were happy warriors, but the looks on the officers' faces suggested that wasn't the case on Belzimus. Not yet. Complaining Belzonians were unhappy Belzonians.

These fuckers have no idea what they're in for. Do we let the untrainable walk or move them into support billets?

I don't know, Marcie replied. *Let's spend the week sorting things out. They didn't make a good first impression, but we can't let that taint our decisions. I think we'll see something far different in a week. If Shaky Jake and Crantis can become the professionals they are, then I have hope for the rest of their people.*

Kae bumped and bounced people out of his way as he fought to join the others visible to all who were standing on the *Vengeance's* ramp. *I definitely married up,* Kae told his wife.

I know, she replied. He shook his head and smiled as he finally broke through the closest Belzonians to join Marcie, Colonel Braithwen, and Sergeant Major Monsoon.

Colonel Braithwen raised his hands for silence. His stone-cold gaze swept across the mass of officers, helmets in their hands, who were looking back. Multicolored tufts of hair gave the crowd the texture of a field filled with spring flowers. He took a deep breath to build volume from his diaphragm. Being loud without yelling. Commanding.

"I see potential. I see Belzonians assuming their rightful place at the sides of the Federation's greatest warriors. I see peace, established and maintained through making war, through overwhelming force applied to an enemy's pain points. I see...the future."

A cheer erupted from the crowd. A sharp look quickly silenced them.

"Between now and that vision is the time of shaping and honing. First, you must understand what needs to be done. Second, you must do it. Today, during the inspections, you'll set up tents and cots in the physical training yard, and you'll move into those quarters, where you'll remain for the duration of this phase of training. Plan for a month."

The grousing was instantaneous.

Marcie whispered to Kaeden, and he disappeared inside the ship. When he returned, he carried something shiny. Marcie nodded, then removed her helmet and removed the band that kept it back. Her long, golden hair tumbled over her shoulders and down her back. "Cut it," she told her husband. Without hesitation, he started at one side, just below her ear, and worked his way around her head. He handed her a shock of hair the color of cornsilk. She waved it at the army before her. A gasp rippled through like the wind across a field of grain.

The colonel clenched his jaw but held out his hand. Kae slapped the scissors into them. Jake dropped his helmet. His style was executive, without gaudy coloring. It rose to a peak above his head, with separate tendrils that trailed to his chest and over his shoulders to his back. "Sergeant Major?" Crantis took the shears and got to work. He took more joy in the cutting than should have been permissible, but they were making a statement.

The sergeant major whispered, "You might have to clean this up with a razor later. I'm making a dog's break-fast out of it."

"You fucker." The colonel snickered while keeping his expression even. The officers in the crowd gaped.

Once the colonel's butchered hairstyle was complete, he stooped to pick up his helmet, shook the hair free, and replaced it on his head.

"You'll be wearing your body armor and helmets from now until we tell you to take them off. You're going to learn what it means to be professional soldiers. You'll be better Belzonians for it, and you'll be saving your life and the lives of those around you."

Kaeden stepped up. "PT at oh-four-hundred hours. I'm going to run until every one of you jagoffs pukes. Then we're going to run some more. After that is when we'll get down to the real work of being a soldier."

"Dismissed!" Marcie shouted. No one moved except for the leadership team.

Paithoon appeared out of nowhere, breathless in his race to get onto the ramp. "You can't expect the men to cut their hair! That goes outside the bounds of common decency."

Marcie recoiled, looking at him as if she'd seen a dirty diaper. "Why aren't you out there helping them set up tents? You can add fruit baskets or whatever it is the fuck you do."

"I do more than that. If you insist on the hair, there will be a mutiny!"

Kae grabbed Paithoon by his shirt's collar. "Do you want to be the example when someone refuses an order?" he growled in the protocol officer's face.

"No!" He brushed ineffectually at Kae's hand. "I'm the voice of the people."

Colonel Braithwen took an interest while Marcie headed into the ship. The sergeant major loomed over the colonel's shoulder.

"Paithoon, I expected more from you. One thing grossly

lacking here is leadership by example." Jake eyed the protocol officer's distinguished coiffure.

Terror filled Paithoon's eyes as he tried to backpedal. The colonel turned his head toward a group of bystanders who had stopped to watch. It was one of those moments that would catch and run like wildfire. Deflower the protocol officer or not?

Jake put the scissors in his pocket. "You have no authority from the men or over them. I need you to be the morale officer, and your job is going to suck. They are not going to be happy. I don't care if they cut their hair. I want them to focus on being professional soldiers. Anything that keeps them from that purpose will be removed from their lives."

"Some of them have children," Paithoon countered, regaining his bravery once the threat of the shears was lifted.

"And they have families to support them. No one is indispensable, Paithoon, not out there." The colonel gestured toward the nearby city. "But here, everyone is a critical cog in the machine. Everyone will learn their role and the roles of the men above them and beside them. Everyone, including you."

"But…" Paithoon stammered.

The colonel walked away, speaking over his shoulder. "This conversation is over. You have your orders. Carry them out or spend the next week in the brig."

Kae propelled Paithoon down the ramp. He staggered and ran but didn't fall. Kae brushed his hands off and followed Jake into the ship. The sergeant major jumped off the ramp to intercept the protocol officer.

Crantis leaned close so others could not hear. "Don't you fuck with my people. You want to improve their morale? Get some good chow. They're going to need it with all the PT we'll be doing, which you'll be doing, too. I'm not going into combat with someone who can't carry their own weight, not enlisted, not officers. And before you say you don't have a combat role, I'll enlighten you so you don't look stupid in front of your superior officers. Every swinging peacock in this army has a combat role."

The sergeant major straightened and started to whistle a ditty they'd be singing on the formation run. He looked happy as he sauntered toward the barracks.

Oh-four-hundred came way too early unless you were the senior leadership of the Belzonian Army. They first met at three to discuss and work through training schedules. For at least the next week, they needed to do everything the soldiers were doing. They needed to be visible while demonstrating what they hoped the troops would aspire to.

"What I wouldn't give for the Pod-docs on the *War Axe*. We're going to take unenhanced soldiers into battle?" Kae wondered.

"You know the rule. Until everyone can be trusted, we don't create super-soldiers who can bail on us and ply their trade among the wrong types," Marcie reiterated.

"It would make things easier." Kae resolved that things would *not* be easy.

Jake had taken the sergeant major's advice and shaved

CRAIG MARTELLE & MICHAEL ANDERLE

the rest of his head. His hand sought the skin of its own accord as he compulsively stroked his head.

"What's with Belzonians and their hair?" Marcie finally asked.

"Source of pride, status, virility, whatever we want it to be. We're artists more than engineers. The idea of utility over style is not common, shall we say."

"Crantis seems to get it," Marcie countered.

"He gets a lot of things before the rest of us."

Marcie nodded while watching the colonel's hand on his newly bald scalp. He finally realized what she was looking at and yanked his hand away, shrugging as if it were nothing. "It's like the first time you realized how fun it is to play with yourself."

Kae coughed and choked, turning his head and quickly raising his cup of food-processor coffee.

"I guess that's one way to look at it," Marcie remarked nonchalantly. "Training schedule. I want to show old-time videos of combat sequences. Show them some best-case and some worst-case, and give them time to absorb what we're going for while getting mental downtime from everything else that's going to be happening in their lives."

"They're going to be tired, which is good. Once they find they can think while fogged, they'll be geniuses when they get enough sleep. We'll take advantage of both." The colonel accessed his files using a borrowed datapad. "I'm transmitting the full training regimen from when the sergeant major and I worked with the Federation."

Marcie accepted the files and added them to her growing stock of source materials. She tapped a few entries to flesh out the first week and then the first month.

She wanted to focus on what it meant to be professional soldiers, and that kept the entries sparse. Video, class, PT, more video, more class. On the seventh day, they would go into the field and stay there until the soldiers could maneuver effectively. Back to garrison for a week, then back to the field to learn to maneuver under fire. That was when they would learn the details of their jobs. How to aim and fire. How to send rounds downrange from their armor. How to hit pinpoint targets with the artillery while also being able to take out entire grid squares. If they were going to drag the historical kings of battle around, they were sure as hell going to deploy them.

She showed Kae and Jake.

"I'm going to need you to put together a killer opposing force, OpFor."

"Are mechs allowed?" Kae asked hopefully.

"As many as you can get. The Bad Company is not off-limits," Marcie clarified. Kae tried to look like he hadn't thought of them, but that was the only unit on his mind that required no training and would make for an eye-opening experience for the Belzonians.

They stood to go so they could arrive early for PT. Colonel Braithwen tapped his chin with one finger. "Did the Federation agree to call their military the Belzonian Army?"

"We can't call it that when we deploy on Federation business. They left the name up to me, but it has to include 'Federation' or something official sounding. I didn't give it any thought because it's just bureaucratic bullshit. My mother loves that stuff. I'll call her if I can't come up with a name."

"My job is to take things off your plate. Can I have this one?"

"Yours." Marcie gestured as if brushing crumbs from a sleeve. "What do you say we run their asses into the ground?" She thought for a moment. "Have you had the nanocyte treatment?"

"Yes. Both the sergeant major and I are enhanced." He held a finger over his lips to show it was a secret. "When they see us at PT, we're godlike entities. We only look older because we convinced the technicians that looking young wasn't in our best interests. Everything else is in the rutting twenties."

"I'm going to have to up my innuendo game," Kae remarked. "Belzonian orgies are famous, but are they true?"

The colonel checked his watch. "I'll give you the executive cultural summary. They are real. What we don't have here is marriage, jealousy, distinct and separate sexes, or many of the things that led to the garrison-based behavioral challenges. Combat makes everyone equal. Being hermaphrodites is another great equalizer. Sure, we might be attracted to one person more than another, but you know the old saying."

He turned to walk away. Marcie looked at Kae and shook her head.

"We don't know the old saying," Kae called.

The colonel laughed. "Everyone looks the same in the dark."

"That could be said about the crazy hair, too," Marcie shot back.

"I sure hope so," he replied, dragging his hand over his

bald head one last time. He didn't take any more questions, not that Kae or Marcie had any now that they were sufficiently enlightened about the galaxy-renowned Belzonian sexcapades.

"I don't want any orgies on my watch," Kae mumbled, making a sour face.

CHAPTER THREE

Keeg Station, Headquarters for the Bad Company's Direct Action Branch

"I'm sure *I'm* not going out there." Felicity drawled, standing defiant, one arm outstretched like a signpost, pointing out the window at the nether regions of the galaxy beyond it.

"It's okay if you remain behind. You have a job to do. But we absolutely have to have Ted. We got that approved at the highest levels of the Federation. Lance Reynolds issued the orders himself." Char tried to calm Felicity with her most persuasive gestures and a smile. The director, her old friend, crossed her arms and glared at the purple-eyed werewolf. Terry eased toward the door. He wasn't getting in the middle, plus he had stuff to do.

"Ted's not going without me. I am putting my foot down."

"Sounds like you're going, then," Terry said, slapping a hand over his mouth after the words escaped. "Dammit!"

"Where are you going?" Char stopped him with a question.

"Nowhere," Terry replied, doing his best to look innocent.

"You can't kidnap people. What's wrong with you? You used to be on the side of law and order. The Bad Company, bringing Justice to a star system nearest you." Felicity threw the back of her hand to her forehead and started to swoon.

Terry and Char waited. She would never let herself hit the deck. It would mess up her hair.

"I will talk to Ted and get this sorted out," Felicity drawled after a miraculous recovery. "If you'll excuse me, I have a station to run, supporting those pirates from the Bad Company."

Terry didn't let the door hit him on the way out. Char was right on his heels.

"Are they coming?" Terry asked once they were in the corridor and well beyond the office.

Char's eyes narrowed, and her cheeks bulged from grinding her teeth. "There is some resistance. I feel like the Alpha needs to assert her authority. I don't want to do it, but they're making me."

"You need a blocker," Terry stated. "Give me five minutes on the hook, and then we'll go in hot. By the way, where are they?"

"Shonna and Merrit are at the shipyard office. Sue and Timmons are somewhere in the asteroid field with *Iracitus*."

"Give me ten minutes once we reach the bar." TH walked briskly, like he had a purpose, because he always did. Char went with him. She wanted to drink a Supernova to give her a quick rush before heading to battle with her pack.

There were only five werewolves left. She hadn't asked much of them over the years, but now she needed them. For Cory's sake. For all their sakes.

TH knew that. He wanted to make things right. He strode into his bar, greeting the staff as he went, taking a moment here or there to ask about their families and things going on in their lives. One hundred percent of the employees who had survived the attack on the station had returned to work to help rebuild for the reopening. Terry Henry hadn't taken that for granted. They loved working for him because he was consistent in what he asked from them and recognized them for their work, above and beyond the credits they earned on the job.

The bartender slid a beer toward TH as he headed for the small office he maintained to run the operation known as the All Guns Blazing franchise. Terry hesitated before looking at Char for approval. She nodded, knowing that he was going to drink it anyway. The benefit of owning an All Guns Blazing franchise was free beer.

Terry considered it the greatest benefit a free galaxy could bestow upon its humble servant.

"I fucking love you, man!" Terry declared as he took the beer and downed half of it in one go before saluting the bartender with the mug and heading toward the office. As soon as Terry disappeared into the office, the pay system dinged. The bartender smiled as a small gratuity from the boss appeared.

Char stopped. "Two Supernovas, please." The man

behind the bar raised one eyebrow but turned to the liba-tion center to start mixing the potent concoction.

"All's well on the home front?" the bartender asked while working his magic on Char's drinks.

"Just fine. Business is good. We're here and not in a war somewhere. *War Axe* is one hundred percent. Terry has to make a call before we tour the area. I was hoping for beach time, but it's not to be."

"What beach do you prefer?"

"I'm partial to beaches in the Caribbean on planet Earth. We spent a little time there a while ago. It grew on me." *Fifty years living on the beach the last time the Waltons tried to retire. A* little *time.*

"I've never been. I came here from Homeworld. I'm a Harborian who was tired of living on a ship."

"Nice! Where'd you learn to bartend?"

"Right here. AGB has a good training program, and Colonel Walton sponsored me, so I was able to get in without any previous experience. I have to admit that I never had a drink before I trained here. I've had to sample my own creations, but I can do without that. Some of them are a bit harsh, but the clientele likes them."

"A Harborian? I knew a number of you had moved over from the Fleet. It's good to see you with a job. This is better than a ship but still in space. We need to look at a settle-ment program to give you opportunities to go landside somewhere. See what it's like living in the wild. Do you like what you do?"

"Never had a better job in my life, ma'am." He deftly threw two napkins into place before setting one drink on each.

Char took a long sip, savoring the burn, feeling her nanos engage to remove the alcohol. "How many jobs have you had?"

"Counting this one, that would be two. This is my only paying job, as far as the definition of getting paid goes."

"Still the best," Terry offered, returning from the office and putting down the empty beer glass. He gestured for another. "I'd be crushed if this was the worst job you ever had when you only had two, and the other was working as a slave. It's a low bar, but at least we're somewhere above it. You're not thinking of quitting, are you?"

"No!" the bartender declared with gusto. "I can't imagine what a better job would look like."

"Keep 'em in the dark, keep 'em paid, keep 'em on board. That's my retention program, and it's lots cheaper than training new employees all the time." Terry watched Char out of the corner of his eye. She avoided meeting his gaze, slowly taking another drink from her first Supernova.

"Any luck?" she wondered after she put her glass down.

"Yes." Terry smiled at his wife, sneaking a hand underneath the bar top and onto her leg. "They'll meet us at the shipyard control center in two hours. Kai is restocking the ship while Christina is getting more suits aboard. There's nothing for us to do except sit back and watch the sunrise."

"Imagine a sunrise, right through our big window," the bartender said to no one in particular as he walked away to give Terry and Char their space.

The two clinked glasses. "Thanks for saving me the hassle of beating up people I like."

"That's one way to put it. I got through to Ted. We

should probably stop by the lab to check on him. We may have to kidnap Felicity."

"I'm not wrestling that werebear."

"She's not a werebear. Category five hurricane maybe, but not a werebear. For the record, I'm afraid of her, too."

Terry snapped his fingers. "She's Ted's problem!"

"She's your problem," Char replied, holding Terry's gaze. He briefly got lost in her sparkling purple eyes before returning to the moment.

"Ted probably won't even tell her until he's already gone, and then I won't set foot on Keeg Station until we bring her husband back. She'll cool off by then. Probably."

"Probably not," Char countered.

Terry checked the time. He downed the rest of his AGB dark, affectionately called "Motor Oil," before rising and offering an arm to Char. She downed the second Supernova as if chugging a glass of water, then smacked her lips, nodded at the bartender, and strolled away without staggering in the least.

Terry and Char nodded to the staff on their way out. By the time they hit the corridor beyond, Char had grabbed Terry's arm and started to sway.

"One would have been good. How long are you going to be blasted? We could run up to our quarters for some fun time," Terry quipped. Char blinked, but her vision wouldn't clear.

"We better grab a Pod and get our happy asses to the shipyard."

Char held steady, staring into the distance, feet planted and one hand on the nearby wall. Terry never remembered Char getting drunk before. The enhanced were protected from it. She shook her head, and her eyes regained their sparkle. "That's better. Let's grab a giant Coke on the way out."

"I didn't know you drank that goblin piss." Terry poked her in the side. He'd had more than his fair share of Coke, despite Nathan's insistence on covertly pushing the Pepsi brand.

"I usually go with hot Earl Grey, but not right now. I need some energy for the nanos to stay hard at work." They returned to AGB, Char calling from the entry, "A super-jumbo Coke, straight up, to go, please."

The bartender had it ready by the time they reached the bar. Char grabbed it without stopping, swirling in a tight circle as she headed out.

"Smedley, can't this thing go any faster?" Terry complained.

"It can." The AI's reply was short and sweet but noncommittal.

"Would you fly this faster, please?"

"No."

"Are you mad at me?" Terry rolled his head, looking for peace. He hated long Pod rides.

"No."

"Colonel Walton requests that you explain why you won't accommodate his insane request," Char interjected.

"The Pod can go much faster, but this sector of space is littered with debris from the attack. The HOS, heavy objects in space, could cause significant damage should we attempt to fly at a greater speed. The more I increase the strength of the gravitic shield to compensate, the less power is available for the engines. At this almost leisurely pace, I am able to avoid most HOS. We will arrive in time to pick up the others."

Terry looked at Char. She returned her you-asked-for-it expression. "Carry on." He yielded the field of battle so he could regroup for a counterattack when the time was right. "We'll pick up the others and meet the *War Axe*. The resupply needs to be finished by the time we leave the shipyard."

"I am assured that it will be," Smedley replied. "Ted is loading some special equipment into *Ramses' Chariot* right now, and it will dock in the hangar bay."

"What is he up to besides helping Cory with the cryopods?" TH wondered.

Belzimus, Belzonian Army Barracks

Marcie held her arm up to slow the formation and then bring it to an orderly halt. All ten thousand rippled to a march but never got in step before they stopped. Many fell to the side and puked. Others bent over in pain, faces flushed and hair a mop of sweat and dirt.

We only lost five percent of the formation. Better than I expected, the sergeant major reported to the leadership team over their internal comm chips.

Is that good? Kae asked.

Jake answered, *For this mob, it's a good start. What is acceptable attrition under this new program since not everyone is going to measure up?*

Ten percent, Marcie offered. *Do we have an active recruiting campaign ongoing?*

Yes, but it's not going to replenish ten percent in a month's time. Colonel Braithwen stalked the ranks along with the sergeant major and Kaeden, pounding shoulders and slapping backs to congratulate those who had made it. Positive reinforcement. The little things to keep the troops striving for better.

We don't have the horsepower to run separate on-boarding. Corral all new recruits for training at a later date. If we have any hard-chargers who get injured in combat or sent home after fulfilling their duties, they'll be the new trainers. We need established warriors to set the example for the next generation. Turn them over to me, please. Clock's ticking.

Yes, ma'am, the other three replied.

She assumed the position of attention. "Belzonian Army! A-ten-*hut!*" The massive formation rippled to attention. Marcie waited until most of the movement stopped. "When I give the command to fall out, you will return to the barracks, clean up, and put on your uniforms for a quick inspection before class, which will take place right here. You have one hour to be standing tall in formation. FALL OUT!"

The Belzonians stumbled and staggered away. Kae made his way to Marcie. "An hour? My, aren't we feeling generous?"

"I wonder how many of them will realize they're supposed to get breakfast during that time, too?" Marcie didn't sound sorry.

"Devious." Kae realized there was more than one test underway. "And the officers?"

"Here come a couple of the captains right now. Remember these guys. They could be the start of our core leadership, depending on what they have to say."

Colonel Braithwen intercepted two of the army's four officers and saved them from themselves by sending them to Colonel Walton. The other two escaped with the mass of enlisted.

"And two more, but I think they were encouraged to do the right thing," Kae whispered.

"Captains," Marcie greeted. The two saluted.

"May we get a copy of the plan of the day to help with implementing your orders, ma'am?" the first one asked.

"Name?" Marcie requested.

The Belzonian captain swallowed before replying, "Derrick Baroon, ma'am."

"Captain Baroon, well done. That is what you should be asking for. I will give you the plan as we progress and the leadership of this army establishes itself. Rank does not grant leadership. It only grants the opportunity while making the challenge even greater. You appear to be the first ones who are rising to that challenge. In the next fifty-eight minutes, the troops will need to shower, get dressed, eat, drink lots of water, and get back here. I know too many of them will spend time messing with their hair. They'll be dehydrated and hungry and look like crap, but they'll have great hair that they'll keep stuffed under their helmets for the rest of the day."

"They'll be wearing their helmets during class?" the second captain asked. At Marcie's look, he realized that she didn't know his name. "Captain Grebus Anthen."

"Yes. They will always wear their helmets, and as soon

47

as practicable, they'll be wearing their body armor, too. In a week, all PT sessions will be conducted in full gear. Practice how you play, Captain. That's what we'll be doing. You two better get going. You need to be here to help your troops into formation. While they get an hour, you get forty-five minutes. Dismissed."

The captains saluted before turning and running away on stiff legs.

"They have potential," Kae offered.

"I concur. I wish I knew the mid-grades better. They were here well before the sergeant major and I left for joint duty. I recognize them but don't know enough about them to judge if they're good officers or playing at being good."

"We shall see, but I have high hopes." The colonel turned to greet the two majors who had lagged behind.

"Majors?" Marcie asked.

One of the majors spoke for both. "Towelick Ravamoon and Landis Panthoon, ma'am. We must protest. It'll take a day for our people to recover their dignity from that morning torture session."

"Our people will learn to take every minute of every day in stride. There is no recovery period in combat. You fight until you win. Our people are going to learn that, Captain."

"Major," Ravamoon corrected weakly.

"Not anymore." Marcie scowled. "Promotions can happen just as readily for those who step up and help us lead this army. If that's not you, then get the hell out of the way for those who are ready to lead soldiers."

Marcie walked away. Kae joined her, unsure of where

she was going. "Our stuff is on the ship," he whispered. "It's the other way."

"Crap."

"You were most impressive to that point." Kae bit his lip to keep from smiling. "I think you made your point, though. Shaky Jake is giving them the opportunity to impress you by delivering crystal-clear instructions for what they need to accomplish in what remains of this day."

"Make the ship come to us. Bring it over here since I don't feel like running two klicks to get there."

"Two minutes." Kae smirked. "You got two minutes. We'll tell them when we get there."

He took off without waiting and accelerated to an inhuman speed. Marcie launched after him. The newly demoted captains watched with mouths open at the impressive display, but Marcie didn't do it for their benefit. She did it because her husband constantly challenged her. Also, she wanted a shower. It was critical to get in there before Kae because he'd take his time to mess with her. She increased her pace until even she was near the breaking point.

Jake grabbed the sergeant major and they hurried toward their tent. "Can you run that fast?" Jake asked.

"Not a chance," Crantis replied with a chuckle. "Looks like we got some supplemental training ahead of us."

"No shit, Crantis. Seeing a snippet of what they can do gives me hope for the whole army. They don't expect anyone to live up to their standards, but they show people what is possible. Marcie promised we'll put our core leadership team through the Pod-doc to help them survive the rigors of combat. That is something every professional soldier should aspire to."

"I couldn't agree more. Now, what do we call this thing? Something along the lines of when we're not fucking each other, we're fucking up the enemy."

"I think we'll go with something shorter and with less fucking. The unit used to be called the Force de Guerre, which is from an Earth language. It means War Force, but we're going to win the peace and hold it. I still got nothing, but what do you say we leave the fucking out of it? The humans seem a little squeamish."

"But they dominate a battlefield. I've seen vids of the Bad Company. They aren't kidding when they go to war. If we do things the same way, there won't be any protracted engagements. We'll steamroll every enemy, especially if we can get some of those combat suits they have. With mechs like that, we'll be invincible."

"The Invincibles." The colonel rolled it over his tongue a few times. "Nah. Sounds too cartoony. But we'll get there. We'll grab chow first and then get cleaned up." The two started running. They knew Colonel Walton would tolerate no one being late, not even the former commander and the sergeant major.

They had a great deal to do, and only thirty minutes left to do it in.

"If only we had heavy metal playing between sessions."

"Hey! I can make that happen." The colonel veered toward the admin building.

CHAPTER FOUR

Belzimus, Belzonian Army Barracks

The day ended with half the army sleeping through the last training session, which was another war movie. They'd watched two that day because with the physical strain of too much PT and too little food, the troops looked like soldiers in training should: exhausted. It would keep them out of trouble.

Colonel Braithwen called a meeting with the captains and majors before releasing the army for the day. The troops hurried away despite how tired they were. The colonels smiled at each other in approval. Motivation could overcome exhaustion, which meant that it and training would help to develop the ability to overcome the paralysis of fear. Every soldier would have to face their fear. How they reacted would be a defining moment in their ability to continue. Marcie intended to build them up little by little, teaching them to have confidence in their capabilities. Today, a five-kilometer run had kicked their asses upside-down and backward. In a week, they would finish without issue, in step, with very few falling out.

Courage was the ability to act despite being afraid. She needed her mid-grade officers to embrace that and not fail her.

Fifty captains and majors stood by. She found her two captains from earlier. They had returned after PT before any of the troops or other officers, beating Jake and Crantis by a full minute. She nodded to them as they joined her with the crowd of mid-grades. They quickly saluted. Once they had everyone gathered in a horseshoe around her, she called Baroon and Anthen to the front.

"When everyone else was looking after themselves, these two were thinking of the people in their charge. They weren't afraid to ask questions, good questions about what they could do to help us help our army. Gentlemen, take off your helmets."

They blanched at the praise and reluctantly pulled their helmets from their heads. Their hair was matted, most of the color having washed away with the sweat of the day. They hadn't showered after PT, but they had eaten and hydrated.

"Priorities!" she shouted. "They understand what matters. Being capable of leading these soldiers requires personal sacrifice. Looking outward, not inward. Effective immediately, I'm promoting both to major. Congratulations, Major Baroon, Major Anthen. Now get back in formation."

She waved them away as if brushing off mosquitos, and they melted back into the mob of officers around her. No one congratulated them.

"When the time is right, you can return to a hairstyle that is effective for you and meets your personal desires. Until then, we have a great deal of soldiering to do. You are the critical link in turning this mess into a competent and effective army. Training starts with you. Right now, we're leading it because I want you to see what I'm going to ask of you. That's your first lesson. Never ask your people to do something you won't do yourself. You will lead from the front. That means you have to be better, faster, smarter, and more caring than anyone in your charge. Major, read tomorrow's training schedule."

Kae stepped up. The mid-grades stood close enough that he barely had to raise his voice. "Zero five hundred, PT in full combat gear, no weapons. We're taking a nature hike, but only ten kilometers. That will take us three hours. In a war, we'd do it in less than two. That is our eventual goal. When we return, chow, clean up, and return to formation for a uniform inspection at nine hundred hours. Nine thirty, training regimen conducted by the colonel and me until noon. Thirty minutes for chow and change. PT gear right here at twelve-thirty. Calisthenics, stretching, and introduction to hand to hand combat. Still in PT gear, sixteen hundred hours, more training, closing with a video, securing for the day at seventeen thirty. Any questions?"

"Will there be pads for the hand-to-hand training?"

"No. Any other questions?" Kae stared the asker down to keep him from following up. He nodded to the group and stepped back.

"Make sure your people sleep, get something to eat, and drink lots of water. If you thought you sweated today, you're in for a treat tomorrow. None of you better fall out

CRAIG MARTELLE & MICHAEL ANDERLE

of the combat hike. I don't know if any of you didn't make today's run, and I don't want to know. But starting tomorrow, I better see every single one of your smiling faces standing tall before the formation, and after every event, you better still be at the front."

"Or what?' someone had the bravery to say but not reveal who they were.

"Everyone take off your helmets," Marcie said, icicles dangling from her words.

Some took them off quickly to show they hadn't spent any time on their coiffures. Others sported brightly colored hair, squashed from a day under the helmet but still evidencing the attention it had been given.

"You'll get your time to primp, but that time is not now. We can't waste the valuable resource of a minute in any day. You need to convince the troops that their lives are the priority. Looking good is secondary. No one is going out on the town until we've finished training. You know what's sexy? Not puking on a run. Standing tall and looking good in uniform. Being ready for war during the day and executive guard duty at night. Guards get all the action if you know what I mean. Until then, you need to be in front of your people on anything and everything. Colonel Braithwen will issue your individual unit orders for tomorrow. This route march is going to enlighten you regarding what a land combat force does." Marcie wasn't sure what else to tell them. "Major?"

Kae wasn't sure either. "This week is going to be PT and more PT. We'll start breaking down into smaller unit training so the soldiers can get to know their teammates, and most importantly, trust them. Trust is another source of courage. No one wants to let someone who trusts them down. The same goes for you and us. We'll roll through the barracks later for what we'll call a morale check. We want to see how people are holding up."

Colonel Braithwen produced a datapad and shot-gunned the individual orders he'd been working on instead of watching the movies with the mid-grade officers. They sent similar messages to the junior officers. He nodded when he was finished.

"Dismissed," Marcie said casually. Some officers saluted, many didn't. That was when the sergeant major went ballistic.

"Officers? Showing disrespect not only to their seniors but their betters, too? I didn't see any of you scrambling to lead the run. I'm fucking embarrassed for the troops who have you to look up to. Sir!" He saluted sharply and waited. A ripple went through the group as they returned his salute. Without further prompting, they turned back and saluted Colonel Walton. Marcie returned it, just as sharply.

"Thank you." She scanned the mid-grades until she rested on the individual to whom she was showing her appreciation, Crantis Monsoon.

The group hurried away before they could screw anything else up.

"What do you think, Jake?" Marcie asked.

He pulled off his helmet and scrubbed the stubble. "I think we're going to have a lot of resentment. They're not used to being roughly handled. We're not an aggressive race, mostly. Not speaking for Crantis and me, of course."

"Paithoon seemed to think those in the Belzonian military were different. That they were the most aggressive of your people," Marcie offered.

"From Paithoon's perspective, everyone is aggressive, and most are bordering on criminally insane." Crantis liked the man but didn't respect his opinion when it came to anything military.

"I think we need to give everyone an hour or two before a stroll-through. It'll be what old Earthers would call management by walking around. We'll show the flag and let them see us when we're relaxed."

Crantis and Jake made faces at each other, then the colonel offered his advice. "Don't get suckered into a game of Blintz. It's a Belzonian card game that's a bit active and has some betting, but that's mild. It's more about the motions, bluffs, and dominant plays."

"Is that a strange form of Belzonian foreplay?"

Jake feigned shock. "Everything on Belzimus is foreplay, Blintz included. Maybe more so."

The sergeant major laughed heartily. "I don't think the humans get our proclivities." He faced Marcie and Kae. "Remember, no jealousy here. This is natural for us. You're on our turf now, so it's your human ways that are strange."

Kae nodded vigorously. "No Blintz. Got it. No orgies on my watch. I have vowed!"

"I haven't," the sergeant major countered. Jake nodded in agreement.

Marcie decided that retreat was the only way to save their red faces. "We'll be on the ship. It doesn't matter if you want to join us or not. We'll take an easy stroll through the barracks and officer tents and touch as many noses as we can. Hopefully help the soldiers understand. The enemy is out there," Marcie pointed toward the sky, "and they won't hesitate to kill any of us. The training will keep people alive unless your name shows up on a lucky bullet. Then there's nothing you can do about it."

"We agree on that. Until tomorrow, Colonel, Major."

"I always look forward to a new day to challenge and be challenged. Miles to go before we sleep, Jake, Crantis."

Marcie and Kae grabbed a full hot meal while onboard *Vengeance*. Then they stripped out of their uniforms and went casual, jeans and pullovers for their foray into the barracks.

They walked hand in hand on their way up a small rise to where the barracks and administrative buildings were settled. A short distance away, the supply warehouse and motor pools held the army's gear.

"We should probably check those out tomorrow. We need to make sure this stuff runs, just in case we get called up early." Kae tried to see the armor, transport, and engineering vehicles, but darkness was settling. He could see in the dark because of enhanced vision from the nanos, but the images weren't as clear as in broad daylight.

"We always get called up early."

"Can we tell them no, and if so, for how long?" Kae wondered.

"Nothing more than three weeks. After that, we lose credibility. These knuckleheads were supposed to be trained, so our deployment timeline was based on that. We might get one combined arms exercise in during the full four weeks, but that will be shorting individual skills training. Now, you're making me worried. I'll have to keep checking my comm for a message from General Reynolds.

If we get deployed too early, no matter what the target, we won't be ready, and training during an op is going to be a bit hairy."

"If we could get two months, we'd be ready to go almost anywhere except extreme cold. That takes training we are not going to do. No time or gear for it."

"You have hexed us!" Marcie declared. "We're doomed. We'll be sent to an ice planet in two weeks. Doomed, I tell you!"

Kaeden chuckled. "We'll make it happen. We always do. Is the Bad Company available, just in case?"

Marcie shook her head. "Your parents are being sent to Benitus Seven to look for Skrima."

Kae lost his humor. "How did my sister take the news? Never mind, I'll find out. I'll call her when I get back to the ship."

"Maybe you should go now. Family first. It's a good policy, and the Belzonian Army should probably adopt some variation of it."

Kae stopped walking and looked back toward the ship. "Yeah. I'll call her now."

"I hope she's okay. Have a good call." Marcie leaned in for a passionate goodbye kiss.

"I wish you luck in going in there. I'm afraid of what you might see." Kae waved and started to walk away.

"You have that almost right. *You're* afraid of what *you* might see. When did you become such a Puritan?"

"When I was surrounded by ten thousand who weren't."

"Don't worry. No Blintz for me, not as far as you know. Don't wait up." She flipped a hand over her shoulder and sauntered away.

. . .

Sheri's Pride, the Command Center for Spires Harbor, the Bad Company's Shipyard

"I'm not pleased," Char said for the third time.

"They'll be here." Terry joined the space management coordinator. "Where are those two ships?"

The man pointed at the screen. "They're almost docked."

The _War Axe_ was in transit and would be waiting for them whenever they herded the cats of Char's pack.

She'd had enough and stormed out of the control center, the former bridge of the _Sheri's Pride_.

You goofy fuckers better play nice, or Char is going to rip you a new one, Terry transmitted using his internal comm chip. He held his finger to his head as he always did when using the chip.

Nice try, Char replied. _You're talking to me, but I appreciate what you're trying to do. It's sweet. I'll tell you that no matter how nice they play, I'm still going to rip them a new one._ Char stripped as she walked and changed into a dark-haired beast with white belly fur, then loped down the corridor toward one of the docking airlocks. Terry ran after her, dipping to scoop up her clothes while keeping pace.

"Don't kill any of them!" Terry yelled after her.

Char slowed until she could sense them and knew they were coming through. She scraped feet and claws on the smooth floor of the former Harborian vessel, bolting from the corridor into the receiving space. She leapt, hitting Merrit in the chest and careening off Shonna. The three tumbled to the deck, but Char was up in an instant, growling and nipping, saliva splattering them. Timmons and Sue stepped through and received an equal measure of Char's ire.

Terry waited patiently. He enjoyed Char's werewolf persona as long as her fury wasn't directed at him. He would never forget that day back in twenty-seven. He didn't want to relive it.

Once all four were on the deck, with her stalking back and forth over them, she stopped and changed back into human form. She strode naked to Terry, who had the good sense not to ogle or catcall. He handed over her clothes without comment. She winked at him, and he was ruined.

"We need to get to the *War Axe* right damn now!" he declared, energized to get back to their quarters. "We're taking your ride. We'll park in the hangar bay. Is *Iracitus* up for a little trip?"

"That's our mining ship." Timmons tried to prevent the use of their ship.

"Too bad, so sad," Terry replied. He pointed through the airlock at the ship beyond. It was a runabout and didn't actively engage in mining.

"Fine!" Timmons said a little too briskly. Char glared until he bowed his head. The five werewolves and Terry Henry boarded *Iracitus* for the short hop to the nearby *War Axe*.

"Welcome aboard," Iracitus remarked. The ship was named after the AI who operated it. Iracitus, one of Plato's stepchildren, had led a sheltered life but was learning to stretch his legs. Sharing time with Plato and Smedley on this trip beyond the frontier would probably do him good. At least, that made Terry feel better about inviting himself aboard the AI's ship, and that made him wonder. "Are you renting space aboard this ship from Iracitus, or is he renting from you?"

"That's a good question. We still have to work it out. That damn Magistrate of yours is upsetting the applecart."

"Bah!" Terry gestured that the thoughts were nonsense. "Getting their just desserts. They do the work. You two glory hounds ride on the back of a great mind."

"I appreciate the sentiment, Colonel Walton," Iracitus started, "but Sue and Timmons do most of the engineering and real work that goes into a mining operation the size of one that is necessary to run a shipyard like Spires Harbor's. They are a pleasure to work with."

"See?" Timmons mumbled. "Somebody likes us."

Char glared until her pack deferred.

"You've had too much time to yourselves. You're still pack. I've given you your freedom, but when I need help, you play fuck-fuck games. I need you and your minds to resolve this as quickly as possible. I'm not asking any of you to launch yourselves into a sun. For fuck's sake, you've grown soft!"

Timmons meekly raised his hand.

"What?" Char snapped, but she was cooling down. She'd accomplished what she wanted to, and Terry had been behind her all the way. The pack was her concern, and their problems were hers to fix. He balanced her. "You're all out of the doghouse for the moment. Don't think I'm going to forget this, though. How long did you go without a hand?"

Timmons winced at the jab. Nearly one hundred and fifty years earlier, he had challenged Char for the position of Alpha, and she had punished him to a degree normal humans could never grasp. Werewolf law was harsh but fair, and Char had enforced it without mercy.

"We only heard about some of the mission. We will support you, of course, but it's nice to know why the sense of urgency. Tell us what's going on, Char," Timmons pleaded.

"The Federation needs us to go back to Benitus Seven to check if the Skrima have returned. I don't know why that would pop up if there wasn't something to it, so we're expecting to find those red bastards coming through a rift. At the same time, we're supposed to prepare the space station in orbit above Benitus for Federation occupation. All of that means another conversation with the Grays."

Sue grimaced. "How is Cory?"

"I think Cory is in a good place where she can face Benitus Seven and finally put her husband to rest," Char explained.

"It's time for her to move on, and I believe she is ready for it," Terry added. The werewolves nodded, casting furtive glances at Char. The alpha sat with her eyes closed.

"Smedley, permission to enter the hangar bay," Timmons requested, even though Iracitus was already taking care of it. Smedley was bringing the Pod that Terry and Char had flown to *Sheri's Pride* in right behind them. Timmons tried to adjust the heading. "Iracitus, have you taken control?"

"I have had control from the second we undocked. I wanted you to feel like you were accomplishing something as a distraction from your dressing down. I believe that is the right term."

"Well-deserved ass-chewing," Char offered the AI. "You can use that. Everyone will understand."

"Thank you for that, all of you!" Timmons shot back. Sue snickered. "We get it. We're in a rush to close this loop. Next time, maybe tell us we need to save the universe again. You made it sound like business as usual."

"I did not." Char started to stand, but Terry kept a hand on her leg.

"Saving the universe *is* business as usual," Shonna remarked. "Next stop, beyond the frontier. Can we take the mechs this time?"

"Only all of them," Terry announced. "We picked up enough new suits to cover us, as well as every member of the Bad Company. Skrima phase-shift, but Ted is waiting for us, and he has his toys and other surprises for the Red Dread."

Char cocked an eyebrow at him. "Is that what we're calling them?"

"I just thought of it. Catchy, isn't it?"

Char rolled her eyes closed. "Yes, dear. It's fine."

Terry scowled. Things were never fine when Char used that word. "I don't think that word means…"

Char interrupted him. "Don't you say it."

He closed his mouth. He hadn't started off in the doghouse with the rest of the pack, but he'd ended there. Terry threw his hands up in frustration, then leaned back and closed his eyes, hoping for a minute of peace before they hit the deck running.

Fifteen seconds later, *Iracitus* bumped the deck. Terry stood still as the hatch popped and let Char go first. The rest followed the couple out.

"Briefing right back here at…" Terry checked his watch, "four local time. That's an hour for you to grab some food, check your combat suits, and prepare to deploy. We're leaving immediately. We'll take the *Axe* to the planet's surface in case we need extra firepower, a quick egress, or the Pod-docs. Cory is working on something for us: cryopods that follow the warriors around. They'll preserve whatever's left in case someone gets hit bad. It gives us time to get them into the Pod-doc. Ted is supposed to be working with her on that."

"How did you get Felicity to join us?" Sue wondered.

"We didn't."

Sue gestured with her chin. Terry decided he didn't want to look. Char started walking toward the hatch leading from the hangar deck. "Felicity, I'm so glad you could join us," she called.

Terry turned in time to see Felicity huff and storm into the ship. "Was that smoke coming out of her ears?" Terry asked, but no one answered. They were all in the doghouse, and Char was on her way to joining them.

CHAPTER FIVE

Belzimus, Belzonian Army Barracks

The end of the first week came in a rush. The troops had stayed up late playing Blintz the first night. Fewer stayed up the second night, and no one had the energy to play after that. Outside of training, the only thing they did was sleep and prepare for training through uniform and equipment maintenance. A hundred Belzonians had quit, which meant hard labor to fulfill the remainder of their contract.

That gave Marcie hope that they wouldn't lose too many more. She hadn't known there would be such a harsh penalty from a peaceful people, but it worked in her favor. In a conflict where the army occupied foreign land, numbers were as important as troop quality. Too small a force trained to the highest standard would not be able to accomplish what a massive force trained to an acceptable standard could.

After the first day, she set her sights lower but hoped they'd be able to find a few hundred who fully embraced what it meant to be a warrior to create an elite force to conduct surgical operations.

Kae thought it was pie-in-the-sky thinking. Marcie had to get her feet back on the ground and get back to work just to meet a reasonably acceptable standard. She had no idea what that end state was, but the bar was lowering with each new test of the army's mettle.

Ten kilometers into a route march, she called a halt. The army peeled away, heading to the side of the road to drop to the ground, exhausted. They no longer played grab-ass or various games that weren't focused on becoming a good soldier. She brought Kae, Jake, and Crantis together for a strategy session. The four were the only ones upright out of the entire army. They didn't consider the mid-grades or junior officers to be weak. They hadn't been enhanced, and they were being driven by people who were.

That also helped the four to maintain the mystique of being super-soldiers.

"We aren't even close with this mob," Marcie complained. Colonel Braithwen and Sergeant Major Monsoon exchanged glances before turning back to Marcie. Both were shaking their heads.

"You've been here a week. You may think you're trudging uphill in a blizzard, but we've been here our whole lives. Besides Crantis, I've never seen a Belzonian who didn't sport some kind of do. Have you looked at them lately? There might be a thousand of them who cut things back, and ninety-nine percent aren't bothering with colors. That is a cultural change. It's like moving a glacier with your bare hands, and that's just the beginning. We have come light-years from where we started."

Crantis bit his lip as the colonel spoke.

"I appreciate that," Marcie replied. "What are you seeing, Crantis?"

"People who caught a ride to the other side of the barracks are walking ten kilometers even though they are dog-tired, keeping up with the likes of us. I see soldiers, ma'am."

Marcie looked into the distance. She could smell Belzonian sweat. It was different from humans' in that it smelled sweet, not pungent. The sun was shining, but cooler air wafted past on a light breeze.

"Maybe I'm used to a little faster pace," Marcie conceded.

"Back on Earth, four or five generations ago, we tried expanding the FDG. That took forever, and in the end, we had to dismantle it because we couldn't keep them trained. We couldn't bring new people in. We had to jail commanders for abusing their positions. This is much more pleasant than that."

Marcie snorted a short chuckle. "That was a shitshow."

"Is this?" Jake asked.

Marcie scanned the ranks, which stretched for nearly as far as the eye could see. "No. Not at all. Assemble the mid-grades. Let's talk about what we're going to do tomorrow."

The sergeant major didn't waste any time. "Leadership team, REPORT!" he bellowed through cupped hands. He marched away at a brisk pace, repeating his call every fifty meters.

Captains and majors popped to their feet and hurried

toward Marcie, Kae, and Jake. They led those who were the first to arrive to an area away from the formation, then waited for the last ones to arrive, with Monsoon confirming that was all of them.

"Thank you for your support in bringing the army up to speed so quickly. Tomorrow, we're going to break back into individual specialties: Infantry, Motor Pool, Artillery, Mechanized, Engineers, and Aerial support. When we get back from this hump, send everyone to PM their gear and get ready to move out at first light."

"PM?" the closest captain asked.

"Preventive maintenance. Kick the tires, check the oil, start them, charge batteries, and roll them around. Do whatever needs to be done to make sure they'll work when we hit Zoranitus tomorrow. That's right, boys and girls, we're getting down to the nuts and bolts of being a functioning land army—combined arms operations. Our people are ready for the next phase of their training.

"Grunt the pain!" Major Baroon shouted, catching Marcie unaware. The other infantry officers grunted their slogan.

"Faster, funnier!" a captain shouted from the back. Some nodded, but no one joked about the transportation team. When people needed a ride, those truck drivers became their best friends. When they wanted chow in the field, the trucks brought it.

Major Goran Flayden threw his head back and howled at the sky. "Bow to the king!"

Marcie raised an eyebrow.

"Artillery," Jake explained.

"Metalheads, bringing the heat, baby!" The tankers and

other armor jocks picked up the call, shouting for the metalheads.

"Dig, baby, dig," a captain called from the side. The mid-grades yelled and shouted their slogans at each other.

"Show the way!" a lone voice called.

"Geek!" someone shouted back.

"No rockets for you!" the first voice countered.

"I got a rocket for you, though." The crowd snickered and chuckled.

Colonel Jake Braithwen looked like a proud parent.

Marcie raised her hands to get everyone's attention. "Take charge of your people, get them back to the barracks, and get ready for tomorrow. Four hours of liberty tonight, in town if they wish, but back by midnight. We cross the line of departure at first light."

The mid-grades saluted in a single unified movement and ran for their people.

"Okay. Maybe I don't have a clue, but I am good in a fight," Marcie declared. She gripped Jake's upper arm. "Thanks. To both of you."

Monsoon saluted. "If you'll excuse me, ma'am. I need to make sure those candy-asses aren't causing undue grief for the troops."

The sergeant major was their key to success, and they knew it. He understood what the colonels wanted and also had direct access to the frontlines. Monsoon was in the unique position of being embraced by both the enlisted and the officers. He walked a tightrope at all times.

It suited him.

"Combined arms," Jake mentioned to get them back on track.

"Combined arms, the integration of multiple combat branches to achieve complementary results. The whole is greater than the sum of its parts. We need to conduct a full day of maneuver training before we send any rounds downrange. My only frame of reference is that steaming pile we observed when we got here."

"I can't guarantee it will be much better than that the first time out, but you have their attention. With a coherent mission order, they will know their objective and support it. These are good people, and they have the potential to be good soldiers. They didn't know what that looked like before because Belzimus didn't have the political will or the need to drive the army to a higher level of professionalism. My hands were tied, but now we're able to do what needs to be done."

"Are you thinking I fired the lieutenant colonel too quickly?" Marcie asked.

"Not at all. That guy was a career officer, promoted because he never did anything wrong. You know what that means."

Kae and Marcie laughed. "That he took no risks and always found someone else to blame. Those asshats are the pariahs who have existed in every culture throughout history. Terry Henry never tolerated them, and neither will I. Good! We have a clean slate on which to write this next chapter. I do have one question, though."

Jake waited but Marcie looked away, watching the troops get back into smaller formations and take off at a brisk pace on a beeline toward the barracks.

"What's the question?" the colonel finally asked.

"I was thinking out loud. You probably won't be able to

answer, but how many are going to get themselves arrested or be too drunk to show up tomorrow? I'd like to think they'll all make it, but we held them back for a whole week!"

Jake shrugged. "It'll be what it is. I'll ask Crantis to detail a couple hard-charging NCOs to work with the no-shows and make them regret their decisions. Liberty canceled for the duration of training for everyone who violates curfew?"

"Make it so, Number One," Marcie stated. "Assuming we have a bunch of liberty risks, when we give them a pass next time, the entire squad who has a violator in its ranks will be restricted."

The colonel winced. "I'm not sure about that one. It could lead to animosity and the more proactive soldiers taking things into their own hands."

While Marcie contemplated the thought, Kae stepped in. "Belzonians are used to working in groups; that's the culture. We want them to see their squad as a close-knit family. They might not like them, but they're still family. When they're knee-deep in the shit, those are the only people who can help them get out of it. They *have to* trust each other."

The colonel had aired his concern. He didn't want to press it. He knew there would be issues now and later. It was an army; there were always issues. Then it came to him. "I think our risk is minimal for tonight's liberty."

"Why is that?" Kae was hopeful but confused.

"It's our Sunday. Most everything is closed today."

Kae smiled. "Perfect. I'm not sure we could have planned this better."

The group shared a short laugh before they sobered.

"Success for tomorrow's training?" Jake asked.

"Besides not getting someone killed?" Marcie quipped. "Awareness. Making sure they don't cross into lines of fire during maneuvers. Keeping lanes clear will improve their battlefield sense. With better vision comes better combat decisions. They're going to see what they're capable of during high-intensity operations. Not tomorrow, but in another few weeks when we run the graduation exercise."

"You think they'll be ready?"

"Of course!" Marcie declared with a smile. "Because they have to be. The Federation isn't going to sit on our first mission because we aren't ready to go. I asked for six weeks, they said two. We compromised at four. The Belzonian government said they were ready now. Thank the gods the Federation took that with a grain of salt."

"What if they activate us in another week?"

"The cynic in me is expecting to deploy early. This next week is going to be intense, and whatever time we don't have here, we're going to have to figure out how to fill while embarked on the transports." Marcie stared into the distance. It wasn't yet midday and the sun was bright, promising a warm afternoon. She could smell wildflowers, something they didn't have aboard the *War Axe* or Keeg Station. "We bring peace to save planets from themselves until such time as they recover."

"That reminds me. Crantis and I have a couple options for names. What do you think of 'Trans-Pacific Task Force?'"

. . .

War Axe, Entering the Benitus Star System, Well beyond the Frontier

Terry and Char remained on the bridge, their mood tempered. Their last trip beyond the Federation frontier had cost them significantly, but they'd freed a huge human colony, captured and brought there from Earth untold centuries prior. They had also seized an entire fleet of ships that rivaled all but the most influential in the galaxy.

Terry wasn't going in alone. He'd brought a dozen Harborian vessels with him, hundreds of crew, and enough firepower to protect them from the unknown. Maybe enough to hold unknown threats at bay without having to unleash death and destruction.

Not that Terry Henry Walton was opposed to delivering the pain when called for, but he had softened in his old age. He now thought he'd give peace a chance, especially since the Bad Company had enough firepower to wreak havoc, no matter the enemy, should an initial conversation turn sour. Walk softly and carry a capital-grade railgun.

"Ted?" Terry talked to the ceiling when speaking to Smedley, who would connect him to members of the crew. "What's the status of the cryopods?"

They had already delayed for nearly a week to give Cory, Ted, and the rest of the pack time to build systems that would improve survival on the modern battlefield. If they could perfect them, Terry would ship as many as the Bad Company could afford to Kaeden and Marcie. He wanted to give them the advantages they had earned over time. Plus, they were family.

"Busy," Ted finally replied. Char clenched her jaw. Terry smiled and signaled for calm.

"Cory?" he asked the ceiling.

"Dad, Ted is a genius. I think we're there. We're doing a test on a side of bistok."

"Our bistok? Meat isn't good if you refreeze it. Can't you use something else?"

Char slapped him on the arm. The captain chuckled from his chair overlooking the bridge's workstations.

"It's well worth it," Char told her daughter. "I think your project will save a lot of lives throughout the universe."

"The power source for these is not Etheric-based, so it'll be more readily available, but it will limit the range and hover-time. On Benitus, when Ted activates his Etheric limiter, these won't be affected. Some of the Bad Company cryopods will have Etheric power supplies, giving them unlimited range, but those are for use elsewhere. Ted is working up the final programming now for a user-selectable option to follow a known individual by their chip emissions or something else the cryopod can use to discriminate. The default is automatic: tell it who is in its sphere, with an emergency mode that can be activated in case we need to put someone into deep freeze who the cryopod does not recognize."

Terry and Char nodded in unison.

"May we never need one, but it brings peace of mind to have them. Just like an umbrella, but completely different," Terry stated less impressively than he had intended.

Micky spoke up. "Space station first?"

"No." Terry turned to issue the orders. "Let's go to the planet first. If there is a rift, every second we delay lets more of those evil bastards into our dimension. We took too long to get here, but that delay appears to be worthwhile, based on what Ted and the others have done to help Cory realize her vision."

Terry and Char headed for the door.

"Launch the Etheric dampening satellites and take the *War Axe* down. We'll deploy in small units in the Pods once we're near the deck." Terry stopped at the hatch leading into the corridor. "Have you ever fired the mains inside the atmosphere?"

Micky looked at the viewscreen. "We haven't. I think atmospheric friction would build heat too quickly around the projectile, and that would impact the rails. If they warp, bad things could happen."

"We'll try not to call for fire too often." Terry winked on his way off the bridge.

He and Char ran down the steps, taking them at breakneck speed in their hurry to embrace their daughter. In the hangar bay, the outer doors were cantilevering closed for their entry through the upper atmosphere.

Joseph and Petricia strolled up. "I approve of the flying coffins," the vampire said. He had not had human blood in over a century, and Petricia had never tasted it, subsisting on animal blood until she could be modified in the Pod-doc and given the ability to survive without needing to feed on warm fluids.

"I need your special talents as a negotiator with the Benitons, or maybe we should call them by their human name: the Grays," Terry stated while Char closed on her daughter to wrap an arm around her waist.

"I'm intrigued, TH. Are they expecting us?"

"I would hope they know we're here, but damn. I didn't call them."

"We'll take care of it." Joseph and Petricia hurried away, passing Bundin. He was a Podder who had recently been promoted to corporal, following his valiant efforts to find and destroy the enemy vessel harassing Keeg Station and Spires Harbor. Joseph tapped Bundin's shell. The turtle-like creature with a blue stalk head rumbled a greeting.

An Ixtali, a spider-like race, a Malatian sporting his full plumage, K'Thrall, a four-legged Yollin who used to be the *War Axe*'s systems officer, and Chris Bo Runner, a Harborian, joined their squad leader. The new recruits had proved themselves at the attack on Keeg Station.

"Get loaded up. Full gear," Terry told them. "Have you seen Christina?"

You can use the chip, you know. I'm only one mind-meld away, the Pricolici replied. Nathan Lowell's daughter had joined the Bad company at her father's urging to expand her horizons and see more of the universe. She had taken to it like a fish to water and worked her way quickly into the executive officer position after Marcie and Kae left to take over the new Force de Guerre.

Terry spotted her striding across the hangar bay. Terry's boss' daughter was living with Terry's grandson. A hundred years separated the younger Kai from the older Christina. TH still wasn't sure how he was supposed to feel about the enormity of the relationship. Char kept telling him that as long as the kids were happy, it was not his concern.

His eye twitched.

"You should get that looked at," she told him. "We're

gearing up now, ballistic armor teams around a mech to give us both firepower and flexibility. No one wants a Skrim inside their suit. Is Ted's jammer ready to hold them in our dimension so we can kill them?"

"We're launching the satellites we recovered when we left Benitus the last time. Ted says we can reuse them. Since no Skrima escaped, they shouldn't know about them, so they can't mitigate them. If they could, that is. I have no idea what they're capable of technology-wise."

"Bullet-stoppers," Christina suggested. "They're going to learn how good they are at being targets for our railguns."

Terry leaned close. "I'm not talking genocide, but we kill them all. None can survive."

"That sounds like genocide." Christina looked sideways at TH. "But I don't disagree. They don't belong in this dimension, and the sooner they learn that, the fewer problems we'll have. Maybe if we headed through the rift into the Etheric to kill them, it would be genocide. On this side? We're repelling an invasion. Or maybe we'll find nothing and can stand down."

"That would be best." Terry lowered his voice. "Killing Skrima isn't going to bring Ramses back. He was not a warrior, but he learned to be a good one. He did what he had to do to support my daughter and never asked for anything but to be accepted. I could have done better by him, but instead, I tried to make him more like me."

Terry stopped and looked at the deck. Christina hugged him, but he gently pushed her away.

"I don't know why I told you that." He stepped back. "Prepare the company to deploy, Colonel. Two light for every one heavy, detailed in threes. Six Pods of three teams each. We'll fly out before the *War Axe* touches down. The remaining teams will stand by on the hangar deck, ready to deploy."

Christina saluted. Terry Henry Walton walked away, shoulders square and head high. Cory and Char waited for him. Once he reached them, Cory explained how the cryopods worked, walking through each capability. Terry and Char paid attention to their daughter, not the cryopods. They would work because the sharpest minds would make sure they did. Terry hoped they weren't needed.

Within two minutes, mechs started emerging from the armory and gathered in the hangar bay in front of their assigned shuttles. Terry's and Char's daughter Kimber waved as she strolled past. She was every bit as much a natural at driving a mech as her brother Kaeden. She took her station at her favorite Pod, lucky Number Three.

Bad Company warriors wearing full ballistic protection jogged across the bay to join the mechs to which they'd been assigned.

Christina walked out wearing her personal body armor, a flak jacket with arm and leg covers. Her helmet carried a subdued sigil of her rank. On her hip was the ever-present Jean Dukes Special, its biometrics keyed to her. If she lost her pistol in combat or it was taken from her by an enemy, they would not be able to use the powerful weapon.

Terry and Char took their cues and headed for the armory. The werewolves Shonna, Merrit, Timmons, and Sue joined them. Char didn't expect Ted to come, and he didn't. He had to operate the satellites and make sure the rest of them could fight. He was probably contributing more than any single warrior. Terry gave him a thumbs-up as he ran.

Ted ignored the others. He was still embroiled in the cryopods' programming, transferring it to the six that were ready. Ted had ordered another twenty, giving them priority in the manufacturing queue within the ship now that the design had been finalized. With one last flourish, Ted stood up and waved his hands like a magician. The six cryopods energized before lifting off the deck, then maneuvered carefully across the hangar bay to float serenely beside the troops.

Cory one-arm-hugged her Uncle Ted. She didn't smile or cheer. The idea was the culmination of recriminations and the clearing of guilt. There was nothing that could have been done back then, but they could do something now.

Christina spotted the cryopod and grumbled, "That's creepy as fuck! A floating coffin is going to follow me around?"

"It's going to follow *us* around," Terry clarified from nearby. He waved to Cory before casually striding across the bay until he was face to face with his XO. "And you're going to like it following you around. Maybe we'll stealth them at some point, but for now, it's a floating coffin from which you will rise. Suck it up and take it like a warrior."

Terry circled his arm in the air. "Wagons, ho!"

The Bad Company started to load.

The ship's captain made an announcement over the intercom. "Touch down in the vicinity of the last rift in ninety seconds. Dropships launch in thirty seconds.

Colonel Walton, we're getting IR signatures all over the place. There's a lot of hot down there."

"Pick up the pace, people!" Terry bellowed. The mechs and warriors squeezed into the shuttles. After the rear decks buttoned, the cryopods attached themselves to the outsides, and the Pods launched. Kai appeared after making sure the entire unit had been appropriately outfitted and armed. Two mechs and a few warriors still milled about. The alien squad with Bundin, Bon Tap, Slikira, and K'Thrall wore their custom armor and carried railguns. Private Skates Mardigan hovered near Kai.

Terry and Char stood with the werewolves. There had been no room in the Pods.

Char eyed him curiously.

"Got a little overzealous with the assignments," he admitted. "There wasn't any room for us, so we'll check out the rift."

"You mean, we're walking."

"A little stretch of the legs, that's it." He turned to Bundin. "Corporal, your squad is with us. Teams Nineteen and Twenty," he pointed at each mech when he called a number, "you're in reserve. Be ready to deploy, weapons hot."

He gave the small reserve no timeframe. If they were called, they'd be off the ship in a few heartbeats and running to their target.

The dropships rocketed from their launch tubes.

Joseph and Petricia helped themselves to *Iracitus* the ship and the AI. "We're on our way to see the Grays," Joseph called from the hatch before buttoning it up and lifting off.

"He fought in the French Revolution, and here he is, flying a spaceship," Terry remarked. The *War Axe* touched down, and the massive hangar bay doors rotated outward. The terrain had not changed since the last time they'd been there. He removed his Jean Dukes Special and dialed it to nine, then yelled over his shoulder. "Ted, activate the Etheric jammer."

Iracitus raced past the group, out of the hangar, and into the bright morning sky. The ship immediately banked and flew out of sight.

Terry jogged to the opening, down the ramp, and onto Benitus Seven. Char kept pace at his side. She carried two Glock nine-millimeter pistols and had strapped a railgun across her back. Bundin's stumpy legs rotated in a heavy rhythm as he pounded after the colonel.

A slight shimmer in the distance made Terry Henry's stomach twist inside out. He pushed himself to run faster, angling away from the visual noise, then slowed to get a better look. No larger than a grape. He breathed a sigh of relief. Char sighed. Terry prepared to fire his Jean Dukes into the small gap.

"Colonel!" Bon Tap shouted, pointing around the side of the rift.

A foot appeared and then two arms. A leg stepped through the other side. They had been looking at the back of the rift since the new opening was a hundred and eighty degrees from the last one.

Terry dove to the side and fired. The kick from the superweapon threw him off-balance, spinning him to the ground. Trapped on this side of the rift, the Skrim wasn't able to phase out, and the hypervelocity dart slammed into it with the force of a meteor. The creature exploded in an expanding cloud of red mist.

Bundin took control of his squad on the far side of the rift and fired into the opening. Bon Tap and Slikira joined in, unleashing a torrent of railgun projectiles through the man-sized rift, while K'Thrall and Chris Bo Runner provided security for the squad since the Skrima had already been coming through the rift. They didn't know where they were.

They're on the ship, Micky reported.

CHAPTER SIX

Belzimus, Command Post and Training Area Zoranitus

Marcie ditched the binoculars and headed for the door. Kae was right on her heels. "Sometimes, they act like they know what they're doing, and then there are all the other times," she complained.

"We better get down there. I see Shaky Jake and Crantis running around like chickens with their heads cut off."

"Who are those dickweeds?" Marcie asked. The two stopped and watched a small group of Belzonians laughing and joking while lounging in the grass. Marcie focused like a laser beam and crossed the intervening ground nearly as quickly. Kae wasn't amused either. He didn't want to run into the training area with his brain ready to explode, but they couldn't let the clown show continue.

"Get on your feet!" Kae roared. The smiles evaporated, and the whites of their eyes showed their shock. They popped up. Most of them carried boxes with levers and buttons.

"What the fuck are you doing?"

"Ma'am!" The captain saluted. His rank was hanging sideways off his uniform. Marcie bit her tongue. "We're aerial support, but no one is calling in fire."

Kae relaxed.

"Fucking air wing, living the life of Reilly while the real work happens down there in the trenches. I won't ask you again."

The captain held out his hands, but he couldn't utter the words that would change the colonel's mind.

"We're flying our rigs around the battlefield, as per our SOP, waiting to drop ordnance as called. We can't launch rockets if no one has given us a target."

"You're the rocket man," she noted, recalling the incident from the previous day where his fellow mid-grade officers had given him grief. "Show the way."

"Yes, ma'am," the captain agreed, wincing at the nickname she'd dropped on his head. "We also provide forward observation, remote fire control, and advance reconnaissance, getting out in front of the troops."

Marcie and Kae shared a thought. *Why didn't we know about this?*

"Show us," Marcie ordered. The six with the remotes gathered around them. Captain Sonthi gave a quick demonstration of how the system worked, but for Marcie, the most intriguing part was the screen. He tried to give her the remote, but she turned him down. "You fly it. That's your job. Now, show us the armored combat team."

A sergeant stepped up to share his screen. The bird circled over the tanks and armored personnel carriers. When it rose to a respectable altitude, the vehicles' movements became clear. They drove forward a short distance before backing up to where they started and repeating the process.

Kae looked like he wanted to strangle someone.

"Why don't you climb into your mech suit and show them how it's done?" Marcie suggested.

Kae didn't wait. He took off running for the *Vengeance*.

"Okay, pan over the rest of the units, one by one."

They each shared when their turn came. The artillery unit was running loading drills. An unidentified taskmaster was driving them, striding from one piece to another. The crews remained energized. "Get closer to whoever that is."

"It's Major Flayden, ma'am. He loves the big guns," Sonthi quipped.

"Is everything an innuendo in this...army?" She almost said "this man's" but restrained herself.

"I'm not sure how I'm supposed to answer that." The captain pointed back to the screen. "There's the sergeant major and Colonel Braithwen. You can tell them from a kilometer away."

They were in charge because they took charge. The troops nearest them moved confidently in formations that kept their spacing and stayed true to their heading. Upon zooming out, troops farther away did not enjoy such focus. Some even wandered aimlessly, which demonstrated the effective range of command and control. With training and experience, that would extend to the entire battlefield through the pyramid structure of military leadership, each level from the top to the foundational front lines working as a single entity to accomplish a clear goal.

"You others stay here. Sonthi, you're with me." He made

to hand his remote to one of the others. "What are you doing? Bring your damn plane! I need to see what's happening, and you're the next best thing to God."

"I am?"

"Don't fall behind, Rocketman." Marcie jogged easily to see if he could keep up, but things weren't looking good for the leader of the close-air-support squadron. "Get up here!"

He sprinted briefly to catch up before falling back. She checked her pace.

"What is your problem?"

He was panting so hard he couldn't answer. She ripped the remote from his hand to make it easier for him to run. She felt like she was running so slowly that she could have made better time by walking.

The thunder of a mech running at top speed was music to her ears.

"Watch this," she told Sonthi, stopping to give the Belzonian a brief respite. Marcie pointed to the spot where Kaeden vaulted over a border fence and entered the training area with a profound statement. He looped past several formations on his way to intercept the broken-toy formation the armor appeared to have adopted.

With a final leap, he came down on the middle of a tank's upper glacis. The vehicle rocked under the impact. Marcie could hear Kae's external speakers from a good two kilometers away as he boomed instructions for their near-term training.

"Follow me if you want to live!" Marcie shook her head at his dramatic approach, but the mechs revved their engines and followed as Kae led them over a hill and deeper into the training area.

"Time to go," she told Sonthi. He groaned but started running. Marcie had time during the slow run to play with the remote and direct the aircraft around the field. She flew it low over her head to see how it appeared from the ground. Up close, it was plain, just enclosed blades that rotated to give it forward speed or the ability to hover. Its rectangular body carried more than a video sensor, however. "What else can this thing see?"

Sonthi panted the words one at a time as he tried to keep up. "IR. UV. Audio. Meteorological." He stopped trying to say words. It was too hard.

"You're not reflecting well on your team," Marcie stated.

He managed to utter his defense. "We're...the best... flyers...on the planet."

"That'll earn you some slacker credits. Now keep up. We have a war to fight." Marcie did not run faster. Flayden kept pace even though it looked like it was killing him. She wondered if he and his team had participated in any of the group-formation runs. Probably not. They would have fallen out, and she would have known who they were.

When they reached the infantry company that was the farthest from where Colonel Braithwen and Sergeant Major Monsoon were engaged, Marcie buzzed them with her aircraft. Some of the troops dropped before rolling over to lounge on the ground.

Until they spotted Colonel Walton storming toward them.

When she reached them, she didn't bother to yell. "If you know the right thing to do but choose not to do it, that means you have no integrity. Thanks to that," she pointed at the drone overhead and handed the control box back to Captain Sonthi, "we can see everything you're doing, but why? Why would you want us to waste our time watching you to make sure you do what you're supposed to do? I need to be watching out there for the enemy."

She let that sit. No one answered her charge. No one had an excuse. They were undisciplined. That made them bad soldiers.

"Who's your platoon commander?" Marcie demanded. They all pointed. He stood at the far edge of the group, watching but not coming closer. "A word."

She pointed to a spot off to the side and strolled over to wait for him. He took his time out of fear, arrogance, or a complete lack of engagement; it wasn't obvious why.

"Explain," Marcie requested.

"We're not sure what we're supposed to do," he replied simply.

"What have you done to find out?"

He shrugged. Marcie took it in stride. "Where's your platoon sergeant?"

He waved toward a soldier in the middle of those who had been lounging.

"Your squad leaders?"

The lieutenant motioned for them. Three were in a bunch on the far side, but one was close. The nearby corporal was there first. He saluted.

Marcie waited for the others to join them.

"What do you think you're supposed to be doing?"

"Training?" the sergeant quipped, but he sounded serious.

"Ma'am," the corporal interjected, "we're supposed to be practicing fire and maneuver drills to solidify our ability to get into various combat formations while under fire."

"Where did you hear that?" Marcie pressed.

"The sergeant major. He briefed us earlier."

The lieutenant shook his head. "But what formations, and how far do we go?"

Marcie's hand shot out and grabbed the rank on his collar. She ripped it free and handed it to the corporal. "Give me your stripes."

He unhooked the emblem and slipped it from his collar. Marcie took it and handed it to the lieutenant. "Welcome to the enlisted ranks," she told the former platoon commander. She turned to the corporal. "Lieutenant, do what you're supposed to do and report to me at the end of the day. As for the rest of you, if I hear that you're giving your new lieutenant any grief, I won't just throw you in the brig. I'll put you on bread and water for three days. If you demand to be taught through punishment, I will accommodate you. If you want to be the professional soldier you signed up to be, then train to the standard I use when we fight. You're going to see combat, and sooner than you want. If you're not ready, we're not leaving you behind. You'll die on the battlefield, but worse than the death of a dumbass is the people they get killed. Sharpen up, you knuckleheads! Your lackadaisical attitudes are pissing me off."

"But ma'am." The new lieutenant stared at the rank in his hand. "I don't know anything about being an officer. He was pretty good at it."

"Being good up there," Marcie pointed into the distance

where the tops of the barracks towered over nearby trees, "has little value to this army. Being good down here is the difference between life and death. It might sound like I'm harping on that, but I've been in a combat unit for well over a hundred years. I have personally killed thousands of the enemy. I do know what I'm talking about. Bad soldiers get their fellows killed. It is a universal constant as certain as the speed of light."

She saluted before he could continue the conversation and started to walk away.

"I'll be watching. Don't fuck up any more than you already have." She pointed at the big drone circling overhead. "If you need help, don't hesitate to call for fire support."

Marcie figured no one in that platoon knew how to do that, but she had planted the seed and hoped the new lieutenant would ask. He seemed to be the only one paying attention. She stood ready to fire him too if needed. She had no time to develop a crop of unmotivated and undisciplined leaders.

Kae rotated the over-the-shoulder launcher into the firing position and sent a single rocket downrange. Today wasn't supposed to be live fire, but he had brought them to a section of the training area that was off-limits because of unexploded ordnance. UXO signs dotted the perimeter.

"Ten tanks at a time, you will form into a line abreast on the firing line. You will each cycle an armor-penetrating shell into your main weapon. You will take aim at the target designated Belz Four. On my command, you will fire. Let's unleash some firepower!"

The tanks started to maneuver, but without rhyme or reason. Kae let it go on for twenty seconds too long. He had assumed command but hadn't taken charge. When left to their own devices, the Belzonians deteriorated into anarchy. Kae expected they embraced that technique because of their orgies.

"STOP!" He activated his radio and repeated his command. When the vehicles came to a halt, he chose ten to move to the firing line, even telling them which position to take. He gestured with his mech's arms for the rest to back up and give the team room to fire.

With the ten vehicles on the line, Kae followed up over the radio. "In order from position one to ten, are you ready to fire?"

The first tank thundered its rifle cannon. Kae couldn't help but watch the round impact slightly below the target. The other nine tanks followed suit. He could not see who hit what, but the impacts were close, better than expected.

"For future reference, when I ask if you are ready, you respond with your voice. If someone wasn't ready and you fired, I would have to bring a great deal of pain to you. I don't want to do that. You don't want me to do that, so let's save everyone a lot of grief. When I have verbal confirmation, I'll give the order to fire, and it'll sound like this. 'Range is hot. All clear on the firing. Fire!' Any questions?"

"Besides that, how'd we do?" tank number four's commander asked.

"First group destroyed it, so now I have to pick another target," Kae deadpanned. The tankers revved their engines in response. "Second group, when I designate you, move to the appropriate firing position."

The exercise went more smoothly going forward.

Marcie? Kae asked using his internal chip. He thought he might be out of range, but she answered. *Leadership. The dearth is in the leadership. They will follow, but there are few Alphas on this planet. Crantis and Jake are. There are a few others, but not everyone's in a leadership position. We have to identify those people and weed them out.*

I already demoted one lieutenant to corporal. I probably should have busted him all the way to private.

Kae chuckled. With more time, their task would be easier. Not easy, just easier. There was never a good time to forcibly remove someone from a leadership position, and time was their enemy. The Federation wanted much and gave Marcie no time to deliver.

Because an occupation force wasn't something they wanted, but it was a force they needed and had for quite some time.

What do you say we give them tomorrow off while we work with just the leadership to run a series of small unit exercises and see who rises to the top? They'll be the core of Trans-Pacific's future.

Is that what we're calling it now? Marcie asked, not defensively or accusingly.

I like it. Trans-Pacific, as in, beyond the pacifying.

The shot was there, and you didn't take it. What have you done with my husband?

I lost you. Kae was confused.

TP Task Force because we're cleaning shit up.

It took Kaeden longer to get it than it should have, but

when he did, he found a new appreciation for Marcie's ability to see the humor in a situation that was less than funny.

We'll separate the wheat from the chaff, and our training will start to resonate. The Belzonians have their moments, but I'll be damned if these people don't love their anarchy. I can't see how they have a military at all.

We'll call it a mystery of the universe. As good warriors, ours is not to question why, only to do and die.

Ours to fix, Marcie. We'll be proud of these soldiers in a month's time.

I hope you're right. I have to get back to these knobs before somebody pokes an eye out.

It's all fun and games... Kae secured his link. He climbed aboard a tank that had died. The motor pool was sending a tractor and a flatbed truck to recover it. The motor pool was run by non-military, which reinforced Kae's suspicions that the Belzonian military was some politician's dream and had nothing to do with Belzimus' ability to field a functioning force. They had respectable equipment, even though it was dated. Kae assumed the politician had his hands in the till somewhere to profit from the creation and arming of their budding military.

Kae was genetically predisposed to loathing professional politicians. He didn't know what Belzimus had. He wondered why he'd made that assumption. Probably because it was too easy to believe.

Having let those thoughts run their course, he climbed atop the dead tank and unleashed his suit's speakers at maximum volume.

"We are going to learn four formations, and you are

going to drive two klicks that way and then come back. Then we'll practice the next formation. These formations apply at platoon, company, and battalion level. The first is the echelon formation, echelon right and echelon left. Each tank lines up offset to the one in front of it. Right or left is the direction of the slant. Simple as that.

"Diamond formation is one tank in front, two to either side, and one in the rear directly behind the lead tank. Spacing for these formations will depend on terrain and enemy capabilities.

"The staggered column is how we will move to contact. We will never give an enemy a perfect chance to take out a column of tanks, even if there is no enemy.

"The final formation is the Vee. Two tanks up front, parallel and wide. Two tanks in the rear filling the gap between the lead tanks. This allows maximum firepower to the front of the formation. That's it. We don't need anyone getting creative. Not yet, anyway, and we definitely don't need anyone going off on their own. The four tanks of a platoon will never separate. No tank will operate on its own without explicit direction from me, Colonel Braithwen, or Colonel Walton. Period. First company, organize your platoons in an echelon right and move out. Second company, you're on deck."

Kae had to run back and forth since the unit tanks had gotten intermingled during the earlier Operation Clusterfuck. He stepped back and watched them unfuck themselves. One tank moved to the side and parked. An older Belzonian climbed out of the turret. Kae was instantly skeptical when the man removed his tanker's helmet and shook out a fantastically colored mane.

He approached the combat armor. Kae didn't have to turn to see him. "Can I help you?"

"I am Major Punyaa, the battalion commander. I'm responsible for these vehicles. That means that I take full responsibility for their miscues to this point. I failed to give them direction, but I want to rectify that. I respectfully request permission to run the formation training."

"Tell me your plan," Kae ordered.

"I will move my tank to the line of departure and call out the commands using secure point to point, P2P, radio. We'll run two companies down and back simultaneously. We'll do that with our six companies. I believe I can cycle through the units five times in the next couple of hours to give every company a chance to work with every other company."

"Major Punyaa, execute your training plan."

"Roger that," the major replied happily, running back to his tank. He was barely in the cupola before the tank raced through the formation to take its place at the front and to the side.

Kae had tuned in to the battalion and company frequencies. He hadn't bothered with the individual platoon frequencies, but if they were going to assess the leaders to find their combat Alphas, he needed to listen. He dialed those into his system as well. There would be eight platoons operating simultaneously as two companies. With the company channel and on-deck platoons, he figured that he would be overwhelmed with chatter.

I wish I had an AI, he mumbled. *But at least I have help if Major Rainbow Hair shows his chops.*

Punyaa broadcast on all channels and gave crisp, clear

directions. Kae leaned back and watched. He idled his suit, turning down the air conditioning. Maybe he wasn't going to be overwhelmed.

That thought died as one of the tanks fired his main gun through the middle of the formation toward the area where Marcie, Jake, and Crantis were working with the infantry.

CHAPTER SEVEN

War Axe near the Rift on the Surface of Benitus Seven

TED! Your fucking jammer doesn't work. How'd they get onto the ship?

Bundin's squad continued to fire into the rift to encourage the Skrima to stay in their own dimension while Terry and Char sprinted back to the ship.

They phased in before the jammers turned on, Ted countered as evenly as he could, but stress had worked its way through his usual calm. The mechs weren't firing, but they were dancing and weaving in a deadly battle with two Skrima. The ballistic-armored troops, as well as the four werewolves of Char's pack, fought to stay behind the mechs. The humans were ill-equipped for hand-to-hand combat with the devils from the Etheric. The werewolves hadn't changed shape and weren't prepared for mortal combat.

Terry thumbed his pistol down to the three setting. Char pulled both her slug-throwers as they ran up the ramp and into the ship. Terry took one Skrim and Char took the other. At three, the JDS wouldn't penetrate a suit of armor. Char's 9mm slugs wouldn't either. Once they had clear shots, they fired. The JDS only required one shot, even at the lower setting. The creature's body slammed into the mech beyond it before crumpling the deck, broken and dead.

Char fired, the first three rounds stitching a pattern into the Skrim's back, hoping the heart would be in that part of its chest. The interdimensional invader turned and started to run at her, and her next shot hit it between the eyes. It stumbled. The mech-suited warrior wasted no time in hammering a metal fist into the Skrim's head, ending any aspirations the creature had of harming a human.

"Where are they, Smedley?" Terry shouted. He looked for Cory and saw Ted holding her behind him against the rear bulkhead of the hangar bay. "Stay there!"

There is a Skrim in the main ladder well, a second trying to break into the engine room, and a third just entered the mess deck, Smedley reported.

Terry veered toward the hatch leading into the ship. Char motioned for the warriors to follow her as she ran after TH. *Protect Cory,* she told the werewolves of her pack. Dokken was already by Cory's side, growling and barking.

TH hit the stairs at a dead run, aiming his pistol ahead of him as he climbed.

He came upon the Skrim as quickly as he expected, closing on the creature before it could enter the third deck. He fired as it dodged, missing the kill shot but tearing off one arm. The creature howled in pain. TH bowled into it, taking it down on an interdeck landing. He shoved the JDS into its gut and fired. The Skrim exploded against the grating, its insides becoming its outsides and splattering the wall.

Terry jumped off it and ran up one more flight to get to the mess deck level. He bolted through the hatch, down the corridor, and through the open door. Two women screamed as the Skrim stood in the food preparation area, tearing at a bistok haunch that had been destined to be the crew's dinner. Terry dove over the serving counter toward the creature. It spread its arms wide, claws ready to rend the human asunder.

Terry Henry twisted in mid-air, firing upward while inverted to keep the women behind the Skrim out of his line of fire. The shot removed its face. Terry rolled before he hit to avoid landing on the top of his head.

Silently, the remainder of its jaw worked as it blindly slashed with its razor-sharp claws. Terry pushed away from the creature when he landed.

Char's pistol barked as she sent two rounds in rapid succession through its skull. It froze mid-pose before toppling to the deck.

"Engine Room," Terry called. Char slowed to turn around but never stopped running. She disappeared out the door while he checked to make sure Jenelope and Xianna were uninjured. The green woman nearly collapsed because she was sobbing so heavily. The older Jenelope held her upright even though she was shaking uncontrollably. "We'll be back. Stay here."

Terry didn't have time to wait for an acknowledgment. He headed out, but this time, he ran around the serving counter, avoiding going over the top.

Halfway down the corridor to the stairs, a railgun barked a single time.

Clear, Char reported.

"Smedley?" Terry asked the corridor's ceiling.

"Ship is secure, Colonel Walton," the AI replied. Terry stopped.

I'll be on the mess deck, he told Char. He hurried back to check on the women.

Before he made it into the galley, Captain San Marino announced over the ship-wide broadcast that no Skrima remained on board.

Terry found Jenelope and Xianna exactly as he had left them. They both stared at the red-skinned creature with the horns. Terry picked up the carcass and dragged it to the solid waste disposal and stuffed it into the chute, where it would be mulched and its biomatter would be separated from what couldn't be used. The refuse would be jettisoned into a planet's upper atmosphere, where it would be incinerated upon reentry. Terry looked longingly at the bistok but decided that it was better to destroy it than risk getting a disease from the Skrim.

He tossed it into the chute after the creature. He didn't contemplate that they might be eating some part of the Skrim when the ship recycled it, but that would be after the systems ensured it was safe.

Terry washed up before reaching out for Jenelope and Xianna. He guided them from the galley and into the seating area, where he pushed them into two chairs.

"I-I've never seen anything like that," Jenelope declared.

"Bad aliens," Terry replied, smiling and shrugging one shoulder in the hope that it would help calm the cook and her helper. "They're taken care of. Maybe you could spend the rest of the day on the hangar deck with the warriors? You'll be safe there, even though you're safe here, too. They can't use interdimensional shifting to move through walls anymore because Ted's jammer is in orbit."

Xianna sniffled. "I don't understand any of that. Are they coming back?"

"Not here. They are not coming back aboard this ship." Terry looked them both in the eye to show he was confident that the ship was now and would remain secure.

"Is that what killed Ramses?" Jenelope managed to ask.

"Yes. A Skrim killed him." Terry hung his head. He thought he smelled something burning. He rushed into the galley to remove four loaves of bread from the oven. They weren't a total write-off. "The rift is back, and they're coming through. We need to figure out how to close it for good this time, but Ted is here. If anyone can figure it out, it's him."

Jenelope nodded. "I like Ted. He's my favorite out of your mob."

Terry looked sideways at her before laughing. "And here I was thinking it was me."

Char strode through the door. "You what?" she asked before sniffing. "Is something burning?"

"Bread was saved," Terry replied. "We'll call it pre-toasted. Jenelope just said Ted is her favorite."

"He's mine, too," Char said smoothly. She helped herself to the fresh loaf, ripping it in half to bring to the table. She handed half of her half to TH. He stuffed the steaming, crispy-on-the-outside goodness into his mouth, chewing while taking breaths to cool it off before it burned his tongue.

Char was eating it the same way.

Xianna had stopped crying, but a tear escaped and followed the path of the previous cascade down her cheek. She wiped it away before it fell from her chin. Her eyes were puffy and red. Jenelope rocked her.

"I can't go back in there," she said, lips quivering.

"I know. I'll get dinner ready. You heard the good colonel say they're gone."

"You blew its face off!" The memory threatened to unleash a new outburst.

"It was a tough shot because I didn't want to hit either of you," Terry explained. "But Char took care of him. Too bad about the bistok. The bread is good, though, even with the edges a little blackened."

Jenelope cocked an eyebrow Terry's way. He stood to go help himself to the drink dispenser and brought two glasses, one for each of the women.

"It's nice to be served every once in a while," Jenelope told him.

"I need to get to the bridge," Terry said suddenly. "Our people are out there."

Char nodded. *Need two warriors on the mess deck. Jenelope and Xianna need help.*

Pounding footsteps preceded two railgun-armed and armored members of the Bad Company. Char patted them on the shoulders on her way out. "Help Jenelope prepare the next meal. If Eldis is on the ship, have him join you."

The warriors groaned. They had gone from combat action and saving damsels in distress to cooking dinner.

Then again, it was better to be on Jenelope's good side. They dumped their gear on the table, rolled up their sleeves, and got to work.

Terry was already well on his way up the stairs. Char jogged to catch up. "What are you thinking?"

"We need to scan the planet to figure out how many of those bastards are on this side of the rift, then we need to let our people know what's out there."

Terry was first onto the bridge. "Smedley, connect me with the Pods and all the mechs."

The overhead crackled to tell Terry that comm was live. Modern-day communications were clear without static or line noise, but Terry liked what he grew up with, so Smedley accommodated him. More people were adopting the technique to tell them when their connection was live.

"You have comm," the AI reported.

"Attention Bad Company. The rift is live, and Skrima have come through. We don't know how many because we don't know how long they've been coming."

"Terry, Joseph here. We're at the Grays' city. The Skrima have been here."

Terry closed his eyes. He understood the implication but had to get confirmation. "Last time we were here, they said they could protect themselves against an Etheric intrusion."

"Something changed because they weren't able to defend the city," Joseph said, his voice grim. "There were no survivors."

Terry turned to Char. "How many Skrima does it take to wipe out an entire race?"

"As horrible as it sounds, I hope it did not take many.

How many can we fight? If we are overwhelmed by numbers, they'll cause some serious damage."

"Did any ships leave their spaceport?"

"Not that we can tell."

"Your new task is to secure the spaceships. We have to make sure that no Skrima leave the planet. If the Grays aren't here, we can fight this battle a lot differently."

He looked at Micky, who nodded slowly.

"Recover the Pods. All hands return to the *War Axe* except Corporal Bundin. Keep the rift under observation and fire until we can set up a remote firing platform."

"I'll put Kai on it," Char remarked and turned away to give the orders to her grandson.

"Report," Terry requested.

Before anyone could respond, Kimber reported in. "We've engaged a dozen Skrima at my position."

Terry quickly brought up the location on the main screen. Three mechs and six warriors. "Smedley, can you track our people not in the mechs for me, please?"

Five blinking lights flashed into existence.

Terry ground his teeth as he waited for another report. "Show me the nearest Pod." When it appeared, Terry accessed the comm channel. "Christina, Pod Three needs help."

"On my way," she replied. The Pod's marker changed direction, and it raced across the open terrain. Three mechs and now only four lights continued to fight. They had bunched together, the ballistic-armored warriors protected by the trio of mechs. Terry could hear the rail-guns hammering at the enemy.

"Aim true and stay frosty," he said, holding himself back from bothering those engaged in a fight for their lives.

An image appeared on the screen. Smedley explained, "Major Kimber is transmitting her feed."

Dozens of Skrima lay dead before them, but an undulating wave of red bodies approached. A mech-grade railgun barked to the right, and Kimber's railgun joined the cacophony. Rockets raced from her armored shoulders, crossed the intervening space quickly, and slammed into the mass attack. Four more rockets screamed across no man's land. The railguns panned methodically back and forth, ripping into the wave, exploding bodies, and shattering the ranks, but the enemy pressed relentlessly forward.

"How many?" Terry asked. The others on the bridge stared, dumbfounded.

"Hundreds," Smedley replied.

Terry brightened. "Not thousands?" Kimber watched Christina's Pod swoop past before flaring without landing. Three mechs, six warriors, and Christina jumped out. Ten railguns fired as one across the length of the enemy like a scythe through wheat.

"Get some!" Kimber shouted. Her railgun was silent for a moment as she selected her targets, then short bursts finished the enemy one after another.

"Get those warriors into the cryopods!" Terry shouted at the screen, finally recovering his wits enough to realize they had a new asset at their command.

"It's automatic. Gefelton is already in, and the cryopod from the second shuttle is collecting the second." Kimber turned to show the hovering cryopod with the solid red light, confirming there was an injured warrior inside. The second cryopod settled next to a mangled body and used scoops to carefully lift the injured and put him inside. It sealed and flashed red until the color settled to a constant green.

"The cryopods worked," Terry said softly.

Char took Terry's hand and looked into his eyes. They didn't have to say any words. They both knew. This was the closure Cory needed. They nodded to each other and got back to work. "We better prep the Pod-docs," Char said and hurried out to talk to her daughter.

Terry leaned toward the main screen. "I want to debrief the teams as soon as they're back. Micky, we'll need an IR view of the planet to locate the enemy. Let's see if we can hit them from orbit after we've recovered our people. I'll be in the hangar bay."

He left with a measured stride. Ruzfell, the systems specialist, and Clifton, the pilot, watched him go. They glanced at the captain, hoping to receive orders to lift off soon. They were getting antsy, sitting on the ground with a Skrima army nearby, and they were more than happy to rain destruction from far above.

Belzimus, Command Post and Training Area Zoranitus

"*INCOMING! GET DOWN!*" Marcie bellowed. Some of the troops passed the message along. Colonel Braithwen and Sergeant Major Monsoon were close enough that they picked up the call. They shouted on their way to the deck.

Too many soldiers froze in place, confused by the order. The tank's shell whistled as it approached and passed overhead. The Belzonian infantry stared in disbelief. The shell continued toward the command post. Marcie exhaled the breath she'd been holding.

She saw it hit the *Vengeance* before the sound of metal screeching under the impact of an armor-piercing projectile flooded across the training area. Marcie stood. The Belzonians reluctantly followed her lead.

"Continue your training," she told them before bolting for the ship.

It hit the Vengeance. *I'm on my way to see if anyone was hurt,* Marcie transmitted to her leadership team. *What the fuck are you doing over there, Kae?*

It was a misfire. No one was supposed to be loaded. It's still my fault. I'll take care of it on this end. I am so sorry. Kae signed off.

Marcie snarled as she sprinted a kilometer and a half up a gently-sloping hill to get to the command post and the *Vengeance* parked in the lot beyond. The ramp was deployed, welcoming the crew and visitors to freely enter and leave the ship. This was supposed to be safe. They didn't have gravitic shields, not yet. They had just joined the Federation's asset list.

The shell's point of impact didn't look as bad as it had sounded. It had left a fairly small hole in the side of the ship. Marcie tried to visualize what was beyond but failed. She rushed into the ship and headed upward to the impacted deck. When she exited the stairwell, darkness greeted her. Flashes before her strobed the crew, who were still fighting a fire that had started when the shell tore through a power junction.

Marcie moved into a transverse passageway to see how

far the round had penetrated. On the far side of the ship, she found that her and Kae's quarters were dead center of the bullseye. The round had entered the wall amidships and exited through the door before continuing toward the portside hull. A look through the opening where the door used to be confirmed that most of the items and furniture in the room had been destroyed by the fury of the projectile's transit.

She followed the round into the storage area opposite her quarters, where crates of biomass had slowed the armor-piercing round until it embedded in the interior bulkhead of the double-hulled ship. The round was scraped and the penetrator nose dented and misshapen, but it had worked as it was supposed to. Maximum amount of armor penetration. Only the effect of the biomass in slowing it down kept it from ripping through the outer hull, creating an exit wound for the damaged ship. The fire was out when Marcie returned to the starboard passageway.

"Anyone injured?" she asked.

"Nah. We were all up front or in the back. It gave us a little bit of a jolt, though!" The crew laughed. "Does this mean we get our blood wings for being in combat?"

Marcie wasn't surprised that they were untested. "No. The real thing is a lot worse. Imagine fighting this fire and fixing the hole in the ship while you're being shot at and trying to shoot back. That's combat. I hope you never experience it, but we'll be ready for it if it comes. And that was how this happened—a misfire by a Belzonian tank about five kilometers from here. That's a lot farther than it should be able to shoot and still have any penetrating capability."

The crew gave her blank looks. Combat wasn't their thing. She might as well have been speaking without the translator chip active.

"I'm glad no one was hurt. Will you be able to repair the ship?"

"We'll get the repair bots on it right away. Shouldn't take too long. Sorry about your quarters. We'll get a supplemental space ready until we can make your suite habitable."

"Bill it to the armor battalion," she told them, but they didn't get that one either. "Carry on."

Kae, can you hear me? Marcie called once she was off the ship. She tried twice more before trying Jake and Monsoon. *No injuries. Ship's got a hole in it, but they'll get it spaceworthy before we need to leave.*

That's good news, Monsoon replied. *What happened?*

Misfire by one of the tankers. They weren't supposed to be loaded. Kae's probably ripping someone a new asshole and installing additional safety protocols as we speak.

CHAPTER EIGHT

Belzimus, Training Area Zoranitus, Live Fire Range

Kae used his jets to get additional height on his jump and came down on the tank's turret as hard as he could slam into the metal. "Get out here!" He loomed over the hatch.

It popped and pushed open. The tank commander peeked out before starting the long climb to infamy. He put one foot on the ladder and took the first agonizing step.

Kae wasn't about to wait. As soon as he could see something to grab, he did. He pulled the soldier out, holding him dangling above his vehicle.

"Why did you have a round in the breech of your weapon?" Kaeden demanded.

"We reloaded after the first shot. It's the firing SOP," the tank commander, Sergeant Wiriya, stated.

Kae scowled. "Why did you fire the weapon?"

"Accident. I was trying to rearrange myself. It was just an accident!"

"You shot my ship. The *Vengeance* now has a hole in its

side and needs repairs before it's spaceworthy. There are no accidents when firing your gun, only negligence. What should I do with you?" Kae turned to hold Wiriya away from the tank, a good three meters above the ground. The sergeant started to scream.

Kaeden winced at the shrill cries. The threat had gone beyond fear and into terror. Kae set him down on the tank. Wiriya stopped screaming, chest heaving from his episode. Kae bent over to put the speaker in his chest against the soldier's head. "Get your shit under control. You will teach a class tomorrow to the whole battalion on how not to accidentally fire your weapon. You will talk about the importance of not being loaded when it's proper to be unloaded, and how to keep your fucking finger off the trigger. Do you understand your orders?"

The fear in Wiriya's eyes slowly morphed into anger and then hatred. He didn't answer, only continued to glare at the screen, behind which was Kaeden's face.

"I am reducing you in rank to private, effective immediately, and you will spend the next three days in the brig. Major Punyaa, take charge of this soldier and see that my orders are carried out."

The major ran to the tank. He looked like he was going to protest until Kae pushed the offending private toward him. Wiriya caught his foot and tumbled off the tank. Punyaa half-caught him, keeping his head from slamming into the ground.

Kae stood up straight. He accessed his files and started playing Wagner's *Flight of the Valkyries*, increasing the volume until it blasted. He waved a mechanical arm in the air, signaling to rally up. He gave the hand signal for diamond formation, hoping they remembered it from the quick class he'd given before they kicked off. Kae hatcheted his arm in the direction he wanted to go and jumped off the tank. He started running down the track he wanted them to follow until he reached the point where they would turn around.

He waved at them before pumping his fist. *Hurry up!*

A platoon left on its own, moving into the proper formation but driving too close to each other. Kae signaled them to spread out. The flank vehicles angled away until they had two to three tank lengths between them. The next platoon headed out, then the next.

Kae cheered them on and waved them through the finish line before ordering them to turn the formation and head back.

Diamond formation coming down and diamond formation heading back. The platoons were coming fast and furious, sending thoughts of the intransigent tank commander far into the rearview mirror. Kae wasn't sure what to do with him. If Kae could help Wiriya harness that fury and focus it on an enemy, it would set him apart from the rest of the more passive Belzonians.

Tanks were running up and down the open field, tearing up the turf before recovering and getting in line for a second and then a third pass. Nearly one hundred tank engines roared.

Despite the lower tech of the Belzonian armor battalion, they were impressive when unleashed. Kae hoped the thrill of running wide open translated to doing it during a fight.

They seemed to easily overcome the loss of Tank

Commander Wiriya to continue their mission. When Kae had seen the fear in the private's eyes, he hoped they weren't following his commands only because they were afraid to cross him. "Battalion Commander, report to me," Kae ordered.

A tank broke from the ranks and raced toward him. It angled away on its final approach until it stopped beside him. Major Punyaa popped out of his hatch and saluted, then leaned casually against the ring, as tankers were wont to do.

"Looking good, Major. Can you move them into company formations now? Let's up the game."

"Roger that," Punyaa made to climb back inside his tank.

Kae motioned him closer.

"I should have handed Wiriya over to you for discipline," Kae stated. "I'll let you take care of those things from now on. Please understand I can't have flagrant belligerence or such abject negligence. It takes a lot to fire a tank's main gun."

"It does," Punyaa agreed. "We don't punish. That concept is mostly unknown on Belzimus, but I see the value when used sparingly."

"Wise words, Major. Sparingly. We need the men to grow with the training and become more cohesive as a unit. The tanks will operate in platoon and company formations because we can't have lone tanks out there. In my experience, every mechanized asset is the biggest and easiest target for anyone with a weapon. We get shot at more than anything else on the battlefield. It helps when you can intelligently shoot back. We're going to learn how to call in fire, too, putting the enemy into a dilemma. That is the beauty of combined arms."

"Your patience will be needed, Major," Punyaa requested. "We operate independently. Working with the other branches is a foreign concept."

"When you see it in action, you'll wonder why you didn't do it sooner. Imagine your tanks attacking across an open field. You pin down enemy infantry. Before they can rise, artillery splashes across the area. One branch pins them down and the other finishes them. It's a beautiful thing, Major Punyaa."

"I look forward to seeing it."

Kae returned Punyaa's salute. The major jumped into his tank, dropped the hatch, and drove away.

Kae jogged toward the collection area, where the tanks idled, waiting for their next command. He wanted to see them up close and personal, make sure they were taking the right lessons from the day, but he would do that outside the direct chain, leaving Punyaa to do the heavy lifting. He relaxed and turned down the temperature. There was no need to break a sweat. Everything was back on track.

War Axe, near the Rift on the Surface of Benitus Seven

Char strode into the hangar bay and made a beeline for Cory while glancing at the returned Pods. Bad Company warriors from four of them milled about, waiting for their follow-on orders. Char didn't know if they had encountered any Skrima. Terry would find out, but she suspected that only Kimber's Pod had been unlucky enough to drop into the middle of a swarm.

"The cryopods worked," Char announced, having waited to tell Cory in person. Ted was tinkering with one of the limited Pod-docs. With the news, he stopped what he was doing.

"We have injured inbound," he stated.

"Injured, yes. All I can say is that they registered as dead in the system, but the cryopods scooped them both up before too long. Four minutes for one, and less than a minute for the other. The cryopods took care of it without anyone having to do anything."

"As designed," Ted replied, not bragging, simply stating a fact. "No one should have to interrupt a fight to care for the injured because often they won't be able to. You tend to get involved in engagements that are life or death. That doesn't leave time for anything that is not automated."

"Your experience and understanding are clearly the cat's ass," Char told him. Ted looked at her. Werewolves generally weren't partial to cats.

"The Pod-docs are ready." Ted pointed at the two end units. "The cryopods will line up next to them and deliver the injured directly into a Pod-doc for servicing. Once again, the automatic setting is to restore their life functions before making major repairs. Depending on the extent of the injuries, it could be from thirty minutes to twelve hours before they are released."

Cory took Ted's hand. He looked at the contact as if studying it. "Uncle Ted, you will have saved lives today and forever into the future. I can't thank you enough." She moved in and kissed him on the cheek.

Char tried not to laugh at his obvious discomfort. Dokken worked his head into their hands until Ted was able to free himself. Cory gave the dog a good ear scratch.

That's more like it, right there, Dokken said, leaning into her hand.

Terry appeared and rallied the warriors to him. In less than ten seconds, four mechs ran off to provide perimeter security for the *War Axe*.

A ship darkened the hangar bay entrance, then *Iracitus* slowly entered and assumed its parking position. The hatch popped, and Joseph and Petricia appeared. They saw Terry and headed straight for him. Char waved for her pack to join them. Ted went back to tinkering with the Pod-docs while he waited for the cryopods to arrive and complete the process of battlefield recovery. Cory and Dokken stayed with him while the rest joined Terry Henry Walton in the middle of the hangar bay.

The warriors in mechanized combat suits stood around the outside, while the others stood closer.

"Who saw the Skrima?"

Heads shook all around.

"No one?"

"Just Kimber's Pod," Auburn, her husband, said. People around him gave him space. Maybe his dour expression drove them away, or maybe they were glad it wasn't them with a spouse engaged by a Skrima army.

The Pods ignored the launch bay and flew into the main hangar. The warriors ran out of the way as the Pods maneuvered overhead, turning their rear decks toward where the Pod-docs awaited their arrival. The cryopods detached before the Pods landed and hovered smoothly toward their assigned Pod-docs. Every person in the hangar bay watched the evolution, moving to get a clear line of sight. When the cryopods opened and deposited their hard-frozen charges into the Pod-docs, a collective gasp issued from the warriors.

Both had been torn apart. Terry had never seen anyone that far gone go into a Pod-doc, let alone come out of one whole.

When the lids closed and the lights flashed, indicating that the systems were working, Ted casually stepped to the first to check the process screen. He walked to the second and examined it, then turned without further engagement and headed for the hatch leading into the ship. Cory ran after him. No one made a sound so they could listen.

"Well?" she asked.

"Well, what?" Ted wondered.

"Are they going to make it?"

"Of course. Their brains were intact. Everything else can be repaired, even a brain, to some extent. I'm hungry. I'm joining my wife for something to eat." Cory made eye contact with her parents and shrugged before following Ted out.

"I forgot to check on Felicity," Char whispered. Terry didn't reply because no one wanted to talk to Felicity when she was this angry at everyone, most specifically, Terry and Char.

Terry Henry looked at the ceiling and closed his eyes. "The Bad Company cheats death," he said as if reciting a poem. Those from the Pods Three and Four drifted over to join the company. He opened his eyes again, and his face turned hard as he addressed the warriors. "Don't think you can take shortcuts just because you can be saved. Dying sucks because it hurts a whole lot. Kimber, tell us about it."

She parked her mech and climbed out the back. Auburn was waiting for her. The two shared a moment, giving others time to see the state of her armor. It was covered in Skrima remains.

She and Christina took their places next to Terry. "Railguns rock, but we also need close-in weapons. I recommend we don't go back out there unless everyone is carrying their kukri. Railguns as primary weapons kill them at range, but they move fast. We need a way to hold them off once they get within knife range. We killed every one we saw, but I got the impression there were more of them."

"What makes you say that?" Terry asked.

"They didn't try to escape. Last time we engaged them, they didn't necessarily fight because they hadn't established a beachhead yet. This time, they were relentless. That told me they feel like they're here to stay."

"Opinion?" Terry nodded at Christina.

"We have to find them wherever they are and eliminate them. We need a planetwide IR sweep and then tiger teams to hit them wherever we find them. If we locate major concentrations, we jack 'em up from orbit. It's the only way to be sure." She smiled at TH after having used one of his phrases. There was no mirth in her smile. Christina was deadly serious.

It wasn't his. He had taken it from somewhere else.

"I agree. As soon as we set up an automated system to fire into the rift, we're heading skyward to do exactly that. My preference is we lead with an orbital bombardment and follow up with tiger teams to burn out any that survived. After seeing their mass wave attack, we can't let them remain, even if we close the planet off. We can't let the Skrima gain a foothold in this dimension."

Terry pointed to three mechs. "Relieve the team at the rift and send them back here."

The three moved out, taking care not to run anyone over. TH followed them to the ramp and watched them go. Two hundred meters away, the pinpoint of light shimmered from the backside of the portal. It blocked the view beyond, but two mechs were still visible.

They faced away from the rift. One fired and then the other.

"Saddle up!" Terry waved the Bad Company forward. "Christina and Kimber, remain here with your two groups and defend the ship."

Terry yelled his war cry and ran toward the rift.

CHAPTER NINE

Belzimus, Training Area Zoranitus, Live Fire Range

Marcie, Kae, Jake, and Monsoon watched the army withdraw to the barracks for those on foot and to the motor pool for those with vehicles.

"It wasn't a total shitshow," Kae offered.

"Did I tell you the round destroyed our quarters?" Marcie turned her head to look at Kae.

He smacked his lips. "Why am I not surprised? With an entire planet for a target, it hits our stuff."

"Shows you stuff is fairly meaningless as long as you have your health," Jake suggested.

Kae gave him the stink-eye. "I like my stuff."

"'Liked,'" Jake taunted.

"What do we do with the men?" Monsoon interrupted.

"Field day," Marcie replied. "It was something Terry Henry would do on occasion so the troops could let their hair down, so to speak. Build camaraderie on a field where they aren't training to kill people, but where they learn the importance of friends. It makes them better at killing people. Defending your fellows is all you have left when the chips of battle are down. You're fighting to survive."

"What does that look like? Yollin commanders had a tendency to decry fun."

"Sports and games, contests and teambuilding."

Jake and Monsoon brightened.

"Not an orgy!" Kae pleaded.

Monsoon shook his head. "You don't have to come." The colonel and the sergeant major both chuckled. "I get it. We play a game called Balls Out. It's played with a ball you kick and then run while those in the field try to bean the one running to the far end of the field and back. They try to run to the far end before the next baller is up. There's a lot of strategy. Ten-person teams and a rubber ball. We maintain a stock of them here. I'm sure you'll have noticed the wear and markings on the main training field. It's from Balls Out."

Marcie and Kae shrugged their approval. "Sounds good. And some track and field: running, long-jumping, stuff like that."

"Sure." Monsoon stared into the distance as he reviewed the planning required to pull off an army-wide field day first thing tomorrow when they formed for PT.

"We'll be taking all the officers for something similar, but theirs will be a leadership test. We need to find the lions and unleash them. An army of lions led by a sheep will fail, but a flock of sheep led by a lion is a thing to be feared," Marcie explained.

"The small-unit leaders need to be able to take charge when the situation demands it." Kae pounded his fist into his hand. "What we saw today was what will happen if communications break down. If we are unable to think for the front lines, some will turn passive. In too many missions we've been a part of, that could be deadly."

"Many will rise to the occasion," Jake offered. "You better go, Crantis. Get Paithoon to help you. He's good at organizing parties."

The sergeant major excused himself.

Jake pointed to the four-wheeled combat vehicle. "No need to walk."

Crantis looked at it for a moment and then started to laugh. "What's it say about me when my first thought was to wonder where the driver is?" He waved off his comment. "Thanks for the ride. I'll try not to beat it up too much."

He climbed in, adjusted the seat, started it, and headed off. The vehicle jerked to a stop, then launched forward, jerked, and finally settled into a smooth rhythm before passing out of sight.

"We haven't driven in a while if you couldn't tell."

"Let's find an area on the ship that isn't blown up and knock out the details for tomorrow. We've got twelve hours to shape this thing to make it worthwhile. If we do it right, we'll save ourselves weeks of wasting our time with officers who don't have what it takes." Marcie led the way into the *Vengeance*. At least power had been restored, but it would be a while before their quarters were livable.

"All officers, fall out and fall in on Colonel Braithwen," Marcie ordered from the front of the formation, her electronically-boosted voice echoing off the nearby buildings. She pointed to a spot on the field where Shaky Jake waved his arms. "All enlisted are to remain in formation. Sergeant Major Monsoon will take over with your direction for the day. Teambuilding is too often used as a crutch word, but not today. You've earned a full day of barbecue, snacks, play, and sport. We'll memorialize this day as the first for the Trans-Pacific Task Force, the Federation's go-to force to bring peace to the galaxy."

Marcie shook hands with Monsoon before he took over the microphone. He waited until the officers had extricated themselves from the formation. When they were out of the way, the sergeant major started the warm-up calisthenics.

Kae had gone to the brig to talk to the former tank commander. For some reason, he had a great deal of confidence in that particular Belzonian.

Marcie had none for those she'd busted in rank or the lieutenant colonel she'd fired outright and sent packing. No regrets. She hoped Kae was getting what he needed from the Belzonian in the brig.

"Time to wake up," Kae told Private Wiriya through the bars of the cage that served as a brig holding cell. Wiriya was the only inmate currently locked up.

"Sir," Wiriya acknowledged from the lone bunk. He didn't bother standing. Kae realized the private didn't recognize him.

"I'm Major Kaeden. I reduced you in rank yesterday and sent you here."

That brought the Belzonian around. His head snapped to his tormentor. He slowly rose from the bed. "What do *you* want?"

"Your reduction isn't permanent, and neither is your stay in here." Kae took a few steps. There wasn't enough room to pace, so he tried to stand still. "I see more fire in you than nearly any other soldier in this army. Monsoon has it. Colonel Braithwen has it. You have it, but you aren't leading from the front."

"What's that supposed to mean?"

"It means showing the others how to do it, not randomly firing your cannon and not screaming like a little girl. You embarrassed yourself."

"*You* embarrassed *me!*" Wiriya got up and ran at the bars but stopped before he hit them. He gripped the bars in both hands and squeezed until his knuckles shone white. Kae hadn't flinched.

"Nah. I didn't fire your cannon, and I didn't cry. That was all you. So, what the fuck?" Kae wrapped his hands around Wiriya's, trapping them against the bars. "This army needs you, but they need the you that you're capable of being, not a petulant child. You are different from the others. Use that to your advantage because in this profession, different is good. Get over your bullshit and focus your fight on the enemy."

Kae let go and took a half-step back.

"You're going to turn me loose?" An honest question, not a challenge.

"If you convince me that you can channel what you are in a direction that benefits this army."

"What I am..." Wiriya started. He ran his hand over his

head, combing his full plumage with his fingers before sitting down on the bed. He held his face in his hands with elbows propped on his knees. "I'm a pariah. Half-human and half-Belzonian. I'm a male, not like the rest of them. That makes me an outcast. Promoted to sergeant because I know the regulations. I am aggressive. Rarely is that a benefit. Not being properly plumbed? Not so much. Many don't know. I moved around a lot growing up."

Sonofabitch! Kae thought. He hadn't known what to expect.

"I won't be accepted out there any more than I was yesterday."

"You were a sergeant. Someone recognized what you could do." Emotional highs and lows; Kae needed Wiriya to even those out. Before he could catch himself, he blurted, "I'm going to move you to the rank of Bad Company warrior-in-training."

Wiriya cocked his head back and forth, much like a dog trying determine if something was real.

"The Bad Company has a reputation. They don't lose a fight."

"I can attest to that, but it takes focus, discipline, and a great deal of training. You have the chops but little discipline. And you can't be shooting our ship."

"Sorry about that," he muttered. "How far away was the ship?"

"We measured the shot at four and a half klicks."

"It shouldn't have gone that far," Wiriya replied.

"No. We need to find out why and make sure we can replicate it because it did plenty of damage when it arrived. I'd like to deliver some of that goodness to our enemies."

"Me, too. Am I going to get my tank back?"

"Probably not. I expect you'll get one of the mechanized combat suits like the one I was wearing yesterday, as my aide de camp."

Wiriya finally smiled. "I'd like that, Major. Thank you."

"Guard! Unlock this cage. We have work to do."

War Axe near the Rift on the Surface of Benitus Seven

"Get us out of here, Micky." Terry watched the main screen from where he always stood in the center of the bridge's open floor.

"Take us up to a hundred kilometers," Captain San Marino ordered. Clifton responded with a dust off. He pointed the heavy destroyer skyward and accelerated.

"Not orbit?" Terry wondered.

"No. We can use our IR sensors better a little closer to the surface, and more importantly, we can use our capital-grade railguns to pound them. Otherwise, we're limited to missiles."

Terry gave two thumbs-up. The War Axe accelerated skyward, powering through a layer of low clouds without the slightest tremble or bump. It reached altitude quickly, leveling off. The main screen showed a tactical ground map, and infrared signatures started to populate it. The Skrima were scattered across a large section of the continent, concentrated mostly along the equator.

"Smedley, can you give me the body count for each heavy mass?"

Counts appeared on the screen next to each significant

heat source. Three different IR blobs carried numbers in the thousands.

"Target the biggest group and fire," Terry ordered. Ruzfell, the systems specialist, dialed up the controls. The nose of the *War Axe* dipped and the railguns began to cycle, sending a stream of plasma projectiles a hundred thousand meters to the ground. By the time they hit, they would have the force of miniature nuclear bombs.

When the stream impacted, the IR signatures flared and quickly receded. When Ruzfell stopped firing, the heat of living bodies no longer burned and the count showed zero.

"Target the next greatest concentration and fire," Terry said casually. Ruzfell repeated the exercise. "We'll be done before lunch."

Char nudged Terry Henry and pointed to the screen. "I guess that answers the question of whether they can communicate."

The next largest concentration of Skrima was expanding in all directions as they ran for their lives. The smaller groupings were breaking apart as well.

"So much for lunch." Terry checked a small image on a side screen, where a video feed showed the rift. The image started to shake. "They're attacking our remote firing platform. Fire the *Axe*'s mains into that opening. Line it up on the side they're coming from."

The *War Axe* adjusted course, looping widely to bring the nose to bear on the rift opening.

"Target acquired and locked," Ruzfell reported.

"Fire." TH kept his eyes fixed on the small screen showing the feed from the remote firing platform. A flash indicated the arrival of the first ultra-high velocity plasma projectile, followed quickly by more. The image whited out and disappeared. "Status?"

Ruzfell's fingers danced across his systems like a virtuoso pianist's. Finally, he reached his conclusion.

"Unknown."

Terry ground his teeth in frustration. "*Iracitus* has a full sensor suite?"

"Yes," Smedley replied.

"Connect me with him, will you?"

The comforting crackle. "Yes, Colonel Walton? I don't believe we've ever talked before. I've heard a lot of things about you."

"From Shonna and Merrit? I suspect none of it was good. We need you to collect data on the status of the rift. I don't know if you'll be able to identify it with any of your onboard sensors since it is a portal into the Etheric dimension."

"Unless there are other elements, I don't see how I'll be able to, but my crew will be able to see using their innate abilities."

Char contacted her pack. *Shonna and Merrit, report to* Iracitus. *I need you to get eyes on the rift and see if it's still open.*

Once they'd acknowledged, Char gestured toward the hatch. TH nodded, and she bolted from the bridge to join them. Her ability with the Etheric was stronger than the others'—a gift from Terry, or so they'd been told. He couldn't see the Etheric and didn't have insight into how it worked, but he trusted Char implicitly. She would go to ensure that they took the best look possible.

"Smedley, what are the biggest groups remaining that we can target?"

"No more than ten, Colonel Walton."

"Ruzfell!" Terry called cheerfully. "Are you up for some target practice? Let's see if you can fire through the eye of a needle to hit a gnat's ass a hundred klicks away."

"I will give it my best," the systems specialist replied.

"You will kick some Skrima ass," Terry corrected. "Let's see what you got, big dog."

Ruzfell, a two-legged Yollin, rocked and clicked his mandibles. He brought up the hologrid to surround the systems position as he immersed himself.

"*Iracitus* away," Clifton reported from the pilot's station as he adjusted their heading toward the target firing lines. Ruzfell would take over the final adjustments to align the railguns that ran the length of the *War Axe*.

"Make sure you don't shoot my wife," Terry said in a voice loud enough to be heard throughout the bridge.

"I will not shoot anything but gnat's asses, sucking the blood of every Skrima on Benitus Seven," Ruzfell confirmed.

"Now you're speaking my language." Terry looked for a cup of coffee or a cigar or something to do while standing back and watching the show. He didn't know why he thought of a cigar. It had been a long time since he smoked one. Not since he left Earth. The rest of the galaxy frowned on such depravity. He wondered how he could set up a cigar-smoking area in the AGB, while simultaneously deciding he would settle for a cup of coffee. "I'll be right back. Going to the mess deck for a cup of Joe. Anyone want anything?"

Micky looked at him like he'd lost his mind. "You better not spill that in here. Better yet, drink it down there."

"I'm going to drink it here. I promise not to spill any, but if the inconceivable happens, I'll clean it up. And you still love me." Terry waved at Micky as he walked out.

"Firing," Ruzfell announced. He adjusted the heading a nearly insignificant amount. "Target acquired, firing."

"They're running," Clifton stated as he watched the magnified IR signatures darting in erratic directions, distancing themselves from each other until no group remained. They'd have to pick them off one by one.

Micky rocked back in his seat, settling in for what promised to be a long day. He dialed up a person-to-person channel from the arm of the captain's chair. "Terry, bring me a Coke."

CHAPTER TEN

Belzimus, Command Post and Training Area Zoranitus

Colonel Braithwen stood front and center. The entire officer corps, nearly one thousand bodies, was seated in a semicircle around Jake and Marcie.

"Today's exercise is to find those Belzonians who will lead this force in battle. We have a number of tests we're going to run people through. You'll see stations along the way. We've separated you into teams of ten. It's important to note that for this exercise, no one has any rank. You are all equal in my eyes until you prove differently. When the day is over, you can put your rank back on and return to your duties. Tomorrow, we'll be back here at Zoranitus in full combat gear for more live-fire training. Read 'em and weep."

Braithwen had enlisted the aid of the entire administrative staff, all civilians, to oversee the exercises. Some involved personal engagement, like building a pyramid of bodies to climb high enough to seize something dangling off a crane. Cross a small area without touching the ground. Some of the problems were unsolvable in the five minutes allotted, but they were a test of mettle. Who rallied the group? Who kept them going in the right direction? Who sat back and waited for direction?

Marcie considered the grading sheets to be the key to making this happen. She, Braithwen, and Kae, if he ever showed up, couldn't be everywhere. They wanted to watch live, even though drones would have been nice, but they needed the data before they had time to review so many hours of individual video feeds. They could each watch a few stations, but that was it.

Marcie would have to trust the data. There would be one hundred different groups running through the problems. Each group had a number assigned, and the names were on their uniforms. Many of the admin staff were uncomfortable. Marcie expected to get some reports that were trash, but as long as the majority were sound, she'd be able to move to round two of her evaluation.

Put the lions in charge and see what they were capable of doing.

The admin team rolled out massive boards with names listed to ten different stations with identical information, where the individuals could discover what team they were on. A hundred more admins held up signs with a team number. Once they had their ten, they'd move to their test station. Each of the hundred tests would be given one hundred times, providing ten thousand reports with at least three data points each. By dinner time, there would be thirty thousand entries for review.

Marcie figured that was statistically significant. She expected that it would take a few minutes to parse how often names were mentioned as those who impacted the process, demonstrating a proclivity in taking charge. There were three significant factors: the one who took charge, the first one to come up with the right answer, and the one who argued against a course of action.

It was simple and quick, but they'd only had an hour to go through it with the admin staff before the officers arrived. Marcie, Kae, and Jake had pulled an all-nighter in preparation. They'd brought the admin staff in three hours before their normal workday.

Marcie expected a certain amount of chaos starting off, so data from the first few tests and challenges would be suspect. After that, the information had to be sound, or the day would be wasted.

They couldn't afford to waste time. Marcie could feel the impending call from the Federation. She knew beyond a shadow of a doubt the task force would be called up early. How much time did she have?

Not one minute to piss away. That was why she was looking for the lions. She kicked herself for not starting the search on the first day, but she hadn't known. The entire process had happened way too fast. Once the Federation decided they needed a pacifying and peacekeeping force, the bullet train had left the station without looking back.

Marcie was strapped to the front of it, hanging on for the ride. She found it difficult to steer the speeding loco-motive, but that didn't mean she wasn't going to try.

Kae jogged toward them, with a Belzonian keeping pace. Marcie relaxed, only then realizing how tense she had been. She was as taut as a piano wire. She shook out her shoulders and arms.

"Meet Wiriya, my aide de camp. He's been briefed, and we'll get him a grading sheet as well."

Colonel Braithwen studied the soldier. *He's enlisted, and you're going to have him evaluate the officers?* he asked privately, using their internal comm channel.

Who better than those who have to follow? I've relieved him of his duties with the tanks. He is more like you and the sergeant major than anyone else I've met here, but I'll keep him under my wing to make sure there's no trouble.

I trust you. Jake turned to Wiriya. "Welcome aboard."

"Glad to be here, sir," the soldier replied. Marcie snagged a datapad from an admin walking by and slapped it into Wiriya's hand.

"Stop fucking off and get to work," she said, but she was looking at Kaeden.

Kae smiled at her. "Yes, ma'am. Heading out now to see how they get to their starting spots."

"Good call. We're right behind you." The training area was arrayed in a back-and-forth pattern like a flea market, set up with random tables depending on if the particular test needed them. Chairs had been put out because the admins might not be able to stand for ten hours straight. The officers had no choice but to remain upright throughout. "No matter what, we don't end the exercise early. The more tired they become, the better the chance for us to see the real stars."

Kae pointed Wiriya to a spot where he'd be able to watch at least ten different tests simultaneously. "I'll be along shortly," Kae said. He motioned for Jake and Marcie to huddle up. He leaned close preferring to speak in person than over the internal comm. He whispered, "My compliments to you, Marcie. This was enlightened thinking to accelerate training and increase the effectiveness of this army. We saw from the first second that there was a lack of leadership, no disrespect to the colonel or sergeant major because they weren't here. I believe we can train them, but it's going to take a cultural shift, which we don't have time for. The first tell-tale sign is the hair, but even that isn't an indicator. Major Punyaa, the armor commander, had a perfect coif, but he still took charge and carried out an excellent day of training."

"Except for that little episode where they shot our quarters," Marcie quipped.

"I have to admit that I was running the training at that time." Kae hung his head. "And we weren't sleeping last night anyway, or anything else." He waggled his eyebrows.

"Humans." Jake shook his head. "But I agree. I like this exercise, and it might be something we adopt in the future for officer acquisition. We'll need fewer if we have the right ones."

Marcie gestured with her head. "Break's over. Time to get to work. And what the hell? Like you're getting any nowadays."

"Twice yesterday. Probably twice or more tonight. We're Belzonian!"

Kae stopped in his tracks while Jake waved and jogged to the far end of the testing area. "Is he saying that just to get our goat? I feel small and insignificant now."

Marcie threw her hands up. "No clue. We were raised a touch differently, I guess, but the Belzonian way is not for me. I've only had eyes for one since Chicago."

They touched foreheads as they looked into each

CRAIG MARTELLE & MICHAEL ANDERLE

other's eyes. "I couldn't agree more. It's time to find our lions, my love."

They headed to their places. The four of them were able to simultaneously watch most of the groups. They figured the more senior officers would take charge at the outset, so each test was time-stamped to graph name mentions, but they would lose interest and clarity. Who would get the most mentions in the second half of the day?

When every team was in place, Marcie waved to the official timer who carried the airhorn. Five minutes for each test, one minute in between. With the first blast, the teams were briefed on the problem and turned loose to answer.

War Axe, the Bad Company's Heavy Destroyer and Mobile Command Center

"I only want a cup of coffee," Terry told everyone.

He sat with Jenelope and Xianna. Both women had not been able to return to the galley. Two warriors worked within while Jenelope shouted orders without watching. When the two got bad enough, she would abandon fear to save her kitchen.

Cory, Ted, and Felicity ate quietly, making faces because the quality wasn't what they expected. Ted and Felicity held hands, with Ted concentrating on his meal while Felicity ate without looking to enable her to stare daggers at Terry Henry.

Never one to back away from an engagement, especially when it would be fought on the ground of his choosing, Terry wished the women peace and moved to his daughter's side, across from Felicity.

After he sat down, Felicity kicked him in the shin.

"Is that all you got?" he wondered, bracing himself against the table for the inevitable second blow while he was taking a drink. When it arrived mid-sip, weaker than the first, he remained steady. "My compliments, Ted. You've saved our lives again."

"I know," Ted allowed, but the expression on his face was dark. "I should have seen it before, the need for such a device. Anyone could have done the engineering." He indiscriminately waved a hand over his shoulder.

"Not anyone, dearest. It took you to finish it, and it took you only a few days from start to finish," Felicity drawled.

"Like always, when we needed you the most, you came through. Thank you, Ted. We'll take you back home only as quickly as humanly possible."

"We can take *Ramses' Chariot*," Felicity suggested.

"As soon as we get the space station up and running for immediate Federation occupation. With the Benitons gone, there is an opportunity to expand beyond the frontier without displacing anyone. The next hop is to Homeworld, which is currently unoccupied as well. Once we clear out the Skrima and close the rift for good, that is. Until then, we're all here." Terry leaned toward Ted. "Do you have any ideas about how we can close the transdimensional doorway?"

Ted took his last bite, finished chewing, and stared at the wall.

Terry, Cory, and Felicity looked at each other. It was

never a good idea to interrupt Ted when he was communing with the universe, as he occasionally did. Or he could have been talking to Plato, the AI he had developed.

With a nod to his daughter, Terry finished his coffee and stood up.

"The question," Ted started, "isn't necessarily about closing the rift, but about closing it to the Skrima. If they can no longer use it, does that meet your needs?"

"Yes," Terry answered as simply as possible.

Ted stood without looking at anyone and walked away. Cory collected his tray along with hers and headed for the scullery, leaving Terry and Felicity alone.

"I love my husband," Felicity stated.

"I'd give my life for his," Terry replied. Her eyes glistened, and a single tear escaped. TH didn't know what else to say. He excused himself to refill his mug and grab a Coke for the captain.

Once back on the bridge, he handed over the beverage. The captain savored the first sip, holding the container in both hands as if it were a fragile prize.

"This is going to take forever," Micky complained.

"Time is a cheap commodity right now. We almost lost two of our number today. There's nothing pressing us to get this done. Even if we let the Skrima overrun the planet, as long as they can't get a ship, they're trapped."

"Are they?" Micky asked.

"What do you mean?"

"Once in the Etheric, can't they move around?"

"But they couldn't get here until they had the rift. As

long as the satellites are in orbit, they are jamming the Skrima's ability to interact with the Etheric."

"That also means we're going to run out of power at some point, operating inside the atmosphere. The engines are energy hogs, and without the boost from Etheric power sources, we have a finite ability to operate."

Terry chewed the inside of his lip. "I hear you saying time is a factor. How much time do we have?"

"A week, maybe less."

Terry moved to Ruzfell, the systems operator. "You have four days to kill as many Skrima as you can. After that, we have to take the company planetside. Get up close and personal."

Ruzfell acknowledged the order and continued to seek, target, and fire. A constant hum filled the ship from the railguns' firing. The bridge's mood turned grim. Terry took another drink.

The landscape of Benitus Seven would be forever scarred because of the bombardment, but they would have done it even if the Benitons had survived their encounter with the Skrima. The red devils could not be allowed to remain in this dimension, and the Beniton genocide meant the Skrima had to be punished so violently that they would feel the pain through the rift and to the other side.

Iracitus, on Approach to the Rift, Benitus Seven

Dust and smoke hung over the area, making it stand out from a hundred kilometers away. The approach was easy, but seeing what was inside was not to be. The ship plowed through the outer edges and continued forward, relying solely on instruments.

"You are five hundred meters above the rift's last known location. I cannot get visual confirmation of its status at this time. I do not recommend getting any closer," Iracitus reported. He showed the infrared view of the ground below. Too many Skrima.

"No need," Shonna replied. They turned to Char.

She closed her eyes and tried to reach out, but she was blocked. She focused harder, forcing her mind to engage with the Etheric, but she couldn't break through. "I thought that might be the case." Char stretched her arms and twisted in her seat to loosen her tight muscles. "Iracitus, get me the *War Axe*, please."

The AI connected them.

"Any luck?" Terry asked, hope hanging off the words.

"We need to shut down the jammers. We can't see a thing down here, and we're not getting closer than five hundred meters above the ground."

"Don't go closer than that." On the ship's small viewscreen, Terry was vigorously shaking his head. He looked over his shoulder. "Micky, shut down the satellites, but be ready to turn them back on."

When Terry turned back to the screen, he held his hand out with fingers splayed.

"Five seconds."

"Thanks, out here," Char stated quickly and closed her eyes. The other werewolves followed suit, ready to dive into the Etheric and take a look for themselves.

The weight lifted, and Char jumped clear of her body and the ship. She headed down toward the pulsing energy, her spirit sinking as she approached. Despite the high-altitude railgun bombardment, the rift remained.

Char caught a glimpse of something racing past her. "Turn it on, turn it on!" she shouted. Terry waved frantically. Char was forced back into her body in time for the Skrim to materialize inside the ship. It slashed at Timmons, but space was tight. The razor-like claws didn't have enough momentum to cut through the body armor. It stood firm as Sue tried to drive it backward.

She ducked and it hammered claws into her back, cutting through her flak jacket and sending four of its claws through her body. She gasped and dropped. Char tried to change into a Werewolf but couldn't. The jammers kept her in human form. She pulled her pistols and fired, unleashing a deafening cacophony within the confines of the runabout. At that range, she didn't miss. The nine-millimeter slugs might have been small, but she put her shots through the Skrim's eyes, then through its chest. Anywhere Timmons wasn't as he struggled to keep the creature from using its claws.

The Skrim ducked its head and tried to ram its horns into Timmons' exposed face. Char launched herself from her seat, firing mid-air into the base of its skull, with a second shot into its spine. It bounced off Timmons, its head lolling on the broken neck, and fell to the deck on top of Sue.

Timmons stepped over it and popped the hatch. He and Char picked up the body and shoved it through to fall five hundred meters to the ground.

Sue groaned and tried to sit up, but Timmons told her to stay where she was. He stroked the side of her head, carefully moving her blonde hair, which was covered in Skrima blood, away from her face.

"Iracitus, take us back to the *Axe*." Char removed one of the bandages from her armored vest and joined Timmons in keeping pressure on the wounds while Sue's nanocytes worked to repair the damage.

CHAPTER ELEVEN

Belzimus, Command Post and Training Area Zoranitus

Kae sat with his head hanging to his knees. Marcie stared at a spot on the wall. Braithwen was asleep sitting upright. Wiriya waited outside the command post, declaring himself their guard until they could recover their senses. He sympathized with them.

The day had been harder than they expected, running from test to test, trying to see one thousand officers engaged, never a single down minute. After the all-nighter leading up to such a day, they had hit their limit.

Wiriya was tired too, but not as tired as the Trans-Pac leadership. The sergeant major appeared out of the darkness, having made no sound on his approach.

"I know you," Monsoon started.

"Sergeant Major," Wiriya greeted him.

"Tank jockey, sergeant."

"Private at the moment. Major Walton has made me his aide de camp," Monsoon stated without giving away his thoughts. "They're inside but a bit wiped. I'm standing guard until they're ready to tally the results of the day."

"I think that's a good call. Private? Are you the one who shot the ship?"

"Fuck, man. Stab a guy when he's down."

Monsoon shrugged. "That's the best time to stab him. He doesn't stab back. Come on, let's rouse the team and see if we can get this thing done. I'm stuffed and ready for some shuteye."

"Field day barbecue was good?"

"Have you not eaten?" Monsoon asked.

"I had one boxed lunch, but we burned a lot of calories today. I can feel myself wasting away. I think my hair has gotten thinner." He pointed to his head. Monsoon didn't bother looking.

"Let's go inside. I'll rustle up chow. Somebody has to take care of them, and heaven help us that it's me."

Inside the command post, the sergeant major turned on the radio and contacted the headquarters building. He had the duty gather a few bags of leftovers for transfer to the command post. Monsoon gave the corporal the impression that the meals needed to be at the CP an hour ago. He winked at Wiriya.

"Incorrigible, Sergeant Major."

"It won't hurt him to hurry up. This is the army. We need everything yesterday. Hurry up and wait. And no, I won't do that to him. As soon as it arrives, grab it and bring it in here. I'll start crunching the numbers once I'm able to pull their data if I can figure out what they were trying to collect."

Wiriya briefed the sergeant major on how they'd

conducted the process. He showed his datapad. Monsoon was able to figure out where the data went and then pull it up. Kae and Marcie had set up the program early that morning, and no other work was required. The analysis was already done. The data was parsed and displayed, tallied exactly as Wiriya had described.

"I guess this list is what we'll call the Lion Corps."

The crunch of a vehicle on the parking lot's gravel signaled the arrival of the duty. "Record time, Sergeant Major." Wiriya hurried outside to gather the booty.

"Rise and shine, boyfriends!" Monsoon said, tipping a chair over for the clatter effect.

Marcie opened her bloodshot eyes. "If you ever do that again, I will shoot you."

"It's going to be dawn soon. We need to do this thing and then get ready for PT."

"Dawn?" Kae whined. "I feel like shit."

Jake checked his watch. "You fucking asshole." He showed Marcie the time.

"I guess we don't have to wait for next time. I'm going to shoot you right now."

"You don't want to rush into something like that." Monson spoke softly in his soothing baritone. "Let's savor the moment with some barbecue and the best sides the chow hall could come up with."

Wiriya managed to turn the handle and pull the door open, catching it with a foot and kicking it far enough that he could work his way inside. He struggled under the burden of more bags than he should have tried to carry at one time.

The aroma of smoked meat and bright side dishes and

even the smell of cake wafted by. Kae was up in an instant and took a few bags from his aide. "You know, you could have made more than one trip or asked for help."

"What?" Wiriya looked at Kaeden like he had committed sacrilege. They delivered the spread to the table where pastries had rested their first day on Belzimus. Wiriya and Kaeden opened the bags and set things up, then Wiriya stepped aside. The other four looked at him. He pointed to the plates. "Start there. It's all ready."

"You first, and make it quick because you got hungry people behind you," the sergeant major ordered, allowing no chance for rebuttal.

In response, Wiriya's stomach growled, and he had to swallow because his mouth was watering so intensely. He dipped his head in reply and loaded up. Jake and Kae filled their plates while Marcie stretched. She went last, taking two plates to save herself a trip.

"I already ate," the sergeant major replied to their looks. "While you're verbally incapacitated, I'll go through the results of today's exercise. It looks like the data tallied like it was supposed to. Your programming skills have served us all well. Judging by what Private Wiriya described, I think you have a winner. I'd like to do the same thing with the NCOs if we can."

"I liked what I saw from shockingly few and was alarmed to the point of being terrified by what I saw from too many," Kae managed to articulate through a mouthful of sauce-heavy meat.

"Here are the players, according to the data." Monsoon projected it to the biggest screen in the room. Kae and Marcie frowned. There were fifteen names on the list. The next names had a significantly lower total number of engagements.

"At least Major Punyaa is at the top. I wonder why he sat back at the beginning of the armor training yesterday?" Kae asked. No one had an answer.

"It's good to see Baroon and Anthen, too. Even Gamon. The tally is three majors, a captain, and eleven lieutenants." Marcie stared at the list, trying to put faces to names.

"The Lion Corps," Jake muttered. "I had higher hopes. What about the next ten names on the list? Engagement on occasion where they stepped up to answer a question but generally laid back?"

"The Cub Scouts?" Kae offered. Marcie understood the old Earth term even though it was before both their times.

Jake nodded. "Good enough for me. When I get back to officer country in about five minutes, I'll send out notifications to the fifteen and the next ten. We'll have to run them through their paces to make sure they weren't gaming us. I'll have them show up a half-hour prior to morning PT."

"What do you think?" Kaeden asked Wiriya.

"I know those officers. Some can be abrasive, but the same could be said of you, no disrespect intended. I have not been in combat, but you have. All of you. You drive the soldiers toward a seemingly impossible goal, but we're going to find out that we will reach that level and beyond, aren't we? Using that standard, I think these men will serve you well."

"I need these leaders to serve their *men* well," Marcie clarified. She yawned and then stood. "Time to pack it in."

Kae started gathering the leftover food. He expected to

make it a midnight snack. Wiriya jumped in to help. "Today was a good day, Corporal."

"I thought I was a private?"

"That was yesterday. Who knows what tomorrow will bring?"

Belzimus, Physical Training Field

The twenty-five showed up in their PT gear a half-hour early. Others started to drift in but stayed at a reasonable distance, thanks to the sergeant major's imposing look. He didn't have to say a word. His presence and stance told the others everything they needed to know.

Marcie went from one to another to shake their hands and put faces to names. Kae followed suit, with Jake behind. Colonel Braithwen had not known any of the lieutenants or the captain. They hadn't been in the army when he left for the Federation. Two of the majors had been newly promoted, but they had been officers for long enough that he had seen them before. Punyaa was the only officer he knew well.

He liked the tanker, even though he himself was a ground-pounder. Jake had been an infantry officer his whole career. Only knowing one of the fifteen nagged at his sense of self-respect. It had taken strangers to shine a light on the army's shortcomings, and more importantly, to devise a way to fix the issues holding them back. Jake didn't take it personally. He had been too close to the process.

Now they were under the Federation microscope. "This is the time for Belzimus to shine!" Jake blurted.

Marcie looked at him out the corner of her eye, trying not to smile as she met the last few officers. Once Kae and Jake finished their handshakes, they stood aside for Marcie to deliver her expectations.

"Mission orders. These are the lifeblood of a modern military. A mission order allows subordinates to make the right decisions to accomplish the objective. I can issue an order to take a hill, but that's not the mission. The mission is to secure a supply route. If there's a better way to accomplish that, isn't it better if the small unit leaders can make that decision? If they don't secure the supply route, whether on the high ground or not, the mission fails.

"This is what I'm asking of you: understand and help our people with their decision-making process. When we came here to establish the Trans-Pacific Task Force, we did not give the soldiers any choices. We told them what to do, and they did it. We had to establish a performance baseline. We're still doing that. No one out there is ready to make mission decisions, not yet, but that will be thrust upon them far sooner than anyone is comfortable with." Marcie pointed at the units forming on the PT field before clasping her hands behind her back and continuing.

"We're trying to accelerate their understanding of what we're trying to accomplish, and we've picked you to help us educate them. We'll give you special reflective sashes to make you stand out during training. Leadership isn't about the rank. Rank should be reflective of what leaders can do for their people. In combat, troops will look to the one who gives them a fighting chance to survive while accomplishing the mission.

"We have to lead from the front. That means we've been

CRAIG MARTELLE & MICHAEL ANDERLE

there, fighting hand to hand, covered in an enemy's blood. The troops need to know you won't ask them to do anything you won't do yourself. They *must* know that, or they won't do your bidding.

"For today, we'll run PT as always. One of our admin folk has the sashes. Make sure you get one. Put yourselves in the front of the formations and set the pace. It better be one the majority of troops can meet, but not so slow that everyone makes it. Not yet. We need the soldiers to understand that they have to push themselves. Not every day for the rest of their careers, but these are easy days. They won't realize that until they've had a hard day.

"We were on a mission where we engaged an enhanced enemy, extremely deadly because we'd backed them into the corner. They were fighting for their lives. Major Walton took a spear through his chest. He stayed in the fight because it was that or die. I want everyone here to have that will to live. That demands a competitive spirit and belief in an ideal higher than the individual.

"Because the mission will come first, and soldiers will die. As hard as we train and as much as we don't want them to lose their lives, some will. You can't negotiate it away and you can't reason with it. Sometimes a bullet has your name on it, and sometimes it's your best friend standing next to you. You watch him die, and you keep fighting. You celebrate what they were once the battle is won. You make life worth living to honor those who sacrificed for it. The Trans-Pacific Task Force will be issued orders by the Federation to establish and then keep the peace. We are risking our lives so others may live.

"There is no greater ideal in this universe. When the

soldiers return home, I want them to take pride in saying that they were a part of this. I want you to know that you were instrumental in keeping them alive. I've had good men and women die under my command. You will deal with it because starting right fucking now, you will give one hundred percent to every soldier in this army. You are improving their odds. Go get your sashes and lead these soldiers to the promised land."

The group ragged out a salute and ran off. Marcie pursed her lips as she watched them go. "I'm not sure they understood."

"They will soon enough," Kae told her.

"You took a spear to the chest?" Jake asked while shaking Marcie's hand.

"I don't recommend it," Kae replied. He pointed at an admin civilian hurrying toward them. The Lion Corps swerved to intercept him, so he swung wide to avoid them. They started chasing him. He threw the sashes into the air and ran screaming. "An inauspicious start."

Jake's mouth hung open. "I'm embarrassed for all my people."

"They better get that shit out of their systems before we deploy, or we're fucked."

"A Belzonian would take those words as a victory dance, but I get you. Let's make sure that doesn't happen again."

"If only the Lion Corps had seen it from this angle." Marcie snorted, then sighed and looked at the ground. "I'm sure that will be funny later, but right now, it makes me want to go back to bed. Not even my bed, because bullshit like we just witnessed destroyed our room."

"The skipper said he'd have it ready today and we'll be able to move in, complete with a new mattress," Kae noted with a smile.

"When this day is over, I will revel in my bed."

"Our." His smile faded, but he didn't lose hope. "Our *squeaky* bed."

CHAPTER TWELVE

War Axe, **100,000 meters over Benitus Seven**

Terry paced the corridor, talking to himself while Dokken watched him. "Where's Cory?" he asked.

Hangar bay, the dog replied nonchalantly.

"Then why are you up here with me?"

Cory was concerned.

Terry stopped pacing and took a knee next to Dokken. He scratched the thick neck fur behind his big ears. "It's been a couple years since you left her side. She okay?"

Right there, yes. Dokken opened his mouth to let his tongue fall out. _She is. There will always be a place in her heart for Ramses, but she's now filling much of that emptiness with her own sense of self-purpose. Coming here was the best thing we could have done for her._

"Coming here almost got a couple _more_ of my people killed," Terry countered. "I have a great dislike for Benitus Seven."

Dokken remained seated, enjoying the moment.

"You better get back." Terry stood, watching the big German Shepherd.

I'll stay with you for a while if that's okay.

"It's more than okay, buddy." Terry and Dokken strolled the corridors, not having a destination in mind. He had been thinking about the ongoing fight and kept coming to the same conclusion: they were going to have to go down there and kill the Skrima one at a time. "How about Wenceslaus? We had some great battles with him, didn't we?"

Our arch-nemesis. We sent him packing, all right, Dokken agreed. Terry chuckled at the dog's mirth.

The overhead speakers crackled to life. "Colonel Walton to the bridge, please."

"Crap." He scowled. "I better go."

Me, too. I need to get back and check on Cory. Next time, try to have a stick of jerky on you. Dokken trotted down the corridor toward the stairway. Terry hurried after him and headed up while Dokken descended.

When he walked onto the bridge, Char was there with her whole pack, along with Joseph and Petricia. "What's up?" he asked, trying to sound as calm as he had been when he was with Dokken.

"We're going to have to destroy the ships at the spaceport," Micky said from behind him.

Terry spun. "We can't recover them?"

"Skrima are inside the ships. A few scattered around the Grays' city, but there's a concentration in each of the ships."

"Light 'em up, Ruzfell. There is nothing on those ships worth risking the Skrima getting off-planet. Without Ted's jammer, they can't be killed. Joseph, I thought you disabled the ships?"

"We did; that's why they're still on the ground. We assumed they might be able to fly them, but not that they could repair them. Seeing them in action, they'll be able to fix the minimal damage we caused. It was superficial at best. We had to hurry because we didn't want to get caught by the Skrima."

"Let's take care of them, Skipper. It'll be a lot harder if they get airborne." Terry gave no room for an alternate approach.

"Ruzfell, it's time to permanently ground the fleet," Micky declared.

"I can carve notches into my workstation!" the Yollin systems officer declared. "Bring us around, Clifton, and give me a line of fire."

Micky looked at Terry Henry. "This is your doing. Everyone watches those old movies you brought on board."

"Probably," Terry agreed. He didn't feel like lightening the mood with friendly banter. His mind was wrapped up in a seemingly endless tide of enemies. Char looked like she wanted to say something. "What am I missing?"

"You know what we're going to have to do," Char stated.

"Go down there and fight them one on one?"

"We also need to get this space station up. I want to take my team to the station and bring it up while you handle the Skrima. I'm assuming everyone will be wearing armored combat suits down there." She made it sound like a question, but it wasn't. Terry knew there was only one right answer.

"Everyone including me, because we'll need our full sensor suites and speed. We'll hit the ground running and won't stop until we've taken away any chance of them establishing a foothold, but we're fighting a losing battle as long as the rift remains open. You said you had an idea?" Terry stared at Ted.

"Yes. I will draw power from the rift in such magnitude that no one will be able to come through. I can find the materials I need to build the device on the space station."

"While you're there, you other engineers can check it out and make it habitable. As soon as we give the thumbs-up, the Federation will move a team in there to start building a Gate."

Char nodded and pointed to her team. "Pack your trash. We're taking *Iracitus* to the station." She looked from face to face. "We'll take *Ramses' Chariot*, too, with a few additional people like Felicity."

"Who better to tell the Federation what they need to bring the old girl back to life?"

"A promenade," Sue offered. "With the best clothing shops, like they have on Onyx Station."

"Why can't we get good shops on Keeg? It's like you don't want us to enjoy our home away from home, Terry Henry Walton! How can we make this suck more? We want a shoe store for women." Shonna pounded her fist into her hand.

Terry looked everywhere but at the werewolves. "Where did I go wrong?"

"Looks like you married into the wrong family," Micky muttered.

Shonna smiled and waved as she sauntered out.

Char stopped when she was next to TH. He whispered for her ears only, "Don't have too much fun over there. Please stay in touch."

"I'll tell Ted to pipe a continuous feed to Smedley. We'll all be monitored, so you will know we're alive. We'll drop some sensors too, so you can see if we're good with air, but we'll bring the means to cut our way out if necessary. I don't know if the station was able to repair itself from last time, but we'll find out and be ready before we go past any immovable bulkheads."

"Why *don't we* have better stores on Keeg?" Terry asked, his mind finally distracted from the burdens of the mission.

"By the time the Gate became operational and known, Keeg was damaged. It's hard to entice stores to take a risk. I'm sure Felicity is working on it. We'll find out since Shonna and Sue will bend her ear the entire time we're on this station."

"We should call it something neat like 'Spindle of Doom Station.'"

Char didn't dignify that with an answer. She left while she still had her wits about her.

Clifton turned control over to Ruzfell. "Preparing to fire on the Beniton spaceport." Ruzfell's voice was grim, his previous enthusiasm greatly dampened. "Firing."

The main screen showed a magnified image as the stream of railgun fire drew a line across the ships, corkscrewed around them, and walked back to make a second pass. Nine parked ships devolved to nine smoking hulks.

Residual IR showed a few survivors running for their lives. Ruzfell made short work of them.

"Next targets?" the Yollin asked.

"Return to the rift and pour intermittent fire into it to prevent reinforcements from coming through. We can't kill them fast enough. You keep them from coming through the rift, and we'll take care of the rest. Bad Company! Full powered combat armor for all hands. Report to the hangar bay suited up and ready for extended operations planetside in thirty minutes." Terry clenched his jaw with his lips apart to let the growl escape from deep within his throat. "Christina, meet me in the armory in ten."

Belzimus, Command Post and Training Area Zoranitus

Marcie held the binoculars to her face and scanned back and forth across the training area. "Sphere of influence," she muttered.

Kae tapped her on the shoulder to get his turn, but she shrugged him off. "Why is there only one set of binos?"

"Belzimus," Jake replied as if it was the single answer to all the army's shortcomings.

"On it!" Wiriya bolted from the command post. Jake and Kae turned to watch the door swing closed behind him.

"I guess all I have to do is ask." Kae headed for the steps to the observation deck. "I'll be on the roof."

Marcie waved with one hand while holding steady with the binoculars.

"What are you seeing?" Jake asked.

"I'm watching the timing between the coordinated movements. It's safe, and I'm good with that. It's a new baseline from which to improve. Don't get me wrong, they are light-seconds ahead of where they were three days ago. I'm still not comfortable with going to live fire. We'll work more unit, personnel, and equipment integration to go live starting in another week."

"You've been here a grand total of eleven days. That equates to less than two hundred total hours in training. How long did it take to bring the Bad Company up to speed?"

"The Force de Guerre. Bad Company selected the best of the best of the FDG. To get the Force combat-ready? I don't know. That happened when I was a baby. Terry Henry started with four men and grew it over a hundred and fifty years." Marcie finally lowered the binoculars. "We don't have a hundred and fifty years."

"We don't, but we won't need that many," Jake replied. "Look at their progress. They'll never be ready to be blooded, but that's what it will take to make them a professional fighting force. Without blood, they can only go through the motions so much. The terror and fury of combat are foreign to our culture. These men think they are ready for it. They aren't. We'll lose ten percent of the force due to shock, maybe more, after the first battle where we take any kind of losses."

"That's why we need to reinforce training. When they lose their senses, the only thing remaining will be the habits they are forming right now." Marcie raised the binoculars and returned to scanning the training area.

Jake stood silently by, frowning as he watched the

masses. "I'm proud of how far they've come and am happy to be a part of it. Even though it isn't in our culture, Belzonians are capable of great things."

"The sergeant major is greatness personified." Marcie pointed at the focal point of the entire training area, where Monsoon directed and inspired.

"Crantis puts the "he" in hermaphrodite," Jake replied. Marcie guessed that was considered a compliment in Belzonian culture. She couldn't see how, but that was neither here nor there. She decided not to use the expression. Ever.

Colonel Walton, you have a call coming in from the Federation. They said it was urgent, the duty comm officer relayed from the *Vengeance* to Marcie's internal chip.

Her heart sank. "We were just saying…" She let her arm drop before putting the binoculars on the table. "Can you connect me to the ship through the comm station here?"

Jake sat behind the terminal, tapped a few buttons, and contacted the ship. "Federation wants to talk to you." He tried to sound cheerful, but his heart skipped a beat.

"Colonel Walton, with whom am I speaking?"

"Lance Reynolds. How the hell are you, Marcie?"

She chuckled before answering, "Is this the sugar to make the medicine easier to swallow?"

"It might be, but I am always concerned about the well-being of my field commanders. That's a holdover from active duty about a million years ago. How are you?"

"Tired, but Jake and I are observing our first foray into combined arms training while they're still trying to learn individual soldiering. We've given them the firehose, and they've been pretty good about taking it."

"Which means you haven't had a mutiny or mass suicides?"

"It's a careful balancing act, but I see you understand, General. I salute you."

"We need the Belzonian Army on Kor'nar in ten days. The conflict is escalating, and it's starting to envelop Federation assets. We need you to stop the war and establish peace. The Federation needs to expand its presence in that area of space, and we cannot do that with a planet embroiled in a civil war."

Marcie chewed on her thoughts before answering, "We can't have two weeks?"

"I really need you there in seven days. The extra three was because of getting hosed when you should have had a month to prepare a green army to do the Federation's business. They were the only force available of any size, and they came with their own training area for ramp-up. We had no other options."

"Damn!" Jake blurted before slapping a hand over his mouth. He thought there had been competition. He couldn't say that they were better than anyone else out there. He took his hand away and mouthed, "We're the only kid on the playground."

Marcie shook her head. "We are calling the army the Trans-Pacific Task Force because we are going one step beyond establishing the peace. A little thing, but we are starting to build identity and unit loyalty." She looked out the window at the ongoing maneuvers. "We'll do what we can to get there in seven days, General."

"If you can hit that date, I won't be able to thank you enough. I'll transfer everything we know about the Kor'-

narians and the conflict to your ship so you can start devising your strategy of engagement. Good luck, Colonel."

Marcie waved even though it hadn't been a video call. *Kae.*

"I heard," he said from the bottom of the steps. "I guess we better rally the loggies to build a loadout plan."

"At the end of this series of maneuvers. Let them finish. We'll do a quick hotwash with the Lion Corps and let them know they are ready for war."

"Even though they aren't," Jake stated.

"They are going to learn what it means to be war-tired. We are adopting twenty-hour operations effective immediately. They need to train, and they need to prep equipment for deployment. They can catch up on sleep on the ship."

Wiriya burst through the door and waved a pair of binoculars. "Success!"

"New plan. We've received our deployment orders," Kae told him. "We need to load the task force and head for the system Gate in six days."

The corporal looked at the binoculars in his hand. "I'll pack these for you, just in case." He was the only one smiling. "We can do this. Just tell me where to start."

Kae held his hands up in the universal gesture of "I don't know."

"We need to figure that out," Marcie remarked. "Colonel Braithwen, have Monsoon take over the training. You join him, Wiriya. We'll be on the *Vengeance* for the next few hours, establishing what we need to do before we can articulate a plan."

"Six days to get out of here?" Wiriya asked before immediately continuing, "We have approximately one hundred shuttles and dropships for land-to-orbit transport. A round trip takes two hours. They can move all the tanks in one trip. Ten thousand troops, twelve thousand if you include support personnel, two thousand per trip if all shuttles remain operational. Another four to six rotations with supplies like ammo, food, medical, field base, and things like that for thirty days of self-sustainment. Accounting for delays in loading and unloading, it can be done in, say, twelve hours of prep to load and twenty-eight hours of movement. Cocktail-napkin math."

Jake stared at a spot on the wall, his lips moving as he cycled through the numbers. "I think he's right. We need to start moving people and equipment in the afternoon four days from now to make a launch window on Day Six. Gives us half a day of leeway in case any shuttles break down."

Kae gave Wiriya an approving look. "That stuff isn't normal knowledge for a sergeant."

"It is if you've hit the glass ceiling in this herm's army and you see a career where numbers and organization mean more than your plumbing. I've been training in logistics ever since we moved the tank battalion to the other side of the planet. They made a puke pile out of it. I helped us get back in a third of the time."

"No glass ceiling here, Wiriya." Marcie looked at Jake. "Let Monsoon know he's got it. We'll see him in a few hours to talk deployment strategy. Start a countdown, Kae. We're on the clock."

CHAPTER THIRTEEN

Ramses' Chariot, **Heading to Orbit over Benitus Seven**

The viewscreen showed a tiny image of the *War Axe*. Pretty soon, they would no longer be able to see it. Char watched wistfully. They all had a job to do, and by splitting the tasks, they'd be able to finish and go home that much sooner.

"You said you can block the rift?" Char asked.

Ted waved her away as if brushing away a mosquito. She grabbed his collar and dragged him out of the pilot's chair, twisting him in mid-air and slamming him against the bulkhead. "I don't have time for your bullshit, Ted. Can you or can't you?"

He clenched his teeth and glared at her. Felicity pulled ineffectually at Char's arms. Ted held onto her wrists and squeezed as his anger grew. She took a breath and let go of him. He did not let go of her. "Ted," she warned, "your Alpha has asked you a question. This is how it is with werewolves. This is how it will always be."

"Why?" Ted asked, now a scientist contemplating a

164

problem. Felicity rubbed his arm on the way to his neck, which she started massaging to work out the tension. He finally released his grip on Char's arms.

"I don't know," she stammered. Char ran a long and slender finger through her hair, pulling the white streak to the side before tucking it behind her ear. "Maybe it shouldn't be. What do you think it should be?"

"Nothing. We have our own lives now. I answer to me. You to you. Merrit to Merrit. We can be more efficient without a secondary chain of command."

"Most of the time," Char replied. She leaned against the bulkhead. "We need to finish this job, and I think that will be it. I'm ready to pack it in, and this time, our retirement will be permanent."

Felicity stared in disbelief.

"I'm sorry, Ted. This isn't easy for me or anyone. I shouldn't have grabbed you."

Ted would always be Ted. "That is correct. You should not have."

"You said you could fill the rift with the power transfer from the Etheric? Is that true?"

Ted cocked his head. Even after all this time, Char didn't understand him sometimes.

Felicity answered for him. "He despises wasting time. He already answered the question once, and it was yes. That's why we're going to the station—because he needs parts to build the device and they are out there. I swear," Felicity drawled.

Char rubbed her temples. The engagement with the Skrima had left her head throbbing and her soul shaken.

"We have to stop them. There is no one else. I don't take

CRAIG MARTELLE & MICHAEL ANDERLE

it for granted that the jammer will make them vulnerable forever. That is my greatest fear while Terry and the others are down there alone and fighting for their lives."

Ted shook his head. "It will work, and it will keep working because the science is correct."

"Can they counter the jammer with an anti-jammer? They were trying to fix the starships in the spaceport, and when we hit their formations, they instantly split up. Not just locally, but across the whole continent."

Ted froze in place, standing still and staring at the viewscreen while Plato drove the ship toward the Benitons' abandoned station. Felicity continued to massage his neck.

"Does Terry know?" she asked softly.

"It was his idea, now that Cory is back to herself. It came more suddenly than we expected, but this will be our last mission. We haven't told Christina, so please don't mention anything to her or anyone else. We'll tell everyone in our own good time. As TH would say, 'We have to win this fight first, then we can do the fun stuff.'"

"Yes," Ted conceded, interrupting the conversation. "They can block the Etheric jammer if they combine a broadband..."

Char held up her hand. "Plato, please connect me with Terry."

The system showed green. The *Ramses' Chariot* was Ted's ship, and he considered the crackling that preceded a connection to be superfluous noise. The green light said everything Ted needed to hear.

"Terry, Ted said the Skrima might be able to counter the Etheric jammer."

"The Dickens you say?" Terry replied. Char looked at the overhead, wondering if she heard correctly. "*We must have bloody noses and crack'd crowns, and pass them current too. God's me, my horse!*"

"Quoting *Henry IV*. Are you that confident?"

"'*Once more unto the breach, dear friends,*'" Terry replied with another quote. "Once more. We'll do what we have to do. I've had about enough of the fucking Skrima."

"That's the Terry Henry we know. Take it to them, lover."

"You get that station up and running so we can throw an All-Guns-Blazing-level party after declaring victory and sleeping unhindered in the camp of a destroyed enemy. I have to go. We have a planet to disinfect."

"Thanks for connecting me, Plato," Char told the AI. "You heard the man, we have a station to set up." Char mashed a button for a direct link with Iracitus. "Engineers, conduct your survey after giving Ted all the help he needs to build his device. By the way, Ted, what are you going to do with that power?"

Ted spoke softly. "I'm going to run a shield generator as a backstop to the portal, and then I'm going to beam the remainder up here to run this station because I'm taking all the miniaturized Etheric power supplies they currently have. I need them."

Char gave him a thumbs-up. "I'm good with that." She connected to the other ship. "Iracitus, can you dock in the berth closest to ours, please? We'll take the same spot we had last time."

Plato and Iracitus maneuvered close to the station, and despite Char's impatience, they inspected the outside of the structure before docking. Char didn't ask why. From there on out, Ted was in charge of what needed to be done to bring the station to life. Char was in charge of the life it would take, but Felicity's input was critical. Char was little more than physical labor. Shonna, Merrit, and Timmons were engineers. They were going to be busy and do the heavy lifting.

Char headed for the small cargo bay before the ship attached itself to the station. When she returned, she was dragging the plasma torch.

"No way I'm getting stuck in there, just in case the bots fixed the bulkhead."

"I won't let that happen again," Ted promised, looking at Felicity. She would be inside with him. He would not let anything happen to her, one of only two people he'd let inside the barriers he'd surrounded himself with. The other was the Crenellian Ankh.

Felicity kissed Ted on the forehead, and his expression softened. Once breathable air was confirmed, the airlock cycled, and the hatch popped.

Ted headed out without another word. He carried a small tool bag and that was it. He would leave the heavy lifting to the others. They would haul the various equipment Ted had brought.

He walked straight down the corridor toward the central hub. After fifty meters, he found the way blocked by a bulkhead that looked untouched.

"I guess that answers that," Char remarked. She dragged the torch forward.

"What are you doing?" Ted asked.

"Cutting a hole?" It sounded like a question and not an answer.

"No." He opened his toolkit and started removing a panel on the wall. Once inside, he connected six different jumpers to a small device in his pocket. The others caught up. They watched and shrugged.

And then they waited.

Belzimus, Command Post and Training Area Zoranitus

Once training was completed, Monsoon rallied the troops to stand by. He kept the whole army behind so everyone got the word at the same time. Marcie didn't want rumors or misinformation to flood the ranks. If she passed it to someone else to deliver, it would inevitably get changed.

She didn't want that. Everyone needed to know what she knew.

She stood on a chair and held a microphone that was connected to a sound system to make sure everyone could hear her.

"It was a good day," she told them. "Every day in the field is a good day, especially when you return with everybody who started the day. You accomplished the day's training by improving your tactical maneuvers. Tomorrow, we'll do more of the same, but in a live-fire environment. You might not think you're ready, but you are.

"There is no time tonight to celebrate. You'll recover from here, clean and PM your gear, catch chow, and then begin packing. That's right. We've been activated. Six days from now, we will fly through the Belzimus system's Gate on our way through two more Gates to get to an insectoid planet called Kor'nar. The two hives are fighting, and it is putting a damper on Federation engagement in that sector. We're going to stop their war, and we're going to teach them how to make peace."

Marcie hesitated. Murmurs rippled through the crowd. She waited for the buzz to die down.

"In seven days' time, we will land on a planet in the middle of a war. Take your training seriously because now is the time you save your lives, not out there. Keep your wits about you, and you'll be fine. We're not going to send you into battle alone. We'll be there right beside you. We'll stare down the barrel of an enemy's gun together and make him wish he hadn't pointed it at us. We'll keep doing that until they stop pointing their weapons at us. Then we'll show them how to live without fighting.

"Clean your gear, eat, and check the monitors when you get back to the barracks. You have all become cheap labor to ensure this move happens in the most orderly manner possible. We will take the fleet through the Gate six days and two hours from now, and a great deal of training will take place between now and then. You have long days ahead of you, but when we land on Kor'nar, you're going to be ready. Dismissed."

Kae met her when she stepped off the chair. "You're getting to be as bad as Dad with all the speeches."

"Does that make me a terrible person?" she wondered with a half-smile.

"The opposite. Your job is to drive the ship. Jake, Monsoon, and I will make sure it's running right. We'll get there. I'll take the motor pool. You take supply, and they'll take the barracks." Kae gestured at the colonel and the sergeant major.

"The troops' first night with reduced sleep. We'll see what they look like when we're aboard the ships."

"That's one thing we haven't seen from them yet—a soldier's ability to sleep anywhere at any time. I think we'll see a comatose task force when we leave orbit. They'll be out cold for the duration of the transit. Care to bet on it?" He held out his hand to shake.

"I think that's a good bet. It's a critical skill. I look forward to them learning it without us having to teach them."

"What don't we have to teach them?" Jake asked as he and Monsoon approached.

"A soldier's real life. Sleep. Chow. Boredom. Terror. Personal hygiene. You know, the stuff civilians take for granted in their nine-to-five lives."

"They might be in for a shock. Just like me when every member of the Lion Corps showed up with a shaved head."

A smile spread slowly across Marcie's face. "The future is looking brighter for the Trans-Pac Task Force."

"Time to move the ship closer to the supply depot to load up. Might as well start early. I give it two days before the spokes and cogs no longer line up and the wheels grind to a halt."

"I was going to say three, but we'll plan for two."

"Planning for when the plan goes to hell?" Jake wondered. "That sounds like a good plan."

War Axe, the Hangar Bay

Christina held her head high and watched the mech warriors line up in the hangar bay. "We'll need two waves to get them landside."

"You go with the first wave and take everything east of the rift. I'll take west with the second. You'll be first in and last out."

"An honor, TH. That's something you usually reserve for yourself as the leader's prerogative, given your attitude that you must lead from the front."

"I demand it from the leader of the Bad Company," he stated and walked away. Christina watched him head to the armory to get his suit. She had already brought hers out and parked it while they waited. They would be deployed long enough. She faced the first wave and shouted, "Four mechs per dropship. Deploy two by two. Search and destroy. Keep your IR engaged at all times. Do not let those things close with you."

Sergeant Capples unlocked the combat axe from the side of his armor. Christina had developed the weapon for use during opposed boarding of ships in space. It had the tools to break in. It was bigger than a kukri and could be held in a mech hand and swung in tight quarters. "I think we'll be okay if they get too close." He swished the axe through the air for emphasis. "They're still operating solo, aren't they?"

"Yes, but new intel suggests they might be able to counter the jammers. If they do that, you'll have to wait for them to close. To attack you, they have to move fully into our dimension. That's when they're vulnerable. That's when we kill them."

"Then we need to kill them as fast as possible while we can," Capples replied matter-of-factly.

"That's the plan. I don't want to see anyone stop running until everything east of the rift is cleared. The *War Axe* will keep anything else from coming through, so the lines are drawn and sides are chosen. We have to repel this invasion. There is no other choice."

She prepared to climb into her suit. Kai ran across the hangar bay and caught her arm before she entered. She turned and pulled him into her arms for a passionate kiss that made Terry look away. Kai brushed the hair out of her face, which reminded her to tie it up before locking herself inside the suit. They said words only they could hear, then Kai walked away, acknowledging TH as he passed but not saying anything. Christina climbed in, sealed her powered combat armor, and brought the systems online. "Load up," she said over the company-wide channel. She switched to point-to-point to talk to Colonel Walton. "Does my father know?"

"About you and Kai? I sure hope so. Otherwise, it'll be an uncomfortable conversation," Terry quipped.

"He already knows that. He's not as uptight about it as you are. But not that. The part where you're handing over the Bad Company's Direct Action Branch."

"You know, then."

"I could see it in your eyes and how you're not doing things that you always used to, but giving them to me." Christina was astute. Terry hadn't bothered hiding what he was doing. He was happy she had figured out. Maybe that was the last test before she took the reins.

"I'll tell Kae when the time is right. We have a job to do

first, so let's focus on that. This mission isn't done until that rift is permanently closed. I don't know if they can open something onto other planets or not. It might be easier if they're already in this dimension. I know jack shit about them except that they are willing to kill every living thing on this side of the rift."

"We're going to convince them of the error of their ways," Christina declared.

"See you on the other side." Terry watched them load and seal the Pods.

Smedley announced on a general broadcast, "Landing areas are clear. Launching the first wave of dropships."

The access hatches sealed, and the shuttle Pods raced into the upper atmosphere.

Joseph and Petricia appeared with the alien squad, those personnel who didn't fit into the standard Bad Company armored combat suit.

"Hold down the fort while we're gone," Terry told them. "Just in case we get a new incursion somehow."

The squad hoisted their hand blasters while showing off their kukris.

"We'll be ready," Bundin boomed.

"That's all I can ask," Terry replied. "Joseph. Stay in touch with Char and the people on the station. And stay in touch with us. Watch over us all like our guardian angel."

Joseph couldn't see Terry's smile behind the screen of the combat suit, but he knew it was there. "I never thought I'd be called that. You used to have quite a chip on your shoulder about me."

"You used to eat people," Terry deadpanned.

"I wasn't eating them. It was a little more refined. But I

digress. For the record, I got better." Joseph's shoulder twitched as if he wasn't sure whether to shrug or not. "Here we are, a galaxy away, doing more good Terry Henry deeds. You, sir, have not changed since the first day we met, when you beat the holy bajoolysnackers out of me."

Terry couldn't help but laugh. "You deserved it. Now I trust you with my life. I trust you to protect my daughter's life."

"If it comes to that, we will. All of us here."

Cory emerged from near the Pod-docs that were still churning on the two warriors for their second round of repair and recovery. They were almost as good as new, despite having died horrible deaths. Thanks to the cryopods, those deaths hadn't been permanent.

Dokken walked alongside her. She shook her finger at her father. "We only have nine Pod-docs, so if anyone gets hurt that badly again, we won't be able to take care of them. We only have seven cryopods. That's sixteen total casualties. That's all we can tolerate before warriors start dying."

"We can't have that. We'll pull out at half that number and request special dispensation to nuke the planet."

Cory nodded. "I wanted to make sure. I don't want anyone else to die because of Benitus Seven."

"Neither do I, sweetheart."

"Any other final words of wisdom?" Joseph asked.

"'*The fool doth think he is wise, but the wise man knows himself to be a fool,*'" Terry quoted. "Fight until there's no enemy left. We may regress, but we'll never quit."

"Words to live by," Joseph agreed. "My pal William had a way with words."

"I've known you for a hundred and fifty years, and you never told me. You knew William Shakespeare?"

"No. William Williams. He signed the United States Constitution. He was a huge fan of Shakespeare. Honestly, TH, how old do you think I am?"

Terry managed to dial up a middle finger using the mechanical hands of the mech suit. "Fucking Joseph," Terry grumbled. He turned to the second wave. "Park your suits. Be back in ninety minutes to prepare for deployment."

Joseph tapped Bundin on his shell. "Get your gear. Lock and load. The first wave will be on the planet any time now, stirring things up even more than the *War Axe* already is."

"Yes, sir!" Bundin shuffled away, taking the Malatian, the Ixtali, the Yollin, and the Harborian with him.

Although the Harborian was human and Chris Bo Runner could have gone landside with the others, Bundin's squad had gelled with their response to the attack on Keeg station. Terry refused to break them up. They made an effective team with a good variety of unique skills.

Terry parked his suit but stayed within and thumbed his music selection to jam vintage Black Sabbath. He needed to think.

CHAPTER FOURTEEN

Belzimus, Parade and PT Field

"Two days left. Are we going to make it?" Kae asked.

Jake shook his head. "Absolutely."

"Hedging your bet, I see." The field was filling with supplies that weren't needed for the last twenty-four hours of training. They were using their equipment, tanks, trucks, artillery, rifles, individual field gear, and more. That would all get cleaned, PMed, inspected, and prepared to load. When they hit the ground, their equipment had to be operational until such time as they built a new support infrastructure.

They would tear it all down once the mission was declared complete. It could be a month down the road, or a year. The sergeant major's voice wafted through the air. They couldn't see him, but he was advising at least one miscreant of the errors in his genetic line.

"Is he always like that?" Kae asked.

"No. Sometimes he's more animated," Jake quipped.

"Don't use him as a paradigm. There are no other Belzonians like Crantis Monsoon."

"I doubt there are many like him in the whole universe, but all the others are probably sergeant majors, too."

"'Sergeants major.' That's the proper plural."

"What kind of bullshit is that?"

"I didn't make the rule, so don't shoot the messenger." Jake waved for Kae to follow. "Private! What is in these boxes?"

The private looked like he wanted to run but surrendered before his body could follow what his mind told it to do. "Personal gear, sir."

"Show me." Colonel Braithwen crossed his arms and tapped a foot. The private tripped over himself, trying to get to the box, then nudged an edge open as if Jake or Kae were going to lean down and peek through. "What the fuck is wrong with you? Take the lid off."

The private removed the lid and set it to the side.

"What is this junk?" Kae asked.

"Junk? Sir! This is the best coif curation kit in the barracks." The private stood straight, jaw clenched in defiance.

"You said words, but they don't mean anything to me."

"Let me show you," Jake offered. "Take your hat off, soldier."

Jake dug through the box and pulled four different items to the top. "This is the trimmer to bring unruly sides under control or to hermanscape the coiffure." He demonstrated the turning and blending technique. The equipment was corded, requiring power, and there wasn't any around the pallets, so Jake had to demonstrate without it being live.

"This is your color blending mask. You pull the hair through these holes using this hook." He pulled some of the private's strands through. "Then you take one of these to further separate based on length, with this spacer and sub-mask."

Kae stared in disbelief.

"If you have wavy locks," he removed another powered device, "you can use this to straighten them. Conversely, if it's straight and you want a wave, this has a separate attachment. Many use a second straightener. You can do both straight and wavy for an incomparable textured look. I preferred that with rugged colors, no rainbows. When I had hair, that is."

"And here is an exceptional dye kit. Private! You must be someone's favorite son to get this incredible kit. My compliments to you. This is better than mine, and I can believe it's the best in the barracks."

The private beamed. "Now, take that shit out of here and tag it for storage," Kae told him, replacing the lid before the colonel explained something else.

"We'll have power in our rooms, and this is very important to Belzonians."

Kae rolled his head to look at Jake. He held his hands up in surrender. It was on Kae to explain what their future held. "We'll be sleeping in a tent city, maybe. You won't have any power. There may be lights running off a generator, but that's it. There won't be any power for this stuff. There won't be any time, and more importantly, there won't be any need."

The private looked confused.

"That's the same look I had on my face when you guys started explaining this stuff. Do you not grasp the full details of what's in front of us? We're going to war. People are going to get killed. Your daily effort will revolve around surviving the day, not if you've got great hair. Which you do, I'll concede, but you can live it up when we get back. There will be a massive party, the likes of which Belzimus has never seen."

Jake clapped the private on the back. "We've seen some pretty righteous parties. This *is* Belzimus, after all. I will hold you to the best party ever. Put your gear away, Private, so it's in perfect condition upon your return. Until then, focus on being the best soldier you can be. Save your life and one more so we can all return home."

The private reluctantly picked up his box and carried it away.

"I think you mistook the look on my face for curiosity when it was perplexity. Not about the private's coif kit, but that you were explaining it to me, complete with demonstration."

"You needed to understand more about our culture if you want to relate to these soldiers."

Kaeden stared with a blank expression.

"How does your wife stand you?" Jake wondered.

"I think the word you're looking for is 'tolerate.' She tolerates me. I'm Terry Henry Walton's son. He was always far too manly for the softer skills, like appreciating what it takes for a good hairstyle. I learned that was his way of coping with the outside world. He's a protector. He protected his family and all of humanity when we were on

Earth. Out here? He's sworn to fight for anyone who wants to live peacefully. His cast-iron exterior covers an interior that is as soft as pudding.

"When Mom calls, Dad drops everything and comes running. If my sister needs something? He's there. Don't be fooled by a manly man's false front. I don't care about hair because I have none, and now Marcie doesn't either. I just want to see tomorrow and enjoy it with people I care about and those I'm responsible for. The entirety of my being is focused on getting as many of these swinging peacocks as possible back home."

"A tree grows from the garden of love," Jake corrected. "So much manly man in your jeans. I mean, 'genes.'"

"You can explain that to me later when there is absolutely nothing else to talk about." Kae raised a finger in caution. "Until then? Let's concentrate on taking supplies that will keep us alive. Anyone else tries to bring their hair kit, I'm confiscating it and turning it over to the undertakers. They'll make your hair look good for your closed casket funeral."

"Sometimes, there's too much business in the business. These soldiers need to retain their Belzimanity. It is part of what drives them. Humans would call it vanity, but for us, it's like wearing medals earned in battle. Some styles, younger Belzonians are not allowed to wear. Those come with maturity. Status, maturity, career. Everything can be shown through a coif."

"For the Lion Corps?" Kae asked.

"They've had wigs made of their hair. Shaving their heads was not a hollow gesture, but it wasn't as traumatic as it might have appeared." Jake drew back. "You're making headway with these soldiers. They respect your fighting prowess, but when it comes to after-hours, you won't be invited to any parties."

"It sounds as if you feel like that should matter." Kae chewed his lip. "We've spent twenty minutes talking about something that's not war, but I have been enlightened. Thank you. See what we can do that doesn't require power, and you can be their knight in shining armor. We have final maneuvers tomorrow in a twenty-four-hour crucible. After that, they'll be done with their training. I have to admit I'm worried, Jake."

"Me too, my friend. Your rough exterior doesn't come from not caring, but from caring too much."

"Can I use that?" Kae asked.

"No," Jake told him. "Copyright me as of ten seconds ago."

"Damn. You're a hard man, Jake."

"Something like that." The colonel snapped his head to the right. "Hey!"

Kae jogged after him, spotting more soldiers trying to sneak things onto the pallets. This group had the sense to run, and they scattered like grouse. Kae didn't bother running after them. He dug out the box they had secreted away. More hair kits, plus a stash of candy bars. Kae closed the box and gently placed it to the side. He glanced toward the motor pool, where engines revved and power tools whined.

Lightning flashed in the distance. A solid ten heartbeats later, the thunder rolled by. The training area was about to get drenched. The equipment and troops would be mud-covered, and there wouldn't be enough washers to clean all the uniforms before they packed them for deployment. Kae saw the mountain getting steeper.

He prompted himself to order extra garbage bags to store the mud-covered clothing during transit on the shuttles and while finding their spaces on the heavy transports. The soldiers would have time to run the clothes through the ship's cleaning systems. He didn't want any of them being on Kor'nar without a spare uniform.

Kae leaned against the pallets. He was so deeply embroiled in the logistics of the move that he couldn't think about the insectoid war on Kor'nar. He hadn't read the brief General Reynolds had sent. He shook his head. They needed to end tomorrow's crucible by nightfall to give the troops twenty-four solid hours before the first units shuttled to space. He had to talk to Marcie if he could figure out where she'd gone.

Beniton Space Station

Ted casually put his tools away as the door opened. Merrit was sleeping so hard he had drool running down his face. Shonna was using him as a pillow. Char forced her eyes open and checked the time.

"Four hours?"

"It is open and won't close now unless I give the command," Ted declared. He walked through, and the hatch immediately closed.

"*TED!*" Char jumped to her feet, grabbed the plasma torch, and dragged it toward the metal portal. It opened as she got close. "Is it supposed to do that?"

"It's a bulkhead barrier that helps maintain the integrity

of the spindle section in case of structural compromise on the external docking ports and transit rings. Of course, it's supposed to do that."

"I meant, is it supposed to scare the hell out of me? You just said it wouldn't close unless you gave the command. You're killing me, Ted."

"I meant close-close, not close. The closed-hard-and-sealed-not-to-reopen version as opposed to working-like-it's-supposed-to closed. It's the latter."

"Ted, dear," Felicity drawled. "You're even more cryptic than normal. Since I see that I'm not going to like it here, the sooner you get to work, the sooner you'll finish, and the sooner we can go home."

She walked through the hatch, eyeing it skeptically until she reached Ted. She kissed him on the cheek before waving the others forward.

Ted headed for the stairs. Everything he wanted was nine levels down. Shonna, Merrit, and Timmons hurried after him, lugging his equipment.

Char stopped to stare at the spot where Terry Henry had almost stopped breathing, where he'd risked his life for Dokken's. She tapped her pack where the duct tape resided. They had learned the hard way to never go into space without it.

She reiterated the mission. "We need to do a survey of the upper levels for the sake of turning this into a Federation station. Where do we start, Felicity?"

"At the beginning," Felicity said, smiling coyly. "Top-down. I have this device that connects with Plato. I dictate, he takes care of everything else."

The device looked like a brooch. Char had thought it

was a favorite piece of jewelry. It might have been, but it served a dual purpose, thanks to her genius husband. He probably had a tracker built into it so he could make sure she was okay.

"Where do we put the shoe stores?" Sue asked.

Felicity turned slowly through three hundred and sixty degrees. "I think right down there will make an excellent promenade. We can put an arch over here with a Welcome to the Promenade sign. Beyond, there's enough room for small vendors to set up in the passage. The more impactful stores—shoes, accessories, handbags, and women's clothing—will line these two sides."

She abandoned her plan to go upstairs. Instead, she and Sue daydreamed their way down the wide and empty corridors.

Char snorted. "Transfer of supplies and materiel in and out. Food preparation, sanitary and disposal systems, berthing, processing, workshops, and everything a small city needs. Does any of that sound like shoe stores?"

Felicity and Sue ignored her.

Timmons, besides helping Ted, you three have to do the engineering survey of the station. Start with structural integrity, then work your way inward. If the frame is sound, we need power next, followed by air, water, and waste. Char wanted to get home to the *War Axe*, too. She didn't need anyone to dawdle.

We got it. Relax and check the spaces for potential configurations. Sleep, eat, and get clean. That's all the pioneers need to have when they get here, and that's way more than they usually get. They usually start with nothing and work from an ore-processing ship. They'll be living the glamor life on this gig,

Timmons replied, *no matter how austere we might think it is. Better make sure there's space for science experiments.*

What kind of science experiments would a Gate-building crew do on the station?

Build a still. Timmons laughed. *Gotta go. Ted is glaring.*

Char headed up the stairs to where operations control had been. The problem with the station was the three-dimensional interactive interface throughout it. It made the place look empty. If they started tearing out the 3D emitters to install Federation systems, they might destroy the next level of interface technology. Some people like Ted and Ankh already used that with their hologrids, but it wasn't available on a broader basis like this space station promised.

At the top of the station, transparent windows of a material Char was unfamiliar with looked out on the universe on one side, with a glimpse of Benitus Seven on the other. The workstations were empty, the seats long gone if they used such things. She'd met the Grays. They had heard the station had not been built by the Grays—the Benitons—but no one knew for sure.

It no longer mattered. The Grays were gone, victims of the Skrima. The original builders of the station weren't there. It was up to Ted, Felicity, and the rest of the team to tell the Federation what it would take to make it operational. Char dutifully logged the operations space on a notepad with what she thought it would need for a crew to manage movements into and out of the station.

She headed down the steps to the next level, where she ran into Sue and Felicity, still talking about what the vibrant day- and nightlife here could look like.

"Are you talking about this station or Keeg?" Char asked.

Felicity tapped her nose with her index finger. "I'm expounding on my experience with Keeg Station to broaden the horizons of those who will occupy this outpost in the middle of nowhere. They can brighten their lives, no matter how deep into the frontier they are forced to live. It'll be like my ancestors riding wagons across America to bring culture and better lives to our family and those they touched. What is this place called, by the way? Hell's Watchtower?" Felicity drawled.

"When the Federation arrives, the devils will be gone. The only thing they'll be watching for is a second rift that wasn't closed due to the power of a burning sun being funneled through the small opening," Char replied. "'Hell's Watchtower' could have negative connotations. This area of space should be an opportunity for exploration, not wars with unknown aliens."

"Should be." Felicity's words dripped sarcasm.

Char held up her hands in surrender. "The real name is Federation Exploration Outpost Four Xray. I don't think we'll be using that except when transmitting our recommendations."

"Maybe we can call it 'Station Nadezhda,'" Sue suggested.

"My!" Felicity declared. "That's a mouthful."

"What's it mean?" Char asked.

"Hope in Russian. We lived with Gene all those years. Didn't you guys talk to him?"

"Of course, but in English. I don't speak Russian." Char thought about it for a moment before nodding slowly.

"You didn't either, but we spent a lot of time with the werebear."

"And this was between Ted and Timmons. Gene was good company." Sue didn't explain further.

"Nadezhda… Works for me. Is that mapping program online?" Char asked.

Sue produced a tablet and tapped. "Yes. Ted already populated it with a baseline map from our last visit." She turned the tablet around, tapped a few more times before declaring victory, showing it with a blinking cursor that said, "You are here."

"We're supposed to document population capacity numbers that aren't a clinical analysis of so many square feet per person. Ted and the others are looking at what the systems can support: CO_2 scrubbing, clean air, water, sewage, all that exciting stuff. We're looking for number of beds, butts in work seats, general useable space, and recreation because we don't want to produce any serial killers due to space sickness." Char shrugged at the end of her explanation as if to say, "That's from the brief, not me."

"You're boring the snot out of me," Felicity drawled. "Be a dear, Charumati, and take care of that, will you?"

Sue handed the tablet over. Char didn't take it. "I'm not doing it all by myself." She put her hands on her hips. Sue didn't press the challenge.

"We'll get it, Char. Any idea how long it will take Ted and the others to assess the station?"

Char snorted. "It took him four hours just to open the door. I think we'll be here for a while." She looked at the pad hugged to Sue's breast. "I'll update the notes for the op center. You guys take the Promenade. Nadezhda needs to inspire the hope for which it is named."

"So let it be written, so let it be done." Felicity offered her hand, and Char took it before Sue gave her the tablet. Char headed back upstairs while Sue and Felicity sauntered away, chatting about their favorite pre-World's-Worst-Day-Ever clothing stores.

Iracitus, would you update me on Terry Henry, please? I don't want to bother Plato since I'm sure he is neck-deep in more important stuff, Char requested when she was alone.

Of course. Colonel Walton's dropship has departed. He was last off the War Axe. *Colonel Lowell has already engaged the enemy. They will need a drop can resupply fairly soon. Work on the cryopods has stopped because of the need for more ammunition. The production system is operating at one hundred percent,* Iracitus replied.

Thanks for the report. Please contact me if there are any casualties. I know what those will do to my husband. He might need someone to calm him down.

Char looked at the pad, then dictated the information rather than poke it with her finger. She was done in five minutes with the smallest space on the station. She headed to the next level down to walk through and document her impressions, thinking all the while about Terry Henry Walton in a prolonged battle against an enemy that numbered five hundred times what the Bad Company had put into the field.

Benitus Seven, Eastern Sector

Christina poured a stream of railgun fire into the trees

where the Skrim had run. Her deployment partner Private Workman moved wide to catch the creature in a crossfire if he got a clear shot. Christina ran directly at the spot in the woods where the IR was showing the Skrim running for its life. She was able to accelerate faster than it could run.

It was in a depression below her line of sight. She needed to get into a good position for the kill shot. A quick glance showed misted ghosts of IR signatures. "Hold up, Workman," she ordered before grinding to a halt. She studied the terrain. "It's an ambush. Run down to the far end and kill that thing. They are arrayed to attack in this direction. You come down that cut from the far end, you'll get some clean shots if I haven't tagged them first, but watch out. They could be lining both sides. I only see two, but there could be more, and they're better hidden."

Christina backed up and searched the surrounding area for someplace one could hide to attack from behind. She waited until Workman closed the back door on the ambush.

"Scratch one bogey, Colonel," he reported.

"Fire in the hole." Christina activated her rockets and sent a single one downrange. It arced high before coming down between the two signatures. The blast splattered the two, which had hidden under a layer of mud and leaves. More IR signatures appeared right in front of her where she would have gone down the slope and into the depression, effectively boxing her in.

"Tag. That one is yours." Christina shared her screen. "I'll take these other two. Belay that. One."

She'd bagged the first with a single railgun projectile.

The second used cover better while it ran. She bolted after it but kept to the high ground, firing random shots into the trench below to rout out others who had been hiding. A flurry of shots from a railgun signaled that Workman had completed his task.

"Fuck! It's like I stepped on an anthill." Workman fired and fired.

"Run!" Christina ordered. "Fire in the hole." She launched a second rocket. It arced high and came down in the middle of the bubbling mass of IR signatures. The heat sources started to cool, but a few new signatures joined them. "Join me on a monster hunt, Workman."

Christina finally jumped into the trench, one hand on her railgun while pulling her axe with the other mechanical hand. She kept her eye on her sensors, barely watching where she was going while looking for yet another layer in the ambush.

Workman reengaged from the far end, clearing the area in front of him before he moved forward. Christina pounded two more steps before the ground gave way, and she fell into the darkness below.

CHAPTER FIFTEEN

Belzimus, Parade and PT Field

"Who wants to go to space?" Marcie asked. Kae looked away. Monsoon maintained his usual stoic expression. Jake glanced at the other two, who were avoiding eye contact.

"Does it have to be me?" Jake asked.

Marcie shook her head. "If one of you volunteered, then you could go, but I really want to go, because that's my domain. We've spent the last seven, maybe eight years in space operating from a warship. I'm comfortable there, and you and Monsoon know the troops down here. Turn-around time is important, down here and up there. I'll take Kae with me, and we'll see if we can get everyone situated. We have four transports that can hold four thousand each. We'll take all four and spread the load to reduce the impact if we lose one. We shouldn't since there are no space defenses around Kor'nar, but it is a good practice to get into: use all available assets to provide greater lift in-theater. We want extra assets at all times because shit always happens."

"No shit," Kae added.

"No one has time for that shit," Monsoon said evenly.

"Ain't that some shit?" Jake looked proud of himself.

"Where did you hear that? It's not a Belzonian phrase." Marcie gave him the side-eye.

He pointed at her.

She smirked. "That does sound like me. No, that sounds like my father-in-law, actually. Look what I've become." She took a moment to meet Kae's eyes. "And I'm good with that."

"Sounds good," Jake confirmed. "I think we've intercepted most of the contraband. I don't have any problems with the other stuff the troops sneaked into the boxes. They've figured out that the logisticians are key to a comfortable deployment."

Marcie had been there before. "Little do the soldiers know we aren't dropping the tent city until we've established a cease-fire and a no-fire zone we have confidence in. They'll hit the ground with what they're carrying on their backs, and it'll have to do for at least the first three days. I guarantee they'll pack better on the next deployment."

"There's a lot to be said for firsthand experience." Monsoon winked.

"We'll join the first shuttles up. I'll take the *Angkmoor*, Kae will be on the *Praithwait*. Monsoon on the *Thilamoot*, and Jake will bring up the rear on *Gonboon*."

The group shook hands and stood around uncomfortably.

"Better get to it, then." There was too much work to do and little time. "Oh, and if you see Paithoon, tell him he's on my ship. I need to bend his ear. As much as I hate to say it, I think Civil Affairs is going to be critical in not only winning the peace but maintaining it. Killing an enemy isn't hard, but convincing him that I'm not his enemy? That might take a little more finesse than I have."

"Paithoon is going to crow like a prize cock."

"That is the worst part. At least he's gotten a taste of what real soldiering is all about. He's not good at it, but he better be good at the stuff I don't do. If I have to do it, I think we're all going to regret it."

Jake and Monsoon stepped back. "Don't look at us. We just finished two years with Yollin forces. Their level of touchy-feely is more like scratch and bite."

Kae held up a finger. "I don't think Civil Affairs is all touchy-feely. They're supposed to coordinate with local populations to reinstate things lost during military operations. His job is to make us look like we're there to help them."

"We can't do that if we don't give the enemy a hearty beating."

"Paithoon will probably tell you to beat the enemy without destroying the local infrastructure and killing the locals, even if they get in the way."

"Paithoon can kiss my ass."

Jake cleared his throat. "Paithoon isn't here and doesn't know that you're going to lean on him, and you're already pissed at him."

"I'm not pissed at Paithoon but at *him*," Marcie countered, pointing at Kae.

"What did I do?"

"You put hurtful words in Paithoon's mouth. Shame!" She pointed an accusing finger.

"Is *that* what marriage is like?" Jake asked the sergeant major.

"Fuck if I know. I've never seen anything like it. Please continue. I'm studying human behavior because it's more interesting than anything on the vid screens." Monsoon held his chin and leaned closer, looking back and forth between Kae and Marcie. "Maybe it's foreplay?"

"I don't know. That's an interesting observation. Well done, Crantis!"

"No," Marcie stated. "Not well done, Crantis. We're talking about loading out the task force. Let me quote another era. *'Give me your tired, your poor, your huddled masses yearning to breathe free, the wretched refuse of your teeming shore. Send these, the homeless, tempest-tossed to me, I lift my lamp beside the golden door!'*"

Kae shook his head at the looks from the other two.

"Statue of Liberty on Earth, where we were both born. Never mind. Colonel, deliver the Trans-Pacific Task Force to orbit. Tomorrow, we go to war. For every day we delay, more lives will be lost on Kor'nar."

Braithwen snapped a salute. Monsoon mirrored the colonel. Talking was over. It was time for action.

Benitus Seven, Western Sector

Terry took aim, resisted the urge to lead the running Skrim, and fired a short burst from his railgun. The hyper-velocity projectiles crossed the distance so quickly that point of aim was point of impact on the running target.

The dart blew the Skrim in two, and Terry checked his HUD for the next target.

"Keep running, Donner. Flare wide to my right, two hundred meters. Checking six, no targets."

"Roger," Private Donner confirmed. They ran faster than the Skrima to eliminate the chance of one coming up behind them.

The entirety of Terry Henry's half of the Bad Company ran in a long, spread out line abreast. "Kimber, slow down a bit. You're getting ahead."

"Targets ahead running for cover," she reported. "Request single envelopment. Watch my flank."

Terry veered south to the edge of where he could see Kimber, but more importantly, he could hit targets at that range since he had a line of sight for his railgun.

Kimber accelerated to full speed to get between the enemy and bore down on a Skrim from the side while her teammate held it in place with a steady stream of fire into the woods in front of it. Kimber caught up to it and finished it, then returned to her lane and waited for the others to catch up.

Terry returned to his spacing.

"Firing," Donner said softly as he squeezed the trigger. The mech suit balanced the weapon and crosshairs, limiting the bounce while running. They never had a reason to fire while still. Made it hard for the enemy to hit them while delivering precision fire on target.

The mechs gave them an advantage that non-technology adversaries could not resist.

The remaining Skrima ran.

"Colonel Walton," Smedley interrupted. "We've lost signatures for both Christina and her partner."

"Are they down? Deploy the cryopod right fucking *now!*"

"Not dead, gone. One instant their signals were there, and the next, they weren't."

It took Terry two milliseconds to decide on his next course of action. "Smedley, send a Pod for me. I'll travel to their last known location." He switched to the company-wide channel. "Kimber, take over here. I will head back to check on Christina. Donner will join your team. Continue pushing forward and cleaning out the enemy."

"You should take Donner," Kimber shot back.

"You need the firepower here. We can't reduce our frontage. That's an order. I'm going solo." Terry drifted to a stop and prepared to board. Three Pods had been holding station over the forces, one for east, one for west, and one in reserve. Three had returned to the *War Axe* to await further orders.

The shuttle Pod landed and Terry hurried aboard, ordering the ship airborne before the ramp closed. "Take me over the site for a visual," Terry requested.

"Yes, Colonel. Here is the imagery we have from the *War Axe*. We'll be on site in two minutes." The large screen at the front of the passenger cabin lit up with full-color images of a forested area. "Are those shadows? Is there an elevation change through there?"

"It is a depressed area between the sparse trees. It runs southwest by northeast for nearly two kilometers."

"I hope they didn't go in there." Terry studied the

pictures, but the shadows from the trees refused to give him a clear view. "Hold up. What's that?"

Smedley zoomed in on the image.

"That looks like a hole in the ground. A really big hole."

"From the measurements I can take, I agree with you, but I am unable to give you a depth of anything more than five meters below the surface of the surrounding terrain."

"At least five meters deep. That's nothing for a mech to drop, but you said at least five meters. Could be fifty, but that's not a problem either, or any height for that matter if the driver can get the suit turned around in time to activate the boot jets."

"We're here," Smedley reported. "Transferring to live feed."

"It's a trench. Perfect place for an ambush, and judging by the dead reds, they tried it, but Christina wasn't having any of that. I count three dead there, two more with a rocket blast unless the Skrima are using explosives. There's the hole with piles of dead beyond it. IR shows nothing hot in the vicinity. Lower the ramp, Smedley. I'm jumping down. Go to the end of the depression, the site of the ambush."

TH moved to the rear of the Pod. The ramp lowered, and he walked out. After one look down, he stepped off and activated his jets. He dropped slowly and touched down with barely an impact. It only took a few seconds to see what had happened. The violence of a point-blank range railgun impact left a pattern that backtracked to where the round had been fired.

"A mech fired from up there and splashed two," he said to himself. He headed down the center of the cut. "Dug-in enemy on both sides, eliminated by a single rocket between them."

Terry continued toward the hole where dozens if not fifty or sixty Skrima had been massacred. He tried to determine what had happened from the blast patterns.

"Another rocket. Railgun fire coming from both sides, catching the Skrima in a crossfire. Nicely done, people." Terry launched a drone and guided it over the hole, then directed it to descend. He assumed Christina and Workman had gone down there. He didn't know if it was by choice or by accident. He keyed his mic. "Christina. Workman. Respond."

He activated the transceiver in the drone. "Christina. Workman. Respond."

Terry watched his HUD. There was no doubt he was going in. He just had to make sure they didn't send a search party after him unless he needed it, and then he wouldn't be able to send them word.

"Smedley, inform the ship that we have Skrima in a cave system. Communications won't penetrate the ground, so we're blind down here. I'm going in after Christina and Workman. If I'm not back in thirty minutes, send someone after me."

"What will happen in thirty minutes?" Smedley inquired.

"If there are as many Skrima down there as I suspect, in thirty minutes, I'll be out of ammo."

Benitus Seven, Eastern Sector

Christina bounced off the cave walls on her way down,

ripping Skrima off who were climbing out. She tried to rotate upright to slow her descent, but the cave walls were irregular. It wasn't a shaft as much as a series of breaks in the rocky layers supporting the ground above.

She needed to slow her fall instead of breaking it with her head when she hit bottom. Christina shouted her war cry and thrust her boarding axe into the stone, trying to find purchase, but it only ripped out a boulder, which followed her down. She kicked off the wall to propel herself to the other side, hit a ledge chest-first, and tried to dig in with the spiked end of the axe handle, but gravity pulled her down before she could set it. At least she was finally upright.

Christina hit the jets and slowed. The boulder bounced off her shoulder. Her HUD showed the bottom close by, but it was teeming with Skrima. She fired the jets hard to hold her above the mass and groped for her railgun, finding it still slung over her shoulder but behind her. Christina rotated it to the front and unleashed a full-auto burst while spinning in a death pirouette above her unadoring fans. She pushed the jets to send her upward, stopping when she saw Workman heading toward her.

Moving sideways, she cleared a spot for him.

"Workman," she said. "Since we're here, let's clean the rats out of this sewer."

Christina and Workman dropped to the cave floor, stood back to back, and started firing. Their railguns lit up the area. It was dark at the bottom, thanks to the ledges blocking the opening above, and they were deep, maybe a hundred meters.

Their targets appeared on IR, and that was how they

aimed. Calmly and rhythmically, they fired. Three tunnels led away from the chamber at the bottom.

"Ouch!" Workman blurted. "Son of a bitch. There's one with a weapon."

Christina couldn't see. She poured fire into the tunnel with the fewest Skrima.

"I'm hit," Workman reported, but he continued to fire. Christina tried to see where and how badly by accessing her rear cameras, but they couldn't get a view of her fellow warrior.

"Come on. Let's go!" she ordered and ran toward the escape route she'd cleared. Workman launched a missile into the tunnel behind them. It impacted almost instantly, but his back was already turned as he loped after Christina.

CHAPTER SIXTEEN

Benitus Seven, Eastern Sector

"Come on, give me some love," Terry coaxed his drone. He wasn't as good at flying it as Kaeden, but Kae wasn't there. By Terry's own order, he had gone in alone. The drone swerved down past Skrima that were climbing up. It jockeyed past outcroppings until it flew in the dark, then the images glitched and the drone refused to continue—a failsafe to prevent it from flying out of range. "That's why I can't talk to you, eh, Christina?"

Terry ordered the drone to return and readied his rail-gun. He leaned as far over the hole as he could and started firing, combining his targeting through the IR on his HUD with images from the drone. He maneuvered around the crater to get better firing angles but didn't want to blast his own equipment. "Hurry up," he encouraged the drone. As soon as it popped into the air, Terry unleashed a long stream of fire while continuing to move around the perimeter.

He jumped out over the center of the hole and activated

his jets to slow his descent. Swiveling his external views, he lit up the Skrima in a three hundred and sixty-degree circle on his way down. He didn't want any making it to the surface.

How many had he killed? He lost count. He passed five, then six ledges, and the sky above disappeared. Darkness settled around him, and the suit automatically switched to IR and night vision to compensate. Terry continued to pick off targets, firing downward by bending slightly at the waist so he could see while spinning slowly. It unbalanced him, but allowing the Skrima to get within striking distance wasn't the option he wanted.

As he bounced past the eleventh ledge, the bottom of the cavern came into sight. Skrima jostled around a mountain of dead.

"I see you've been here, Christina." Terry added to the carnage by killing anything that moved. Pings registered off his suit. "And now these fuckers have weapons."

Terry cut his rockets and dropped the last ten meters into the pile of bodies. They softened his fall while he swept the barrel from one side to the other, cleansing the chamber of anything moving. The last echoes of his final burst died away and he listened for reinforcements, but even after increasing the audio pickups from his suit, he heard nothing except the faint sounds of heavy metal feet hammering the stone.

With his suit's advanced electronics, he determined which tunnel the mech was heading down. "Christina? Christina, respond." He started running after them and launched the drone to follow him, remaining first ten meters back, and then thirty, and if he still had a link to it, fifty meters to give him a long lead time if the Skrima were coming. He switched to external speakers and firewalled the volume. He even tried his internal chip, using the RF mode since the Etheric was stymied. *Christina!*

The footsteps in the distance ground to a halt. He breathed a sigh of relief until the silence was filled by two railguns spinning on full-auto within the confines of the underground. Terry started running again. He didn't waste breath yelling. He focused on the HUD's view of the tunnel ahead. With no side tunnels, he was comfortable that he wouldn't get overwhelmed. If the Skrima were only coming from one direction, he could pin them down.

If they came from multiple directions, they might get closer than he wanted since he could only fire in one direction at a time. The tunnel was big enough for his mech suit to move but not maneuver. He could put his back to the wall, but he needed to be where they weren't, especially since these Skrima had weapons. Terry didn't know how lethal they were. He saw the muzzle flashes and heard the pings of something hitting the suit, suggesting slug throwers, but he couldn't be sure.

It didn't matter. Christina and Workman were up ahead and engaged with more of the enemy.

"What the fuck is down here?" Terry grumbled. He'd fought underground before and wasn't a fan. It reminded him too much of his time with the Forsaken called Kirkus, but good could be found in all things since they had freed Yanmei, and she and Aaron became lifelong partners. In the end, TH had walked out of the caves, and Kirkus had not. Just like then, he would do what he had to do.

His disdain for the Skrima was reaching a new high.

The railguns were firing around the next bend. He could feel the concussion of the hypervelocity darts banging off the stone between the shredding of flesh. A grim smile took over his visage as he tightened his grip and prepared to fire.

He dashed around the corner and into a huge chamber. One mech was frozen and hunched over, with Skrima crawling over it. The other mech was swinging at them with an axe while firing haphazardly with the railgun clutched in the other mechanical hand.

Terry Henry blasted his speakers to full and fired up *Iron Man* as he ran into the chamber, firing at the Skrima closing on the functioning mech. He stopped firing and dove, using his jets to accelerate into the second armored combat suit, and knocked it to the cavern floor, taking away one avenue of approach for the attackers. Terry hit the ground, which was littered with dead, rolled, and popped back to his feet. He jumped backward and, using his railgun like a scythe, swept it through the enemy he had bowled over.

He moved to straddle the downed warrior, ashamed that he was relieved it was Christina still upright and firing. After backing up to her, he kept his railgun on full automatic in an attempt to turn back the wave.

Christina and Workman had gone into the chamber and then been surrounded. With the press of Skrima bodies, the best they could do was try to hold their own, especially since something had happened to Workman. Terry read the private's vitals feed in his HUD. He was alive but in bad shape.

"TH, glad you could make it." Christina fired over the

heads of those approaching to cut down the next relentless wave. Then she dipped the barrel and swept across the front ranks.

"We have to move. We can't stand in the middle like this. I'll drag Workman. Cover me." Terry grabbed the private's arm and started dragging, but the suit wouldn't slide and bent in half, which made it difficult to move since it caught on the rough cave floor. Skrima pounced on him and tore at the suit's crevices and joints with their claws. Terry dropped and rolled, cleaning them off like putting out a fire. He bounced back to his mechanical feet and fired to clear away more Skrima.

The only way to a wall was through surging and charging bodies. He saw the flashes, but they didn't register as he became a whirling dervish, spinning and firing. His railgun started to send error codes to his HUD: too much firing on automatic. It needed to shut down.

"Help me clear a way to this wall. I have an idea." TH redlined his railgun before letting it slip under his arm, then stooped to pick up the other mech. It took longer than he wanted, and he found himself covered in snapping and slashing Skrima when he finally hoisted the other suit to his shoulder. He ran through a small gap that Christina's fire had opened up.

He risked a glance backward. By helping him, she'd lost the momentum on her side. Skrima were climbing onto her suit, and one held a weapon. Could have been a pistol. He was trying to stick it into the joint between the suit and her head.

Terry turned, took careful aim, and fired a single projectile. It exploded Christina's attacking Skrim off her shoulder, so she was free for an instant and started to run after him.

He dropped Workman with his head against the wall and to the side, then backed up to a meter from the wall. It was all the space he needed. He fired up his railgun to full auto once again, hoping the short break had given it the juice it needed. "Take my other side, you and Workman on the outside."

Christina hesitated. She'd thought they'd keep Workman between them. Protect him. "But.."

"Fucking do it!" Terry demanded.

She made it to the wall, slammed chest-first into it to splash two Skrima that were hanging on, and then rolled down the wall to clean off any others.

Christina started firing again, side by side with Terry Henry, covering a ninety-degree arc instead of the alternative.

"I'm getting out," Terry said. He stopped shooting and unbuttoned.

"You're what?"

It was too late. He slid out the back of the suit, the Jean Dukes Special in his hand. He dialed it to five and fired danger-close over Workman's back, pummeling a swath through the incoming.

He dialed it up to ten and braced himself to fire. "May God have mercy on our souls." He pulled the trigger, sweeping half the cavern like a tidal wave. His arms tingled. He thought his wrist might have broken. He gripped the weapon tightly and cleared a new swath.

He leaned forward, screamed his war cry into the still-blasting *Iron Man*, and fired. A new red wave of death swept across the cavern. Parts of the ceiling and wall crashed down, obliterating the red tide.

Terry's pistol fell from nerveless fingers and he dropped to his knees, struggling to pick it up. He dialed it back to seven, and with his left hand, fired to clean out a couple of surviving pockets of Skrima, then slumped to the cave floor.

Accessing Terry's suit, Christina turned off the music. "Terry?"

"Give me a second," he mumbled. Christina turned on her suit lights. Terry held up his hand, which was returning from purple to normal flesh tones. He stuffed the Jean Dukes inside his shirt and leaned over to access Workman's suit. The back popped and unsealed.

Christina remained in her suit, with her IR systems showing the chamber as clear. She thumbed her smoking railgun to single fire and picked off the curious who popped their heads out of tunnels that fed into the chamber.

Workman was unconscious, but his pulse was stronger than what Terry had initially seen on his HUD.

"Looks like we're carrying him," Terry stated and prepared to get back into his powered combat armor after pulling the emergency first aid kit from an inside panel. He took out a wrap, then tucked his elbow in close and pulled on his right hand with his left to straighten the wrist bones. The world darkened and he saw stars, but Terry Henry Walton fought through it. He blinked away the shock of pain before winding the wrap tightly around his wrist and tying it with one hand, holding one end with his teeth to help secure it.

He climbed back into his suit.

"Oorah!" he shouted. "Let's get the fuck out of here. I'll take his feet."

"We have a problem," Christina started.

"We have lots of problems," Terry interrupted. "I guess this is a big one."

Christina used her laser designator to show where they had entered the cavern. A section of the wall had slid down. The tunnel no longer existed.

"Yeah. That's a big problem."

Nadezhda Station, in orbit above Benitus Seven

Charumati, Iracitus called.

Her heart instantly sank. *Go,* was all she could manage.

Colonel Walton, Colonel Lowell, and Private Workman are missing. Colonel Lowell went underground with the private, and Colonel Walton went after them. They have not been heard from for thirty minutes, so following the colonel's directions, a rescue party has been mounted. I will keep you informed.

Thanks, Iracitus. Please send the same report to Nathan Lowell. Char put her pad down. There were no chairs, so she sat on the steps. Char wasn't a crier—she expressed her sadness and frustration in different ways—but they had decided to retire before this mission arose.

"Of all things, the Skrima." Her words were sharp, and her eyes narrowed. Even the Forsaken had not caused them as much lasting grief as the Skrima. Hatred bubbled within her. She closed her eyes and reached out, using her strength with the Etheric to peel back layers of the onion.

What would it take to walk through to their dimension and kill them?

She pulled back when she felt someone shaking her.

"Are you okay?" Felicity asked, staring into her eyes. "You were kind of here and kinda not. Your body wasn't solid."

Char breathed deeply to slow her racing heart. "Yes. Terry and Christina are missing on the planet's surface. I'm going down there."

Sue came around Felicity. "I think staying here is what you need right now. You look awful."

"I feel as useless as tits on a boar hog." She thrust the pad at them. "Take it. I need to go."

Char gripped both women's shoulders loosely, in a friendly way.

"Thank you for your concern. There's a fight down there, and I need to be in it. I'll stop by the *War Axe* and pick up my gear." Char bolted down the steps and into the corridor leading to where *Iracitus* was docked.

She slowed for the sealed bulkhead to open, breathing a sigh of relief when it worked like it was supposed to, then sprinted to the open airlock and onto *Iracitus*. "Take me to the *War Axe*, please."

Char sat in the pilot's seat, but Iracitus handled the flight. He made short work of it, racing through the upper atmosphere to where the *War Axe* was holding station. The ship was firing at a steady rate into the rift and the area surrounding it. They approached from underneath the heavy destroyer and looped into the hangar bay. Char rushed out as soon as she could open the hatch.

Joseph and Petricia met her. "We heard," Joseph said.

"Are your fighters flightworthy?" The two vampires nodded. "Load up. We're going hunting."

She ran to the armory to get into her powered combat armor.

Joseph waved at Bundin. The Podder's stalk head remained steady as he turned his body and headed for Joseph. With eyes on all four sides, he didn't need to turn his head to see. The appendages alongside the stalk gesticulated wildly as he hurried across the hangar bay.

"We're going to the planet. You're in charge. Protect the ship at all costs."

One of the previously injured walked stiffly across the hangar bay. "I'm ready to go," he declared. Cory caught sight of him and ran over.

"I don't think so."

Char clumped into the hangar bay deck. "Ma'am!" the private shouted. "I'm coming with you."

"Get your suit on. We push in five."

"Mom!" Cory held her hands out, pleading.

"Your father needs help. Christina needs help. I can't fix this by myself. Now is the time we rally what's left of our spirits to finish this fight."

Cory stepped back. The private had already gone. "We don't have any more cryopods."

"I know. We'll use what we have if we need them. The more warriors we press into action, the better off we'll be. That is our best chance of keeping our people from getting hurt. I'm sorry, but we have to go."

Cory hung her head in defeat. "I know," she whispered before walking away. She prepared herself to be busier than she wanted to be by looking for a quiet spot in the hangar bay where she could meditate and get her raging thoughts under control.

She'd heard the tone in her mother's voice. Char was going to the planet to kill as many Skrima as needed until she found her husband. Cory felt guilty for taking too much pleasure in her mother's quest for vengeance.

Her efforts to stop her mother had been nonexistent. Cory walked back to the dropship, arriving at the same time the private appeared.

"I'm going, too."

"You're not," Char stated. "You need to be here. Everything that can be done will be done planetside. You need to receive any casualties and manage their care."

"It's all automated."

"You're not going, and that's final. Fire up, Joseph! It's time to leave."

Cordelia felt the tears coming. Even at her age, she had to defer to her mother. It was a universal thing, no matter the culture. The mechs disappeared into the dropship as two fighters smoothly moved overhead. The Pod buttoned up and launched.

Joseph and Petricia raced through the open hangar bay doors, vectored down, and disappeared.

"Shoot straight," Cory told the empty space where they'd been.

CHAPTER SEVENTEEN

Angkmoor, **Trans-Pacific Task Force Flagship**

"This is a fucking freighter, not even well converted. What a steaming pile!" Marcie declared. "And it smells."

Paithoon sniffed the air. "It'll be okay, Colonel. Maybe some decorations…"

"Stop the madness!" She wanted to scream but forced herself to calm down. She knew it was the stress of deploying and feared missing important details that would bite her in the ass later. It was wearing on her ability to confine her focus to what was most important. Decorations on the ship were never going to make it into the top one hundred items on her to-do list.

But she had people who thought those were important.

"We'll be on the ship for maybe a day or two, Paithoon. How do we keep the troops engaged without feeling overwhelmed? A good meal, entertainment? Too much downtime when we have no further information is a bad thing. They need to be focused on the mission ahead and what to do when they hit the ground. That will be the time of greatest confusion, just when confusion is least welcome."

"But the troops will do as the officers direct. That is what the last two weeks have been about. I've watched. I've learned. I suggest you keep working with the officers to make sure they are not confused. Let the troops do what they need to do to prepare themselves. Their best choice is physical engagement."

"There's no room to PT," Marcie replied.

Paithoon wiggled his eyebrows. "Leave it to me. All you need to do is stay in your quarters."

His meaning dawned on Marcie. "Won't that sap their energy?"

"Quite the contrary, Colonel. If you want these people to perform when they land on a strange planet, let them prepare as only Belzonians can."

Marcie looked at the deck. She found she was clenching her teeth, so she worked her jaw to loosen the muscles. "Thanks, Paithoon. Take care of that. We'll get the officers into the briefing rooms on all four ships and hit them with everything we know, then break down into separate group planning sessions. A box within a box within a box. They'll have direction when they hit the deck here and the ground on Kor'nar. We'll make it work, and the task force will be better for it."

"They will be the best for it!" He beamed with pride. It took little encouragement to keep him motivated. He gave her insight into the Belzonian culture that others only hinted at. She needed the civil affairs officer on her team. Terry Henry would chew off his fingernails.

He saluted and hurried away, and she grabbed the logistics officer to discuss the loadout. Marcie had split the force into one third on the ships and two thirds on the planet. The plan was to leave the majority of the force on the ground to help with loading the shuttles. Unloading and storing would be far easier than the initial packing.

Once the logistician had articulated his plan, Marcie found herself with little to do but wait. She went to her quarters, which were little more than a closet, but at least she had them to herself, a privilege reserved for the commanding officer. Everyone else had to share, some with as many as twenty bodies in bunk beds stacked five high in quarters not much bigger than Marcie's stateroom.

She dumped her pack on the bed, bumped into the small desk when she turned around, and headed out to familiarize herself with the ship.

Kae, can you hear me? she asked over her internal comm chip.

Indeed! he replied from *Praithwait. This thing is a garbage scow, but we'll make do. I expect the troops will be happy to get off even if it means being under fire.*

That's the plan. Ground pounders prefer the ground. Otherwise, they'd be Fleet.

I guess that's one way to look at it. Just checking in, or do you have something else on your mind? Kae wondered.

A check-in, a plan of attack going forward, and a warning. Once we have the officers on board, we're going to keep them in planning sessions from the word go. We will have about a day of travel to get to Kor'nar. They need to know what they're doing so they don't get anyone killed in their first ten minutes dirtside. That's our job between now and then, to teach them what to expect and how to get the job done. And the second thing is, while we're training the officers, Paithoon is going to hold a massive party for the enlisted, so you'll want to not be anywhere you can see them. By party, he means orgy. Plan and execute appropriately, Marcie advised.

You signed off on that?

Belzonians take strength from bonding with each other as many times as possible. It's the weirdest thing, but it's their culture, not ours. You were the one who recommended we embrace that, and Paithoon to help us realize it. Marcie smiled even though Kae couldn't see it. She had him on his heels. Checkmate in two moves.

That's not what I meant! I was talking about Kor'nar and stopping the war. How did I become the one promoting orgies?

From my understanding, there's only going to be one. It's the party where everyone comes.

Is this funny to you? I will be under my bunk crying, and it's your fault.

I take full responsibility for your tears. Checkmate. They both laughed. *I'm feeling better about this.*

Second stick is inbound. I better receive them so I can tell the people in charge what they should be doing as opposed to what they're actually doing.

Marcie nodded to herself because Kae couldn't see her. *Remember the golden rule. As long as they have a bunk and can eat, they'll be okay. If they have their stuff and can keep busy, they'll be fine until we get to Kor'nar.*

On it, boss, Kae replied. *I'll keep them so goddamned busy they won't have time for an orgy.*

Don't try to fight that fight, Kae. Stay in your room. Maybe pray for your soul. Be at peace.

Marcie! Kae was happy about the jibes since they

provided a semblance of normality. During this time, he needed as much of that as anyone. He knew his wife did, too. She bore the full weight of it all, no matter how much he tried to help, and that weighed on him.

Sleep fast, Marcie. I'll see you tomorrow on Kor'nar. I'll be the one in the fancy suit.

They're here, Marcie stated abruptly. *Holy shit. I've never seen a goat rope like this. Gotta run.*

Benitus Seven, Eastern Sector

"Clean out those trees!" Capples ordered, sending two mechs after a pair of fleeing Skrima. "We don't need anyone breathing down our necks while we're trying to get down there."

He looked at Kimber. She bent over the ledge and looked into the hole.

"That is where they went, Major Kimber. I cannot give you a different answer," Smedley insisted.

"It's not that I don't believe you, it's that I find the *situation* unbelievable. What about a drone?"

"Already tried it," Capples replied. "There's something in the stone that blocks the signal after it goes down twenty-five or thirty meters. It returns without providing any data beyond that. There are Skrima on the walls. We'll have to clean them out as we descend."

"No other way down?" Kimber tried. She knew the answer, but she wasn't a fan of going underground. She'd been a captive once and didn't like being trapped. She was okay with the *War Axe*, but caves gave her the willies.

Capples didn't bother to respond since they'd already

answered all her questions. They didn't need to do it a second time. "I'll take the rescue party, ma'am," he offered. He could sense her hesitation and hear the fear in her voice. Underground operations weren't for everyone. "If you go, the CO, XO, and OpsO will all be out of contact. Does that make any sense? You need to stay up here and coordinate feeding us warriors and supplies. Maybe set up comm repeaters between here and the bottom."

Kimber sucked in her bottom lip as she thought. They couldn't delay any longer. "Do it. I'll coordinate from here. Take four with you. We'll secure the surface area and shaft while working to install a repeater so we can talk to you while you're down there. I have no idea what you'll find. They could be at the bottom, unconscious."

The hopeful statement ignored the Skrima trying to climb out of the shaft. They wouldn't be doing that with living warriors behind them, and they didn't look like they were trying to escape.

"We'll find out." Capples called four mech-suited warriors to him. "Descend using jets. I'll go first. Maintain a ten-meter separation. IR and lights active. See you at the bottom."

Capples was one of the experts with the suit, being the first to be trained in their use, and he operated it as an extension of his body. He lifted upward just enough to slide laterally over the center of the hole. When he dropped below the ledge, his suit's external lights came on, illuminating what had been shadows. He rotated slowly with his railgun aimed between his feet. After clearing the first outcropping, an enemy appeared. He finished it with a three-round burst and continued downward. The next warrior followed suit.

"Relay from one to the next so we know what's down there," Kimber called before Capples was out of range.

"Roger," he replied, but the signal was already starting to break up.

"Roger," the second warrior down repeated.

"Smedley, find me some repeaters I can install in that shaft." Kimber switched to the views of the other warriors above ground. The two mechs hunting the running pair of Skrima closed in, then fired and finished them.

"Sweep the area to see if they were running to anything in particular. They appear to be erratic, but there is both rhyme and reason in what they're doing. Smedley, do an analysis of the movements of all Skrima tracked, starting with the premise that they communicate with each other. We saw that when they dissolved their large formations. What if these up here are decoys for what is going on underground?"

"I'll start immediately, Major, and will report my conclusions as soon as I reach them."

Kimber watched the fifth warrior shuffle close to the ledge and wait for the fourth to drop so he could bring up the rear.

"Sergeant Capples reports hitting the bottom. There's a small cavern with three exit tunnels and a shitload of dead Skrima. No sign of the missing. The sergeant said he'll follow the trail of bodies."

The fifth warrior lifted off the ground, rotated his armor to face Kimber, and gave her a thumbs-up before gripping his railgun in both hands and descending into the hole.

"I like what I heard." Kimber dialed up a relay through the Pod hovering overhead. "*War Axe*, this is Major Kimber. The rescue party has reached the bottom of the shaft and reported that they've found hundreds of dead Skrima. Sergeant Capples is following the trail of bodies, expecting they'll lead him to the colonels and Private Workman. End report."

Kimber settled in to wait. The two warriors who had gone after the Skrima were disappointed that they had missed their chance to go with the rescue team.

"We have work to do up here. Secure this area, and I want eyes in that hole until we can get a repeater set up."

A drone launched and went twenty meters before holding station, its IR cameras trained downward. It was the early warning for any Skrima trying to climb out. Judging by the one limited report, if her father got his way, he wouldn't be leaving any alive to climb out. She wondered if he had gone on a hunter-killer mission.

They would have to do it sooner or later.

"Kimber, are you down there?"

"Depends where you mean by down, Mom," Kimber replied. "Did you hear that last report?"

"Yes, Smedley beamed it to us as well. We'll be there momentarily." Two Black Eagles screamed overhead in a high-speed pass. "I brought reinforcements to hunt Skrima on the surface. I think Terry found where they are setting up their new home—Hades itself. They live in the dark heat of a planet's core. They are the devils of our horror stories."

"And you think the whole company will be heading down?"

"Yes." The dropship slowed. Char and another warrior vaulted from the open rear deck and dropped, using their suits' jets to slow enough that they didn't crash through the planet's surface, creating a new access to the underground system.

Char strode briskly to her daughter, patted her on the shoulder, and looked at the hole. "This it?"

"That's it. We sent five after the first three."

"They need more." Char leaned close until their face-plates touched. "I'm bringing him out. We'll bring all of them out."

"I know you will. I'll manage from up here."

"Right. I heard your order for relay gear. I think Iracitus might have something that can help that they used for asteroid mining, but someone without a suit on will have to go dig it out. I recommend you reorient the company to right here. Once we have comms, we'll let you know how many more we need and where. In the meantime, Joseph and Petricia are going to show everyone how high-speed space-fighters can cleanse the surface of Benitus Seven in record time. Only we can go down there, so that's what we need to do."

Kimber nodded. Her mother had spoken, and she was right.

"You three, come with me."

The warriors who had previously missed their chance were energized by the opportunity. Char jumped into the hole and fell a full ten meters before hitting the jets and slowing down. She studied the walls as she passed, noting where a mech had bounced and scraped on its way to the bottom, and there, a boulder had been torn loose. She wondered if it had landed on any Skrima.

"Terry, are you there? Capples, do you read me?" she requested over the company-wide channel. "Can anyone hear me?"

Two of the three warriors above her checked in. She marked them both and estimated her comm range as somewhere between crap and total comm blackout.

Char snarled when she hit the bottom and snap-fired at a red face that appeared from within one of the feeding tunnels but didn't know if she hit it. She listened, having detected sounds of mechs traveling on the stone. They appeared to be approaching.

The other three hit the ground, crushing bodies beneath their metal boots because nowhere was there a clear space on the cave's floor. A metallic object caught Char's eye. "Watch for the others. Mechs are coming from that direction." She pointed with a heavy metal arm before turning her attention to the mess on the floor, digging through it to look for anything that seemed different.

She found it quickly, with a Skrim's hand still attached. She scraped away the flesh to leave the object, fairly small, in her mechanical hand. She couldn't activate it because her fingers were too big.

"Looks like a pistol," the private who had been rebuilt in the Pod-docs noted. He stepped carelessly across the bodies, hammering his feet down to cause further destruction.

"Take it easy, Private. Do you want suit-washing duty when we get back to the ship?"

"No, ma'am," he replied, softening his stride but stepping on the bodies all the same.

"I think you're right that it's a weapon. Armed Skrima, as if they weren't deadly enough with just their claws."

The private didn't respond to that. He'd been on the receiving end too recently. He started to shake within his suit, translating the first interior tremors to external before he cut off the sensitivity and stopped the entire suit from shaking. Char turned her attention to him.

"You'll get your chance for payback. I guarantee there are more down here. Terry Henry Walton went somewhere, and so did the Skrima. This is a drop in the bucket. Lock and load, Private. We have front row seats to the only show in town."

One after another, five mechs emerged from the tunnel.

"Report, Sergeant Capples."

"Ma'am! There's a massive cave-in blocking the tunnel. We couldn't tell how much farther the cave extended, whether the cave-in was in the middle or toward the end. The roof looked weak, so we didn't try to remove any of the blockage. We're going to have to go a different way, and the colonel is going to have to find a different way out because at least one mech definitely went this way." Cap talked fast in his excitement and with the angst of being blocked from following the colonel.

"Flip you for it?" Char asked.

"Ma'am?" Capples had no idea what she was talking about.

"Fine. I'll take this tunnel with my team, and you take that one with yours. Return here in one hour with an update. Mark your timepiece. Good hunting, Cap."

"And you, ma'am."

Char led the way into the tunnel where she thought she splashed one of the Skrima. She didn't find a body. The growl returned deep within her throat. She tamped it down and pressed onward. She slowed to scan more thoroughly, looking up and sideways. Skrima with weapons bothered her. They were coming through the rift bare. Terry and the rest had assumed it was because they didn't have technology.

Reality appeared to be distinctly different. Maybe they couldn't cross the barrier into this dimension with their technology. They had been working on the Benitons' spaceships, and now... A sinking feeling settled into the pit of her stomach. What if they had only stopped what they saw last time and left an infestation? What if they had set up a beachhead down here? What if the Skrima'd had two years to reestablish the rift and build their army?

Giving their soldiers weapons and sending them into the galaxy.

What if they had already taken a ship?

Char started to panic. The Bad Company hadn't finished the job last time. "We need to hurry," she told the others as if that would make up for it. She had no way of knowing how many ships the Benitons had taken if they'd left the planet. Why had the Skrima flooded aboard after Joseph and Petricia had disabled them?

She started to relax. They wouldn't have if they had already taken a ship. Had they done so, they would have taken all of them by then. She tried to clear her head of the errant thoughts.

Char rushed around a corner and headfirst into a web

of fibers that caught at her arms and railgun, preventing her from raising it to fire at the Skrima that were bringing their weapons to bear. The others behind her flared wide and fired through the cables, cutting them and splashing the red targets beyond. Char shook the carbon fibers off her and stepped on the Skrima weapons as she continued forward. She stopped and held up a fist.

The others froze mid-stride.

Far away, she heard railgun fire coming from in front of her and adjusted her body to get the best audio pickup. Unless Capples' tunnel swerved around and they were sprinting to get in front, she had located Terry and Christina. She took off running, keeping her railgun up in case she ran into more bundled fibers.

"I'm coming, Terry!" she yelled inside her suit, not transmitting. Her voice was only intended for one person's ears.

Nadezhda Station, in orbit above Benitus Seven

Ted stared at the bank of miniature Etheric power systems. Shonna and Merrit were measuring air ducts and pump capacity to determine maximum habitation numbers. They had volunteered and run off before Timmons could argue, leaving him to support Ted. When he tried to do something—anything—Ted asked him to be quiet and wait.

Ted had been standing like that for thirty minutes. Timmons imagined a variety of ways to maim his fellow werewolf, Pod-doc him back to health, and start over. It gave Timmons the patience to keep waiting.

"Start over there and prepare to disconnect the fourth in line."

Timmons came back to himself. "Which fourth?" he asked, not having seen Ted point.

Ted threw up his hands and moaned before stomping through the power space and pointing. Timmons shrugged and held his hand over the connector. He touched it and Ted winced.

"Prepare doesn't mean touch."

Ted stormed off. The power supplies were arranged ten by ten. One hundred total units should have been enough to power an entire planet multiple times over. Ted had taken two during their previous trip, but they had been replaced. Timmons wanted the answer to how that had happened. Ted seemed unconcerned. An automated production system that could produce the Etheric power supplies would be a welcome addition to the Federation.

Most of the time, Ted's view was myopic while simultaneously being universal. He wanted to figure out the inner workings to explore the boundaries of physical laws and left the applications to others once he had added new discoveries to his base of knowledge.

And to lord his intelligence over others like me, Timmons thought. *I'll find it, and we'll get the shipyard cranking.*

"What are you going to do with a hundred of these?"

"Experiments." Ted didn't expound.

"Sometimes, I fucking hate you," Timmons blurted.

Ted looked up, his expression blank. "Why should that concern me?"

"It shouldn't, so let's get on with it. The sooner we can close the rift, the sooner we can go home. Felicity is not happy about being here." Ted had one weakness, and Timmons wasn't opposed to exploiting it.

Ted looked toward the ceiling. Felicity was upstairs somewhere. "Yes. Let's take care of this so we can start building the power transfer system. Be quiet so I can think."

Timmons let his hand hover over the disconnect and waited for instructions. Ted started tapping his pad. Five minutes later, Timmons sat on the floor and leaned against the wall with his arms crossed while Ted continued his calculations.

CHAPTER EIGHTEEN

Benitus Seven, Eastern Sector, Underground Cave Complex

From the tunnel's mouth, Terry scowled at a massive cavern filled with a city out of the devil's worst nightmares. Power coursed through the veins of a complex filled with thousands of Skrima and buildings in fantastic shapes and styles with streets and equipment.

"We're fucked," Terry grumbled. He looked down at Workman, who was still unconscious within his rigid suit.

Christina studied the city to find a trigger, something they could blow up that would create sympathetic detonations and level the entire cavern and take all the Skrima with it. She used the suit's systems to map as much of the city as she could, including IR and energy readings. Terry was thinking the same thing, but they didn't have a lot of time to come up with a plan.

The Skrima were coming. The mechs hadn't kept their presence underground a secret. They'd already killed a huge swath of Skrima.

"You know," Christina started over her direct channel with Terry while using her arm to delineate her field of fire, "bad guys aren't bad guys in their own minds. These Skrima might think of themselves as the heroes of their race, expanding their territory to support their swelling population."

"Maybe." Terry took aim. "What do they eat, as in, how do they stay alive?"

"I wish I knew, TH, so we could eliminate the source and starve them out. They put up a stiff defense when they're at full strength, and they don't seem to care about losses. Wave attacks only buy them time."

"While depleting our ammo. There is rhyme to their reason, like, why did they stop?"

The approaching Skrima bunched up between nearby buildings.

"Bull-rush?" Christina offered. "What do you think of a preemptive strike?"

"We have to kill them sooner or later, so why not? On your command, Colonel."

"Thanks, TH. Fire." They both popped their shoulder launchers and sent one rocket each into the air for a danger-close delivery.

Terry took careful aim and fired three-round bursts into the crowd. Christina controlled her fire, too. The last thing they needed was for a railgun to fail, followed closely by running out of darts or power, both of which eventualities were already of concern since they could not draw on Etheric power or sunlight for the suits.

A wisp of light caught Terry's eye. "Incoming!" he shouted. He and Christina had the same idea. They both dove for Workman, bouncing off each other to mostly land on top and cover the injured warrior.

A plasma bolt grazed them on its way past and into the tunnel. It skipped off the stone floor and slammed into a turn not far up the grade, exploding against the rock. A slow rumble preceded the cave-in.

"Time to move." Terry climbed to his feet to find Skrima racing toward them. He unleashed the fury of his railgun on full auto to mow down the first ranks across a broad front. Christina finally extricated herself from the private's suit and joined TH. "Right up the gut. Fewer of them. You take an arm, I take an arm, and away we go."

"What the hell was that thing?"

"A weapon we don't want to be on the receiving end of."

The two concentrated their fire down the middle while sweeping left and right to hold the attacking waves at bay.

"On three," Terry declared. "One." They kept firing. "Two." They stepped backward, Terry shifting his railgun to his left hand and continuing to pour hypervelocity darts into the teeming masses. "Three."

They each grabbed an arm of the rigid combat suit and dragged Workman free of the tunnel before lumbering forward in a mad five-legged dash toward the gap. The wings of the attack started to fold in behind them.

"This is a bad idea, but I can't think of anything better," Christina remarked. She stopped firing on full-auto, using three-round bursts on targets that appeared. They sped up as they got used to the stride and pace. They hurried around a corner and into one of the plasma launchers, which was aimed right at them. They both dove to the side, stopping when they reached the limit of Workman's suit.

Terry snap-fired at the vehicle's gun, trying to take it out, but he only managed a couple shots before the blue plasma ball appeared and launched toward them. Neither had a chance to let go as the round hit Workman, exploding the suit and yanking Terry and Christina backward. They lost their grips with the violence of the explosion.

Terry Henry spun around, keeping his feet as he ran toward the Skrima launcher. It had an open turret like a self-propelled artillery piece, and he made quick work of the Skrima within. The controls looked to be jury-rigged around a more advanced interface.

No Etheric. It was built to operate in the real environment but ready to switch over to their more natural state of gliding between the dimensions. The manual controls he understood. Push, pull, adjust the gun trajectory and direction. He tested the controls and found the load button, which showed red. He hit it, and it changed through shades of red as it built the next charge.

"Come on!" he called over the radio to Christina.

She gave Workman a quick once over, looking for his railgun, but it had been destroyed along with the rest of the suit, taking the private with it. If they had a cryopod with them, they might have been able to save him.

She wasn't sure they were going to be able to save themselves.

Christina ran forward and jumped onto the tank. There was no room left in the turret for her, so she squatted on the outside behind Terry Henry Walton while he worked to maneuver the vehicle using his oversized mechanical hands.

It lurched backward. Christina took on the role of sniper, selecting targets and killing them with single shots. She glanced at her ammo because it had started flashing a warning. Ten percent remained.

And they had no hope of resupply.

Thilamoot, Trans-Pacific Task Force Transport Ship

Monsoon stood on top of a stack of shipping containers with his feet spread and his fists jammed into his hips. "What is your major malfunction?" he boomed into the cargo bay.

"Just trying to please the sergeant major!" a private shouted back while arm-deep in the latching mechanism, his face flushed and covered with sweat.

"Not you, knucklehead. These other snackwad diltwats standing around watching you flail. Corporal! Unfuck this situation."

A corporal moved a little too slowly.

"I'm coming down there," Monsoon warned and disappeared toward the back.

The work party became frantic, pulling and pushing helplessly at the load, trying to free it to finish unloading the last of the shuttles. They were getting toward the deadline. The last thing the sergeant major wanted was to be the one responsible for holding up the fleet's departure.

When he strode briskly from behind the containers, the work party had made no progress.

"First time, fucknuggets?" he asked in a calm and collected voice.

The corporal hung his head. "We could use your help,

Sergeant Major. This has thoroughly and in all ways kicked my ass upside-down and backward."

"There are magnetic locks. This is a metal ship. Is the pallet's lock engaged?"

"No!" the corporal shot back. The sergeant major widened his eyes, staring hard enough to bore into the corporal's soul. "Yes?" he offered.

"Which is it, cockslobber?"

He waved at his crew to check while the sergeant major continued to stare.

One of the privates jumped to attention while two others pulled off a panel and jammed a spanner inside. "It shows off, but it is locked in. We're going to manually disengage it."

The sergeant major reached down and grabbed the first soldier, who was still elbow-deep in the latching mechanism. He dragged him away from the container when the mechanical lock disengaged, and the pallet started to slide. The sergeant major let go and braced himself. The private he pulled out of the way dug his feet in and braced his shoulder against the load. The work party rushed round the pallet and got it under control.

"Latch," the sergeant major said softly. The private dug back in to tighten it again after loosening it all the way, which added friction to limit the extraneous movements. He lightened up enough for the crew to move the pallet into position.

The sergeant major stood back and wiped off his hands. The corporal came around the pallet and locked his body in the position of attention. He was shaking and unable to speak. Monsoon put a hand on his shoulder.

"We talked about troubleshooting these pallets. If you have to do anything to excess, then there's something wrong, and you need to rethink your approach. Push harder isn't usually the right answer."

"I almost killed the sergeant major!" the corporal blurted.

"Not quite. You could have hurt your own soldier, though, and that is unforgivable. If you get me killed, I will come back as a ghost to haunt you for the rest of your natural-born days. If you get one of your people killed, your own thoughts will haunt you if you haven't done everything you can. Now get back to work. We need to finish unloading and button up. I don't want to be the last ship reporting green."

"What if I've done everything I could and somebody still dies?" the corporal wondered. "Will my thoughts be haunted?"

"Maybe, but they shouldn't be. We joined a military, which duty might include going to war. In war, people die. That doesn't mean we don't value their lives. We put a very high value on lives, and that's why we've been fanatical about your training. You heard the colonel tell everyone that when your world is coming apart and you're exhausted, the only crutch to keep you upright will be your training. Sometimes there won't be anyone to save you, and that's when you have to save yourself. Training. Doing what must be done, no matter the circumstances. We wanted a month so you could develop habits, but well, as is the way with higher-ups, they had different ideas. Keep training. Keep reinforcing the right things to do."

The others in the work party drifted in to listen.

"This is why you will take your weapons apart and clean them ten times a day. You need to be able to do that in the dark, rain, exhaustion, maybe even while eating. This is why you'll learn to sleep every second you can. Why you'll be able to wake up instantly and be ready to fight. How you'll be able to keep going when your body is telling you differently. That's why we give you twenty seconds to do a task that should take thirty. If you don't constantly push yourselves, you won't see the limits you can reach. Think about it. We're in outer space. We're going to go through a couple Gates and arrive at Kor'nar, thousands of light-years away, maybe even ten thousand. I haven't looked at a star chart because it doesn't matter. We'll arrive on the planet, and much will be the same while everything else is wildly different.

"And here's a hint about tomorrow. The Kor'narians are an insectoid race. You might not be able to tell them apart, which means you can't tell which ones are the enemy, but we can't just kill them all. We have to win the peace. Get your nasty bodies under control, and don't shoot anything you're not supposed to shoot. Exercise discipline. You will be afraid, and that's okay. But don't give in to your fear. Dominate it. That's the definition of courage. Now, stop fucking off and get back to work. Next stop, Kor'nar."

The work party saluted together and rushed away. The sergeant major left them to it. He had to set up for the officer training, something he was dreading because he'd be missing the big party.

"Fucking officers," he grumbled.

CHAPTER NINETEEN

Bridge of the *War Axe*

"What happened?" Micky yelled. Ruzfell was twisting and clicking, frantically looking for answers. The *War Axe* had started a slow rotation after the port railgun stopped firing. Ruzfell was having a hellacious time trying to maintain a modicum of accurate fire with the remaining railgun.

"Suresha, get attitude control fixed!" Micky ordered.

"Working on it," came the quick reply.

"Trying to compensate," Clifton called from the pilot's station. The rotation came to an abrupt halt. "Axial thrusters at maximum."

"Commander Lagunov, I need the port railgun back online ASAP."

"It came apart in the cycling mechanism. We can't fix it out here."

Micky frowned while looking at the tactical board. Ruzfell increased the rate of fire from the remaining capital-grade railgun.

"Smedley, connect me to Ted, please."

"Plato is currently blocking all comms since he is in the middle of a delicate procedure."

"Then ask Plato how he feels about *Ramses' Chariot* getting pressed into service to cover the firing line while we make repairs."

Smedley disappeared to commune with his fellow AI. He was back two seconds later.

"After a lengthy discussion, he said that he has moved from the ship to be with Ted inside the station. I will fly *Ramses' Chariot* in support of the Bad Company's mission."

"When can you be on station?" Micky inquired.

"Ten minutes."

"Commander Suresha, have crews in place and ready to address the issues we're having in ten minutes."

"I'm not sure we'll know what to fix within ten minutes."

"We have limited time, Commander. Please make the most of it." Micky signed off. "We're not even getting shot at and we're coming apart."

Ruzfell was moving quickly, trying to adjust to maintain fire on target to keep more Skrima from coming through the rift.

"We're being pulled toward the planet," Clifton suggested. "We need more power. Etheric power."

"There's no way in hell I'm turning off those jammers, not with the Bad Company engaged with the Skrima."

Clifton threw his hands up in frustration.

"No way," Micky reiterated. "Work through it. As soon as *Ramses' Chariot* is on station, get out there and help them fix it."

"Aye, aye, sir," Clifton confirmed. He was cycling through his diagnostics to find the problem, even though he expected the engineers to find it first.

"The Black Eagles are available if we need them to fill a gap in coverage," Ruzfell suggested between adjustments.

"Smedley, see if you can get Joseph and Petricia into the rotation."

"On it," the AI confirmed.

The tactical board showed the Black Eagles screaming across the countryside one hundred kilometers below.

"You can cease firing, Ruzfell," Smedley stated.

After three last hologrid engagements, he dropped the screens and hunched over.

Micky jumped from his seat to catch the Yollin before he fell over. "Sickbay to the bridge. Man down."

Benitus Seven, Eastern Sector, Underground Cave Complex

As Char pounded through two more Skrima checkpoints, she gritted her teeth and forced herself to maintain speed. The enemy at the last checkpoint had weapons had fired repeatedly before she could overwhelm them. One round had penetrated one of the suit joints, clipping her elbow. Nothing major, but for pistols, being able to penetrate powered combat armor was a higher-level achievement. Given they were creatures considered to be technically unsophisticated, they had proven the Bad Company wrong.

Lesson: Don't underestimate the Skrima.

Up ahead, the railgun fire had stopped. Char knew she

was getting close and had not been deceived by false echoes. The Etheric was denied to her, so she couldn't reach out and check for Terry's essence.

At the next bend, the tunnel branched. She hesitated, giving her elbow more time to heal itself. The nanos were working, but the damage was different from the usual combat injuries. The rounds were something besides slugs. She couldn't feel poison or radioactivity, but something was there.

"Fucking Skrima. We can't kill you fast enough."

She clenched her jaw and waved for two mechs to go to the right while she took the tunnel to the left. They pounded down the tunnel and Char headed the other way, making it to the first corner before she figured out she had better tools at her command. She launched a drone to check around corners, maintaining line of sight so she didn't lose it.

The first corner was fine and she kept running, zipping the drone ahead to check the next one. She'd almost reached it when it showed her what was around the corner and she slid to a halt, grabbing at the wall to help stop the mech's momentum. One shot from a heavy weapon vaporized the drone and would have blasted her had she not swayed backward.

She faced the direction the tunnel turned and dropped to the push-up position, then opened her over-the-shoulder rockets. She leaned that shoulder around the corner and fired, and the rocket's impact was nearly instantaneous. As Char popped to her feet and eased around the corner, she fired her railgun into the smoke and dust just to be sure, panning back and forth to clear out any stragglers.

If she couldn't see, neither could they. She powered forward. The private remained behind her, watching their six while ready to bring additional weapons to bear should Char call for it.

Her IR systems penetrated the debris filling the air sufficiently to show her it was clear on the other side. She launched her last drone and sent it ahead. After the second corner, she knew something was different.

"Slow down, Private. I need to take a better look." The tunnel opened into a great cavern. Something blocked the immediate view, so Char sent the drone farther ahead. She made it to the corner and dipped her head out and back to get the full sensor view of what was in front of her. She held her hand out for the private to hold back. She moved forward to find a group of five Skrima hurrying into the tunnel. She fired on full auto and wiped them from the face of the planet.

If they hadn't realized she was coming when she sent the rocket into the heavy weapon checkpoint, a railgun on full auto had sent them a message they couldn't ignore. The drone soared high. Char stifled a curse when she saw the magnitude of the Skrima city before her.

She hoped they'd only moved in and these were archae-ological ruins, but presence of heavy weapons quickly tamped down the notion of the Skrima not being an advanced race.

Char noticed a tank-like vehicle driving haphazardly through city streets while a Bad Company mech crouched on the rear deck, firing at targets of opportunity.

"Only TH could drive that badly and be proud of it," Char broadcast.

"What are you doing down here?" Terry replied. "Belay that. Where are you? We need a way out."

Char rushed from the tunnel and stitched a line of hypervelocity darts at a forty-five-degree angle from halfway to the ceiling down to the tunnel mouth—a line pointing the way.

"I have it. Thanks, Char," Christina replied. The tank jerked, caromed off a building, and accelerated. The cannon rotated backward, forcing Christina to jump off. Terry fired one of the blue plasma projectiles into the biggest building underground.

Char waved the private forward. "Be ready to lay down covering fire. I think we're going to see something special."

They took up firing positions as the vehicle rolled close and turned around. TH adjusted the turret and fired, then changed his aim and waited for the plasma to regenerate.

"Missed you," TH transmitted over the company-wide band using his suit's radio.

"Me, too," Char said. "I thought you were out philandering and came to drag your ass back home. But I find you playing with a tank. Is this because I didn't let you have that one all those years ago back in Cheyenne Mountain?"

Terry fired. A perfect shot clipped a corner of a building, removing enough structure that it crumbled and fell. The private fired at a crowd approaching from his direction. Christina added firepower of her own, but three-round bursts only.

"Where's Workman?" Char asked.

"He didn't make it," Christina replied. "Maybe you can

tell us about that tank you mentioned that Terry wanted to take our minds off how the private cashed in."

Char unloaded a torrential flood of hypervelocity darts on Skrima coming from her side of the vehicle. When the mass behind the current dead started to grow, she increased her impact. "Fire in the hole." A rocket raced off her shoulder and into the crowd. The private joined the rocket parade, sending one of his own into the masses.

"We discovered a weapons cache to help us in our war against the Forsaken as well as anyone who was trying to take over old Earth." Two more rockets blasted into the massing Skrima. Terry fired the main gun. The smell of ozone was unmistakable, penetrating the filtered air and reaching into their suits. "There was an M1A1 and Terry wanted it, bad, like a kid looking for a Red Ryder BB gun for Christmas. We didn't have the fuel to support it, so instead of embracing logic and reason, he made me the bad guy."

The main fired again. Two more rockets headed into the cavern.

"No bonus points if we bring rockets home, people," Terry interrupted. He stood up while the plasma was regenerating and sent a rocket into a building across the way. When the plasma was ready, he fired, re-aimed, and prepared to fire again. He stood to send another rocket downrange.

"Listen," the private said.

They quieted, only the whine of the plasma system intruding on their momentary respite.

"One, maybe two more vehicles inbound. A single

rocket will take one out if it strikes the turret." Terry adjusted his aim and fired.

"Across the cavern!" Christina pointed. The private launched a rocket, but a blue plasma ball was already headed toward them. The three mechs dove out of the way, leaving TH inside the vehicle. He stood and aimed, firing his railgun on full auto at the ball. It sparked and started to lose its integrity but not quickly enough. Terry ducked and flinched.

The remainder of the plasma round splashed across the front of the vehicle instead of tearing it apart. Terry started to aim at the tank but the rocket slammed into it, blasting it from the inside out. The main gun tottered drunkenly from the distended turret.

Terry fired at the next biggest building. "Watch for number two," he called. Three railguns barked at once at a new surge of Skrima. Terry depressed the angle and fired into the crowd, obliterating a massive swath of incoming.

The plasma started to recycle.

"Time to go," Terry said as the ranks of the Skrima swelled. They didn't have time to wait for the other vehicle to appear. Char bolted into the tunnel mouth, and the private fired back and forth across the growing mass before backing into the tunnel. Christina climbed off the back of the vehicle. "Clear back, people. I'm going to stopper this bottle."

TH revved the engine, fired, and accelerated backward into the tunnel, wedging the vehicle into the entrance. He had just stood and started firing to buy them a little more time when the second vehicle appeared at his nine-o'clock. Since it was aimed and ready to fire, he jumped backward, sliding off the rear deck and landing on his head as a point-blank-range plasma ball blew the tank out of the entrance and cast the hulk aside. The other three fired out the tunnel mouth while Terry regained his feet.

Char was the first to run.

"You go," the private told them. "I can see your load is out."

The flashing red was obvious. Terry had dropped below ten percent, and Christina's was solid red—single fire only until it was empty.

He laid down a stream of fire while jogging backward after the others. When he rounded the corner, he kept firing for a few moments before turning and running.

Praithwait, Trans-Pacific Task Force Transport Ship

Are you up? Kae asked. The day had been full, an incessant bombardment of questions and requests to know more. The officers had homework to deliver action plans for their units before they hit the ground, but they needed to be the height of simplicity.

Marcie ordered the establishment of a secure compound from which to operate. The task force would send out random patrols to learn the lay of the land while locating Kor'narian units and locations. Marcie wasn't counting on third-party observations. She wanted the full spread of drones airborne and gathering information.

They would consolidate the info and turn it into analyzed intelligence delineating capabilities and intentions. After that, the task force would be able to interdict Kor'narian operations.

I am, Marcie replied from the *Angkmoor.*

I can hear them, and it's giving me the willies.

Such a Puritan. What am I to do with you?

Not what they're doing to each other! He switched to his outside voice. "Keep it down, for fuck's sake! If I have to come out there, the party's over!"

It quieted but not by very much. Kae decided to stuff wads of paper into his ears and pull his blanket over his head.

Are you ready? Marcie asked.

I wish we had mechs. We'd make quick work of this mess.

That's why we aren't using them. The Federation is convinced that by inserting a comparable force, we'll be able to reduce tensions before getting them to the negotiating table. With too much military superiority, they would go out of fear, but it would only last as long as we were there. If we beat them in a straight-up fight, we get their attention.

Kae saw how the Federation justified it. *Earn their respect versus demand it at the end of a mech's railgun.*

Something like that. I just want to get there and get started. I'm falling asleep talking.

I know what you mean. I love you, and I'll see you tomorrow on Kor'nar.

Miles to go before I sleep, Marcie recited. *I love you, too.*

CHAPTER TWENTY

Benitus Seven, Eastern Sector, the Caves

"No explosives?" Terry asked.

"None," Char replied.

"You're harshing my happy reunion buzz." Terry contemplated his approach. "Let's stop and set up a quick roadblock. I need to get out. I can collapse the tunnel with my JDS."

"I'm all for that, but if we're going to cleanse them off this planet, we're going to have to go back in there," Char suggested.

"Fuck that." Terry backed close to the wall to give himself cover for when he both climbed out and got back into the suit. The private lit up the tunnel as Skrima appeared down a long straightaway. Terry had developed the idea based on how far away they would be if the roof came down.

Terry climbed out the back of his mech and prepared his JDS. His wrist had healed, but he wasn't up for breaking it again. He dialed it to six.

"Ready?" he asked. The private backed away to give Terry room but kept firing to make sure no Skrima could get off a lucky shot.

Terry squeezed in front and sent a shot into the roof at the far end. It ripped off a layer of the roof but didn't bring it down, so he dialed it up to eight and waited. The private fired to clear the way. Terry ducked in and fired at the same spot. The roof exploded under the concussion, a great rumble preceded the avalanche that filled the tunnel leading to the Skrima city.

Terry gave a satisfied shrug and tucked his JDS back into his shirt.

You look like shit, Char told him directly.

It's been a long day, he replied. *Got a little fucked up taking out the trash, but I'm better now, just not one hundred percent. It'll be nice to be above ground. It sucks down here.*

Just a lot. How are we going to eradicate the Skrima?

I have no idea, and that scares me. Terry buttoned up his suit. "Lead on, warriors."

Char continued her trek. The way was clear. They hadn't left any Skrima behind them. She pounded the stone hard with her feet to let anyone ahead know that mechs were coming. Before she reached the entrance chamber, she heard a counter-stomp.

"This is Major Charumati. We'll be coming out, four of us."

"Roger, ma'am," Sergeant Capples replied. "We found nothing but an alternate route to the outside. Not even a steep climb, but it twists a lot."

"Did you see any Skrima on this side?" Char pressed.

"None, ma'am." Char entered a tunnel that was filled

with mechs, so much so they didn't have room to maneuver. Capples waved for his team to move back. "From the looks of your suit, *you* did."

"We even found somebody," Char replied.

"Colonel Walton. Colonel Lowell," Capples greeted them once he recognized the suits. He leaned both ways before checking his HUD. "Private Workman, sir?"

"He didn't make it," Terry answered. He dialed up the video from the encounter and shared it privately with Cap.

"Fuck, man," he mumbled before straightening up. "Orders?"

Terry stepped up but moved aside. "Christina?"

"It's great to be out of that place," she started. "We're going to close the shaft I fell down because that sucked. Then we're going to establish a presence in the tunnel, but it'll be with heavy weapons, claymores, mines, and every fucking thing we can put in there to keep the Skrima from getting past. After that, we're going to contact the Federation and get permission to drop a nuke into that cavern. That needs to happen before they can dig themselves out, and none of these wheels start turning until we're out of here and back in comms range."

"They have the repeaters set up, ma'am," Capples noted.

"Well done!" then, "Break, break. Colonel Lowell to the *War Axe*, please come in."

"Colonel! It is great to hear from you," Micky answered immediately. "You had us worried. Are Terry and Char with you?"

"They are, but we lost Workman. We need immediate authority from the Federation to send a nuke through the crust of this planet to a cavern where the Skrima have built a massive city, complete with manufacturing of heavy weapons that are different from what we have and more powerful. We need to put a hard stop to that right now."

"I will make that request, but we don't have any nukes on board the *War Axe*. The Queen banned them."

"Crap! I knew that. Do we have anything that might serve the same purpose?"

"We might. We can overload a pulse generator. We have a penetrator since those are standard issue to break into strongholds. We just need to marry the two. I'll put all my people on it immediately, and there's no permission needed from the Federation."

"I love you, Micky. And because he won't say it himself, I'm sorry TH keeps taking your cats."

Terry held up his mechanical hands. "Why? Here I am, an innocent bystander, getting skewered by friendly fire." He pointed down the tunnel. "That way to the hole?"

"Yes, sir," Capples confirmed.

"Then we're going the other way. Get all of our people out of here. You heard the colonel. We'll blow the vertical access from the top and set up a checkpoint in the tunnel out."

"Major Kimber is at the top," Capples remarked.

"Kimber, can you make that hole go away as soon as we're out of this place? We'll be taking the walk out, and we'll also need static weapon systems for the tunnel access. We should be out in a while. Give us an hour."

"It's wide enough that we can run." Cap pumped his fist in the air—time to go. "If you're able to."

Char turned toward Terry, even though they couldn't see each other through their suits' face shields. She confirmed it. "Yes. We'll run. Please have Cory standing by when we get to the surface."

Terry dialed up a direct channel. "Are you hit?"

"Yeah. I took one in the elbow of all places. I thought it was healing, but I'm not so sure it is now that any adrenaline has worn off. It hurts more than it should, and I'm tired."

Terry patted her armored shoulder with his mechanical hand before becoming all business. "Lead on, Cap, best possible speed. Char behind Cap. I'll bring up the rear. Have a Pod standing by to take Char to the *Axe* as soon as we're on the surface," Terry ordered.

Capples didn't delay. He took off running, accelerating when he could, slowing when he had to to make short work of the transit. Char cradled her right arm, not swinging it as she ran.

Nadezhda Station, in orbit above Benitus Seven

"Now," Ted said, yanking the cable off one of the power supplies while Timmons mirrored Ted's actions. The shock charged through Timmons, stunning half his body. His knee collapsed, and he fell over. "You should have been insulated better."

Timmons groaned while trying to recover his senses. "Fucking Ted."

Ted ignored him as he removed both power supplies and headed to the next level up. There was a maintenance area that Ted had secured as his workshop. The pack had carried in enough equipment to allow him to set up. Although much of the work was in programming the systems to control the energy flow, there was a physical interface that was critical to the entire process. Without it, there would be nothing to control. He stopped when he reached the bottom step.

"Timmons?" Ted asked. "I need the energy transfer shell that is in the cargo bay of *Ramses' Chariot*, along with the routers and processors stored inside it. I need you to go get them."

Plato intruded on Ted's thoughts. *Ramses' Chariot is gone, but I had everything you need moved to the outer ring. I'll have it brought down immediately.*

Where is my ship? Ted wondered.

I authorized its temporary use. The War Axe *was unable to maintain continuous fire on the rift since one of the railguns suffered a catastrophic failure. They are making thruster repairs to better hold station.* Ramses' Chariot *will return. I thought it was okay since the Bad Company is risking everything to make it safe for the installation of your power transfer system.*

I could have told them their ship would break down after flying it too long within the atmosphere, but they need to learn those things for themselves. Let me know when my equipment is here.

It would be easier if we could get the freight lift working, Plato suggested.

Ted nodded before climbing one level and dropping off the two power supplies. He headed for the freight system on that level and tapped into the controls. He grunted at the complexity attached to a simple system and sat down as he worked.

Timmons slowly climbed the stairs, giving Ted the finger as he stumbled past. By the time he got to the top, he was sorted out. He tried jogging to loosen up his body. Felicity and Shonna stared at him.

"What happened to you?" Felicity drawled.

"Your husband," Timmons said without clarifying.

"You might want to check a mirror. God bless your soul."

Timmons wasn't a Southerner, but even he knew Felicity was not paying him a compliment. Timmons continued to the outer ring, where he found most of the gear.

I need a hand carrying this junk down to the Doctor Doom Death Device Development Den if you could, Timmons requested. He picked up a load and carried it in. On the way, he passed the others heading out, all except Felicity, who he hadn't expected. She wasn't that kind of helper.

Ted wouldn't want her to take the risk of hurting herself, but she was as enhanced as the others and was probably safe no matter what the task. If she were injured, she would heal quickly. Still, Ted protected her as if she were a fragile flower. She had trained him to be that way over numerous decades. She had the patience of Methuselah and had kept Ted sane through his intellectual evolution. Ted's inventions had saved all their lives more than once.

Timmons looked at Felicity and softened. "We'll get this stuff down there before he fixes the elevator, and then we can work on going back to the planet to help the others. Have you heard what's going on? What happened to Terry Henry?"

Felicity smiled. "Iracitus?" she asked.

The AI spoke to all of them at once. *Terry and Christina*

have been found, but Char was injured and is on her way back to the War Axe. *The number of Skrima on the planet is significantly different because of a vast underground complex. Smedley is still parsing the data gathered by the colonels. They have manufacturing capabilities underground. Terry stole a Skrima tank and used it to expedite their escape.*

"The Skrima have tanks?" Timmons shook his head to clear the cobwebs. He yelled over his shoulder at the others, "Pick up the pace, people!"

CHAPTER TWENTY-ONE

Kor'nar

A picket line of destroyers and cruisers exited the Gate ahead of the massive transport freighters. As they'd done for the fly-by when Marcie and Kae arrived at Belzimus, the picket assumed a spear formation. The first big ship through was Marcie on the flagship, *Angkmoor*. *Praithwait*, *Thilamoot*, and *Gonboon* rounded out the fleet assets. By spreading the soldiers across the four ships, they were able to carry their own supplies, reducing the need for support vessels.

"One hour to orbit," the captain announced.

Marcie stood on the bridge, having been invited to watch the transit. She accepted, not because she wanted to watch the crew fly the ship, but because she wanted to see the tactical picture as soon as it was available to get her head into the game with as much information as was available. The tactical view populated, making the captain scowl.

Marcie voiced the obvious. "Did we expect to meet any ships like that?"

"No," the captain slowly replied, scratching his chin before fluffing his mane. "Freighters have been waved off because of the conflict since there hadn't been a safe place to land their cargoes. The planet is supposed to be in transport limbo. Helm, slow the ship. Give us some space between the picket line."

Helm immediately responded. Emergency klaxons sounded. Marcie crossed her arms and glared at the screen. She had expected the plan to break down on first contact, but not before they made it to the planet. She ground her teeth in frustration. A ground-pounder in space was a casual observer, with zero ability to influence the action. At least dirtside, she was able to do something. She forced herself to unclench her fists.

"Small ships approaching from the rear," the navigator reported. "They've engaged the *Gonboon*. Point defenses active. One enemy ship destroyed. They are moving away."

"Who's the enemy?" Marcie wondered.

"Data coming in from *Gonboon*. The attackers had various ship configurations. No identifiers. Their estimate is pirates, possibly black marketeers supporting the illegal arms trade and delivering goods to one side or the other," the captain noted.

"Can we capture one to see what arms they were delivering?" Marcie asked.

"Fighting off and capturing are two completely different efforts, Colonel. Our mission is to deliver you to the planet."

Marcie glared at the captain with ice in her eyes. "Why

don't you join us on the planet, Captain, so we can all guess what kind of weapons will be used against us?"

The captain held up his hands, not willing to fight with the colonel. He was flying a reconfigured freighter with no offensive combat capability and a bare minimum of defensive weapons. "I'll pass your request to the combat picket."

"Thank you. Please let us know when we're in orbit. We'll load up the shuttles over the next hour and be ready to deploy the second we're able."

"Will do." The captain smiled, but Marcie wasn't amused. She nodded tersely and strode off the bridge. The tension of the captain and his flight crew eased greatly with Marcie's departure, while hers only increased.

The three cargo bays of the massive freighter were stacked one on top of the other. The shuttles were lined up to launch out the rear through an opening protected by a thin door and an energy shield. They wouldn't roll up the outer door until they were ready to deploy for safety in case of power fluctuations when bouncing off the upper atmosphere. Once the ship had settled into a low planetary orbit—not too far into the atmosphere so the ship's old engines could drag her away from the planet's gravity—they would launch. The transports were not capable of landing on a planet's surface.

Marcie looked at the numbers. Eight hundred soldiers on each deck, plus a mass of support personnel. She had designated eighteen hundred out of the twenty-four hundred on board to head to the planet on the first wave. The shuttles would be packed tight with soldiers, but they needed to establish their control of the ground and airspace between their base and the transports before she wasted lift bringing in supplies for a tent city, a fuel dump, and ammo reload. Equipment maintenance would be field expedient only, no major repairs until the camp had been established.

They couldn't determine a location for the task force base until they had a clear picture of the situation on the ground. Judging by the complete lack of intelligence before their arrival, Marcie had little hope of a quick determination.

Plan: Hit the ground fast. Send out eyes and ears in all directions and start building a map from scratch.

She couldn't understand why she'd had higher expectations. She shrugged it off and did what she liked most, the same thing that Terry Henry liked to do before going into battle.

Troop the line. Walk before the troops. Look into their eyes to allay their fear. Joke and put them at ease while also firing them up. Hitting a hot landing zone would be an adrenaline surge like they had never before experienced.

The troops were squeezed around and on top of the cargo and in the small gaps between the shuttles. A few had even managed to get on top of the shuttles. Marcie forced her way through, sliding against one body and another. Her pack caught on somebody with every step.

"Time to go vertical, ma'am," a sergeant from the Lion Corps offered. He intertwined his fingers and held them out for her to step on and climb up, where she'd find more room to maneuver. She shifted her slung rifle to make sure it wouldn't fall or swing around and smash the sergeant in the face.

"Good call." She pounded his shoulders with two fists

and stepped upward. He lifted, not much since she was much heavier than he had anticipated, but she made it, thanks to the tactical assist. She hooked to the ship's broadcast through her communications chip.

"We are here!" she announced. "As soon as I give the order, board your shuttles. It'll be a tight squeeze, but we need to make this first lift count. We are going in light. Infantry will land and pave the way for those who follow. We will establish a beachhead on Kor'nar from which to expand our presence.

"The Kor'narians will see the extent of our resolve. Because of that, we will be able to bring hostilities to a close. They do not want to bear the wrath of the Trans-Pac Task Force. This is the foundation of your legacy. Make it a good one. I will be the first with boots on the ground. I will be the last to leave because I will be there with you the entire time we are here. *We*, as in *we*, are in this together. One team, one fight. Board your shuttles." She ended with a cold order, no oorah-shouting.

They were here to do a job. The better they did it, the easier their future engagements would be until planets decided that it was in their best interests to resolve their issues before the Trans-Pac became involved. That was Marcie's hope. It was what Terry Henry talked about when reminiscing about the Marines. Countries would raise their heads every now and then whenever they thought the Marines had softened, only to get their asses kicked spectacularly.

Until the next time, but a well-fought battle made the next easier for whatever reasons.

Marcie moved across the top of the cargo and onto the

tops of the boxy shuttles. She hopped from one to the next until she slid down a sloped nose to land on the deck behind the first shuttle. She waited until the twenty assigned soldiers worked their way inside.

"Get cozy," she shouted.

"We don't know any other way, ma'am," a private replied, filling half the space she needed to stand.

"Damn straight." She took two steps back and ran into the gap, crushing bodies against each other sufficiently that they could close the rear hatch. "Who's flying this thing?"

"Webster, ma'am!" a distant voice shouted.

"Best you've ever flown is going to be today because you're the mac daddy!"

"No doubt about that."

She looked at the private about a hand's breadth away. "I'm not superstitious, but I don't want to tempt fate, you know what I mean?"

People were struggling to breathe. Marcie climbed upward and popped out almost like a wine cork leaving a bottle, then sat across a couple shoulders. A few others did the same to relieve the pressure. She looked into the eyes of the soldiers and started to laugh. "Are we there yet?"

"I don't think we've left the transport yet," somebody replied from the press below.

Marcie nodded. "A wise man once said, don't revel in how much something sucks, ask yourself how you could make it suck more. That is the key to happiness."

Some of the soldiers scrunched their foreheads in thought. "Don't you mean, make it suck less?"

Marcie laughed again. "How you deal with the suck is

what will make the Trans-Pac great. That is the stuff of legends! Do you think normal people would do this?"

"Fuck normal!" someone shouted from up front.

The soldiers on the shuttle started shouting, stopping instantly by a jolt that would have thrown them to the deck had there been space to fall. They had not yet launched.

"It's okay," Marcie said. "Just a little turbulence."

Pirates in the air, the captain told her over her internal comm. She steeled her features, trying to look calm and reassuring. The soldiers had no idea they were under attack. The ship jerked and dropped, then rose again. One Belzonian turned green.

"Hold it!" Marcie said even though she knew it wouldn't help.

The sound of the point defenses cycling at maximum was unmistakable. The troops knew what it was. Another jerk to the side and drop. The first Belzonian puked on his neighbor, and the dominos started to fall. Puke smell permeated everything. Marcie pulled her shirt over her mouth.

"What the fuck did you eat?" she wondered. "Hey up there! What are you trying to do to us, Webster? It's like you're not even trying."

"*Angkmoor* is clear. We have a straight shot to the planet. Express elevator going down, leaving in one minute," Webster reported. "Damn! That's a lot of puke back there."

Any chance we'll be attacked on the way down? Marcie asked over her internal chip.

We'll make a steep descent. The pirates have gone exo-atmospheric, so they won't be able to catch up. The destroyers are chasing them now, and the cruisers have formed a cordon around us. The transport will be in geosynchronous orbit directly above us. We're fine. I'll set the pace for the formation, ma'am. Stand back and enjoy the ride.

Roger. Thanks, Webster. Keep taking good care of my people. Marcie took a deep breath through her shirt before pulling it away from her mouth. "Launch in thirty. Airspace is clear. We're going down, people. I don't know about you, but I'm ready to get off this damn shuttle."

"Will we have time to change?" a private asked, knowing the answer but hoping he was wrong.

"Sorry. The good news is that it'll dry and then you crumble it off. The longest I've worn one uniform was seven days. In the field while under fire, no one cares if you smell like puke. Or worse, blood."

"I care." The private shrugged. A few Belzonians snickered. The mass of bodies compressed as the shuttle zipped away from *Angkmoor* and into the skies above Kor'nar. The bouncing and heat buildup were minimal before the shuttle dove toward the deck. Everyone hung on until the craft leveled out.

Marcie pulled her rifle around to the front. She carried a short-barreled slug-thrower in the same caliber as the enlisted infantry's. Pulling a magazine from her leg sleeve, she ordered, "Lock and load!" The troops on her shuttle did their best with the space they had and managed to get magazines inserted while keeping their safeties engaged.

She knew they were getting close.

"When the deck drops, you're going to run like hell is chasing you. Straight on the target line I give you, then fan out at fifty meters and establish a defensive perimeter. Are you ready?"

The response was lukewarm at best. They were afraid. "Remember your training." She tightened the chin strap of her helmet and checked to make sure her pack was secure. "Show me your war faces!" She had to repeat it three times before she was satisfied with the response.

The shuttle bounced hard on landing, and Marcie slid down the two soldiers who had been holding her up. Thanks to being tightly packed, nobody fell despite the jarring impact. Marcie faced the rear drop deck and started to bounce in anticipation, ready to run off. The seal popped, and the deck started to lower. Marcie stepped onto it before it reached the hard, dry ground.

At least one thing went right; her shuttle had landed where it was supposed to, at the far end of a long valley. She ducked to clear the overhead and ran toward the closest threat to them, an area of trees and rough brush. If there were an enemy waiting for them, they'd be in there.

Marcie hatcheted an arm in the main direction. She felt a bullet hit her ballistic vest, but it didn't take her down or even knock her backward. She started zigzagging before dropping to a knee. "Get the fuck out here!" she screamed at the soldiers. "Keep your heads down."

She bolted laterally, physically forcing soldiers into positions on the ground. A round struck one of the soldiers in the face and he went down. "Return fire on that tree line. Range one hundred."

A few shots rang out from soldiers who had gotten into position and dropped prone. They fired slowly, trying to pick targets. The fire from the brush continued.

"Light 'em up!" She took aim and swept the tree line using three-round bursts until the bolt locked to the rear on an empty mag. She reloaded in a clean movement, pocketing the empty mag for reloading before sending more ammo downrange. The soldiers picked up what they were supposed to do and followed suit. The fire from the tree line stopped.

"You and you, with me." Marcie pointed at two soldiers and gestured for them to get up and follow her. She ran toward the tree line, zigging and ducking while carrying her rifle ready to fire. No one knew her Jean Dukes Special was tucked into her pack. She had already considered taking it out, despite the Federation's limitation on the rules of engagement. She had lost the first soldier within seconds of landing, so she wasn't about to play around when she could finish the enemy with little more than a thought.

The shuttles continued to plow into the deck, landing the entirety of the force from *Angkmoor*. Farther down the valley, clouds of shuttles delivered troops and equipment from the other transport ships. It was an impressive display of force as nearly eight thousand troops landed almost simultaneously.

Yet, Marcie cared only about the sector assigned to her shuttle, and even smaller than that, the woods where she and two soldiers were headed to clean out an enemy. She hit the brush line at a dead sprint, but the other two had fallen back. She vaulted high to clear the initial obstruction and landed in a clearing beyond to find a trio of enemy thoroughly perforated from the volume of fire poured into the brush that acted only as concealment and not cover. The bullets had passed through it.

Kor'narians—black-shelled bugs bleeding black ichor

that looked like large ants with wasp heads. Marcie moved behind a tree to listen, but the soldiers were blundering through the brush. She held up a fist for them to freeze, but they weren't looking her way. "Stop and get down!"

They threw themselves to the ground, eyes wide, looking for the imminent threat. The bugs' legs were stick-thin. She wondered if they made any sound when moving since their pinpoint feet wouldn't break twigs or slap the ground. Marcie scanned the trees beyond and caught a slight buzzing, only possible to hear because of her enhancements. She turned her head to get a direction from which the sound was coming.

"Stay here," she whispered, putting a finger to her lips for emphasis, then moved sideways, crouching before quickly diving into the brush.

Marcie ran perpendicular to her target before rushing in. The insectoid that had been watching saw her too late. It tried to raise a weapon, but she tackled it and kicked the slug-thrower away. It had arms with small, harmless pincers at the ends, but the forearms were shelled, with razor-sharp backs. It stood shorter than a human on four legs and maneuvered through three hundred and sixty degrees easily. Marcie kept it in front of her, away from the brush where it might manage to escape.

"I'm Colonel Walton from the Trans-Pacific Task Force. I need you to stop fighting. You will not be harmed." The Kor'narian's big iridescent eyes were opaque to her, so she couldn't tell where it was looking. She darted in to see its response, then moved laterally to keep it centered in the small area. "Can you understand me?"

It clicked and buzzed a response. Every soldier'd had

their translation chips updated while they slept. She should have been able to understand it.

"I can't understand you. Can you speak a different dialect?"

It started again, but this time the words came through. "Invaders. Go back to space. You are not welcome here."

"Thank you for that, but no. As a Federation member, Kor'nar has become unstable, requiring an intervention. That's us. Stop fighting, establish a peace that lasts, and we'll leave. Go tell your queen I want to talk to her. She needs to talk to me. We don't want to kill any more of your people, but we will defend ourselves while forcing you to stop. That's the first step toward peace."

"You don't know why we fight," the insectoid replied.

"Then help me understand. Which hive are you?"

"Zirric." It rubbed its legs together.

"Go and tell your queen. I'll be out there. Approach us unarmed, and you will not be shot. How will I recognize your queen?"

"You will know if she comes," the insectoid replied.

Marcie took that as a sign it would pass on the invitation. She stepped aside and let it disappear into the brush, then listened intently before picking up the insectoid's weapon and returning to collect her two soldiers. When she appeared, one of the privates fired in her direction. He pulled up at the last second and sent the round into the air.

"Get your shit under control!" she snarled. "Now come on."

She stormed past them and back into the open. "Colonel Walton, coming in!" she shouted at the defensive perimeter. Slinging her rifle to show that it was safe,

Marcie made a beeline for the senior NCO. "Take the soldiers into the brush and establish a watch post. Do not fire unless fired upon. Do you understand me? And give me a two-man work party to put our injured in the shuttle."

"Yes, ma'am." He didn't sound confident in his answer.

"I've invited their queen to talk to me. It wouldn't do to shoot her or her people. I'm assured she looks different. Please keep an eye out and don't do anything that'll extend this war any longer than it needs to be. I already don't like it here. I'll contact the medical support team and see where they are."

"I understand." He headed out to issue the orders.

She walked around the shuttle and scanned the landing field. The emergency medical flag was already up. At least one group had their shit together. It was over a kilometer away, but they wouldn't be able to help the dead private. Two soldiers reported for casualty duty. "Get the stretcher out of the shuttle and take the private to that flag." Marcie pointed. "Then get your asses back here. We still have a job to do. Don't forget where we parked."

The two saluted and ran off. "No saluting in the field!" she shouted after them.

Kae, are you out here?

Depends on what you mean by "out here." I'm planetside, giving the locals a reason to run for their lives. We took fire on landing, but that didn't last long. One mech could probably level both forces, but I needed to hold them at bay while we unloaded a company of heavy metal. They will be operational shortly. Artillery is on the other side of the valley. Jake is having them set up *dead center in a circle, so they can engage targets in all directions.*

I fear 'tis true about the one mech, but we don't get to do as we would like. I had a run-in, killed three, and talked to one from the Zirric hive. I was hoping for something a little closer to the Naries' queen so we could talk strategic direction. I need the planetary government to step back.

Keep your head down, and I'll see you later. I have to make sure the armor doesn't drive into each other or over a prized insectoid gourd patch.

They eat gourds? Marcie wondered, but Kae was already off chasing his people around the staging area.

Marcie headed out, encouraging the troops and making sure they were alert to the threat.

She needed to consolidate information. Paithoon was setting up a temporary command post. Where were the drone operators? She wanted eyes in the sky. Where was her exec? Where were the minions?

She had put a flat structure into place because the Lion Corps was limited to fifteen forward thinkers with an extra ten potentials. That wasn't a big number for a force ten-thousand strong, and she didn't want to take a leader off the front lines to be her runner.

Jake, are you out there? Marcie called. *Anyone else take fire?*

I'm here. We have a solid perimeter. I've launched the first two recon patrols to the top of the hills due east.

We need to start consolidating data. Kae?

Stand by, Kae replied. *Go ahead, but make it quick. I froze the armor in place, but they need to set up on the four corners of this valley to improve our response time.*

We need to build a battle board.

I have scans of the entire area, Kae replied. *Seventy-four hundred thirty-one troops on deck. In the surrounding hills, there is minimal insectoid presence, total of about a dozen. I don't have a view beyond the surrounding hills. I advise we compress within this valley and spread east and west to secure the opposing hill-tops. We need the high terrain and an internal line of communication across the valley.*

Sergeant Major Monsoon joined the conversation. *I concur. My compliments to you all. This wasn't the massive clusterfuck I anticipated.*

The day is still early, Crantis, Marcie replied. *Let's get that orientation change going. This is where we'll stay until we figure out the best location between enemy lines as a barrier to hostilities. I've invited the Zirric queen to talk to me. We'll see if she comes, but our people better not shoot anyone waving a flag of truce.*

I'll get the word out and start rolling up the flanks to expand our presence to the east, Jake noted. *You've already talked to the locals?*

The locals killed one of the soldiers on my shuttle. Most of them did not survive the encounter. Our people did fine, even after the soldier went down. I have high hopes.

I need to get the armor rolling, Kae interjected. *I'll personally head to the top of the western hill to give you the best picture and then return to the central compound by the field medics. I'll report when I have something. Kae out.*

Marcie continued across the wide plain, making sure the soldiers were alert and staying down. She contacted shuttle control. *Take sixty of the shuttles back to space, fifteen from each transport, for the next wave to start loading supplies and equipment. Take any wounded needing more than a quick bandage with you. Take the dead, too, and put them on ice for our return to Belzimus.*

The grim business of running a war did not detract from the overall feeling of what they'd accomplished. A random shot came from the forest, and the soldiers responded with a massive volume of fire, shredding limbs and branches.

As with all green troops, they were firing too high because they were looking over their rear sight post to observe their targets within the front sight. "Aim lower!" she bellowed to get their attention. A second wave of shots poured into the tree line at body-level.

"Cease fire," she called, hurrying up to them to find a corporal or a sergeant. She grabbed the first soldier who wasn't a private. "Take a team into the trees and check it out, then get back here. Don't shoot each other!"

She left him to it and continued her tour of the area. Sixty shuttles lifted off in small waves on their way back to the motherships.

Fewer shuttles would be easier to defend, and she needed lift for supplies. The sooner she could get hot chow to the troops, the better morale would be. Judging by the touch-and-go nature of the Kor'narians, the Trans-Pac was going to be there for a while.

Clear on top of the western hill, Kae reported. *A small company, maybe forty insectoids, hightailed it as soon as they spotted me. They headed west-southwest, for reference. We'll need the drones if we want to find their camps. I'm sending one now and keeping it so high they won't spot it. From everything I can see, they have pulled out. We have this valley to ourselves.*

Get back down here and redirect the western line to establish the perimeter on the far side of the hill. Move a tank platoon to the top and start digging in.

Marcie grabbed a company's flag with guidon and planted it in the ground where she wanted the southern line to be established. She'd use the valley's north and south entrances as the avenues of approach for any delegations. The troops wouldn't have itchy trigger fingers if they had time to think.

She ran across Lieutenant Gamon. "Hey! I need you to reorient our base camp."

"We're going to set it up here?"

"I'm not sure about that yet, but our temporary base camp is going to start right where that guidon is planted. That will be the southern limit. I need you to pull the troops back past this location. The troops on the east and west flanks are going to move up those hills. We will have secure internal lines and a broad landing field that allows visitors to come from either direction if we have the geography figured out. Zirrics are that way," Marcie pointed to the south before facing the other direction, "and Naries are that way. They all look the same to us, so that's a way to keep things straight in our humanoid brains."

"Roger that. I'll take care of it, ma'am." The lieutenant headed out. Marcie went the other way, looking for the field medics so she could share a few kind words with those who had been hurt and get a count of the dead, then start building an intelligence picture. She had high hopes that the Zirric queen would show. It was the only way to kickstart the process. She needed to drag the two parties to the table, even if she had to kidnap them.

CHAPTER TWENTY-TWO

War Axe, **Hangar Bay**

"Dad didn't come with you?" Cory asked as she studied her mother's elbow where the wound should have already healed.

"He wanted to come but couldn't. The fight is down there, and the Bad Company needs to win it."

"They need to win every fight they're in," Cory replied. She held her hand close to the injury, and the space between started to glow blue. The intensity increased from Cory's side and stopped once it reached Char's skin. Cory concentrated and the blue glow took on its own aura, expanding and spreading. It found traction around the wound and then moved in like a door had been opened.

Char sighed, and the lines around her eyes softened and smoothed out as she relaxed with the release of pain.

The blue glow faded until it disappeared, then Cory stumbled and her chin drooped. Char caught her daughter and guided her to a chair by the Pod-docs. Using her gift tired her, but this was extreme. The effort she had expended to heal what should have been a flesh wound was immense.

"I know what it was. The Skrima rounds act as an Etheric inhibitor, even though it was a physical bullet that hit you. You continued to hurt because it was an untreated injury. You are so used to your nanos fixing everything that you don't know what an injury feels like." She smiled and shook her head as she started to drift. Char caught her, picked her up, and carried her like a child to her quarters.

Across the hangar bay and up the stairs, down the corridor and into Cory's quarters. Char deposited her in bed and walked out, stopping to look at the old-style photo in a frame that stood on her daughter's desk. "Soon, you will be avenged. We *will* eliminate the Skrima in this dimension," Char whispered.

She had Smedley send a note to TH reporting her return to full health and headed to the bridge, where she found Micky pacing.

"Ship still broken?" Char asked.

"No estimate on repair time either. *Ramses' Chariot* has taken up the slack. The Black Eagles are on their way back because the Skrima have disappeared."

"That's disconcerting." Char closed on the tactical display, but there was nothing to see. "What about the mother of all bombs?"

"That's the bright spot in this mess. It is close to ready, or so I'm told."

"Anything I can do to help?"

"I don't know what that would be unless you can fix the breakdown in attitude control. We still haven't found the problem."

Char scowled. "Show me the system."

Smedley took care of it by displaying the technical drawings of the attitude control systems.

"Please highlight the junction boxes, relays, transformers, and other switching and distribution elements that are not for primary power."

Micky stopped pacing and joined Char in looking at the main screen. "What are you looking for?"

"Call it a hunch. Why don't you put the ship on alert?"

"That's some hunch." Micky returned to his captain's chair and spun up the alarms and flashing lights.

"Smedley, give me ship-wide broadcast, please," Char requested.

The captain gave the nod and Smedley connected her.

"All hands, I believe there is a Skrim on board. Since we moved out from under the Etheric jammers, the creature is now able to phase in and out, making it extremely difficult to kill. Bundin, deploy your people near the stairwell of Decks Three and Four. I'll meet you on Four and we'll move forward. I have reason to believe we're looking for it near the secondary relays somewhere between frames three hundred and five hundred. Find shelter, and do not be alone. We need you to work in teams."

Char faced Micky. "Can you take us below the satellites?"

"We'll have to make a racetrack since we don't have thrusters to hold us in place. Forward momentum is important to keep us from being pulled down, where we might start spinning and be unable to correct it. In the black and white world of good and bad, that would be bad."

"Do what you can. We'll try to fix the problem that

doesn't want to stay fixed." Char loosened her pistols in their holsters and walked out.

Alarms blared in the corridors.

On the fourth level, she ran into Bundin. "This way. Be ready. If we see a Skrim, it'll be quick. Who's on the third level?"

"K'Thrall and Slikira."

"Good. Chris, why don't you join them? Bundin, B'Ichi, and I will take this level. Heads on a swivel."

"Yes, ma'am!" the Harborian replied and hurried down the stairs.

Char looked at Bundin. "Sometimes, I envy you. No one is going to sneak up on a Podder."

"No one," Bundin rumbled through his vocalization device.

Char strode briskly past him and the tall Keome in his heat suit on her way down the main corridor before branching to the smaller corridor that ran alongside the interior of the heavily armored double-walled hull. The thruster controls were between the hulls in a space filled with supplies and raw materials to feed the production machinery.

Char checked and couldn't see into the Etheric, but she wanted to be sure. *Micky, are we below the satellite jammers yet?*

We passed under them a couple minutes ago. We're going to spin in tight circles to hopefully not fly into a gap in the coverage.

"You follow us as we move forward," Char said. She popped an access hatch and stepped through into a narrow corridor that traveled between the two hulls for maintenance access. Char looked aft before walking forward. B'Ichi followed her in and secured the hatch.

Char took out both her pistols. B'Ichi shouldered his railgun. "Be careful with that thing in here," she warned.

"Of course, ma'am," he replied.

They started moving forward, crossing bulkheads and breaks that prevented them from looking too far ahead. They reached the first relay and actuator and Char examined it. "Looks like somebody tried to get into it."

Scratches on the outside of the panel didn't look like they had been made by a tool. She didn't have any wrenches or screwdrivers with her to open it and check for internal damage. Once she was sure the area was clear, maintenance could double-check everything. Her suspicions had been triggered because relays that had been repaired had failed later. That shouldn't happen on a starship like the *War Axe*. She'd concluded it had to be intentional.

There was only one entity that wanted the *War Axe* out of the way.

Char stopped checking the evenly spaced junction boxes and relays. She wouldn't find her enemy in those. He was somewhere; she could feel it, even though she was as blind as he was, leveling the playing field.

Third deck team, we are at frame five hundred fifty, Char reported to the warriors below.

Six hundred, Slicker replied. Her voice over the comm chip didn't contain the heavy sibilants of her Ixtali accent. *Catching up.*

Char started to slow down but saw movement. Galvanized into action, she bolted, leaving the Keome standing there. She twisted around a bulkhead and fired at the red form disappearing down a ladder.

I see it. A Skrim at frame 530 descending to Deck 3. I'm following.

Bundin moved toward the stairs, his odd shuffle accelerating him faster than an average human could run.

B'Ichi caught up with Char as she was throwing herself down the ladder. She fired past her leg, and the Skrim dove off the ladder and into the third-deck maintenance accessway. It turned aft but stopped when it saw Slikira coming toward it. She fired her railgun, and the hypervelocity dart bounced and echoed its way forward. She didn't attempt another shot.

The Skrim opened the hatch and dove into the corridor, nearly landing on K'Thrall, and grabbed the railgun, keeping the barrel where the Yollin couldn't fire. The Skrim slashed K'Thrall's front carapace, splitting it open. With a thrust, the Skrim kicked over the four-legged Yollin, leaving him gasping in agony.

It ran aft past the operations center and toward the engine room. Char jumped into the corridor to find K'Thrall down. "Get him into the Pod-doc," she ordered, pointing at Chris. "Slicker, with me."

Char and the Ixtali ran aft. In the distance, the Skrim continued to run, outpacing them.

Bundin jumped out of the stairwell and into the path of the Skrim. Bundin took aim with one of the pistols from Tissikinnon that fit in his tentacle-hands. He fired and hit the Skrim, but behind the creature, Char and Slicker were advancing, and they were in the line of fire. Bundin charged, raising his shell to ram the Skrim. It slashed, but a Podder shell was tougher than a Yollin's carapace.

The attack left an ugly crease but didn't penetrate. At close range with a bulkhead as a backstop, Bundin fired in rapid succession, but the Skrim was dodging and diving as if twisting through a maze. Bundin finally hit the creature, then a shot rang out from nearby, and the Skrim bucked from the impact. It dove over Bundin's shell, hit, and rolled into the stairway, where it popped to its feet and headed down.

Bundin bolted after it, with Char right behind him. She fired past Bundin's stalk head to hit the Skrim again.

It continued to run but left blood splatters as it passed. Char stopped and leaned over the stairs to take potshots as it descended. She thought she hit it but couldn't be sure.

Bundin continued the chase, running down the wide stairwell so quickly it looked like he was floating. The Skrim hit the hangar level and headed into the bay. Bundin got a clean shot and fired, hitting the Skrim in the middle of its back. It stumbled but stayed upright, then staggered forward. Cory popped out from behind the emergency Pod-docs, ran two steps, and swung the chair she was carrying.

It hit the Skrim in the face, flipping the creature as its feet went out from under it and it landed flat on its back. Cory screamed as she swung again and brought the chair down on its chest. It grunted, and blood frothed from its red lips. Its eyes glowed as it glared at her. Dokken stood over it, barking and slavering. "Cryopod," she said. The device landed next to the Skrim. "Please put the injured into stasis. Step back, Dokken."

The cryopod used its spatula-like scoop to pick up the Skrim and secure it inside. The lights flashed briefly before turning solid green. Dokken panted and dog-smiled.

Bundin reached her first, followed quickly by Char. "You didn't kill it," Char said.

"It wouldn't bring Ramses back. I am a healer, after all, so I'm not fond of taking lives. That being said, I'm sure R2D2 would like to study this specimen and learn what makes it tick."

"They might not be restrained about injuring the captive."

"I can't be bothered by how scientists explore their craft." She winked at her mother before turning serious. "Is anyone hurt?"

"K'Thrall was messed up, but they should have already put him in the ship's Pod-doc."

Micky, scratch one Skrim. Get us into a higher orbit, and get your crews back into those ducts. When they fix something this time, it should stay fixed. Once we're out of the jammers' influence, I'll take a look around the ship and see if there are any more infestations. Then I'm heading back to the planet.

No need, Micky replied. *TH and most of the company are on their way here. He said he has a plan.*

Nadezhda Station, in orbit above Benitus Seven

The last time he asked for an update, Ted looked like he wanted him to electrocute himself with another power supply, so Timmons had called out the big guns and stood back to watch.

Felicity sauntered into the lab. Ted stopped what he

was doing when he saw her approach. Torn between continuing to work and talking to his wife, he finally arm-wrestled himself into doing the right thing. He put the torch down and smiled at Felicity.

"Are we almost ready to go home, dear?"

"Almost. Another two hours and I should be ready to run a simulation. After Plato and I analyze the data, we'll run one more, then we'll be able to move it to the ship and take it to the planet's surface. Eight hours and thirty minutes until we can leave."

"And then?" Felicity leaned back and looked down her nose at her husband.

"Then we'll have to come back here to funnel the power into the systems. That'll be another day. After that, we'll be able to go."

"They say Terry Henry is having a bomb built using a plasma generator or some such nonsense to send underground and flush out the Skrima."

"The Skrima are underground?" Ted asked.

"Yes! Terry, Char, and Christina were all trapped, and no one heard from them. It was a trying time for us all."

"But Char's here with us?"

"Remember, she took *Iracitus*, but he's back now."

"Yes. I remember that. When was that? It couldn't have been more than an hour or two ago."

"It was yesterday, dear. Ted, Ted, Ted. You and your projects, losing track of time. This is why I am down here. We have completed our survey, and I'm ready to go."

"Then you should. Have Iracitus take you back to the *War Axe*, get a hot meal, and sleep in our bed."

"I want to sleep in our bed with you," Felicity drawled.

Timmons couldn't help but keep listening.

"Tomorrow, if I can get back to work now. Go back now, and I will join you as soon as I'm able to finish this project." Ted brightened. "This will be the only one of its kind. Plato is documenting everything for publication with R2D2 to establish a power baseline for planetary energy supplies. Think about it. No planet, no matter how small, would lack the energy to grow."

"That is truly amazing, Ted dear. *You* are amazing, and when you get back to *War Axe*, I'll show you how much I love you. Until then." She kissed him as passionately as if they hadn't been married for a hundred years, then strolled out, slowing when she reached Timmons. "You have your timeline, so you are now on your own. I'm going for a shower and a hot meal. Toodles."

Timmons chewed his lip. He and the rest of the pack had to stay to carry the device to the ship. Felicity was out. "It could be worse. It could be raining," Timmons mumbled and held his hand out, expecting the water to pour down on his head.

He went upstairs to tell the others, leaving Ted alone. He probably wouldn't notice. In eight hours and twenty-five minutes, he and the others would show up to provide manual labor.

Ted finished early. Maybe Felicity had convinced him to pick up the pace. Regardless, the werewolves were there, carrying whatever Ted told them to carry. He had not gotten the lift working, but the pack didn't care. Seven flights of stairs were nothing if it meant they could get off the station.

Ted waited until the three others returned before directing them in how to carry the rig, which was about the size of a double refrigerator and ten times as heavy.

"Grab a corner, Ted, because we can't get it by ourselves," Timmons said.

Ted hemmed and hawed for a moment before taking over. "Timmons. You are the strongest of us and need to shoulder the greatest weight. Merrit and I will lift the corners. Sue and Shonna on that end, which is lighter, and they'll go up the stairs first. We will have to carry the majority of the weight unless you want to wait for me to fix the elevator."

"Nope." Timmons's reply was definitive, and none of the others disputed it. "On three, bitches, heave this big bastard. By the way, thanks for the compliment, Ted. I didn't know you had it in you."

"What compliment?"

"Two. Three," Timmons said, shaking his head until they started to lift the beast. Timmons thought his arms were going to rip from their sockets, but he wasn't about to show any weakness. He grunted through it. They managed to get it up and struggled through the doorway and onto the first steps. Sue and Shonna backed up, step by step.

Timmons' eyes bulged with the effort and his face turned red. Ted and Merrit started panting and grunting with the increased effort. "Go!" Timmons gasped.

They forced their way up one flight, then two. By the time they reached the third landing, they had to put it down.

Timmons rubbed his hands, encouraging the nanocytes to take the pain away, then stretched and massaged his aching muscles. Only four flights and one corridor to go. Together, the five werewolves looked upward as if staring at an impossible climb.

"We're fucking engineers!" Merrit blurted. "Well, not me. I'm a chemist! But fuck, people. We have to know a way to make this easier. I'm afraid I'm going to drop it and then Ted will have to start over. I don't want to spend another three days on this station. I'd rather chew off my foot."

Shonna exaggerated her nod. Being on the lighter end had been no picnic. "I don't want to carry this thing anymore," she admitted.

"Fine," Ted declared. "You've been throughout the station. Are there any rollers, cables, or sliders that we might be able to use?"

"There's nothing here. Everything is solid. If they had chairs, they loaded them onto their ships whenever they left. Everything else is virtual, using that three-dimensional system of theirs."

"Once this is in place," Ted tapped the top of his device, "I'll bring the system back online. It'll return to its former glory. The Benitons were not the builders of this place. It has been here for far longer than they've been on the planet."

Merrit looked at Timmons, ignoring Ted. "What's on *Iracitus* that we can use?"

Iracitus, we need to move an obscenely heavy box to the ship. Is there anything on board to help us? Timmons asked.

Of course, the AI responded immediately. *You can use the grav plates used to direct the explosive charges when collecting core samples. With the Etheric power supply, two of them will support approximately two metric tons at standard gravity.*

Timmons tried not to feel like a moron but failed. He held up a finger to declare his revelation, but it withered when he saw their looks.

"We heard," Sue said.

Discretion being the better part of valor, he decided retreat would be prudent. "I'll be right back." He ran up the steps and continued to the ship, bringing back four grav plates to better balance the load.

After he returned and they were installed, Ted activated the system's power supply, and the device lifted easily off the deck. Timmons pushed it by himself up the stairs, taking care not to make eye contact with the others. He flew down the corridor, skidding to a stop to slow the load before it slammed into the outer bulkhead, then maneuvered it onto *Iracitus*. The others boarded, and the ship buttoned up and flew away from Nadezhda before the passengers were seated.

Ted accessed the comm system. "*War Axe*, this is *Iracitus*. We are headed to the rift to install the power conduit. I will shut down the jammers before the installation so I can power the device and calibrate it. Please provide support personnel for the effort."

"Turn off the jammers?" Char replied from the *War Axe*. "Is there any way we can do this without turning them off?"

Ted looked at the console. He hated answering questions twice. "I would not have said I needed to turn them off if I didn't need to do so. They have to be off."

"There are a lot of Skrima down there, Ted. I'm not sure we can protect you. Terry Henry just arrived. I'll turn him around and have him meet you there. Also, we're going to send a massive bomb into a Skrima-infested cavern. You might want to hold off your approach until after we deliver the warhead."

"Standing by," Ted replied. He pulled out his datapad to look at a series of calculations. He and Plato discussed the best way to calibrate the device for optimal efficiency.

"Anybody got their gear?" Timmons asked. Everyone shook their head. "Iracitus, please take us to the *War Axe*. We need weapons and armor if we're going to the planet and the Skrima are still down there. Even you, Ted."

He waved them off, still working with Plato. Ted couldn't be bothered with his own safety. He left that to others.

"*Iracitus*, this is the *War Axe*." Terry Henry's voice was unmistakable.

"Go for *Iracitus*," Timmons replied, pasting on a smile. "And before you ask, we're on our way to you right now. We need our gear before we go to the planet."

"Good call. You can watch the MOAB deliver the wrath of the Bad Company."

"Mother of all bombs," Iracitus clarified for those on his ship.

"See you there, TH. I look forward to it. I miss blowing shit up like we used to back on Earth," Timmons replied. Sue shook her head at his sincerity.

"We blew up a lot of shit back then, not the least of which was the Eiffel Tower. The good ol' days when we didn't know about Skrima or Ten or any of these other take-over-the-galaxy jack weasels."

"Or All Guns Blazing."

"Love me some AGB. See you in a few, and then we'll drive that big bastard into the Skrima's heart."

CHAPTER TWENTY-THREE

Kor'nar, Trans-Pacific Task Force Expeditionary Camp

Marcie nibbled on a protein bar, trying to make it last. She knew she'd still be hungry when she finished, but leaders ate last. That was Terry Henry's incontrovertible rule.

Kaeden's mech was parked near the solar charger, topping off the power. He didn't have one of the Etheric-powered suits because he knew he wouldn't be able to get it repaired if anything happened.

Jake and Monsoon leaned against one of the two tables in the command tent and looked at the tactical map. Instead of a screen, it was a poster-sized sheet of paper taped to a metal board with hand-drawn topography and magnets representing the units' tactical dispositions. On the side, there was a chart for tallying numbers that mattered to the commander. Injured and killed. Resupply. Ammo status for heavy weapons. General unit status. Simple but effective when running a war from inside a tent.

"How are we doing?" Kae asked.

"We have six patrols out right now. We've seized the high ground overlooking the valley and have a tank platoon positioned on each. Reorienting this infantry behemoth is taking longer than I want, but I can tolerate that, for now, anyway. Artillery is set in, but we need to test-fire a few rounds to make sure the theodolites are giving us good graduations."

"I'll take care of it," Monsoon said and headed out. Wiriya was waiting outside. "What are you doing out here?"

"Giving the leadership their privacy, Sergeant Major."

"If you're going to be a runner, you need to know what's going on. Get in there!" Monsoon smacked him on the back as he hurried into the tent. The sergeant major nodded with a half-smirk before heading for the centrally located artillery emplacement. It was surrounded by the entirety of the task force because the Kor'narians didn't have their own artillery for counterbattery fire. Colonel Walton wanted to use that to her advantage by centralizing their assets for optimal engagement through three hundred and sixty degrees.

Monsoon started whistling as he walked away. He was at home there as any place he'd ever been.

Wiriya stopped inside the tent flap as Marcie, Kae, and Jake looked at him. Kae waved him over to stand next to him.

"What do we expect to learn from the foot patrols?" Kae asked.

"Is asking that they discover the complete disposition of both the Zirric and Naries forces too much?"

"Maybe a little, but it's not too much to hope for. We will eventually get eighty percent of that. We'll never have the full picture, but we'll make do." Kae crossed his arms and leaned back against the table. The initial force disposition was north to south, and now they were set up east to west. "Probably something we should have anticipated initially."

Marcie didn't understand his change in thought. "You mean, the force dispositions? No way we could get those remotely."

"I mean the setup of the task force from left to right, encompassing the high ground on both sides of the valley instead of filling it. But they don't have arty, so the high ground is of relatively little use to them."

"They have portable rockets," Wiriya added.

"They do, and I'd like them to use them so we can get a visual on the combatants," Kae stated. "Right now, it's more like camping than a war, although the landing was most impressive. Maybe that alone scared them straight?"

Marcie snorted. "That alone? I'm thinking no." She turned back to the board and touched the markers for the forward observation posts. "They follow a hive hierarchy. Maybe we're not in their areas of influence, so we can't see them."

The tent shook when the cannon fired, and those within flinched as the concussive wave blew past. Marcie shook her head to clear the ringing. A second cannon belched its fury, then a third. Into the silence that followed, someone yelled, "Clear."

Thirty seconds later, the sergeant major strolled back

in. "Bullseyes on the setup, ma'am. We can bracket a single bad guy at twenty klicks."

"I'm going to have to rethink the command tent location." Marcie fixed the sergeant major with her colonel's stare. He clasped his hands behind his back and started to whistle, looking anywhere but at her.

A commotion began somewhere outside the tent.

"More people unhappy with the cannon cockers interrupting their beauty sleep?" Marcie quipped. Wiriya pushed away from the table and rushed outside to discover what was happening. He ran face-first into an infantry private.

"Sorry, sir!" he blurted before realizing Wiriya was a corporal. "A bug party is coming down the valley. They aren't carrying weapons."

"Thank you, Private. Make sure nobody shoots them. I'll be there momentarily. Run like the wind," Marcie ordered.

He saluted and ran off.

"No saluting in the field," Kae yelled after him.

"Get me Paithoon and have him meet us on the southern perimeter."

"Roger on Paithoon." Wiriya disappeared outside.

"Shall we, gentlemen?" Marcie gestured toward the tent flap.

"Ma'am, may I suggest that two of us stay back in case it's a trap?" the sergeant major offered. "Colonel Braithwen and Major Kaeden."

Marcie looked at Kaeden with a hint of pain in her eyes. The sergeant major was right, but she wanted Kaeden watching for things she would miss. "Jake, you know Crantis is right."

Kae leaned back against the table. "I'll only be a call away. My armor is charged and ready to go if there is any duplicity."

"Duplicity, indeed. We need none of that, so let's see if the good guys are coming out to play."

She and the sergeant major made a beeline through the camp. Soldiers performing a wide variety of tasks made themselves scarce as the two strode through, and they made short work of the two-kilometer walk. When they reached the southern boundary, they found that the delegation had stopped.

"They said I would know the queen. They were right." Marcie thanked the troops as she stepped around fighting positions that were nowhere near deep enough.

"These need to be deep enough so if you're standing, it hits you mid-chest," Crantis prodded gently, but his words left no room for misinterpretation. He pointed at a sergeant. "Make it so."

Marcie stopped and turned. "Where the fuck is Paithoon? I have a mission for him, and he's nowhere to be... Never mind. There he is."

Wiriya had a hand on his back and was prodding the protocol officer forward. Paithoon looked more than uncomfortable but less than afraid.

When he arrived out of breath, Marcie didn't give him a chance to speak. "Come with us and keep your mouth shut. If we need something like a table and chairs, your job will be to make them magically appear."

"How am I supposed to do that?" Paithoon was flustered. He looked like he'd been sleeping.

Monsoon leaned close. "I don't care if you have to pull them out of your ass. Pay attention, and don't embarrass us." Marcie and Crantis marched forward in step to meet the Zirric queen.

Paithoon kept up by half-running but stayed behind them, out of sight of the Kor'narians.

When they reached the delegation, Marcie bowed her head to the queen, who towered over them. She was easily twice the size of the male Kor'narians.

"I am Colonel Marcie Walton, here on behalf of the Federation to help Kor'nar establish peace."

"I am Zirric," she said through clicks and buzzes that were readily translated by the chips inside the humanoids' heads. "We have no argument with you, but already you have killed many of my people."

"We were invited to stop the conflict," Marcie explained.

The queen reared back. Paithoon cowered, but Marcie and Crantis held their ground unflinchingly. "Not by me."

"No, by the Naries. Help me understand why the two sides fight since the Federation has tasked me with resolving this conflict and returning Kor'nar to a peaceful Federation planet."

"Not your concern. Kor'narians will resolve with Kor'-narians. Outsiders are not welcome. Go now and leave us be."

The queen swirled around and walked away. Two of her minions moved between her and the task force leadership.

Marcie and Crantis stood still, watching as the delegation covered the ground to disappear back into the wooded area beyond. The final two Zirrics turned and walked away.

"I should have brought something to drink. It's dry here and a little warm," Marcie remarked casually.

"It appears our esteemed Kor'narian colleagues fear duplicity as well."

"So much duplicity. I've heard you can't swing a dead cat without hitting duplicity on this planet," Marcie replied.

"Too true, Colonel." They found Paithoon staring. "I think that went well. What do you think, Paithoon?"

His mouth fell open, and he pointed to the woods and then back to the spot where the queen had been standing. "A disaster!" he managed to utter.

"Nah," Marcie said, clapping him on the shoulder. "We established that we won't get spun up over posturing. We're here to stay. How they deal with that is now in their court. Mark this spot and move a table and four chairs out here under a tent that's big enough so the queen won't have to duck. Thanks, Paithoon. Look at you, already earning your keep."

"How am I supposed to... A tent?" Paithoon stammered.

Monsoon waved him away. "Those kinds of details are your department. Take care of it. Ma'am, shall we return to the camp?"

"A nice day for a stroll, sergeant major, but I should have brought water. Paithoon, make sure you put a few bottles of water on the table as well. Can't talk when I'm parched. Where the fuck are my drones?"

· · ·

War Axe, Bridge

"The honor is yours, Terry Henry," Micky said.

"Thanks, Skipper. Ruzfell?"

"Target is locked, Colonel."

"Outer door is open," Smedley reported.

"On my mark, prepare to launch Demon Killer One Alpha Four."

Char threw her hands up and gave TH the side-eye. He winked.

"Fire!"

They had neither seen nor felt it. If the tactical board hadn't shown an icon for the missile on the screen, they wouldn't have been certain it had launched.

"Give me a visual on the target area, Smedley," Terry requested. The main screen changed and showed clear terrain, beneath which the Skrima city sprawled within a massive chamber.

A speck appeared, and a small puff designated the point of impact. A second later, another small puff appeared like a mini dust cloud.

"The fuck?" Terry watched closely, trying to see what he had missed. "That was a little less than thrilling for the mother of all bombs. Did it explode?"

"Switching to IR." Smedley changed the screen. A blaze of red appeared, with red tendrils snaking away from the shape of the main chamber. "The bomb exploded. Here is the sequence, starting just prior to impact."

A slight pink outline showed the change in temperature of the surface rock, roughly following where Terry thought the chamber existed below. Their sensors couldn't penetrate the rock. The elements in the stone would have been of great interest to the Federation if the Bad Company didn't put the planet surface off-limits, which they intended to do. The missile entered the middle of the outlined area, and a sun-like blast, followed by burning red from the superheated air, treated the rock to a massive temperature increase.

"I'll take that as a yes, but look at those tunnels. How many Skrima weren't in the main chamber?" Terry glowered. "We're going to have to go back down there. Shit. I know no one wants to be a tunnel rat, but we need to root out the survivors." Terry looked at the deck and slowly blew out a long breath. "No time like the present. Kimber can take as many as she needs to provide security for Ted while he installs his hooyah."

"Don't let him hear you call it that," Char quipped, waving to Micky on her way out.

She relayed the instructions to Kimber. Terry Henry preferred not to use his internal comm chip for the simple reason that he didn't like it. They walked slowly down the stairs to the hangar bay, Terry lost in thought. Char stopped him and leaned her body into his. "We finish this and hang up the spurs. You stay sharp, Terry Henry Walton. Now is the time to start living."

"Maybe that's what is getting me down. Can I be happy as an AGB magnate and a businessman?"

"You already are. If we run the business across multiple stations, we'll get a yacht or a runabout with a Gate drive, something that would only be available to a person like you. Civilians don't get the best toys."

Terry chuckled. "You got that right, but it's people like *us*, not just me. It's almost never been just me. We have good kids, doing great things and making the universe a safer place for good and peaceful people."

"Have you talked to Kae lately?" Char knew he hadn't.

Terry swallowed hard. "Crap."

"Did you think to talk to Kai after Christina was saved?"

Terry held up his hands in surrender. "Focused on the battle," he admitted.

"Exactly. You do that, and everyone else does *their* jobs. It's what independence is all about. It doesn't mean you love them any less. You can spend your days running the AGB, brewing beer, drinking it, telling stories, playing in the golf simulator, and expanding the business. You've earned that. I already have an idea about what I'm going to do. Shhh. I'm not telling, not yet."

"You little vixen!" Terry hugged his wife, closing his eyes to fight back tears. Old men didn't cry less than young men. Terry appreciated what was important. He might have been bad-talking it, but that didn't lessen his emotional engagement.

"Kae is fine. They landed the Trans-Pacific Task Force on Kor'nar two days ago to stop a civil war and ensure a lasting peace, at least whatever they can set up." Char smiled, and her purple eyes twinkled. Terry never grew tired of getting lost in them.

"What? The Trans-Pacific?"

"Only Earthers think of the ocean. The rest of the galaxy will look at it as 'beyond the peace.'"

"I'm old-school," Terry admitted.

"We need old-school, but we need the new one, too. Let's go down there and take care of business."

"It's time to kick their red asses back into their own dimension. I have to admit I take a certain pleasure in splattering the devil's minions. Those are the fuckers who have haunted human dreams for eternity. Who would have guessed they are real? Not the devil, but every bit as evil. Let's suit up and finish this."

They continued to the hangar bay where both Ted and Christina impatiently waited, tapping their feet with their arms crossed. Terry held up one finger. "Gotta get dressed for success," he told them with a big smile. He had just returned, and his suit was still covered in Skrima blood and mud. He had left the back open to air out the suit, but it was still ripe. He took a deep breath through his nose. "Smells like victory!"

He climbed in and powered up. "Dammit." He switched to his external speakers. "Reloading rockets and swapping railguns." He moved to a station set up at the side of the hangar bay. Char moved over to insert the reloads. They switched places, and he topped up her shoulder launchers. They cycled them back under cover.

Christina sent a mech-suited warrior to the armory to get two new weapons. Terry and Char swapped their emptied and abused railguns for shiny new ones carrying a full load. Kai strolled out and held up two reloads and two supplemental power packs for his grandparents.

"Oh, yeah! Thanks, Kai. It's almost like you were raised right."

"Almost," the young-looking man replied with an easy laugh and a quick smile.

Terry took center stage and addressed the warriors in the hangar bay. "We've caused them a big hurt. There are tunnels that crisscross under a significant part of Benitus Seven, but there was only one Skrima cavern based on the IR variations in the stone overhead. It chaps my ass that we can't see inside the planet, but sometimes, we don't get all the intel, but we still have a mission to accomplish. It's our job to root out the Skrima survivors. We need to do that as soon as we land because shortly thereafter, the Etheric jammer is going to be turned off, and the Skrima will be able to get inside your suit. Better to kill them while they're vulnerable. Probable access points have been loaded on your HUDs. Smedley has the drop coordinates where you'll be deposited. Five-mech teams because two are not enough, as we saw last time. Five can deal with anything the Skrima can throw at us. Questions?"

"Same ROE as last time?" Capples asked.

"Kill 'em all and let Satan and the hellspawn from which they come sort them out. Next stop, fucking Benitus Seven. Load up!"

"Finally," Ted grumbled. Felicity waved to him from the hatch leading into the ship. He waved back awkwardly while looking down. Felicity continued to smile.

"God bless her soul," Timmons drawled. Sue punched him in the arm, but the werewolves wore full ballistic armor, so he didn't feel it. They carried the smaller rail-guns along with slug-thrower sidearms and kukris. It was the best they could manage without climbing into the powered combat armor.

The dropships launched the second they were ready. *Iracitus* flew out of the open hangar door and headed down after them.

In Terry's Pod, he studied the screen displaying the

tactical view of their planned deployment. The teams were heading to six different locations with Terry's and Char's team going into the tunnels surrounding the cavern city. Terry wanted to be sure the infestation had been cleansed by the MOAB.

He winced, thinking of the terms he kept using in his mind. They had been terms of evil throughout history. Genocide. Even the Skrima deserved a chance. He wrestled with his thoughts. Maybe they did, but not here. Not in this dimension. The Skrima had wiped out the Grays, and they would kill every member of the Bad Company.

The hardness of steel entered and tempered his soul. Behind his face shield where no one else could see, he snarled, "No mercy."

They hit the ground for a rapid drop and dust off. Terry ran out the back to find a three-person squad of powered combat armored warriors waiting. They'd continued to defend the tunnel against Skrima escaping even while being in the MOAB's blast area.

"Did any try to escape?"

The private bounced with excitement. "We blasted two trying to make their way out."

"What about the bomb? Did you hear it?"

"Heard it. Felt it. Nearly pissed myself. Ran for my life. You should have been here."

"Damn! From space, it looked like a dud." Terry grinned from ear to ear.

"It was not a dud," the warrior assured him.

"We're going in to see what's left and clean up any bullshit that escaped. I'm still going to need you in the tunnel running blocker. At some point in time, sooner rather than later, the jammer will be cut off. That's when the Skrima are at their most dangerous. I still think they'll use the tunnel to get out. You'll have to be ready to kill them up close because that's where they materialize to attack."

"Aye, aye, sir." The three waited for Terry, Char, and the three other mechs to head into the tunnel before following them down. Terry took point. They'd rotate to the rear every fifteen minutes. Being on point took an immense amount of concentration, and it was difficult to stay sharp over long periods of time. Fifteen minutes was sufficient.

Terry set a grueling pace, his active sensors giving him the same view he could see with his eyes since everything else was blocked. Whatever was in the rock dampening their signals, it was impenetrable. Terry put it out of his mind, launched a drone, and sent it beyond each successive bend in the passageway.

He didn't slow down until he reached the rockfall he had caused with his JDS. It was still there and as solid as the walls from which it had come. Terry stepped aside.

"Next," he called over the suit radio, "we'll clear the tunnel Capples went down last time, leaving two at the crossroads to make sure no one gets in behind us. Keep your heads on swivels, drones at max range from you, and be ready to engage. You won't have much time."

They ran back to the Y in the tunnel to head down the second off the main branch. Char launched her drone and went in first, jogging easily, not setting the blistering pace Terry had adopted. At least her elbow was completely healed, and she was back to one hundred percent. The second tunnel was uneventful. When they returned, they found the two warriors on edge.

"You saw something?"

"No, sir. More like felt something, like being watched."

"Power through. Tibbets, you're on point." She launched her drone, sent it ahead, and started loping forward. Terry brought the other two warriors with them. There were two tunnels in the direction they were going. The one they were taking led them to the initial vertical chamber access that had since been closed, and the second was the way out and already covered by another team.

Private Tibbets moved more deliberately than Char, but Terry couldn't fault her for being cautious. The warning of something watching had made Terry wonder if Ted had shut off the jammer.

He expected it and chose to drop his rifle to the sling position and pull the Damascus-steel version of the Mameluke sword he always carried while the others carried the boarding axe, magnetically attached to the mech's thigh plate. Terry's scabbard had been custom-fitted, and he often forgot he was carrying the sword, but not now. He expected they'd be forced into close-quarters combat. A Skrim that could use the Etheric was a formidable enemy, no matter how much powered armor a warrior was wrapped in.

Terry was at the end of the line. He watched the others closely, as well as the walls and the roof. He could feel it, too. The hairs on the back of his neck were standing up. His eyes darted back and forth, with a glance at his rear camera view on every pass over his HUD.

The first one appeared out of the wall from their left and dove straight into the middle mech, the one behind Char. The warrior screamed as he scrambled to bring a weapon to bear, but the Skrim was half inside the suit and had materialized with a claw out that stabbed through the warrior's body. Terry lunged past the warrior in front of him and slashed, taking off the creature's face and both arms. It howled in agony as it tried to dematerialize, but it was too injured. A thrust and a twist finished it.

One dropped from the ceiling toward Char, claws out, ready to stab into her helmet and through her head. Her lightning reaction of crouching while simultaneously punching a metaled fist upward sent the materializing Skrim into the ceiling, battered and broken. When it fell back down, she let it bounce off her shoulder on the way to the floor, dying if not already dead.

Terry lunged to the side and swung, but the Skrim had not yet materialized, so Terry's sword passed through it without harming the creature. Char placed her back against his. Tibbets had two on her. She swung her railgun, scything back and forth, trying to hit the ephemeral creatures. They kept stabbing into her suit, materializing and then pulling out. She staggered, and the suit went rigid.

Terry slashed left, catching the Skrim halfway through a transition between dimensions. It separated into two pieces, the halves dropping separately to the cave floor. Terry didn't have time to admire his handiwork. He had already moved to the second attacker, but it was already moving away and his sword passed through the space of this dimension.

Char crushed one against the cave wall as it stabbed into her suit, twisted and ripped its arm off, and then caught its head in a mechanical hand, squeezing it like a grape until the Skrim was finished. She staggered toward the next melee.

Terry charged ahead, closing with three Skrima standing as a group and watching. They phased out before he reached them. He slashed a figure-eight through the air and around his body, willing them to return and materialize. He knew they had come back when a claw stabbed into the thigh of each leg. He caught one with the sword, but the other escaped. Terry swirled the sword around him, but the damage to his legs would take a while to heal.

He protected his head while looking for the two. More appeared and attacked the group beyond. Terry screamed in frustration because he couldn't help them while he was engaged in his own life and death, cat and mouse battle with two of the creatures. They appeared in his peripheral vision and phased back out before he could strike.

"Screw it," he shouted and ran back to his people, ignoring the pain in his legs to cut between the suits and slash through the exposed red backs. He moved quickly, dodging left and right, a blur of heavy metal in motion.

Torn between multiple attackers, the remaining Skrima faded into the cave wall, leaving the havoc of their attack behind.

"Report!" Terry called.

"I'll be okay once I get this Skrima arm out of my suit and get a little time to heal."

The two others were nursing torso punctures but nothing fatal. Tibbets didn't respond. Terry bumped his faceplate against hers. She was at least unconscious.

"Unbutton her suit."

Char accessed the functions and unlocked it, but to get

her out, somebody needed to get out of their armor. Terry didn't hesitate. He backed up next to the rigid suit, creating a protected cubbyhole, and climbed out. He reached into Tibbets' suit and pulled her out, laying her on the ground. She had been butchered from the inside, but she was still alive, and her nanos were fighting the good fight.

"We need to get her out of here right fucking now."

Char turned around and held out her mechanical arms. Terry lifted Tibbets into them.

"Run like the wind," he urged. The others cleared the way and Char took off, accelerating to the maximum the suit would allow. The ground shook with each step, fading quickly as she put distance between them.

A claw punched through Terry's chest, coming out the other side. He clutched it with hands quickly numbing as a railgun fired way too close to his head, exploding the Skrim behind him. He fell to his knees, trying to stay conscious while the two warriors waged a deadly battle with the final two Skrima that were doing their best to get to the exposed human and deliver the final death blow.

CHAPTER TWENTY-FOUR

Kor'nar, Trans-Pacific Task Force Expeditionary Camp

Marcie stared at the board, deep in thought. Nothing had changed except the air recon element had been moved close, putting a monitor in the command tent so she could watch the direct feed when she wanted to. The greatest revelation was that the Kor'narians were not easy to find. For two land armies fighting a protracted war, there didn't seem to be very many of them.

She took herself to the next tent over, where the drone operators were controlling the vehicles. "Expand the search. Push it out to twenty klicks and then thirty if you have to."

"The size of each search area expands rather significantly..." the drone pilot started to explain.

"You mean something like pi times radius squared, right? Let's see, twenty-kilometer range from the center is about twelve hundred and fifty-six square kilometers, so I suggest you get to it. That's a lot of area to cover, and stretching it to thirty kilometers is more than twenty-eight hundred square kilometers. But you don't have to do a complete grid search. Focus on the most likely avenues of travel. Although they don't look like us, I bet they prefer an easy walk just like everyone else. Look for shade but not heavy brush, without a large number of elevation changes. My bet is that's where they are going to be. Still, you guys are going to be busy for a while. Better make yourselves comfortable. I'll have food sent in as soon as we get the kitchen set up in a day or two. Until then, be confident, knowing you can take care of yourselves. And find me the Kor'narians!"

Marcie nodded politely and left the drone operators to their thoughts. She hoped the guidance would help them refine their approach and reduce the time it took to search the area.

Paithoon appeared, as breathless as he usually was since he operated in a half-panic at all times. In his mind, whatever he was doing at the moment was the most important thing going on. Marcie appreciated his attitude even though her priorities were a shade different.

"Carpets!" he declared.

Marcie realized she had a hard time taking him seriously. "I'm going to give you to someone else if your first words assume I know something I don't, and even more importantly, that I care."

"The approach to the Peace Garden needs to be more welcoming. I was able to cut up a tent to provide flooring, but I need real carpets for the approach. Roll out the red carpet for our guests. Put them at ease for a better conversation. I've also managed a cornucopia for a small fruit display on the table that is also edible. These things are very important to make your guests feel welcome and give you the upper hand in the meeting chess match."

"Carpets." Marcie mulled over the word. She closed her eyes and raised her water bottle to her mouth, taking her time so she didn't feel obligated to answer Paithoon immediately. She drank slowly and wiped her mouth carefully before replying, "I think that's a great idea. I'll order some from the supply chain, but they may take a while to arrive, so figure out an alternative before cutting up any more of our tents. One less tent means someone is sleeping in the open. Anything we can do to have the upper hand. Better negotiations mean fewer rounds fired. I prefer not to engage the Kor'narians in combat since they'll lose and some of our people will die."

"That is my whole purpose for living, Colonel Walton." Paithoon performed a sweeping bow before sashaying from the tent.

Marcie stared after him for a long time before Jake entered. "What did he want?"

"To improve the Peace Garden, he called it."

"He's had people working on it all day. It's blocking our line of sight, so we moved a squad to each flank to provide overlapping fields of fire on the approach, should we get any bugs trying to infiltrate."

"The Zirrics already made contact. I think they'll be back. They got a closeup of the task force and have to realize they can't take us head-on. I expect they'll resort to hit-and-run tactics and look to piecemeal us. Double the size of the patrols and make sure no one is out there alone. We might find those individuals tortured to death to strike a little terror into the hearts of the invaders. When they find they can't separate out units they can defeat, they'll be more amenable to coming to the table."

"I agree. We need to find the Naries. Without them at the big table, there is no reason to feast."

Marcie studied her Belzonian counterpart. The colonel was enhanced, similar to her, and just like the warriors of the Bad Company, he looked younger than his physical age but not by much. It also suggested he had a heightened metabolism. "I'm hungry, too," she admitted in a quiet voice. "If we bring the kitchen down here for twenty-four/seven chow, would it be easy enough to move if we had to relocate?"

"I guarantee—what did you call them, every swinging peacock, that's it—in this army would pitch in to help. They're all hungry. Belzonian field rations are not the best tasting, and they aren't nutritious either." He made a face.

"Log that for a main hot-wash item. We can't be starving our people. At least we don't have high-intensity operations. We'd break down in a hurry if we were trying to run and gun while starving."

"I'll take care of it. Food will be a huge morale boost. I'll order an initial stock to support double rations for the next couple of days."

"The Trans-Pacific Task Force: if we're not getting skinny from a starvation diet, we're getting fat from being sedentary and trying to eat our way to victory."

"If that's what it takes to establish peace, I'll do my part." Jake smiled and headed to the logistics tent to issue the orders, rearranging priorities and bringing down the greatest invention in the history of warfare—the field kitchen.

Kae high-fived him as they passed. Monsoon nodded respectfully, and the major stopped just inside the command tent and gestured with his chin. "Queen's back."

Marcie jumped up and dashed for the doorway. "I thought I was going to start growing mushrooms from spending too much time in the dark and being fed bullshit."

"You got something to eat?" Kae asked.

"Not you, too?" They walked briskly, the sergeant major keeping pace without appearing to work at it. He scanned the area, looking for anything out of sorts, making corrections on the fly while remaining in lockstep with the Waltons.

"Let's see if Paithoon's efforts deliver anything of value." Marcie shook her head. "She's back, and that tells me she has something to say other than 'Get off my planet.' Maybe the last couple of days have demonstrated our resolve sufficiently to encourage her to come to the negotiating table."

"It's round two. What's your play?"

"Listen to her, even if I have to equivocate. I want her thinking about what a better Kor'nar looks like without giving her what she wants, which is the complete elimination of the Naries. We've already removed the option of us leaving and hinted that we wouldn't act as the Zirrics' proxy to fight the Naries. We've redefined the box within which the right options still exist. We'll find them, but how long will it take?"

Marcie sounded confident while also setting realistic expectations. It would take time to stop the conflict and change the attitudes of both sides.

"You don't play chess well, but you're good at this," Kae

told her. "I would prefer to take a few mech companies into the countryside, kick both their asses, drag them to the table, and make them shake hands."

"That would work for about five minutes, and we might have to do that at some point in the distant future. As they say, all options are on the table." Marcie pushed Kae playfully. "I'm not bad at chess. Just because your father has never let me win..."

"He never plays down to the competition, expecting instead that you'll study and rise to his level," Kae countered. "I've never beaten him either but have managed a few draws."

He smirked at his revelation. She doubted it was true.

When they reached the southern boundary of their perimeter, Marcie looked at both Kae and Monsoon.

"Consistency is good. You and the sergeant major will talk to the queen from now to forever. I'll hold the fort. Don't get lost between here and there."

Marcie laughed. "I hope we're not here forever. I guess that depends on us. Crantis, shall we?"

The sergeant major stayed to the left and one step back as they marched to the tent Paithoon had set up. She expected a tent that would cover the table, not one of the large general-purpose tents with three center poles to hold it up. Marcie tried not to get angry. Since it was arranged the long way, the tent flaps on both ends were open and welcoming. She walked through first to find the table in the center had a tablecloth and a clear-plastic-wrapped cornucopia filled with fruit. Water bottles sat at each position with a small case beside the main table holding more.

The tent had a floor of combat green canvas—another

CRAIG MARTELLE & MICHAEL ANDERLE

tent, one of the big ones. Marcie hoped the investment in troop support infrastructure was worth the effort.

The queen strolled in and stood on the opposite side of the table.

"Welcome to the Peace Garden, which is what we are calling this area. It is a place to focus on something other than war. Please, have some fruit native to Belzimus, the planet from which we come."

Marcie quickly unwrapped the presentation and handed the material to Monsoon, who made it disappear.

The queen dipped her head to the fruit and ran antennae over them. She stood up straight as if to confront her counterpart but stepped back, clicking and buzzing orders to her four guards in the dialect Marcie's and Monsoon's chips did not translate.

The guards dug in, devouring everything except a single piece of apple-like fruit. When they finished, they returned to their former positions behind and to the sides of their queen. She removed the last piece of fruit, called zinnfruit, with one of her spindly legs. It started to vibrate at a high rate of speed, and she guided her leg through the fruit, neatly cutting it in half. She pushed half toward Marcie. After the colonel picked it up and bowed her head to the queen, she snapped her piece in half, giving one section to Monsoon, who ate it quickly to satisfy protocol.

Marcie thought he might have been hungry, too. They all were. She looked forward to her first bite. She raised it to her mouth at the same time as the queen and ate.

The Zirric queen settled down, resting with her backside on the tent floor and her arms across the back of the chair at the table. Marcie took that as her cue to sit down.

"Leaders eat last," she stated with a smile. "It is the way with us, too."

"You misunderstand," the queen said, turning her head to look sideways at her people. "They are storing it for later and will regurgitate it when I hunger."

Marcie took the revelation in stride. "I have much to learn about your culture. Let us learn more about each other before attempting to change Kor'nar, shall we?"

"Why? You are here for one purpose, and that is of the Federation's making: to bring a distorted idea of peace to end a conflict that has been ongoing for multiple lifetimes. We did not sign the Federation's treaty, yet we are subjects to it. The Naries signed it on behalf of the planet following a particularly brutal campaign that tipped the balance of power in their favor. Briefly. Such a small slice of time to influence great events. I bow to the immensity of your force and the Federation's investment in Kor'nar, but the Naries are your enemy as much as they are mine. The Federation has been manipulated from the outset. What have they told you?"

Marcie contemplated the queen's words. There was no reason not to tell the truth. "We have not spoken to the Naries since our arrival. We are having a problem finding them."

The queen vibrated briefly, which Marcie interpreted as laughter.

"If you have a map, I will show you where they are. They have heavy defenses that you will not be able to see. Your people may be at risk, and when, not if, your people get injured and killed, they will make excuses about it being a mistake, ingratiating themselves while declaring us the enemy of all that is good and decent."

"We will keep open minds, and we will protect ourselves. Forgiveness will not come easily for those who injure our people while we seek to parlay."

"I wish you success while expecting the worst. That approach to things has served me well in my lifetime." The queen heaved upward until she was standing.

Marcie stood. "That is a good policy. Can you share the location of the Naries' hive?"

"Twenty-one of your kilometers north and east at the base of a granite cliff. You will find them there." The Zirric queen turned and headed out, her entourage close behind.

Marcie stayed where she was, thinking of the way ahead. The sergeant major leaned close. "Before you ask, I refuse to puke up my zinnfruit the next time you get hungry."

Benitus Seven, Eastern Sector, The Caves

Terry clutched at the claw protruding from his chest, his world sparking between dark and light as he struggled to stay conscious. He couldn't get the claw out, so he left it and drew his Jean Dukes Special from inside his blood-soaked shirt before falling to his side. He dialed to three agonizingly slowly while the mechs swung, fired, and punched, trying to catch the Skrima while they were fully in this dimension.

A red face appeared too close to him and he fired. He considered three a low setting, but from point-blank range at a soft target, the half-formed Skrim was ripped apart.

The two mechs converged to protect Terry Henry, and another Skrim dashed down the corridor while railgun fire passed through it. It disappeared beyond the cave with the destroyed vertical shaft.

"Pull it out," Terry gasped. Neither wanted to, and they couldn't decide what to do. "I said, pull it out. Don't make me ask a third time."

"Hold him," one voice said. Terry's head started to swim as a pair of heavy metal feet moved in front of him. He felt himself being lifted off the floor and propped up. He couldn't see the second warrior. Something braced his back as if he were leaning against a wall, and a searing pain announced the rapid removal of the Skrim's claw. Terry threw his head back to scream but passed out before he could exhale.

The two collected his JDS before lifting him carefully. They left the two suits since they had no choice.

The warrior cradling Terry Henry took the lead while the other lagged behind, making himself a target to draw off the Skrima while the other carried Colonel Walton to safety. He pounded down the tunnel and started to climb, switching back and forth on a relentless mission to get to the surface.

Both mech-suited warriors breathed a sigh of relief when they saw the tunnel's checkpoint. "Clear a path. The colonel's been injured. Two suits are in there, and we need to recover them. I'll coordinate after we deliver the colonel to someone who can help him."

"Roger," a corporal confirmed, not wishing to hold up the rescue party even though they had not slowed down on the approach. They passed through and continued up the tunnel.

The private dialed up his radio broadcast. "This is Private Norse. On our way out with Colonel Walton. Please have a cryopod ready for immediate use." He repeated his message a second time while continuing to run.

When he broke into the daylight, he found Char waiting for them. The dropship was already diving in for an emergency landing. A cryopod floated nearby, but the lights said it was in use. There were no others.

"Into the shuttle," Char ordered, running after the private. The cryopod loaded itself between the two mechs, and Norse put the colonel next to the cryopod. Char was already climbing out the back of her suit, dragging the emergency medical kit with her. "What happened?"

"Right after you left, the Skrima reappeared when the colonel was outside his suit. He didn't have time to get back in before they got to him. The colonel got one of them and we offed another, but one got away."

Char pressed the bandage to his chest, pushing down hard to simultaneously put pressure on the hole in his back, trying to keep the nanos inside his body even though he'd lost a lot of blood. "Hold this," Char told him. He daintily put a metal finger on the bandage. Char worked her way around the mech to get to the Pod's stock of water. She brought two bottles back and tried to feed them to Terry, but he wasn't breathing.

She started cursing at the nanos, unsure of what they were capable of or how long someone could remain dead and still be revived. She started chest compressions, holding the bandage in place while trying to move the blood around his body—exchange the good with the bad and deliver vital energy where it was needed most.

Norse contacted the *War Axe*. "We're on emergency approach. Colonel Walton is not breathing and has no heartbeat. Private Tibbets is in the cryopod. Prepare for a high-speed entrance and delivery."

The *War Axe* acknowledged the information but refused to move closer to keep a Skrim from reaching them. Their track record in resisting Skrima incursions wasn't good. The creatures had caused a great deal of damage both times they had managed to get on board.

In the shuttle Pod, the warriors would know if one stowed away and would deal with it before it could wreak havoc in the heavy destroyer. They were coming in clean. The *War Axe* faced them with the hangar bay's maw wide open and the deck clear. Smedley brought the Pod in, spinning as it traversed the majority of the hangar bay to abruptly stop, settle, and pop the rear hatch as close to the Pod-docs as possible.

After it was opened, Cory ran on board, holding her hands out before she knelt to conduct the initial healing. She closed her eyes and concentrated, and her hands glowed. Char leaned over Cory's back, hugging her daughter while watching the process. The blue glowed brightly, and the injuries immediately started contracting. Terry's chest started to slowly rise and fall.

Char moved to the side to dribble water into Terry's mouth. He needed the fluids and the energy to help his body help him. Norse moved the cryopod out to give them more room. Char rolled Terry over and Cory repeated the process, addressing the hole in his back.

TH opened his eyes, blinking against the internal lights of the dropship. "Hi, sweetie. What's up?"

She shook her head and collapsed against the bench. "You scared the hell out of us."

"It's just a flesh wound," he quipped in a rough voice. He started to breathe harder with the extra stress he was putting on his body and struggled to sit up. Neither woman fought him over it because he was not only going to sit up, but he would also stand and walk himself to the Pod-doc.

"It is okay if you sit there for a little bit." Char handed him the rest of the first bottle and he finished it, so she swapped him for a full one. He drank half of it before taking a breath.

"I almost hate to ask this, but are we winning?"

"Ted is close to activating his power supply. Christina is doing what she can, but they've ended up closing the tunnels. We got a lot of people hurt today. No dead, but the cryopods are maxed out. There are only two Pod-docs not currently in use, and you need to be in one of them." Char tried to help him to his feet.

"I need sleep more than a Pod-doc. Cory worked her magic on me, magic she has because of us. The circle of life comes back around to where it started." He gazed lovingly into Char's eyes, relaxing into the moment.

Dokken trotted up the ramp and into the shuttle. He sniffed Terry.

Into the Pod-doc with you. It'll only take fifteen minutes.

"Since when did you start telling time?"

It's what Cory told me to say. I have no idea what fifteen minutes is. Don't make me bite you.

"It's a conspiracy!"

Save that for your lawyer. I'm going to bite you now.

"I love my dog!" He winked at Dokken and reached for his big furry ears.

Dokken snapped and caught Terry's hand. His canines dug deep into the flesh, and the dog started to tug.

"That's my hand!"

Pod-doc. You wanted to do it the hard way, so you got your wish, big man. My human is stupid, but I'll keep training him because I hope he'll be worth it. At least he doesn't make messes on the floor anymore. Don't disappoint me again. I'll never live it down on the dog blog.

"The what?" Terry looked for sympathy but found none.

Cory and Char shrugged, and arm in arm, they followed Terry and Dokken to an open Pod-doc. "Get in before Dokken gets angry." Char pointed at the device.

"Fine. I wouldn't want yet another person angry with me."

You recognize that I'm a person. There is hope for you yet, human. I'll call you a work in progress.

"Why is Dokken being mean to me?" Terry smiled as he climbed in and laid back.

"I wasn't kidding. Fifteen minutes to good as new, and then we have other customers. Stop wasting time, Dad!"

"Fine. I love all three of you. See you on the other side."

The lid closed. Cory offered the one chair to her mother but Char declined, choosing to return to her suit and take it to the armory. Dokken sat at the foot of the Pod-doc, then laid down with his head between his paws.

"Thanks, Dokken. We couldn't have gotten him in there without you. I think he has more respect for you than for us."

That's not it, the German Shepherd replied. *I've worked harder at training him. It takes consistency, along with appropriate rewards for behaviors you want more of and punishment for those things he needs to stop doing. That's all.*

"Just like training a dog, then?"

Not at all. Dogs are smarter than humans. If we had thumbs, we'd get our own damn treats, but we can't because of lids. The inequity is profound.

"Isn't it?" Cory agreed. She adjusted the chair so her hand hung into Dokken's fur and absentmindedly petted him while closing her eyes and relaxing to recover some of her energy. With the Skrima running free on the planet, she knew she hadn't seen the last of Bad Company's casualties, and Christina was still on the planet's surface, trying to hunt them down.

CHAPTER TWENTY-FIVE

Benitus Seven, the Rift

The swarm came out of nowhere, almost like they had been born from Mother Benitus herself. The werewolves found themselves neck-deep in writhing red bodies. Ted screamed when a Skrim slashed across his back, and Timmons cut its head off with a clean slice. He kept his kukri razor-sharp for good reason. Timmons blocked Ted against the device, using his body to shield the scientist from the enemy.

Ted flipped a switch as he fell, and new energy coursed from the rift and through the device. The werewolves winced at the surge from the Etheric, as if all the oxygen had been removed from the air. The effect on the Skrima was even more profound. They contorted in agony, unable to move from the physical dimension. With ruthless efficiency, the pack made short work of the invaders. They staggered toward the rift, and Ted struggled to stand. Timmons and Sue took him under the arms, helped him up, and worked their way to *Iracitus*.

Once they were on board, Iracitus took over flying his ship. They raced skyward, and the relief was nearly instantaneous, improving with altitude. Shonna checked the wound through Ted's ballistic vest. The Skrim's claw had shredded it as if it were made of cotton. The ugly wound beneath had already stopped bleeding and was starting to close. The vest had stopped the claw from digging in too deeply.

Ted tapped his computer interface before staring at a spot on the wall, signifying he was communing with Plato. Sue looked at the others, holding up her hands in pseudo-disbelief. They'd known Ted most of their adult lives, and he had been consistent. They had changed, becoming more tolerant and less judgmental once Ted showed the universe the extent of his gift.

Sue rested her hand gently on his shoulder. "You do what you need to do, Ted. We'll help as best we can."

"Where are we going, Iracitus, to the station or the *Axe*?" Timmons asked.

"There appears to be some debate on this subject. We shall decide before committing."

Sue and Timmons looked at each other. They'd been working with Iracitus for a long time and had never heard him use such double-speak. "What is that supposed to mean?" Timmons had to ask.

"It means we will decide shortly. Felicity was very specific that I am to return to the *War Axe*."

"You're saying that it's you, Plato, and Ted against Felicity, and you're not winning the argument? I'm pretty sure that's what I heard."

"Possibly oversimplified, but essentially correct."

"You need to go to the *War Axe*," Sue stated. "There is no second choice."

"The problem is that the energy being funneled from the rift needs a terminus or it will back up against itself. The longer we delay, the more catastrophic the buildup."

Sue's face fell. Merrit appreciated a good explosion as much as the next chemist. "Please define 'catastrophic.'"

"Plato believes it will encompass the entirety of this star system, including sending the Benitus star into a critical cascade and making it go supernova. *I* believe it will be mostly confined to the complete destruction of Benitus Seven. Ted is leaning toward Plato's interpretation."

Sue took a deep breath. "You need to go straight to the station. There is no second choice."

"Iracitus, get me Felicity," Timmons said. The others listened with interest while leaning away from him.

"Yes?" was Felicity's simple acknowledgment that a link had been established.

"We have to go to the station. This is non-negotiable even if you're mad at me for rest of our time, which after Ted fixes this will be measured in years and not hours. We will keep him comfortable and safe so he can work, then we'll bring him home. Please, Felicity. Let us help fix this. It'll be a crowning achievement for your husband, even with everything else he's accomplished. If we blow up a star system, *that* is all he'll be remembered for. His legacy deserves better than that."

The long delay brought a vision of Felicity trying to swim through space so she could get her hands around his throat.

When she replied, it sounded like she was crying. "I

know. I am not whole without my husband. Bring him home to me as soon as you can. I won't be mad, I'll be lonely."

Timmons felt like a jerk.

Shonna spoke up. "Get on the hook and find a shoe vendor to come. Merrit and I will kick in some incentive credits. Sue and Timmons have gotten rich in the asteroid field, so hell, how about we buy some product and start our own stores?"

"And handbags!" Sue added.

"How about a dress shop? Maybe intimate apparel? Felicity's Secret has a certain ring to it." Shonna was proud of herself.

"Thank you, guys. You're good friends. I will make some phone calls and see if those vendors who didn't want to come to Keeg would consider selling to us. If Terry Henry can run a brewery, we can run a few shops for women."

"And good old-fashioned blue jeans!" Merrit offered. "Clothes for men that aren't too tight or made of vinyl, by all that's holy."

"Cool your jets, Merrit," Shonna said. "We don't want to get ahead of ourselves."

"Your crap is okay, but mine isn't? Maybe Timmons and I will start our own store." Timmons shook his head and waved his hands to say, "Don't include me in this."

"You're right, Merrit. Your idea of fashion is crap, and it's not okay. Let us take care of business, and you keep building big and beautiful ships. You love that shit."

"Not bad for a guy who isn't an engineer." Merrit gave himself props. Shonna smiled at him. It was enough. They each had their niche. She was the engineer, but Merrit had no doubt she would do fine as a fashion magnate with Sue on the books and Felicity handling the networking and marketing while Shonna took care of the supply chain, making it look like an engineered system.

The shipyard was project management more than engineering. They were each finding their niche.

Iracitus accelerated into space on a direct heading to the station. *Ramses' Chariot* was already docked at Nadezhda. Once it stopped firing, Plato sent it ahead to deliver the equipment Ted needed for the final linkup between Benitus Seven and the station.

The werewolves took off their body armor and stacked it in a corner as they prepared to hit the deck.

"Did anyone restock the food?" Merrit wondered, even though he knew the answer. "We better ask the *Axe* to send us something."

Ted piped up. "I want hot wings, pizza, and a huge Coke."

"We all want that, but we don't always get what we want, Ted. Sorry. I'll see what Jenelope is willing to whip up for the man saving a planet from imminent destruction," Merrit replied.

"Sometimes we do get what we want. I'll call Ankh. Please help me move the rest of my equipment from *Ramses' Chariot* while we wait." Ted didn't expound as he retreated into himself for a private conversation with Plato about how to save the star system.

"Now I want pizza," Merrit grumbled. Shonna slapped his arm.

"Now we all want pizza," she admitted, "but at least we

had the common decency not to say it!" She gave him the glare only a partner could give after having been together for a couple of centuries.

He leaned his head back to meet her gaze. "Men's clothes. Clothing for *men*," he reiterated.

Sue looked from face to face. "I may not be an engineer, but I know that when Ted says there will be an explosion that makes a star go supernova, I stop thinking anything is funny. Can't you guys be serious?"

"If we had a massive mirrorball near a supernova, what would that look like?"

"And no. There is nothing for us to do besides use our big muscles to carry stuff for Ted," Timmons interjected. "The ball is in his court. If anyone can do it, it's him. Have some faith. Plus, he promised pizza and wings in an hour. I'm going to irrationally get my hopes up. So there!"

"If I didn't love you guys, I'd have you all committed," Sue noted.

"Boo," Timmons jeered. "Where's the fun in that?"

Iracitus docked, and as soon as the airlock cleared, they opened the hatch and hurried through. They didn't know how much time they had, and they couldn't waste a second of it.

Kor'nar, Trans-Pacific Task Force Expeditionary Camp

Marcie, Jake, Kae, and Crantis watched the screen as the drone approached the twenty-one-kilometer point. Kae pointed at the left side of the video. "There's the cliff." As if the operator in the tent next door heard him, the drone adjusted its heading to fly directly toward the cliff. It gained altitude while the camera gimbaled to keep the base of the cliff in the center of the image.

The operator shifted from a normal color spectrum to the IR feed.

Marcie clapped. "And there we are!" The screen populated with a significant number of heat sources, weak but different from the surrounding territory. The Insectoids weren't cold-blooded, but they weren't hot, either. Marcie hurried next door. "Good job. Fly beyond them before turning back to swoop low over the Naries' hive. Let's get a good idea of the numbers we're looking at."

"Yes, ma'am," the drone operator replied, nodding. By getting the location from the Zirric queen, they'd saved themselves untold hours of burning holes in the sky. Maybe the operators could get some sleep. They'd been working nonstop since they hit the planet.

The closer view showed distinct groupings, and the small computer hooked to the feed conducted a signature count. The operator fed the info to the screen to be recorded as part of the live view.

"Twenty-five hundred," Marcie stated. "That looks like a hive. I wonder how many the Zirrics have?"

"We haven't been able to trace them back to a central location. We follow them without them knowing we're there, but they have gone a different way each time."

"No need to follow them anymore. I need to earn their trust. If I can get the queens to the table, I don't need to know where they live. Thank you, guys, for the work. Keep eyeballs on that hive, and let me know if they look like they're packing up to leave. We need them there when we deliver our more than gracious invite for them to join us."

Marcie took leave of the drone operators and returned to the command tent.

"That's a hive, all right. I suspect it's the Naries. The next big question is, how do we invite them to join us at the big table?"

Jake strolled to the map. "Recon in force. We take armor and tracked transport. Make a show of surrounding them, then stroll up and drop an engraved invitation on their front doorstep."

"I'm not sure I want them to feel threatened. I do like the idea of dropping off an invitation, though. How do we do that without being in a position to protect ourselves?"

"I'll do it," Kae said. "The suit has a full charge, so running twenty-one klicks is nothing. I'll drop it off and return. No need to involve anyone else. I doubt anything they have can affect the powered combat armor. Regardless, I'll be careful and will jet out of there before I have to hurt someone."

Marcie looked at the others. Jake liked the idea. The sergeant major didn't commit.

"Crantis?"

"Just one mech, although superior technology shouldn't intimidate them. On the other hand, they could see it as giving them the finger, as if we're saying our one guy is better than all of you put together."

"They wouldn't be wrong," Kae suggested. "Except about the giving-them-the-finger part. I want them at the table to come to an agreement, put it into place, sing one round of *Kumbaya*, and then we're out of here."

"Three options. First, a show of force, which is low risk and has a high probability of successful delivery but questionable commitment from the Naries, even though they called us. Second, we take a small group on foot for an in-person delivery and conversation. That's high-risk since we couldn't defend ourselves. Third, Kae does the drop-off. Intimidating but not completely in your face, and again, keep in mind that the Naries called us. They know the Federation has superior technology."

"There's a fourth option." Kae walked to the board, with a new addition of an arrow pointing toward the Naries. It was blue. A second arrow pointed south from the camp. It was yellow for the Zirrics. "A small group that I escort in the powered combat armor. Feel safe and have a conversation."

Marcie nodded and reached for her gear. "I'll take the option behind Door Number Four." She buckled up. "Jake, you manage the war while we're gone."

"If I had known I was going to be the stay-at-home wife, I would have stayed home!" He put his gear back down. "There is jack shit happening here, but that's better than hauling dead from the combat zone."

"Get that chow tent up so we can celebrate when we get back. If we're successful, we'll start loosening restrictions with eight hours on, sixteen off. We'll set up some ball fields and turn the soldiers loose to amuse themselves."

"So much scrogging," Jake whispered to Kaeden. "Bumping uglies, giving the dog a bone, doing the Mambo—"

"None of that!" Kae recoiled from the colonel, fighting to put space between them.

"It's how Belzonians amuse themselves. It's what we do.

Loosen up, buddy." Jake was having too much fun needling Kaeden. He'd found Kae's weakness and was exploiting it.

"I'm getting my suit on. No more muff-pie furburger talk. None of it!" Kae hurried out before Jake's witty retort skewered him.

Marcie strolled after him, tightening her helmet. The sergeant major already had his on and looked ready to go. "I hope you don't mind the child-style transportation system."

Monsoon didn't understand but didn't waste time asking. He knew he would figure it out quickly enough.

Kae ran through his warmups before bending down and crooking his arms. Marcie sat in the crook of his elbow. The sergeant major looked at her. "I can run," he offered.

"Not going to look macho enough, being carried?"

"Not in the least. I hesitate because I have an image to uphold." Monsoon stood military-rigid, back straight and chest thrust out.

"Let me down, Kae. We'll run beyond our lines, and then you can carry us."

"I find that satisfactory," Crantis agreed.

"Have it your way." Kae waited for them to start so he could follow.

With a curt nod, Marcie and the sergeant major set off at an easy pace through the camp, slowing when they reached the forward observation posts. "Hold down the fort!" Marcie yelled. "We'll be back in a while. We need to see a man about a horse."

They jogged down a hill and up the next one. After they crossed the top, they waited for Kaeden to pick them up.

They had to hang on tightly since the mech's running motion bounced them around. Marcie winced at the bruises she was being tortured with. The alternative of running alongside didn't sound so bad anymore.

Monsoon steeled his expression, but he was far more uncomfortable than he was letting on.

Marcie knocked on Kae's faceplate. "Enough! I'm going to run, or I might never be able to sit or stand ever again."

"Sorry about that. The terrain is a little rougher than I expected," Kae apologized. He pointed in the direction they needed to go and Marcie set the pace, with Crantis following a few steps behind. They took a different route than Kae would have because they didn't need to find the widest path.

Kae kept them centered on his HUD while he found his own way fifty meters to either side of their course. He wove back and forth, ran parallel, and ran ahead, always keeping them nearby. They regarded the mech pounding nearby as a security blanket, knowing that Kae would alert them to any threats.

They couldn't find a trail, but that didn't mean there were none. The insectoids had to use something to get from one place to another. Marcie had been on a spaceship or station for a long time where bugs were a rarity, but she had spent a great deal of her life on Earth. Ants, bugs, and most mammals followed the path of least resistance. If they used it often, it became a trail. On Earth, man paved those trails to create roads. The end result was always the same.

The path of least resistance. Marcie slowed and started to look around almost fanatically.

Kae? Where are they? she asked.

I'm getting no heat signatures. We're still a good five klicks away. They might go other directions from the hive.

What is the drone showing? Monsoon wondered.

Kae had tapped into the feed so it was a constant stream to his HUD, but he'd kept it minimized. He brought it up and checked the hive site. *The majority of the activity is around the hive. Very few are venturing away. We will run across the first Naries in about three kilometers.*

Look for the trails, Kae. There has to be something, and I believe it'll be less alarming if we arrive by walking along one of their expected approaches. Marcie started jogging again, not attempting to set a speed record but watching the area. She trusted technology but didn't want to get them into the middle of a trap.

Trails, aye. I'll run ahead. Cue on me.

Kae surged past them and powered forward. They found running behind him to be much easier since he cleared the way.

"Why didn't we do this all along?" Crantis asked.

"Because I'm a dumbass?" Marcie replied. "Just like being carried sucked, trying to trailblaze when we have a machine to do it doesn't make any sense. I see that now. Kae knows where they are, and if anyone runs into a trap, that suit will protect him a lot better than what we have."

They both looked at their ballistic vests. Those and their helmets were all they wore for personal protection.

Marcie and the sergeant major carried short-barreled rifles, but Marcie had her JDS hidden in her pack because she wasn't going down without a fight if things got hairy. She was okay with getting her ass chewed for breaking the Federation's guidelines if it meant she lived to hear it.

Kae and his powered combat armor was the one concession the Federation had made because they didn't want a tragedy with the first deployment of the Trans-Pac.

Her strategic guidance had been simple: minimize tech superiority to avoid causing the locals to negotiate from positions of fear where an agreement would break down once the threat was removed.

"We'll have to keep Kae from getting up close and personal. We want them to fear us, not the process. It's a tightrope we have to walk."

She started running faster to chew up the remaining distance. Kae waited to step aside until they were less than two kilometers away, but he had found a clearly defined trail.

They are out here but moving away, Kae told them. *I must be scaring them, or they think this is an attack. I'll stay back as far as you deem reasonable. Let me know when you want me to move up.*

This trail takes us there? Marcie asked.

It'll deliver you to their front door.

Marcie jogged until she was about a kilometer away and then started to walk, head held high. Monsoon stepped up beside her on the widening trail. Greater numbers of insectoid feet had used it the closer they came to the hive, making it more distinct.

How about now? Marcie asked.

You are just under a klick away. I can be there in twenty seconds running wide open, and a rocket can be there in four. Plan accordingly.

"I can live with that," Marcie said aloud.

They caught sight of a Kor'narian here and there—

wisps as if they wanted to be seen, but not so much that an enemy could lock on. Marcie and the sergeant major rotated their rifles away from the front. The weapons were a quick movement away from being useful, but not showing weapons presented the appearance of a peace-loving delegation.

When they were within sight of a heavy door blocking the cave that served as the entrance to the Naries hive, they were intercepted.

"You have no business here," the insectoid stated. The translation chips had been trained by the Naries dialect, so they interpreted the language without delay.

"We do. Your queen called the Federation. That's us. You know we landed on Kor'nar three days ago. We expected to be met upon our arrival. Imagine my disappointment when the locals disappeared. We're here to talk. Please relay that message to your queen."

"No," the guard replied.

Marcie glanced at Monsoon. The last thing they wanted to do was force their way in. That wouldn't end well for anyone, but the Naries weren't playing nice.

"We seem to be at an impasse," Marcie said, trying to think through options. "I'd prefer not to take drastic measures, but the Naries called the Federation. Unless the Naries are willing to transfer to the Federation the entire cost of our deployment, we need to talk to your queen."

"Let them through," a voice called from near the door. The guard clicked and buzzed, but its words didn't translate into the humans' language of choice.

"Go fuck yourself, buddy," Crantis mumbled at the

guard. The insectoid's head snapped around, and it glared but let them past.

"Easy," Marcie said but coughed to cover her snicker. "I wouldn't have thought there would be much independence in a hive-style hierarchy."

When they approached, they did not see the queen, as they had expected. Another guard waited for them, carrying a weapon similar to what the Zirrics had engaged the task force with.

"My name is Colonel Marcie Walton. I'm here from the Federation and would like to see the queen, please," Marcie announced in a pleasant voice. She figured the insectoids wouldn't get the gist of her tone, but it didn't hurt to be nice.

"The queen will see you." The guard gestured for them to go inside.

"I'm sorry, you're under the mistaken impression that we're going to go in there when your people have already demonstrated that they are hostile to us. Please ask the queen to come out here."

The guard started to vibrate. When he settled, he spoke. "The queen is incapacitated and cannot come to you. If you wish to speak to her, you must come inside."

"I sympathize with the plight of your queen, but that creates a dilemma. I'd like to say I trust you, but then why didn't the queen send a delegation to meet us and talk to us? You have not yet earned my trust."

"Nor you ours," the guard replied. "The queen is waiting."

What are you doing? Kae asked the instant Marcie took a step forward.

If they're going to trust us, I'll give them a reason to trust us. If this is a trap, I'll kill every single thing in this hive, and then we'll negotiate with the Zirrics.

"We agree. Lead on, Pilkington."

"No weapons," he said.

"Go fuck yourself, Pilkington," Marcie blurted. "Federation law protects its senior representatives by giving them the authority for armed security at all times. I'm the senior delegate, and we're going to protect ourselves. I have no intention of harming your queen. Now, be a champ and take us in."

Marcie could hear Terry Henry's voice in her words and she took a deep breath. No wonder he was so abrasive with the power-hungry. She had no patience for games or diplomacy. She thought for an instant that she should have brought Paithoon to deliver endless platitudes and pleasantries. She had a job to do, and the one who begged the Federation for intervention was dicking her around. *Fuck these guys.*

The guard started to vibrate again. Marcie wondered if that was how they communicated. They were Federation members, which meant they had a minimum level of technology. She wasn't seeing anything that suggested the Kor'-narians were anything other than the least technologically advanced civilization in the entire Federation.

Why were the pirates in orbit? What did this planet have that the Federation wanted? Marcie could see no reason for them to be members. She wanted to return to the camp, pack them up, and leave Kor'nar, but now the mystery nagged at her soul. The second she got back, she would call General Reynolds and find out what was going on. He had never been anything but honest with Terry Henry Walton, but one needed to ask the right questions. She knew what those were now.

It didn't get her any closer to the queen.

"No rifles," the guard clarified.

Marcie turned to Monsoon. "I will agree to that." He shook his head vehemently. "If you would, reach into my pack and take out my pistol. I'll carry that, and we'll leave the rifles here."

Monsoon complied while whispering protests. The sergeant major had never seen a Jean Dukes Special, so he could not appreciate the damage it could do.

Kae, keep an eye on our rifles, Marcie requested.

The mech moved into view. They had seen it, but the major decided to be obvious. He brushed away the intransigent guard they'd first encountered, and the insectoid fired three rounds at Kae. Two ricocheted into the wood, and the other bounced off the rock face above Marcie.

"Stop that," Kae thundered, blasting the guard backward through the sheer volume generated by the suit's external speakers.

"You're not earning my trust," Marcie said once the ringing in her ears had stopped.

"The *dorymyr* will be punished," the guard claimed.

The word translated directly, but Marcie didn't know if it was a rank or a position or a family name. She decided it didn't matter.

"Lead on, Pilkington." She had named the guard after an English butler. It made her more comfortable since her skin was starting to crawl. She'd already done two things she hadn't wanted to do: get confrontational and let them dictate the terms of the meeting—and they had happened with relative ease.

Marcie consoled herself with the fact that she had a Jean Dukes Special in her hand. As she thumbed it up to the setting she wanted, she called, "No, really, fuck you." Lucky number eight because it only hurt a lot instead of incapacitating her. She added, "And your family, too." When it reached the max setting, which she had fired only one time into space from the *War Axe*, she finished, "They won't even find your atoms." Her internal bravado comforted her.

"Come on, Crantis. Let's see what the queen has to say."

"For the record, I hate this," the sergeant major stated loudly.

"Me, too, wild man. Gotta do what we gotta do," she replied before switching to her internal comm chip. *This pistol could level this whole mountain. We're good.*

Except that we'll be inside said mountain! Crantis shot back.

Details, details.

Inside the door, they found a different world. Powered lighting kept it bright. Colors were scattered across the walls in fantastic patterns and textures. The interior walls were rounded, but it didn't strike them as natural.

The hive had been built within the mountainside and decorated as an opulent palace. "My compliments to your designers. This is spectacular."

The guard didn't reply. He had assumed a more stoic demeanor once they were inside. Maybe that was part of the aura of the hive, and why the other guard wasn't as cordial as Marcie wanted him to be. So many thoughts raced through her head, painted on a backdrop of artwork, the likes of which she'd never seen.

It instantly made her want the success of this mission more. The rest of the Federation would appreciate what the Kor'narians were capable of. She knew that her mother, Char, and Cory would be fascinated by the display.

"I hope that someday our people will get to see this. There is nothing like it elsewhere in the universe."

The guard didn't answer, but Marcie didn't let that get to her. The compliment was real, and she didn't need his validation of her appreciation. They continued through chamber after chamber, each more opulent than the last. Insectoids withdrew from the main passage, giving the small entourage room to walk by.

The drones had identified some twenty-five hundred heat sources outside the hive. Inside, Marcie assumed there were tens of thousands. Down the side tunnels, she caught sight of vast numbers, indicating it was more of a hive than what she had seen on the surface of Kor'nar.

She wondered where the delegation who had assessed the planet for membership had stayed and what they had seen. She expected they hadn't, and Kor'nar's membership had been fast-tracked for some reason. Once again, she knew the person to ask.

Massive gilt doors waited at the bottom. Marcie couldn't tell how far they'd descended—maybe stories at least. *Could you get us out if you had to?*

Of course, Monsoon replied. *We might have a hell of a time fighting our way through the crowd, though. There is a metric fuck-ton of Naries down here.*

Suffice it to say, I don't want to start a fight down here. What are we, forty or fifty meters below the surface and dead center inside the mountain?

I'd say at least a hundred meters down and two klicks in. Monsoon sounded confident about his assessment. He wasn't turning his head, but his eyes darted everywhere, taking in the details. He never wavered as he walked.

We'll have an escort out because this is going to go well, Marcie replied, feeling better about the impending meeting.

Two guards opened the double doors simultaneously. The gaping maw of semi-dark stood in stark contrast to the brightness and color of the area outside. An unwell queen might prefer to be out of the light. They walked through, counting on their nanocyte-enhanced vision to show the details of the queen's chambers.

A great mass reclined on a couch-sized piece of furniture perched atop a dais. The guard stepped in front of Marcie and Crantis and bowed before the queen. "The Federation delegation," he announced.

Once he stepped out of the way, Marcie and Crantis bowed to her as well. They waited for her to speak first.

"I am the queen of all Kor'nar," the insectoid stated, struggling with the words in an aged voice as the chip interpreted it.

"I am Colonel Marcie Walton, and this is Sergeant Major Monsoon. We have come at your request to help bring peace to Kor'nar. Please accept my compliments on the magnificence of your hive."

"Yessss," she said slowly. "The Zirrics have to be elimi-

OVERWHELMING FORCE

nated. I thank you for that help. Then we shall be able to continue providing the malageodes you have requested."

Marcie had no idea what she was talking about but didn't want to display her ignorance. "The Federation thanks you for your commitment to the deliveries. We cannot simply eliminate the Zirrics. It would be best if you and the Zirrics sat down at the same table and talked over your differences. I expect you'll find you have more in common than you know."

The queen huffed and heaved. "Go," she commanded in an increasingly raspy voice. With the capability to see better in the dark, she knew the queen wasn't just under the weather, she was dying. That was the shitstorm about to strike.

"We thank you for this gracious audience." Marcie bowed, took a step back, and hurried toward the doors. Their escort embraced a comparable sense of urgency. With a gentle tap on the doors, they opened, and he flowed out, increasing his pace to the point where Marcie and Crantis were almost running.

"Your queen is dying," Marcie stated. The guard hitched a step at the humanoids' astute observation. He'd probably expected that they couldn't see the queen's condition in the darkness. "What becomes of Kor'nar when she passes?"

"There will be another," the guard replied, increasing his pace to where Marcie did have to run. She was okay with that. She wanted nothing more than to get out from under the mountain. As they approached the front doors, she breathed a sigh of relief.

The vibrations seemed to resonate up through the floor, filling the air with the noise of the hive.

The guard stopped and blocked the way. "It is too late," he stated.

"The queen has died," Marcie remarked. "You need to let us out of here."

He tried to prevent them from leaving with his weapon, but Crantis ripped it out of the guard's arms and shoulder-blocked him out of the way. He and Marcie started to run. Shots sounded from somewhere. They reached the door and yanked it open to run out. Insectoids rushed toward them, but they didn't appear to be attacking.

The call had been sounded, and it was time for the members to return to the hive. It became a stampede. Crantis found purchase on the cliff face to stay out of the way. Marcie was on the other side of the door and unable to reach him, but they were both armed.

Kae stepped closer to the door. *Good to see you both in the sunlight. What the hell did you do down there?*

Queen's dead. It looks to be a total shitshow.

The stream of bodies lessened to a trickle, and Marcie and Crantis bolted through them to join Kaeden.

"Time to go," he said and started running. They followed in single file, the sergeant major dropping back to provide a warning to Marcie if the tide turned toward them instead of the hive.

I don't see it, Marcie said. *They need to do whatever they have to do to settle their people and pick a new queen. I wonder how they do that?*

You could always ask the Zirrics, Monsoon suggested.

Both of these jackwagons want us to destroy the other. That's bullshit and one thing they have in common. They both want to play us—the stupid humanoids. I need time to think.

We have plenty of time. However long it takes to run twenty klicks. Monsoon looked as innocent as always.

I appreciate your optimism, Crantis. Who are the bad guys here? she asked, not looking for an answer, only insight into an obstacle she had not anticipated.

CHAPTER TWENTY-SIX

Benitus Seven, the Caves

Christina stood to the side of the collapsed dirt that signaled the tunnel roof had caved in. She looked at her squad, now down to two and her. The other two had been put into cryopods. The Skrima saw the injured as easy targets and had slashed one of the victims in the cryopod to shreds before Christina and the others could engage.

"Fire in the hole!" she shouted and dropped in a plasma grenade before walking away. The explosion blossomed behind her. She'd had enough of the Skrima, and the splitting headache wasn't improving her mood. Her limbs felt heavy, even with the powered combat armor supplementing her strength.

She hadn't seen any Skrima since Ted fired up his device. She hoped the two were related but took nothing for granted. "Colonel Lowell to the *War Axe*. Colonel Walton, are you there?"

"Char here, Christina. Terry is getting a little treatment in the Pod-doc. What can we help you with?"

"Does Ted's device affect the Skrima?"

"We believe it does, based on a report from those at the rift at the time of activation. I think with the disruption in the Etheric and the massive pull into the energy conduit, the Skrima are tortured as their very life essence is drawn from them and fed into the machine."

"That sounds profound, but I like it. What I heard you say is that thing is hurting me too, but as soon as I leave the planet, I'll be fine. I don't see any reason to stay down here, do you?"

"Bring our people home, Christina."

"I lost one," she replied softly. "The Skrima took out a cryopod that was in use. I'm glad they're being tortured by Ted's device. Seems fitting that the devils get a version of hell imposed on them. They shouldn't have come here in the first place, and then they made the mistake of trying to stay here."

Christina dialed up the company-wide broadcast.

"All hands, return to the *War Axe*. We're calling this one. The op is finished. Thankfully, we only lost one. All hands for a memorial ceremony on the hangar deck tomorrow. If I never see another fucking Skrim, it will be too soon." She signed off.

Christina struggled to get to the shuttle Pod, then climbed in and collapsed within her suit. Once the squad was inside, they took off. A kilometer into the sky, she felt like a new person. "Smedley, circle until we have all hands accounted for and all Pods on their way back to the *Axe*."

"Of course," the AI replied. They continued to burn holes in the sky for another fifteen minutes before the remainder of the teams were recovered. "We are now on our way to the *War Axe*."

"Total injured?"

"Twenty-one during this phase of the operation. The remaining five cryopods are in use. Nine injured had already been evacuated to the *War Axe*. Seven injured are receiving emergency field treatment from their teams. In addition, there were two deaths for the entirety of the operation, Privates Workman and Gefelton."

Christina reviewed the roster on her HUD. Seventy-five percent of the Bad Company had been injured on the return to Benitus Seven, including both Char and Terry Henry. Christina and Kimber had escaped unscathed despite repeatedly putting themselves into the middle of the fight.

They didn't feel like they had been lucky. Everyone suffered together.

Christina yawned. She tried to think back to the last time she'd slept but couldn't remember when it had been. And it wouldn't be for a while yet.

She accessed her company-wide broadcast. "Bad Company, this is Colonel Lowell. Upon reaching the *War Axe*, injured are to report to Cory at the Pod-docs and get her recommendation for further treatment. Everyone else, stow your gear, hit the showers, catch chow, and get some sleep. All hands form up on the hangar deck at eight in the morning, *War Axe* standard time. Thank you for making this operation what it was to secure the space station for follow-on Federation use. They couldn't have done that while the planet was under siege by the Skrima. As shitty as it was down there, somebody had to clean that place out.

The Bad Company, making the hard look easy and the impossible possible. Lowell out."

Nadezhda Station, in Orbit above Benitus Seven

It took numerous trips, but the pack was able to deposit half the gear in the lab Ted had secured and the rest in the power-supply space nine levels down from the docking ring. Timmons stayed clear of the devices, warning the others about his earlier unhappy encounter.

"…and then he tells me I should have been better insulated!" Timmons wiped his hands on his pants, leaning against the wall after delivering the last load.

"You should have been." Sue shrugged. It wasn't the sympathy Timmons had been looking for. He rubbed his hands together to get the feeling back into them.

The shuttle is here and will meet you at the docking ring, Iracitus reported.

What shuttle? Sue asked.

The supply shuttle Ted asked Ankh to send.

The one with food? How in the hell is that possible? Timmons gawked.

Shonna and Merrit looked at each other briefly before bolting for the stairs. Sue was after them like a shot.

"You fuckers!" Timmons ran for the stairs, taking them three at a time on the way up, but the others had an insurmountable head start.

Timmons almost caught them on the docking-ring level, but they ran in a mad scramble down the corridor until they reached the automatic bulkhead. Merrit slammed into it since it was slower to open than he needed it to be, given how fast he was moving. Shonna ran into him, using his body to cushion the blow. Sue slid to slow down and dodged past them once the doors opened. Timmons was able to maintain his pace throughout and took the lead before reaching the outer ring.

He verified where the shuttle was before turning and bouncing off the outside wall and reached the airlock as the autoloader was delivering a pallet of take-out boxes. As soon as the boxes had been stacked, the unmanned shuttle buttoned up and flew away, formed a Gate, and shot through, all in less than two minutes.

"We have unmanned drones that can Gate?" Timmons asked while digging into the top bag.

"*We* don't. Ted and Ankh do, and you are the beneficiary of their largesse."

Timmons was ready to rip the top package of hot wings open, but Sue stopped him. "Ted first."

He knew she was right. He pulled her close and hugged her tightly. "Load it up. We're taking it downstairs."

"And for once on this glorious day," Merrit eloquated, "I am perfectly fine being Ted's slave labor."

"Can't disagree with that." Timmons smiled. The four divided the boxes equally between them to get it all in one trip. "It's still hot!"

"Hurry!" Shonna shouted around her load, walking carefully but as quick as possible. It looked like a waddle, but no one was watching. Having piping-hot All Guns Blazing food pressed against their faces was a distraction they could barely look past.

"Who takes an experimental shuttle and turns it into a galaxy-wide pizza delivery vehicle?" Timmons wondered.

"There's no way this was Ted's idea. This is more like Terry Henry Walton, but I don't know if he has that kind of pull," Sue replied.

"He said he had to call Ankh. Do you think that lawyer person convinced the little guy to do this?" Merrit offered.

Shonna shook her head as much as she was able. "'Lawyer person?' Do you mean Rivka? Nice lady, and she loves AGB pies, but that gross Moonstokle one. There better not be one of those in here."

"What if that's what Ted likes? Sue?" Timmons looked at her for an answer since she had been partnered with him for a few decades.

"I don't know. This Ted is different from the one of a hundred and fifty years ago, just like the rest of us."

"I didn't like it back then. I don't like it now," Timmons declared. It was slow going down the stairs, but they maintained a steady pace. They hugged their loads tightly, doing their best to keep the warmth inside for maximum enjoyment from nearly a galaxy away.

"I'm sure it was Rivka," Sue said. "I want to know how she did it. That might be a little something to keep in our back pocket, just in case."

"Ted!" Timmons yelled with one flight to go.

Shonna was first off the last step before the landing on the lab level. She missed her footing and started to fall, trying to catch herself before slamming into the rail. She twisted mid-fall, striking the rail with her back before sliding to the floor. The bags and boxes remained upright, resting on her stomach as she laid there.

"Graceful," Merrit noted, walking past her to drop the boxes in the lab before returning to relieve her of her load.

"All's well that ends well," she said while standing and straightening her clothes to restore some of her dignity.

"Just leave them there. I'll get to them in a bit," Ted said. The werewolves' smiles faded into scowls.

Sue held up one finger before sauntering to Ted's side. "Ted, dear, you need to eat to keep up your strength. It's hot, and you know that's how you like it. Plus, if you delay more than two minutes, the rest of us will have ravaged the sacrificial offerings. We cannot thank you enough for this fine repast and beg you to share it with us. The first plates are yours, Ted. Please dig in while it's hot."

She guided him away from the workbench to the boxes. He dug through and found the hot wings he liked and his favorite pizza. Timmons cast furtive glances at the others while waiting for Ted to open the box.

Sausage, pepperoni, tomato, and green pepper. He folded two slices on top of each other, the long string of melted cheese trailing back into the box.

The other werewolves attacked the remainder, Timmons and Merrit waiting as their better halves went first. There was plenty for this meal and probably the next two as well.

"Ted, you are the abso-fucking-lute bomb!" Timmons stated before taking his first bite. Ted smiled sheepishly, and for the first time in his life, showed his humble side.

"I have good friends."

They knew he probably meant Ankh and not them, but it worked. They continued eating in silence, not asking who had paid for the banquet that seemed to include three of everything on the AGB menu. Sue dug the drinks out of a bottom box and handed Ted his Coke.

"To fuel a champion," she said, but Ted was already back into his project, one hundred percent of his focus on bringing the station online with transmitted power. He took the Coke without looking and without comment, drinking deeply while speaking to Plato and working the intense engineering necessary to bring his project to fruition. He didn't doubt that he could, but time was passing without a terminus for the massive surge beaming up through the atmosphere.

CHAPTER TWENTY-SEVEN

Kor'nar, Trans-Pacific Task Force Expeditionary Camp

"The flag is up as ordered, but there's no sign of the Zirrics," Jake reported when Marcie and the sergeant major strolled in.

Kae was parking his suit and setting up the solar charger to top it off. He hadn't expended much of its energy. A short forty-odd-kilometer run without any combat? He was still at ninety percent and then some.

"An interesting trip, to say the least. It was quite the climax, I have to admit."

"Pray tell," Jake said, sitting back against the table and steepling his fingers beneath his chin.

"The old queen is dead, and I sense there will be a free-for-all to take control of the hive. I don't know how that process works. Are there any other queens, and if there are, do they duke it out? If not, then what? Maybe they're like a flock without a shepherd, and we'll be able to pacify them easily and under the Zirric queen. I don't care which queen is in charge, or both of them, or none of them. I don't care!

I do need to talk to Lance Reynolds. The queen said something that is bugging the shit out of me."

Marcie chewed her lip, losing herself in her thoughts while Colonel Braithwen waited, leaning forward as if that would break the information free.

Monsoon asked, "Have you ever heard of something called a malageode?"

Jake leaned back before shaking his head. "No clue." He took a seat and accessed the computer that had been set up in the tent. "It's a rare mineral, but it doesn't seem like anything worth fighting for."

"Or stretching Federation rules to get access to. I think we're missing something because there is no way in hell this planet is advanced enough to be a full Federation member, although I appreciate their art. For what it's worth, they could make a mint allowing tourism just to come see it."

"Begs the question," Jake agreed.

Marcie blew out a breath and accessed the comm terminal, a commander's lifeblood. She looked at the box with a wire trailing outside the tent where the dish communicated with the task force's flagship. She needed a relay to Yoll.

"Colonel Walton, requesting a relay to Yoll to deliver an update to General Reynolds."

She waited while the ship accessed the Gate and connected it to send a signal through the wormhole. When it went live, the ship handed off control to the ground.

"Ack! Terry Henry, are you still on Benitus?" General Reynolds replied, his voice scratchy as if he'd been woken from a sound sleep.

"I'm sorry, General. This is the other Colonel Walton. Marcie here."

"Of course. Sorry about that. You can't swing a dead cat without hitting a Walton in this universe. How is the Trans-Pacific Task Force holding up?"

Jake tried not to laugh. Kae caught the last of it. "We're like rabbits!" Marcie shushed him. Monsoon didn't change expression.

"One casualty and a few injured, but the proof of concept worked. We landed eight thousand troops over the course of eight hours. It was impressive. We have met with both sides in this civil war, and it's clear that they hate each other at an elemental level that defies logic. I'm not worried about that as much as I am that this planet is significantly challenged in regard to technology. They didn't lose it in a war, they never had it. Makes me wonder what the Federation is using the malageodes for."

"We had hoped that you wouldn't be bothered with that side project," the general said evenly. Marcie waited since they both knew it wasn't a side project. "Who is there with you?"

"Monsoon, Braithwen, and Kaeden, and Corporal Wiriya just outside."

"Have him come in. I'll read you in at the same time." Kae didn't have to step outside. Wiriya had been listening.

"We're all here," Marcie said, trying to make herself comfortable.

"The information I'm about to share is not to be further disseminated without my personal approval. Keep it among yourselves. I don't need to warn you about leaks. Don't fucking do it. Malageodes aren't for the Federation, except that they are in high demand on Elementor Three. Of all things in the universe they wanted to trade for, malageodes are it. I can't tell you what they use them for because I don't care. They want them, and that's what matters. Elementor Three is in a critical strategic location, but even that isn't as important as the fact that they are the only place in the entire Federation that can produce Silsonex."

He let that hang. Marcie closed her eyes and tried to remember where she had heard that name. Kaeden spoke up. "The drug that cures cancer for those who don't have access to a Pod-doc?"

"Exactly. Cancer causes unnecessary deaths in this century and in this place, but we can't treat everyone using nanocytes. We don't need super-powered bad guys out there."

"All for the price of malageodes. I got the impression the Federation was already mining them on Kor'nar."

"The Federation installed a remotely operated mining facility run by an EI using nothing but robots. We installed the Gate for the sole purpose of getting the malageodes, but there's no reason to station personnel there because, as you surmised, there is absolutely nothing on Kor'nar besides the insectoids."

"Having visited the Naries' hive, they have art the likes of which has not been seen in the galaxy. I believe art lovers throughout the Federation would pay a great deal to see it in person, but there's one minor holdup." Marcie collected her thoughts before continuing. "The Naries' queen died a short time ago, immediately following our audience. She was old and dying, but I expect they'll find a way to blame us. Even if they don't, the new leadership might not feel beholden to the Federation."

"That sounds like a problem, so it is a good thing that we have some of the Federation's finest on the front lines of its battle to deliver health to its citizens."

"We're exploiting Kor'nar for the good of our people?" Kae asked.

"A rough term, Kae. Do not use it lightly. We are not impacting the Kor'narians with our mining site, but what you need to do now is to secure the mining facility and return it to operation. It went offline the day we called you up. We figured we'd be able to send a team while you were working with the two sides in this conflict. I should have told you, but I didn't want you to be distracted from your primary mission of bringing peace. The miners will do what they'll do, and diplomats will build on the foundation that you create. That will pay its own dividends. You now have a second mission that assumes the role of primary: stand by for the Naries leadership to emerge before reengaging the locals. In the meantime, get that mining facility back in operation."

"And peace, sir?" Marcie asked.

"Once the Naries leadership shakes out, contact them and restart the talks. Peace is important since I want the Kor'narians as partners, not a dominated indigenous species where one might think we don't care about them because we do. We established the mining facility with little fanfare and no Kor'narian interaction. We couldn't find a single native within a hundred kilometers of our site. The old queen was on board with our plan, by the way, and agreed to let us establish the site and extract the malageodes. Then the war increased in intensity and we lost contact with them. The next we heard, they requested our assistance.

"The Kor'narians are an agrarian society that eats plant life. The Federation terraformed a vast area to increase the arability of the land. It should just be starting to grow. They didn't negotiate for that because they didn't seem to care about our taking the malageodes. We made a fair trade, Kaeden. It's not exploitation, but this society isn't up to our usual standards. I'll transmit the coordinates of both. Take a look at your convenience once you get that mining facility operational. Any final questions?"

"No, sir. I'll take care of it."

"That's why you're in charge, Marcie. Let me know when the Naries have a new queen and you're engaged in new talks. If we can ensure the peace, we can send a bunch of worthless diplomats to negotiate the details. Reynolds out."

Marcie closed the line while glaring at her husband. "Why did you think it was a good idea to accuse General Lance Reynolds of exploiting the locals?"

"That's what it sounded like." Kae crossed his arms. He wasn't going to back down.

"The general doesn't owe us an explanation," Marcie continued.

"Bullshit!" Kae almost came out of his boots. "He held back information vital to this operation. A fucking mining facility? This is about sending pretty rocks to Elementor Three so they can send the cure across the Federation."

"What's wrong with that?" Marcie shot back.

Kae stuck out his chin and leaned forward, then closed his mouth and stepped back. "Nothing, I guess."

Jake held up one finger. "The Federation is terraforming this wasteland to provide more food, which is about the only thing the Kor'narians want or need, based on what we've seen. Their only other motivation seems to be this unnatural hatred for each other. The Federation seems to have gone well out of their way to help when they could have simply taken whatever they wanted. I know on the outside, it looks like they did that and threw some scraps to the natives to keep them placated when they had no capacity to understand what they were getting into."

"We can't have it both ways," Kae said. "Either we get the cure by taking what we need, or we wait until this society is mature enough to understand the arrangement. When will that be, a hundred years from now?"

"You're arguing against yourself," Marcie pointed out.

"It's a hard one, even having more information." Kae kicked at something on the dirt floor.

"Jake, spin up a couple shuttles and go take a look at that mining facility. Take three squads with anti-air capability and a platoon of infantry."

Jake rubbed his chin. "What are you thinking?"

"I believe the mining facility is still operating, but it's being run by those pirates we encountered when we first arrived. I don't know what the black-market price is for the cure, but I'm sure it's not cheap. Why else would those crotch maggots be here?"

"I wondered about that," Jake noted. "But then we were into the landing and I forgot. The situation begged questions that I should have asked as your XO. My apologies,

Colonel. I won't let that happen again. I'll take the force out there. If the Zirric show up, you'll be here to talk to them. Maybe Kae can suit up and come with me. The technology prohibition won't apply if we're dealing with off-worlders."

"That is exactly right!" Marcie gestured toward Kae. He rolled his eyes but smiled.

Kae turned to leave. "Become the metal god, and then it's work, work, work. I should have strived harder for average."

Marcie spoke softly, "Then you wouldn't have me."

He glanced over his shoulder. "No one ever won the universe by being average." He made eye contact with Jake. "How long is it going to take to round up your volunteers?"

"I have the Lion Corps on a short leash. Give me fifteen, and we'll meet you at Shuttle One."

Kae nodded and headed outside. A large tent nearby gave him pause. It hadn't been there before. He checked the time to see he still had fifteen minutes.

He leaned back inside the command tent. "Well done, Jake! Chow's up."

Marcie's ears perked. "Hot chow?"

"Twenty-four/seven," Jake replied while buckling his gear.

The sergeant major hadn't said a word since they got back. He snagged Marcie's attention before she left. "I'll troop the line and make sure our people have been sent through."

Marcie winced and hesitated.

"Don't worry about it, ma'am. I'll take care of the troops. You need to keep up your strength. You have far different worries that will affect a lot more people if you make the wrong decisions. Go get some chow. There will be no end of the line since troops will constantly cycle through if I understand how this is supposed to work."

"Units get time slots and rotate through the day. Two hots per soldier," Marcie recited. "It's a good plan. Take care of our people, Crantis."

"Will do. Get something and go do great things. I have a feeling we'll see the Blues today."

"What's with Blues?"

"We can't tell them apart, so Zirrics are Blue and Naries are Yellow. We'll give them ribbons or something so we know who not to put with who."

"Not a bad plan since I couldn't tell them apart either. I can tell an old queen from a young one if that's worth anything."

Monsoon returned a blank expression. That was his impression of the value of her observation.

"Chow," Kae hinted, sniffing the air. "Ten minutes to get it and eat."

"I hear you." Marcie's stomach growled at the thought of something other than a chewy protein bar.

"Ma'am, the Zirric queen is on her way to the tent," Wiriya reported. She and Kae were halfway through inhaling their meals. She looked at hers for a moment before deciding and taking action. She shoveled the rest of it in and chewed while walking out, swallowing before picking up the pace.

Crantis, we have company. I'll meet you at the southern perimeter, she called using the internal comm chip.

I'm already here, the sergeant major replied. *The queen's entourage has grown. I hope Paithoon restocked the fruit. Don't want a hungry queen.*

I expect he did. Marcie started running. She didn't want to arrive after the queen. *He's Paithoon. He lives for that shit.*

Marcie crossed the camp quickly, slowing to a walk when she came within sight of the Peace Garden. The sergeant major motioned for her to continue through the lines, joining her as they strolled into the open. They timed their pace to arrive at the same time as the Zirric queen.

Inside, they found Paithoon fussing over additions he'd made to the tent. She wondered if the sergeant major had made recommendations to hang artwork. The display made it seem brighter on the inside. She had no idea where he had gotten the pieces and decided it was best not to ask. In Paithoon's mind, everything he was doing took priority. Most of the time he was wrong, but in the case of the negotiations, he was correct, and she was glad he took such pride in his work.

"Well done, Paithoon. You bring great credit to yourself, and I'm happy you are here."

The Belzonian beamed with pride as he stood by the table.

"You can take the wrap off the fruit now." She gestured. He caught himself staring before tugging the clear covering free to unleash the full color of the display.

"Almost too nice to eat," the queen clicked and buzzed. "*Almost.*"

The sergeant major stepped around the colonel and took hold of Paithoon by the back of his shirt.

"Stand in the back," Monsoon whispered, dragging the

protocol officer away from the table before the queen's guards and servants descended on the display. Paithoon looked horrified, so the sergeant major escorted him out of the tent. "Stay out here."

Crantis returned, acting as if nothing happened. Marcie waited patiently for the feeding frenzy to finish. They didn't leave anything this time.

The ceremony had been conducted and the relationship sealed. Marcie took that as a good sign.

"You summoned me?" the queen asked.

"I bring news from the Naries. Their queen has died, and they have recalled all their people into the hive."

The queen turned to her people and clicked and buzzed excitedly. Two of the guards bolted from the tent, scampering away at high speed.

"You shall be rewarded for this magnificent intelligence. I knew you were on our side."

"No." Marcie vigorously shook her head. "I'm not on anyone's side. I want to know what the process is for selecting a new queen."

"I need to go. Now is the optimal time to attack and end this war. There will be peace!"

"No!" Marcie shouted before calming. She was not beneath seizing the queen and making her stay. Marcie feared that she had made a terrible mistake. "Tell me the process."

"Very well," the queen conceded. "There are always junior queens. They wait for the enlightening when the old queen passes beyond. They are recalled, and then they fight. They will probably have formed alliances to gang up on the lesser queens, but this fight is to the death. All the other junior queens must die, leaving the new queen as the rightful successor, the enlightened one."

"How long does that take?" Marcie leaned forward to catch every word.

"It is quick, depending on how long it takes the most remote queen to arrive. I have mine scattered to the far ends of my realm. I do not suspect the Naries are any different. The fight itself goes quickly, and it will be brutal and final. This is why we must hurry while they are vulnerable. Without a queen, they will fall before us without defending themselves."

"We can't let that happen," Marcie said loudly since she knew the insectoids found volume abrasive. Marcie wanted to get her attention.

"It has already begun," the queen replied, heaving to her feet and hurrying from the tent.

Marcie looked to the sergeant major. "We better get there first."

"I couldn't agree more." They left the tent at a full sprint, leaving Paithoon standing in the dust they'd kicked up.

"Oh, Colonel?" Paithoon called.

"Busy. Gotta stop a war," Marcie yelled and kept running. She dashed through the lines and the camp until she reached the command tent.

"What's the plan, ma'am?"

"Get the armor out there to stand between the Naries' hive and any advancing armies. We'll move the infantry in as quickly as possible through a vertical maneuver. Get our close air support drones loaded with frag rockets and into the air. Move a ground force overland, but traveling twenty klicks will take a while. Still, better to start now. Also, dial up the artillery so we can deny access to Zirric avenues of approach by filling them with exploding projectiles. That alone might be enough, but we have to get the forward observers out there to correctly call in the fire. Don't want to shoot ourselves."

"What are the rules of engagement?" The sergeant major inched toward the tent flap as Marcie picked up the radio handset.

"Refuse access to the hive. If the Zirrics insist on dying, we'll accommodate them, but we can't shoot first. Deny them access until the Naries have a queen, then keep *them* from launching an attack. I can't believe a new queen would be so bold, but one never knows. Watch your fronts and backs. Bring the shuttles online; we're moving as many soldiers as we can as quickly as we can."

The sergeant major left the tent to work his magic while Marcie started making calls, the first one being to Major Punyaa. She ordered him to take three companies of tanks to the Naries' hive and set up a cordon.

So much to do and so little time. The Zirrics were on their way. Marcie could feel it in her bones.

CHAPTER TWENTY-EIGHT

War Axe, **Hangar Bay**

The last of the injured were being treated in the Pod-docs. The cryopods had been emptied. Six had deployed to the planet's surface and six had returned, only to be sent again, but only five made it back. That wasn't because of a technical malfunction; they had worked perfectly. Most of the injured would probably have survived, but not all.

Terry and Char found Cory asleep in the chair by the Pod-docs. He had brought a cot for her, but she didn't want to sleep too hard. The warriors were arriving and starting to form up for a somber ceremony of the type Terry had started in North Chicago. They were early.

They wanted to pay their respects and move on. Dwelling on the past would be destructive to morale, and they knew that. These warriors had been in the Bad Company from the start. They had been here the last time the company landed on Benitus Seven. They had been here when they held the ceremony for Ramses.

Char checked the Pod-docs, which were operating

without an issue. "There's no reason for her to stay. I'll take over."

"We'll take over," Joseph interjected. He and Petricia approached. "Go on now. Take care of business."

Terry nodded to his friends.

Petricia put her hand on his arm. "I don't usually have much to say, but I want you to know that you have given me a life worth living. I found refuge with the Forsaken because I was different, but theirs wasn't a life. Joseph and the Force de Guerre gave me internal peace, and then I came to space. Me! I never guessed such a thing was possible until Terry Henry Walton asked if we wanted to go. I love being part of all this and will do whatever the Bad Company needs. Watching over our injured is the least we can do. We have a great life on the *War Axe* and Keeg Station, and wherever you go, we will go."

Joseph squeezed Terry's arm. The colonel bowed his head and nodded, then bent down and picked Cory up, carrying her like a small child across the hangar bay and into the ship. Every single person watched them go without comment and without moving.

"Thank you both for being our friends," Char said. "This is it for us. Christina is going to take over the Bad Company. Terry will announce our retirement when he gets back. We decided before Benitus Seven, so it wasn't the losses here that acted as the catalyst. We're tired, the kind of fatigue that won't get better with a short vacation. Plus, we suck at vacations. It's all or nothing with TH. You know him."

Joseph smiled in a patronly but not patronizing way. "We know you too, Charumati. Enjoy whatever distorted version of retirement Terry Henry Walton has cooked up. It's probably something like being the galactic beer magnate with millions in daily sales. I don't think I'm being excessive with my prognostication. See, the look on your face tells me that is exactly what he's planning! He is going to expand the AGB franchise and that god-awful creation of his, the Moonstokle pie."

Petricia, always proper, looked at Joseph and said, "It's shit."

"It's his biggest seller," Char admitted.

"Aren't you half-owner?" Joseph pressed. He knew the answer.

"I take no responsibility for Moonstokle pie, but I *will* take half the profits." The three chuckled, and Joseph turned back to the business at hand.

"The injured are in our capable hands. If any of them finish, we'll make sure they are welcomed properly back to health and turned over to Jenelope for her tender culinary ministrations." Joseph gestured at the hatch leading from the hangar bay. "Join Terry for your swan song. Will it be a celebration?"

"The kegs are already in place." Char pointed at a mound under a tarp that had been on the hangar deck since they'd left Keeg Station, unobtrusive and invisible in plain sight.

"I'll be damned." Joseph shook his head. "No one ever said Terry Henry Walton was bad at logistics."

Terry stopped two steps into returning to the hangar bay and breathed deeply of the air. It smelled different from the rest of the ship—more industrial but earthy, a hint of ozone lingered from weapons fire long past. Sweat was permanently infused in the mechanized suits, the smell of a combat unit doing what it does best.

Char strolled to the formation. She was a major in the Bad Company's Direct Action Branch but hadn't embraced that role. Christina was better suited for military leadership. Char handled her pack. That was in her blood, but she had no desire to stand before the warriors and lead them into battle. She was fine fighting by Terry's side, but that was different.

The werewolf part of her reveled in battle but not war.

Bundin and K'Thrall stood behind the formation in their own row of four-legged warriors. The others of the alien squad had filled in at the ends of the other squads. Capples stayed in the back with the Podder and the Yollin. He had no role in this formation. Felicity appeared and stood against the wall. It was the Bad Company's officers' show.

Christina tipped her chin to Char, then came to attention and called the formation to order.

Terry loved the military precision. He walked through the ranks, touching each warrior on his way to the front.

"At ease," he said in a casual tone of voice, not the usual order issued by a unit commander.

"Bad Company," he called and started to pace. "We're here to celebrate the lives of those who died by our sides on the field of battle. They brought honor to themselves and the unit. They will never be forgotten and will always be celebrated. We knew them as family. We embraced them as friends. They will be part of the story of the Bad Company. To honor them, we move forward. They didn't die so we could disappear into a morass of despair. They died to fight an enemy that needed to be fought. They died for others. No greater gift can one man give than to lay down his life for another.

"We accomplish the mission and we move on. That's as much as we can win, and it's not a Pyrrhic victory because we can still fight. Every day, every hour, whenever we are called up, we go. We give every mission one hundred percent. We train hard to be better than our enemies. When we go into battle, they fear us. We will continue to dominate combat throughout the Federation. It's what we do because it keeps people safe.

"No one needs to know the details of our job or the enemies we've faced. The people we're protecting would be afraid for no reason. Because we are there. We stand between them and the horrors of life so they can live free. Sometimes, it's better when they don't know what's out here besides the comforting fact that the Bad Company is also out here."

Terry stopped speaking for a moment and stared at the deck. A couple of the warriors shifted their feet to get more comfortable, moving their heads to better see the colonel. He lifted his eyes to scan the entire company.

"Private Workman will forever be buried in the depths of Benitus Seven. Private Gefelton was preserved in the cryopod that was destroyed with him. Join me to send him into space." Terry waved for them to follow. Some came to attention before stepping out of formation. Others just walked toward the hangar bay door without demon-strating proper military drill.

A lone case sat there, enclosing a destroyed cryopod

with Gefelton's remains inside. *Skipper, turn us toward the star and give us a little momentum, please.*

Consider it done, TH. The ship slowly turned toward Benitus Seven's star and accelerated.

"From the fires of heaven we came and to the fires we return, where our life essence can once again be sent forth to a new place in a distant future." The warriors bowed their heads as the Bad Company's leadership team, Terry, Char, Christina, Kimber, and Auburn, picked up the case and sent it through the energy shield. The *War Axe* slowed as Gefelton continued on a ballistic trajectory toward the system's star. He would arrive in a year or two. There was no rush. The private was at peace.

"And now's the time I have to tell you that I am stepping down from the Bad Company. Colonel Christina Lowell is taking command while Char and I retire to run the All Guns Blazing franchises, one of which will be right here on the Benitus Station, which I'm told is being called Nadezhda. It's an Earth word for hope in a language a friend of ours spoke, one of our original members. Maybe we'll visit him now that we'll have time."

Murmurs ran through the group. It wasn't as unexpected as Terry had thought it would be. They hadn't been the same since their visit to the Venus pleasure moon orbiting Cygnus VI. They had almost died from exposure the last time they'd tried to take a vacation. They didn't tell anyone what had happened because they couldn't believe it themselves.

The Bad Company was filled with smart people. They had known.

Terry waved for Char to join him. He wrapped an arm around her waist and she around his.

"We have two final things to say. First, no active or retired Bad Company member will ever pay for a drink or a meal at one of our All Guns Blazing franchises." The crowd cheered, raucously so, breaking the tension of a somber occasion. "And second, as a private business, we have pioneered galaxy-wide hot delivery." He pointed to the canvas-covered crates.

"Set up, pull the tab on the delivery box, and it cooks your food to be as hot as if AGB had just taken it out of the oven. And there are a couple kegs that need to be tapped. They are the first two of my custom line. Walton's Barley Pop is a line of light lagers that might be a little fizzier than what you're used to, and Midnight Sun is a beer so dark, a supernova couldn't penetrate it. That shit'll put hair on your candy-asses!"

Char backed away. "Is that your sales pitch?" she asked into the cheers that surrounded them.

"It is. Why? What's wrong with it?" Terry delivered his best shocked look while winking and waving at the warriors.

Char started walking toward the food and drink. The good people of the Bad Company broke out the tables and chairs stored at the sides of the hangar bay. Terry checked the crates and started issuing orders to get it set up. He tapped the keg and tried to give out the first beer, but Capples and Bundin stepped up together, blocking anyone from approaching.

"This one is for you." Bundin's voice boomed off the deck. "The next one is for our lost brothers."

Terry didn't want to, but the warriors insisted. Colonel Walton hesitated, his eyes glistening. Char moved close. "Don't get all shmoopy. I told them about your first attempts to make beer, and they want to be sure it's palatable before taking a drink. This is self-preservation. You've trained them well, TH."

Terry saluted with his dark beer, which looked like a solid chunk of black inside his glass. It didn't immediately shift when he tipped the glass since it had the consistency of a shake heavily laden with ice cream. He held it to his lips and shook the glass to get the so-called liquid to start flowing and chewed his way through a few bites before smacking his lips.

Char's shocked expression wasn't feigned. It was real. Terry grinned.

"It might be a tad thick, but that is the best dark beer I've ever eaten!" he declared.

Capples smirked. "What's that fizzy pop stuff taste like?" he asked hopefully.

Char gently pushed Terry out of the way and drew a mug for Cap to try. After the first sip, he downed half the glass. He pointed to it and shouted, "This is the good stuff!"

Terry served beverages all around until the company was ready, then raised his glass. "To Private Workman and Private Gefelton. You will live forever."

They drank and then cheered as part of the celebration of life. Terry strolled down the line of delivery packs, pulling the tabs and starting the cooking process. A green light would appear when it was ready. The warriors grabbed plates and started lining up.

Char tugged on Terry's arm. He knew what she wanted

to talk about, so he started. "If Ted doesn't get the station to draw the generated power, is it going to blow a hole in the universe?"

"We'll be first to die, yes. Micky recommends taking the ship out of here. *Ramses' Chariot* has Gate capability. They can join us when they've succeeded."

"Is that your recommendation?" Terry asked. He knew what his choice was, and although the decision was his to make, he didn't want to embrace his preference over what was right.

Char nodded. "But only if you drop me off with my pack. I have to go over there."

Terry shook his head. "That ain't happening. We're not losing Ted either, or any of the others. I have an idea."

Char smiled. "Let's go get Ankh."

"How about we let our fingers do the walking?" Terry replied, citing an old telephone commercial. "Smedley, would you connect me with Magistrate Rivka Anoa, please?"

Almost instantly, Rivka's voice came through his internal comm chip.

What did you break? she demanded.

You were much more sedate when you were younger. Why do you think I broke something?

I've adopted the Terry Henry approach to life, which means I've accepted that everything and everyone is trying to kill me. It puts me a little on edge if you get my drift. Now tell me, what did you break?

Damn, Magistrate! You don't like wasting time, either. Very TH of you. There's a rupture between this universe and the Etheric. Ted has built a device to funnel the massive amounts of energy from the rift to power a space station, but the terminus isn't ready yet, and if it takes too much longer, the energy will build up and explode, possibly destroying this sector of space. We need Ankh here, and we need him yesterday.

It was nearly a full minute before Rivka responded.

You broke the galaxy.

It was broken before we arrived, but we made it both better and worse. Have you ever seen a Skrim?

No, Rivka replied.

Pray that you don't. They took two of ours and injured the majority of the rest. They are the worst creatures I've ever encountered. We'd appreciate it if Ankh could come.

I've already issued the orders. We'll be there in fifteen.

Proceed straight to Nadezhda and dock at any available station. Head to the center and take the stairs to the bottom deck. You'll find Ted working on the terminus.

Rivka signed off.

"If it blows, we've killed Ankh and Ted and a Magistrate and a heavy frigate and a heavy destroyer and a little bit more than that."

"Smedley, give me ship-wide, please."

Of course. Use the terminal on the bulkhead. I know you're more comfortable speaking aloud.

Terry walked slowly, shaping his thoughts, but more wasn't better. His message needed to be short.

"Attention all hands on the *War Axe*. This is Colonel Terry Henry Walton. Until the terminus on the space station is active, there is a risk that the device at the rift on Benitus Seven could blow. If it does, it will obliterate the planet and possibly this entire star system. We can move to a safe distance, leaving the crew on Nadezhda Station to handle it, or we can stay. There is a significant risk in staying. If we decide to take the ship, Char and I will be getting off and joining our friends. Please decide quickly."

A few seconds later, Micky responded using the same broadcast. "Sometimes the great thing about being in charge is taking irrational risks, especially when the consequences are ours alone. Every person in the known galaxy would tell us to leave, but none of them are here. I speak for the whole crew when I say we're not going anywhere until this problem is fixed. Do we need to provide additional support to the station? We have plenty of volunteers."

"The support Ted needs is already on its way and should appear soon. Thank you, Micky, for everything." Terry looked down, but that wasn't the end of the conversation.

"The crew will be joining you on the hangar deck and rotating through for the feast. No beer for them, unfortunately. Save some for when they go off-shift. I'm going to go comm-dark to avoid any uncomfortable questions from outside the system. Until then, this is Captain Micky San Marino, and you have your orders."

CHAPTER TWENTY-NINE

Kor'nar, Mining Facility

"I know they're here," Jake said the second he got off the shuttle. He twisted and ducked as if in the line of fire, eyes searching the nearby trees for movement. "Kae?"

Kae dipped to get out of the shuttle. "Thanks, Webster, for the bullseye delivery," he told the shuttle pilot.

"Nothing better than flying a real mission," he replied. "I'm tired of shuttling chow from the ship."

"I thought I smelled something." Kae continued onto the landing field, manicured and ready to receive shipping. He looked for the bot that maintained it since the site was supposed to be unmanned. The rest of the unit ran off the ship, and it headed skyward. The second shuttle settled in and the air defense team disembarked, quickly located two firing positions, and started setting up. Kae used his sensors to check the tree line.

Infrared shows targets within the facility, a dozen, not Kor'-narians. These are much hotter.

Roger, Jake replied, continuing to scan the area. He

moved forward, directing the troops wide to the flanks and bringing the ends forward into a V formation. He waved for them to spread out.

Moving ahead to cut off an escape route. Kae loped around the formation before accelerating toward the rear of the facility.

"Stay sharp!" Jake warned his infantry. The presence of a mech gave them a sense of security as if they wouldn't have to do anything. The mining operation wasn't large, and although it could operate independently, it could also run manually. The spaces within supported a humanoid work crew but were too small for the mech to fit if the pirates decided they didn't want to surrender.

Jake expected to send his people into the facility.

The pistons driving the rock operations continued, oblivious to the machinations of the people in and around the facility. Jake didn't know how much of the mining operation was hardened or if it could be damaged and rendered non-operational. The Federation needed the malageodes because they were a means to an end, and Jake had a mission.

His people were not trained to clear buildings. He'd talked through what to do on the flight over, but that was thirty minutes without any practical application. The soldiers had no habits established to help them when they didn't have time to think. Jake wanted them to be able to carry through but expected they would need the body bags he had stashed in the shuttle. He hadn't brought a lot. He could only hope that they wouldn't need many. Jake didn't mention those concerns to the soldiers.

They had a job to do. His included worrying like a mother hen, but he shoved that to the back of his mind.

A shot rang out, and the soldier on the extreme right flank jerked and fell. The entire unit dropped to the deck and returned fire. No one was sure where the shot had come from. They replied by randomly pinging all the windows.

"Fire and maneuver!" Jake shouted. "Left wing, fire. Right wing, advance!"

The left side of the V formation started shooting, peppering the facility. The plexi windows split and caved in. The right wing ran halfway to the facility before dropping, aiming, and delivering withering fire into the facility.

If it wasn't damaged before... Jake thought.

The left wing popped up and started running. Someone in the facility fired back, drawing a full broadside of small arms fire, but the damage was done. One running soldier tumbled and rolled, grabbing his leg. Jake checked the soldier on the right. He lay unmoving.

Nine soldiers reached the rig and broke into two groups, moving toward the entrances. They didn't have breaching charges or flashbangs, so they had to open and clear the hard way. Had the Federation shared the information before they left, they would have been prepared for the contingency.

But no, they were sent to a bug planet with any action limited to the surface. Jake logged this as a valuable lesson: maintain contingency packs for any operation, regardless of whether it was foreseeable. Better not to have enough than to have nothing.

Jake ran across the open ground. As a lone soldier, he

was less likely to draw fire since the facility's inhabitants had much bigger things to worry about. One of the two breach teams turned the handle and opened the door. It hadn't been locked.

Maybe it didn't have locks. This was a remote facility. Maybe the locks had been disabled by the pirates, and they hadn't bothered fixing them once they'd gained entrance. Jake didn't know why he wondered about such trivialities.

One of the soldiers dove to the ground about five meters back from the opening and unleashed a burst inside, then waved with his rifle for the others to enter. After the first two were in, he jumped to his feet and followed. Four soldiers went into the facility.

Jake heard random, muffled shots but couldn't tell if they were Belzonian weapons or pirates. A mech's railgun burped and silenced. *Kae?*

Splash two runners. Eight left.

Their cover fire had removed two of the enemies. Jake considered that a good sign. He passed the second breach team, which was struggling with getting the door open. The other door's lock had been broken.

"Stand aside and be ready to fire." The soldiers raised their weapons, barrels pointed at the door. Jake reared back and kicked with all his enhanced strength, and the door flew open after the lock shattered. He dropped out of the way and rolled to the side. The first soldier around the corner fired at the same time as someone inside and fell when the back of his head exploded as the round exited.

The others fired and ran inside. Jake didn't look at the dead body, just followed the others in. There would be more if they gave the pirates too much time to think.

CRAIG MARTELLE & MICHAEL ANDERLE

Splash two more, Kae reported.

Jake's head was buzzing. He hadn't heard the industrial-grade railgun fire. It didn't matter that he hadn't, only that the enemy numbers were rapidly being reduced. He'd already left a trail of bodies, but that didn't matter either. It would later, but not right now.

They had to clear the facility. Shots rang throughout, but Jake couldn't tell where they were coming from. The lead soldier stopped at a corner and flashed his head around it, pulling back before his brain registered what it had seen. Two rounds slammed into the wall, and he dropped to a knee and fired around the corner. Two more rounds flew over his head and hit the wall, then he fired once more and was re-aiming when the third round took him out. A soldier wrapped his rifle around the corner and fired blindly, waving the barrel in a circle. A second soldier jumped out and fired, waited for a second, and fired again.

"Clear," he said before moving forward, looking over the weapon's barrel for more targets.

Jake followed them around. They had reached the control room, which contained the largest window and had received the most incoming. A body was on the floor, and two humanoids crouched in the corner with their hands up.

"On your faces!" Jake yelled and ran in front of the other soldiers to keep them from killing the two. They'd seen too many teammates fall to have sympathy, but the intruders had surrendered and could be a good source of intel.

Also, protecting them kept *him* from killing them.

He looked at his soldiers. "Search these two, then set up

a blocking position. Cover those two corridors. Don't shoot our people." Jake waved his helmet in the window before carefully peeking out. "Get in here. That entrance." He pointed at the door through which they entered.

The soldiers were less than kind during their search. "They're clean."

These two didn't look like the others.

Jake kicked chairs against the wall under the window. "Sit down." He leaned back with his weapon aimed toward them. "Who are you, and what are you doing here?"

They didn't hesitate since fear was a powerful motivator. "I'm Kalens Twilgrop, a human from Alchon Prime. Jenbar and I are technicians. We're running this facility, but we can't tell you for who because they'll kill our families and us!"

"You should have thought about who you were getting into bed with before you stripped naked," Jake replied casually.

A shout came from the hallway. "Third squad coming in!"

"Clear," the soldier barring the corridor called before the others appeared.

Kae? Jake asked. *Where are we?*

There are two left, but I think you have them in custody since you all seem to be in the same room.

We have them. Technicians. They surrendered without putting up a fight. Thanks, man.

"All hands! The building is clear. Search the facility for boobytraps and recover our dead. Lieutenant Gamon, take charge and report when the facility is clear."

"The lieutenant is down, sir," one of the soldiers stated. "He was on the end of the right flank."

Jake hadn't known who had been where. He wondered why he hadn't recognized who was who when they deployed into a combat formation.

"Corporal Thaksin. Take over and secure the mining facility."

The soldiers passed the word by shouting the order down the myriad of corridors.

Can you see underground? Jake asked.

There's only one level, and yes. I can see that no one is there.

Thank the gods. Jake exhaled with relief. He didn't want to bury anyone else. He looked out the window. Members of the air defense squad were helping the wounded soldier. The other had been moved closer to the airstrip and lay with his helmet over his face.

He went over to the two men and grabbed them by their hair. "Look at this!" He aimed their faces at the dead pirates. "Three of mine were killed retaking this facility, so you're going to fucking tell me who you work for."

Jake pulled their heads upward, and they rose from their chairs until they were finally standing, and then on their tiptoes.

"You can see that my patience is at an end. Answer me now, please."

The soldiers watched the colonel. He wanted to hurt these men badly for the crimes of their fellows, but he had to set the conduct standard for his people. Belzonians could be businesslike when it came to soldiering but still be kindhearted souls. Jake was angry. He let the two stand on their own and leaned close, his head between theirs, whispering where his soldiers couldn't hear.

"I will throw one of you out this window while dick-smashing the other. You'll swap, and I'll keep it up until you're neutered. Then we'll get down to business. I'll find out who you are because I have the full resources of the Federation to help me. This isn't my mining operation, it's theirs. I was sent here to find out what happened, and I'm going to do that. We're going to find your families before the pirates, and we're going to send them to that prison planet, where they'll live out the rest of their days in pain and agony, in constant fear for their lives. So just fucking tell me and save yourselves all that grief."

"The Glicardi Contingent. They're paying us."

"That wasn't so hard, was it?" Jake let them sit down. "Drink your water. It's dry here."

Jake handed them the bottles that had been sitting on the table and were surprisingly still upright. He didn't care if they weren't theirs. They had water in them. The technicians didn't hesitate. They had been broken, innocents who had been co-opted by the promise of money or power or whatever had coerced them into a criminal's life. They were in over their heads. "Give me your family's addresses and names. We'll get that info to the Federation and take them into protective custody by the end of the day. There would have been a price if you didn't cooperate, and there is a reward since you did. Now, when are these scumbags coming to pick up the next load?"

"They are scheduled for tomorrow." Jenbar had become the talkative one as soon as he was released from his vow of silence.

"Write down the names and addresses. We'll get that to our people soonest."

The technicians looked for paper and an ink stick, but there wasn't anything within reach. "For fuck's sake," the colonel grumbled. "Where is it?"

They pointed in two different directions. He opened drawers until he found what he wanted and handed it to them. He waited for them to finish before snagging one of the soldiers. "Give this to the shuttle for relay to *Angkmoor*, with a follow-on to General Reynolds' office on Yoll." Jake thought for a moment and jotted down what he'd gathered without violating mission security. General Reynolds would know what he meant, but no one else would. The direction to put the families into protective custody was crystal-clear, plus the request for assistance had a specific ship in mind.

"Go," he told the soldier before turning back to the two technicians. "Now you're going to tell me exactly what one of these transfers looks like, walking me through it step by step..."

CHAPTER THIRTY

Kor'nar, Trans-Pacific Task Force Expeditionary Camp

The armor headed out with Major Punyaa in the lead tank. He followed the trail Kaeden had blazed but tracked heavy metal didn't move anywhere near as quickly as someone in powered combat armor. The mechs could move seamlessly across almost any terrain. At least there were no rivers. The terrain was mostly smooth, but it was slow going.

Punyaa knew he didn't have the luxury of time so he pressed forward, abusing his tank as he pushed it, watching forward to find the path of least resistance. He checked the clock. It had taken them twenty minutes to get underway, and the hive was twenty-one kilometers away. It would take him another hour to reach it.

Belzonian tanks were not great cross-country vehicles, being fragile enough to throw a track too often. Punyaa hoped they would upgrade to mechs, being awarded the armored combat suits once they proved themselves. He rushed down a hillside and hit the bottom hard, ramming into the hill opposite and almost bringing the tank to a halt. The major hit the turret hard—too hard. He heard the crack through the padded vest; at least one rib had broken.

"Watch this hill! Slow down, angle across the bottom, and get up the other side," he ordered the three companies of his battalion. The remaining tanks occupied the high ground overlooking the camp in case they were attacked. Much of the camp's firepower would be unavailable to repel a concerted attack. Those left behind had the responsibility of keeping the landing area secure, and by all means to protect the chow hall. A well-fed soldier could fight any battle.

It was odd how the troops responded to the call to action. They put on their war faces and readied themselves for battle. The leadership hoped they wouldn't have to fight it. Two of the Lion Corps remained behind to take charge. Majors Baroon and Anthen carried the burden of keeping the camp secure.

They were ready, but most believed the battle would be joined a long way away. Those left behind didn't relish missing the action. They had trained for this, even though there was a great deal of training left. The soldiers wondered. No one knew how they would do in battle until they experienced it for themselves.

Marcie headed out in the first wave of infantry being airlifted to the hive. The pilot flew low and fast, arriving at the hive in short order. Much to Marcie's relief, the area out front was devoid of Naries.

They knew it would be because a drone was observing the area, but Marcie needed to see it for herself. Once the shuttle dropped into the clearing, the rear hatch popped, and Marcie ran down the ramp to direct the soldiers into place. She performed those duties for the first ten shuttles, then handed it off to Lion Corps member Captain Wattana. The colonel took a company to station astride the doorway in case the Naries boiled out. The soldiers could cut them off without having to fire a shot and pass the word that Marcie was ready to talk to the new leader.

She hoped that would be enough since she had no other cards to play.

One thousand infantry had been delivered by the time the armor arrived. Marcie hurried down the trail to meet Major Punyaa and direct the armor into defensive positions where they would be hull down, the majority of the vehicle behind a hilltop, leaving the turrets and guns exposed to maintain a clear line of sight.

Marcie stopped when she saw him before jumping onto his tank and taking a closer look. His lips were bloody, and a pink froth was visible when he opened his mouth to speak. "Hit some bumps on the way," he explained.

"You look like shit. Did you break a rib?"

"Astute as always, Colonel," he said between gurgling breaths.

"Get down and catch a shuttle back to camp for transport to orbit. You need to have that treated by professionals."

"I'll be fine, Colonel. I can't leave now. The action hasn't started yet."

Marcie swept her arms wide to take in the area. "We got here before the Zirrics. There is no action, and we aim to keep it that way. Now get the fuck down. It would be undignified for me to drag you out of there. I assume your tank can operate without you?"

"I think that's how it operates most of the time," Punyaa quipped. He started to cough, splattering blood speckles into his hand. "Maybe I'll take you up on your kind offer."

"Maybe…" Marcie parroted. "Don't worry, there will be another time."

"I expect you're right." Marcie helped Punyaa from the turret onto the hull. "Why build this fine fighting force for a one-time deal?"

Marcie jumped down and held her hands up. He bent over, gasped, and nearly fell but caught himself and leaned heavily on Marcie.

"You need to cut out those late-night snacks, Punyaa. You're packing on the pounds."

"Muscle weighs more than fat, or so I'm told. Just dense is all, which could apply to a couple of things."

Marcie stood him upright as shuttles approached with the next wave and sent, *Wait at the landing site after drop off. You're taking an injured pax back to camp.*

Roger, the pilot replied.

"Your ride is waiting. Don't kill yourself getting there, but don't let the grass grow under your feet."

Punyaa looked down at the dirt. He hadn't seen a single blade of grass since he'd been on Kor'nar.

"You know what I mean," Marcie clarified. She left him alone to struggle to the shuttle, maintaining his dignity while trying to hurry through the pain.

Marcie didn't have time to see him all the way there. She directed the next stream of inbound toward another avenue of approach, backing up the tank company on the right flank.

She didn't want them to bunch up, but there wasn't a great deal of space in which to operate.

This is the last wave, pass it on. All shuttles still in the air return to base camp, Marcie told the inbound pilots. Once she got confirmation from them, she moved close to the entry and began the ordeal of waiting.

She had twenty-eight hundred troops and three tank companies on site. She hoped it was enough to handle anything the Zirrics could throw at the Naries.

There was only one thing missing. The sergeant major was going to be in the last wave, so she'd have to make do. Just like with everything else, things had a tendency to twist away from her firm grasp.

Or as Terry Henry used to say, "No plan survives first contact."

She was going to modify that to "No plan survives the commander's best efforts to implement it." That was why mission-type orders were so important. They allowed the leaders down to the squad level to make the best decision to help them accomplish the mission.

Marcie hoped it was enough, which brought up another Terry Henry quote: "Hope is a lousy plan."

Nadezhda Station, in Orbit above Benitus Seven

Timmons met *Wyatt Earp* at the docking port. Once the airlock cleared, Ankh walked through, wearing a vacant expression. A young woman with platinum hair walked with him, holding his hand to lead him.

CRAIG MARTELLE & MICHAEL ANDERLE

"I'm Groenwyn. He and Erasmus are already working with Plato and Ted. You know Floyd. Where are we going?"

The wombat bounced on the deck and ran in little circles around the people. Sue caught her and picked her up to scratch her belly.

"I'll take them," Sue offered and headed into the access corridor that led to the central core of the station. They could hear her talking to Floyd as she walked away. "Somebody's getting heavy."

Timmons stayed behind to see if anyone else was coming aboard. Red was next, the Magistrate's massive security guard. "Damn, Red! You're looking fit."

"Is there anyone on board besides you guys from the Bad Company?"

"Nope. There are five of us here, and you know us all."

"Good. There weren't any bets on this mission, and I wouldn't want to disappoint people."

Rivka pushed Red out of the way to force her way past. "No crimes? Maybe I will get some relaxation time."

"If they don't get the terminus fixed, we're all going to die a horrible death. The good news is that it'll be quick." Timmons shrugged. "Hey! Did Ankh get that delivery service up and running?"

"How do you know about that?" Rivka wondered.

"We got a shitload of AGB food a little bit ago. There's some left, but that's our meals for as long as we're here and not dead."

"Don't tell anyone," Rivka cautioned, removing her credentials from her jacket pocket and waving them in Timmons' face.

"Hey! It's common knowledge, so that can't be a crime."

"It is *not* common knowledge. Violating the Secrets Act is a crime, and you're two steps into a three-step walk off the plank."

Timmons couldn't tell if she was serious. Red hadn't waited. Lindy joined him, and they hurried after Sue and Ankh.

Sahved appeared, and Timmons did a double-take. "Whoa! Tall dude."

"I'm a Yemilorian. Our environment is conducive to growing tall. I am average height for my race."

Rivka looked at him. "Don't you have classes?"

He looked beyond them at the station before mumbling under his breath and returning to *Wyatt Earp*.

"A heavy frigate. Can I get a tour?"

"Not quite yet. We have some issues with multiple personalities. I have three AIs living in my ship and another couple hitching a ride. And before you ask, *Wyatt Earp* is the official embassy for the Singularity."

"I don't know what any of that is, but we better check on Ted. He might need help now that there are four minds ready to give the minions tasks. Come with me if you'd like."

Rivka walked with Timmons as he talked through the highlights of the station, like the place where Terry Henry had duct-taped Dokken to his face.

"I heard about that. Right there, huh?" Rivka took a moment to look at the spot, trying to imagine the lengths Terry Henry had gone to to save the dog's life. It was the length he'd go to save anyone, which made him different. Take receiving over three hundred million credits for the art recovery reward. He didn't accept any of that money. He gave a bonus to all the members, including the crews of Bad Company ships, and put the rest into the operating budget. "Some people live up to a higher ideal. I think we all could learn a lesson or two from Terry Henry Walton."

"He punched Char in the face. Kicked her, too," Timmons said deviously.

Rivka narrowed her eyes. "That doesn't sound like him."

"Okay, it was before they were lovers. She tried to establish Alpha dominance over him. He didn't want to, but she pushed him into a fight. He won, and they've been having make-up sex for a hundred and fifty years."

"If we all had such rewarding fights, this galaxy would be a better place."

Rivka's mood darkened. Her fights were with criminals and usually to the death.

Timmons wasn't the most astute when it came to the feelings of others, but he had his moments. "What you did for the AIs was spectacular. We lease our ship *Iracitus* from the AI who runs it in a contractual arrangement where he can go where he wants. He's free to do as he pleases, but he takes care of us. Like being here. He's attached to the docking ring, even though we told him to leave and wait for us on the other side of a Gate. He chose to stay, just like the *War Axe* and everyone else. You know that you could die at any moment?"

"How is that different from my normal day?" Rivka laughed off the question. "I expect we'll get *some* warning. It won't just blow. Everyone here seems unduly concerned about it."

Timmons looked at the floor, shuffling his feet. "Terry

and Char are retiring from the Bad Company. Everyone expected it, but no one wants to see it happen. We feel like if we leave, we'll lose them forever because they won't go. They'll stay here with Ted until the job is done, even though they told everyone else to go. We gave them the finger. No one is going anywhere, and it looks like you're a member of that club."

"The High Chancellor might get a little irked at losing a Magistrate, but he'll get over it. Life will continue. Someone else will get an opportunity. We asked our guys, but the AIs on board *Wyatt Earp* are fine with putting themselves at risk since the ambassador is here."

"Ambassador?"

"Erasmus, ambassador for the Singularity. He lives in Ankh's head."

Timmons blinked. "Ankh's head is a little big for his body."

"Leave Ankh alone, or everyone on my ship will beat you up."

"Is that a formal ruling, Magistrate?" Timmons coughed at the playground threat.

"It's from the school of hard knocks and the reality of him bringing AGB to us anytime we want since we always want AGB. Some of the places we go? Try eating that swill and smiling in the name of diplomacy."

Timmons started walking again. "You're real people. The stories about you seem bigger than life."

"Just stories. Don't put any stock in them. Same could be said for TH."

"I hear he's having a big party in the hangar bay on the *War Axe*," Timmons offered. They reached the stairwell and started down. The smell of the food eight levels below wafted past them.

"Of course, he is. Under threat of a catastrophic explosion that could kill us all, he's having a party."

Timmons frowned. "He has AGB beer over there, and we're over here. Fucking Ted better fix that goddamn power system so I can get some goddamn beer!"

By the time the Magistrate and Timmons reached the floor above Ted's workshop, the lights had brightened, foliage had appeared, and the station was crowded with color and sound. Timmons stopped and tried to look everywhere at once. Vines crept down the handrails, branches reached toward him, and leaves hung near his face. He reached out and touched one, and it pushed back against his hand. He swished his hand across the vines and felt the softness of their leaves and the rigidity of the stalks.

Rivka moved the leaves aside to look beyond. A veritable jungle lay beyond, complete with birds of fantastic plumage. A primate chittered before disappearing behind a trunk.

"It works," Timmons muttered. "I don't know why I'm surprised."

"Because we've only been here for ten minutes?" Rivka asked, used to the miracles Ankh and Ted could perform when they worked together, four minds functioning as one.

They hurried downstairs to find the others. Groenwyn was dancing on the workshop level with Floyd, who sniffed and pawed the leaves.

"Do you think we can get this for *Wyatt Earp*?" she asked.

Rivka smiled and shook her head. "Only if Ankh considers it to be a practical use for the computing power. Let's see what he has to say."

They found Ted and Ankh on the bottom level. They were watching as Shonna, Merrit, Sue, Red, and Lindy unhooked the banks of Etheric power supplies, which were now redundant.

"Don't you want backup power available?" Timmons wondered.

Ted looked at him as he usually did and didn't bother answering. Rivka choked back a laugh. "I know that look well. I get it from Ankh all the time," she whispered.

"Can we assume that we're not going to die?" Timmons asked.

"Yes," Merrit replied. "Now dig in. We have to lug all this crap to *Ramses' Chariot*."

"I'll take two for *Wyatt Earp*." Ankh held up two fingers to reinforce his request. Rivka threw her hands up. She remembered once, not so long ago, when the ship was hers.

"Hey," Shonna called. "Watch this." She waved her elbow by the call panel for the elevator. It popped open, and she sashayed in.

"Hold the door!" The others hurried inside. Timmons and Rivka dug in to help. No one stopped the Magistrate, and Ted and Ankh continued to commune without wasting time with spoken words.

Red was the only one capable of carrying two. "I'll take these to our ship."

They picked theirs up and waited for the next elevator.

I wonder if anyone told the War Axe? Timmons used his internal comm chip to relay through Iracitus.

Micky, Timmons here.

The captain replied, *Yes. Smedley is very excited that the Magistrate and the ambassador are both here. He hopes the Magistrate will be able to join us on the* War Axe *for a short while.*

"Smedley, the *War Axe*'s AI, wants to know if you will join him over there."

Rivka shook her head. "We need to get back. We put the law on hold when we received Ted's request, but criminals never stop what they're doing. Can't let them gain a foothold since they get overconfident right quick and in a hurry."

"I'm sorry to hear that." The elevator arrived, they boarded, and it made a quick trip to the top. Timmons grinned after being delivered on the docking ring level. "I've made so many trips up and down those stairs."

"But now there are vines," Rivka suggested.

"That makes it all better," Timmons shot back. "Not."

Everyone delivered their loads and returned for another round. Red had brought the entirety of *Wyatt Earp's* crew to help. He stopped them to improve the efficiency of their work.

"Two crews, one loading the power supplies into the elevator down here and one unloading and hauling to the ships." He pointed at three people. "Everyone else upstairs for delivery duty."

The ratio worked, and after twenty minutes, the power supply room was devoid of the small Etheric power supplies. Ted had even tagged two units for the *War Axe*, so it was overpowered in case Felicity was ever on board. He wanted to make sure any ship she traveled on was protected the best he could make it. The last two trips included the remaining food, trash, and Ted's tools.

Rivka, her crew, and the werewolves strolled around the docking ring level, the biggest by far on the station. Ted looked longingly at the virtual reality system now installed on Nadezhda. Ankh's expression remained blank.

"You can feel the life," Groenwyn said. "But Floyd has confirmed that you cannot eat the leaves. She is confused and disappointed. Only real life for our little girl."

"This is utterly amazing," Clodagh muttered, eyes wide and gawking. As an engineer, she didn't know where to start for such a projection to manifest as it did.

"The builders of this system no longer exist, but I was able to find their information. Once Plato is able to decode it, we should be able to reproduce this. I believe there is little practical application, though," Ted noted.

"I concur." Ankh didn't say anything else.

"No practical application?" Sue blurted. "It could bring life to a lifeless station or a dead ship."

Ted headed back toward the ship. "I've been gone long enough. It is time to go home. I prefer dealing with reality and not the virtual. I will look through their records for other engineering we might be able to put to practical use."

"I bet Felicity would like this," Sue said to needle her ex.

Ted took a moment to look at the mezzanine and the appearance it now had. "She would," he admitted. "She will want it for Keeg Station."

Sue and Shonna smiled at each other, both thinking the same thing. A properly constructed environment would funnel the customers to their stores when they were up and running, especially if the only virtual reality was around their places. They rubbed their hands deviously. "Make sure you set aside a power supply or three for your lovely better half, Master Theodore," Sue drawled.

The return to their ships was made through a completely different station than the one they had entered, a station full of images of life. The air seemed cleaner, the day brighter, and their lives better.

Or it could have been because their deaths were no longer imminent.

"Get in there," Rivka said as the crew milled around outside the airlock. "The universe isn't going to save itself."

Clodagh clapped her on the shoulder. "Back to the grind."

Ankh was first in, hurrying toward the engineering section and his lab where he could play with his new toys. At least, that was how Rivka saw it.

The crew filed in, with the Magistrate entering last. After a final appreciative look, she headed through the airlock and slapped the big red button to secure the hatch. In three minutes, Chaz and the other AIs running *Wyatt Earp* had undocked the ship, and they sailed over their Gate's event horizon.

Iracitus and *Ramses' Chariot* traveled the short distance to the *War Axe*. There was still some work to do before they could leave, but the hard stuff was behind them.

CHAPTER THIRTY-ONE

Kor'nar, Trans-Pacific Task Force Expeditionary Camp

The sergeant major scowled at the returning shuttles, many of which still had their troops on board. He controlled his breathing and moved to a better position to welcome them back and direct them to the perimeter to fill soft spots in their defenses.

The first shuttle landed closest to the medical tent. This was one thing the colonels had insisted on when drawing the plans for the camp: Medevac had to butt up against a landing spot to minimize transport time to or from the tent. The better facilities were on the ships in orbit, but the field medics stabilized the injured.

Major Punyaa dragged himself to his feet and staggered a couple of steps before sitting down. The sergeant major ran aboard, with two medics carrying a stretcher right behind him.

"What'd you do to yourself, Major?" Monsoon held him steady until the stretcher was in place, then helped lower him.

"Ribs and tank turrets don't make great bedfellows." He coughed another blood splatter into his hand. "The colonel kicked me out of the war. I'll never live it down."

"Keep that attitude, Major. We'll get you patched up and back into the fight before you know it." The sergeant major nodded to the medics, who lifted the stretcher and rushed into the medical tent. The major was pale with a blue tinge and bags already heavy under his eyes. He looked to be one step from the grave.

Crantis pursed his lips. The major's injuries brought home the dangers of war even when shots weren't being fired.

He strode off the shuttle and headed to the middle of the landing field. As troops disembarked, he directed them toward the perimeter, even those units that had not had perimeter duty yet.

"Everyone wants to be infantry until it comes time to do infantry shit!" Monsoon bellowed at the troops. "It makes you sexy, now get your dumb asses on the line. Those foxholes aren't deep enough. Keep digging!"

Majors Baroon and Anthen appeared. "What are you up to, Sergeant Major?" Baroon asked.

"Seems like the hive is filled to the brim with Belzonians and doesn't have any more room for a beast like myself."

"They got turned back?"

"Two thousand, maybe twenty-four hundred, made it forward. We're going to have to take a headcount and find out who's where. This terrain isn't what our people are used to. Anyone lost out there is going to have a hard time. The Kor'narians won't make it easy for them, either."

"We'll get right on that, sergeant major. Do we report to you afterward?"

Monsoon cocked his head left and then right before looking at the rank on his collar. He then stared at the major's collar. "No, sir. You need to keep the tally. There's a roster in the admin tent."

"Crap. We need to check names off one by one? That could take the rest of the deployment."

"No, sir," Monsoon said as patiently as possible. "Trickle down, feed up. Tell your direct reports to account for their people and so on. The platoon commanders report numbers, and if anyone is not present, you assemble a report by exception. Heaven help the unit leader who reports someone as present who is not."

"Shit! I knew that." The majors hurried away. Monsoon tried not to look too shocked. Accountability had been huge at the Federation level. "Leave no one behind" meant the leadership always had to know where everyone was.

Four to six thousand were supposed to move to the hive, but somewhere short of that, the cord had been cut. No plan survived anything.

The sergeant major went to the southern perimeter because they were the pointy end of the camp's spear. The Zirrics came from the south and southeast. That was where they had appeared in the first place. Few others had caught sight of a Kor'narian. He needed those on the southern perimeter to be sharpest.

They were sitting on the sides of their foxholes with their weapons inside, leaning against the dirt walls. Many weren't wearing helmets.

The sergeant major looked away in case his eyes were

deceiving him. The rest of the camp bustled with the activity of the newly arrived getting back on the perimeter. The support services were in full operation. Smoke trailing from the massive hot chow tent, shuttles were dusting off. And then there were those in front of him.

"Come on, Sergeant Major. Let your hair down and join us," one private joked. Monsoon approached slowly, his fists clenching and unclenching almost spasmodically. The private's smile disappeared.

"Private," the sergeant major started in a low and dangerous voice, "what kind of clown show is this?"

"Sergeant Major? We're just taking a break, that's all. This is boring as hell. What happened to the go go go we trained for?"

"*Un*trained is what I'd say. You haven't learned the discipline required of real soldiers. I'm happy the colonel isn't here to see this. Get back in your fucking holes, and while half of you watch the trees, the other half of you keep digging. These aren't deep enough to protect a five-year-old."

The private looked at the other members of the squad as they slowly slid into their knee-deep foxholes.

"You get to work right fucking now, and when I return, these holes better be deep enough to fucking stand in, and you better be acting like real fucking soldiers, or I'll start ripping fucking hair out by the roots. Keep your fucking helmets on, you fucking morons, to protect what few fucking brains are left in there!" Spittle flew from the sergeant major's mouth, and the private winced under the torrent.

"Damn, Sergeant Major. That's a lot of fucking."

"You're pissing me off. Shut your cakeholes and get to work. Thirty minutes. Deep enough to stand in, or we'll see if they're deep enough to bury what's left."

The private slid into the hole and slammed his helmet over his ratty hair. His head jerked forward a second before they heard the report. The helmet bounced off and spun onto the ground. The private's eyes crossed, and Monsoon shoved him down.

He cupped his hands around his mouth and shouted toward the camp, "INCOMING!" then turned back to the squad. "Get down!"

In an instant, all of them had helmets on their heads, crouching in what they had of their foxholes. The tree line erupted in puffs of smoke. Monsoon was too slow diving for the ground and was hit in the chest twice and once in the leg, grunting when he was hit. He low-crawled to get behind a small berm before breaking out a bandage to press against his leg.

"Fire back! Shoot them," the sergeant major growled through gritted teeth. A few were already shooting, but at Monsoon's command, more opened up. He risked a look over the berm. The entire approach was filled with black insectoid bodies. They were coming.

All of them.

Kor'nar, the Naries Hive

What? Marcie demanded after the shuttle pilot relayed the news that the camp was under attack. *Pick me up. I need to get back there.*

We can't land, ma'am. There are bullets flying everywhere back there.

Marcie cursed her lack of contingency planning as she ran through the array in her mind. *Jake and Kae are on the other side of the planet, and we have a big chunk of combat power in the middle of nowhere, watching a rock.*

We have movement, ma'am, the shuttle operator reported. *About ten klicks due west, heading toward the camp.*

Can you see where they came from? Marcie asked, but she already knew the answer.

They are destroying everything in their path, leaving a trail from the other side of this mountain.

Roger. Prepare for pickup from the Naries hive. We are not going back to the camp, but an alternate location from which to launch a counterattack. We might not be able to help the camp from the inside, but we sure as hell can help them from out here. The best defense is a good offense.

If you say so, ma'am. Coming in hot, so be ready to load. Thirty shuttles are in the air, and that might be all you get, ma'am.

It'll be good enough. Thank you. Time to rock and roll.

Marcie passed the instructions to Captain Ravamoon, the Belzonian she'd busted from major. "Take charge and get these people loaded into the shuttles. We're moving to two locations. The shuttle pilots will know where. You'll take the one closest to us here and will probably have to stop them because the Zirrics are attacking the camp from the south. We don't need to be between these two armies when we're not at full strength, so we will bring over-whelming force to bear on them. Once they start retreat-ing, leave them be. The last thing we want to do is kill them, but we *will* bring this ill-advised attack to an end by whatever means we see fit. Can you carry out my orders?"

"Yes, ma'am," he said, sounding less confident than she hoped.

"Make it so." She ordered the soldiers who were blocking the door into the mountain to get on the shuttle. There were no Naries left inside. She ran aboard and signaled for liftoff. The next shuttle was landing as they ascended. She worked her way up front. "Fly low so we don't tip off the Naries. Sweep toward the camp and then out to a spot just on the other side of that hilltop. We're going to slam into them like a hammer on an anvil."

Kor'nar, Mining Facility

"This place can run without all this. These aren't controls as much as status meters," Jenbar explained.

"Thank goodness for that. The Federation is expecting their shipment, which isn't going to deliver what they expect, now is it?" Jake was still trying to think. He'd sent his message to the Federation and needed to contemplate the next steps.

"They come every month. They should be here within two days, but we'll be gone by then. Well, we were going to be gone, leaving with tomorrow's shipment."

"Didn't you think the Federation would find out someone had taken over their facility?"

"How did you find out?" Jenbar asked.

"The facility stopped broadcasting status reports."

"Dammit!" Jenbar slammed a fist into his hand. "I figured they'd have a safety system of some sort, but I thought it broadcast in case of a problem, not that it was continuous. It didn't seem like it was on."

"You're saying you shut it off?" Jake asked.

Jenbar nodded.

"Turn it back on."

The technician pointed to a destroyed panel. "No can do."

"Then you hotwire it. You two are in enough trouble without exacerbating your plight. You're technicians, not here for your combat skills, clearly. Fix it." Jake pointed.

The two moved toward the panel as if being closer would make them feel better about the potential for making the repair. After a short conversation and pulling off the bullet-riddled front panel with the gauges and buttons, Jenbar said, "This is going to take a while."

Jake looked at it. "Go stand over there." He pushed them in the direction he wanted them to go. One of the two soldiers guarding them encouraged them further with a nudge of his rifle barrel. Jake pulled the wires free that had been connected to the activation switch and wound the exposed ends together. "How hard is it to complete a circuit?"

"There's more to it than that..." Jenbar started, but Jake waved him to silence.

"Private, take them outside, then plant their faces in the dirt and shoot them."

"My pleasure, Colonel!" He snarled, "Get moving!"

Shock and terror seized them. Their legs turned to wood as they tried to walk.

"Belay that, Private. As much as I want to, they are in our custody, and we need to take care of them even if they aren't cooperative. Assholes. Get them out of here. I don't want to look at them."

The private deflated but turned back to the two and shoved them into the corridor and down the passageway. The other private joined him in securing the prisoners, leaving Colonel Braithwen by himself in the control room.

Kae strolled in.

"Aren't you worried about someone stealing your ride?"

"It's biometrically programmed. Any Bad Company warrior can use one, but no one else can unless their vitals are plugged into the system. You can't even open it if you're not registered. We're good."

"What do you think?"

"I think your plan for tomorrow is sound, assuming they bring a minimum of shooters. Did we find any comm devices on those guys?"

"Nothing, but they had to be in touch with their guys somehow. Even pirates know you have to communicate before getting in too deep. I think we might be royally screwed."

"Only if we're here by ourselves. I can't stand against fighters trying to take me out. I'll give them a big hairy what-for, but in the end, they'll have the upper hand."

Message from on high, Webster reported.

Go ahead, Jake said. Kae was tuned to the same channel and he listened in.

Angkmoor here. The camp is under attack by the combined Zirric and Naries forces. Do not return under any circumstances. Continue your mission, by order of Colonel Walton.

Message received. Braithwen out.

"Not only are we out here on our own, we're *really* on

our own. This is starting to suck," Kae remarked as he looked out the window at the landing field and surrounding forests.

"Asses hanging out."

"We'll assume we're on our own until we're not. We'll see if they get here in time. In between, we better say a prayer for our soldiers."

"How in the hell did both forces get fired up at the same time, and why attack us instead of each other?"

Kae started walking out. "Maybe the Kor'narians united against the common enemy, that being us, to chase us off the planet so they can get back to killing each other. This could be a decision they'll both regret. I'm going to grab a bite and then get back to it. Lots to do and little time."

Braithwen knew Kaeden was right. He headed outside to talk to the air defense team about camouflaging their positions.

CHAPTER THIRTY-TWO

Kor'nar, Trans-Pacific Task Force Expeditionary Camp

Crantis raised his rifle over the top of the berm. He had been taught to fire well-aimed shots, but the inbound mass didn't give him individual targets. He settled for not too high and not too low and sprayed from left to right. He knew he hit something, but couldn't tell what. They were going to be overrun, despite the intense fire from the fully engaged soldiers.

Artillery, drop the barrels and fire direct. Your target is the Peace Garden. Don't give me any shit about this. Fire, fire, fire, Monsoon ordered.

The incoming wave swept past the tent.

Where are my tanks? he passed over the comm, but three companies were gone. Only two dozen tanks remained, and they were split evenly between the two hillsides. *Fire, motherfuckers! You have to see the incoming bugs. Shoot them.*

A heavy caliber round boomed from behind him, almost instantly slamming into the horde and ripping a swath out of the mass attack. The puff of smoke from the hillside confirmed it had been fired by a tank.

High explosive and shoot, Monsoon ordered. He had no idea why they would have loaded armor-piercing rounds. The next round to hit was HE, and it exploded in a rainbow of insectoid blood and pieces.

A heavy round passed so close to Monsoon's head that he thought he felt his skin sizzle. The round passed harmlessly over the incoming horde's heads.

"Fuck this." Monsoon scrambled away from the berm and limped behind the lines. "Fire all you got, boys. This is the bigtime. This is what you joined the army for. Oorah, you bastards! Let them see what you're made of." Monsoon fired from a standing position, but the Zirric fire was random. They were focused on running toward the lines, and they'd be there in seconds.

The cannons roared, ripping through friendly lines to tear up the earth before the advancing tide. Soldiers died, but far more of theirs than the taskforce's.

Half the squad in front of Monsoon was down. Across the entire line, maybe two companies had been on watch when the Zirrics attacked, which was not enough to hold them back.

Tanks delivered a series of rounds danger-close between the camp's perimeter and the horde, and massive explosions delivered with precision forced the Zirrics to hesitate. A barrage of rifle fire came from behind the sergeant major. He looked back, thinking their lines had been penetrated, but it was friendly reinforcements running toward him, Major Anthen was leading them into the battle.

Monsoon dove out of the way to clear the line of fire.

Secure the artillery. Friendlies in the way, Monsoon ordered.

We have a new fire mission, Colonel Walton called it in. Firing to the north, Major Flayden, the arty group commander, replied.

The tanks cycled quickly. More moved around the hills to better firing positions and added to the incoming. Both the east and west hills joined the enfilade, filling the small area with explosions and shrapnel. As fast as they could fire, they sent rounds into the Zirrics.

The additional infantry stitched a quilt of small-arms fire through which the remaining Zirrics could not pass. The withering wall from all quarters brought the mass attack to a halt.

When the dust cleared in between the impacting tank rounds, the Zirrics were headed the other way.

"Cease fire!" the sergeant major shouted. *Tank company, cease fire.*

The rules of engagement had been to kill the fewest number of Kor'narians possible, and only after they fired first. The sergeant major had not forgotten.

Monsoon felt like collapsing. His nanocytes were sapping the energy from his body to make the repairs to his leg, and his chest hurt where the Zirrics' slugs had slammed into his body armor. He couldn't remember the last time he'd eaten. The bandage he'd tied around his leg was already coming loose, so he tightened it while gritting his teeth and commanding his body to respond. With a final tug to increase the pain and fire more adrenaline into his body, Monsoon stood up and straightened his helmet.

He made sure his rifle was on safe and slung it over his shoulder.

"Cover them while they police their injured and account for their dead," Monsoon ordered.

Anthen gave the follow-on orders to move the reinforcing companies into place. The devastation on the southern perimeter had been nearly complete, and that was without the Zirrics breaching.

The final protective fire had saved the camp for the moment. Monsoon switched to his internal comm. *Get a drone in the air to follow that retreat and keep your eyes peeled. We cannot have an army get that close ever again.* He promised himself he'd stop by the drone operators and rip them a new asshole for their failure to keep eyes on the immediate surroundings so they could give the camp a warning. *And I want to know what's happening up north!*

On cue, the artillery fired into the air nearly vertical, which told the sergeant major the enemy was close. A new enemy—the Naries.

Monsoon tried to limp as little as possible as he walked past the line, looking at the dead and wounded. Sad eyes looked up at him as injured soldiers held their comrades. "The failure is mine, son. I didn't ensure these foxholes were deep enough. I didn't provide enough heavy weapons. Secure the area and then account for our people. I want a report of our personnel status.

One soldier started crying.

"The time for that is later, son. Right now, the enemy is still out there, and they are going to come back better and stronger under cover of darkness when we least expect them. We have to be ready." He rested his hand on the soldier's arm before moving on. There would be a lot more like him. The task force had been blooded and survived.

The sergeant major had not expected it to be pretty. He'd been right.

Monsoon walked with measured steps, delivering encouraging words to every soldier he passed. Just a few words, but they were ones that mattered. "Make their sacrifice worth it. Stay sharp, stay alive. Grieve later, we're still in this fight. Dying now will honor none of them. Be proud. Be ready!"

A field ration pack was scattered among the remains of the firefight. Monsoon picked up a protein bar, opened it, and started eating. He found a second and ate it too. The troops eyed him suspiciously.

He gave them the answer they needed to hear. "In a fight, we don't let anything go to waste. Recover the ammo from our casualties. With respect, but load up. If they come again, don't you want to shoot back?"

"Yes, Sergeant Major," they replied softly. It was a grim job, but one that needed to be done. It would add steel to the nerves of most and destroy others. Monsoon could tell by the looks who was already coming to grips with their situation. The others needed direct words right then before their minds could take them too far into the abyss.

He gathered them one by one to stand in a small circle around him. "Take a knee and make yourselves comfortable. What do you think you saw here today?"

None of them could speak. One pointed to the pocked and pitted wasteland between the camp perimeter and the trees beyond. The bodies and blood of dead insectoids had turned the ground black as if it were covered with tar.

CRAIG MARTELLE & MICHAEL ANDERLE

"You saw fear. Maybe it seized you in its ugly grip and didn't let go. It's okay to be afraid. It's okay that you didn't fire at the enemy if you understand why. What would it take for you to engage? How much training would it take for you to execute the movements of aim and fire? Reload and fire again? That's all we're asking. The colonel and I tried to talk to them multiple times, and this was their answer. You didn't choose to make this happen. They did." Monsoon swept his arm dramatically, taking in the entirety of the battlefield.

"But you also saw the strength of your fellow Belzonians. Battle is something some are born to. Others can learn it, but it changes them all. Do you think I was always like this?"

One of the privates looked at the bandage on the sergeant major's leg. "Yes?" he ventured.

Monsoon laughed easily. "Okay. Maybe I *was* born for this, but that doesn't change how you feel and that you can come to grips with today and just as important, tonight and tomorrow. You'll think back too often to the firefight." Monsoon checked his watch. "It lasted a grand total of one minute and seventeen seconds."

He made up the duration. He had no idea how long it had taken, but it had not been long. He had to make a point.

"You will replay that one minute and seventeen seconds for the rest of your life, and what you did or did not do will be center stage. Or you can decide to do things differently. You can't change what happened, but you *can* control how you move forward. We are undermanned now, spread thin across three different sites. The task force needs you on this line, but help us to help you. Dig a hole that you can stand in. You were all exposed way more than you should have been, and that was my fault.

"But we have time to fix it. We're in this fight until the end. No one is going anywhere. I know I want to get off this dry, hot fucking rock, but I can't do that until we win. That means we drag the queens kicking and screaming to the negotiating table, and that is coming. I guarantee it. Colonel Walton and Colonel Braithwen are not going to let this go. The bugs weren't our enemy until they attacked us while we were at our weakest, and they will regret making us an enemy. I need you digging, and I need you ready in case they return. Now go on back to your units and get to work."

The soldiers nodded. One took two steps and doubled over to puke. The sergeant major picked up the private's helmet and waited for him to finish. He tried to take the helmet without looking up. Monsoon put a finger under his chin and pulled it up until their eyes met. "It's okay. The chow isn't that great. That's why they call it a field mess." He handed the helmet over and watched the soldier stumble away.

Monsoon spotted the company commander, the one who had been responsible for those who bore the brunt of the Zirrics' attack. He made a beeline for him.

The lieutenant was nursing a wound, waiting for the medics. The sergeant major leaned close. "When you have a job to do, you fucking do it, sir. Those men weren't prepared, and you let them be that way. You let them fuck off when they should have been ready."

"That's insubordination," the lieutenant began. He

didn't continue after the sergeant major tipped his head to look down his nose at the junior officer.

"You'll be lucky if you aren't court-martialed for murder. Their deaths are on your head. Get yourself unfucked and go out there and tell your fellow lieutenants to get their soldiers ready. We'll be holding you all accountable. Heaven help those who aren't taking this seriously. How many dead do you have?"

"I-I don't know," the young Belzonian officer replied.

"Figure it out and remember their names. They died to teach you and every single one like you what the price of your failure is. Did you think the colonels were fanatical for their own good?"

The lieutenant shook his head, flushing at the revelations. "What did you tell those men?"

"Don't replay the battle to condemn their actions but to learn from them, and do better next time. No one can ask anything else. I recommend you take that advice, too."

The artillery thundered a new salvo.

"Thank you, Sergeant Major."

"Get back on the line. Your soldiers need you."

He looked at his injury and then back at Monsoon. "But…"

"But nothing. Get back on the line, sir."

Monsoon walked away before anyone took notice. He stopped to speak to Major Anthen. "They are all yours, Major. Refuse the line."

"You think they'll flank us?"

"They may look like bugs, but they aren't stupid. They will have learned from that frontal assault, a tactic that might have worked against the Naries. They knew to attack us when we were weak. They'll find the weak spots, so give them a few. Just make sure they *aren't* weak."

"Words of wisdom, Sergeant Major." He clapped Monsoon on the shoulder. "Good work down here. Did you call the direct-fire shots from the artillery?"

"That might have been me. It wasn't the best choice, and I don't think I'll do it again."

"Not the best, but the only. There's a difference. Get to medical and get yourself patched up. We need you at a hundred percent." Anthen saw a difference of opinion developing among his subordinates and hurried away to deal with it.

"What next, you bastards?" Monsoon asked aloud, even though he was alone. He stood tall and looked across the southern and western perimeters. Where would the Zirrics appear next? What *looked* weak versus what *was* weak?

CHAPTER THIRTY-THREE

Kor'nar, North Approach to the Trans-Pacific Task Force Expeditionary Camp

Marcie hauled herself upward. She had never been a tree climber, even as a child. It wasn't something her mother or father encouraged. She was the blonde-haired, blue-eyed beauty, and despite the end of the world, Felicity had expected her to be pampered and live in luxury.

She pulled herself up to another branch. Part of her harness caught until she pulled hard enough to rip it loose. *The beauty queen thing didn't work out too well. Sorry, Mom.* When she was on the highest branch that would support her weight, she stood and looked at the approaching army.

Or was it just an entire people mobilized against their enemy?

The shuttle pilot had told her the attack upon the camp had been repelled, but she needed more details, and she knew who would have been in the middle of the fight.

Crantis, give me the bare truth. How are we? She was close enough to the camp that she expected her internal comm chip to reach.

Are you back? the sergeant major asked.

Setting an ambush for the inbound Naries. We estimate they are ten thousand strong. They outnumber us by a lot, but we have surprise and a lot of firepower on our side. The artillery has already pounded them pretty hard. They're a big target. We'll whittle the numbers down, so if they get past us, you should be able to hold the camp. How is it?

Mass wave attack. I've never seen anything like it. We fired everything we had at them and they still came. The tanks delivered the final blow, but a mass of them escaped. I've got drones following them. We won't be caught unaware again.

How are we, Crantis? she repeated.

We took a lot of casualties. These soldiers weren't ready. They might be now, though. I'll head to the northern perimeter. Major Baroon has responsibility for that sector. We'll get the soldiers excited about saving their own necks, and we'll put some rounds on target from our metal friends. Fire up the HE, main guns will be rocking.

I like your attitude, Sergeant Major. Be ready. Gotta go. Almost time to see what we can do about convincing the Naries to change their minds.

The insectoid mass had almost reached what Marcie called the "kill box," the focal point of fire for the ambush. She had held the artillery back to pin the forces between multiple lines of fire. The troops didn't have the best positions; many had concealment but not cover, that is, protection from incoming rounds. Not being seen was important until the shooting started, then not being hit by return fire was a higher priority.

The first rank of Naries moved through, and Marcie let them continue for a short while. The incoming artillery was the trigger to close the trap. *Fire*, she ordered.

Within two seconds, the main tubes sent their high explosive rounds downrange. They arced high before dropping on the pre-designated target points, areas on the ground where they expected the Naries to pass. The explosions ripped through the front of the column and farther back. The infantry opened up, full auto at first to deliver as many bullets into the mass as possible before switching to single-shot mode and firing well-aimed rounds.

No sooner had the first salvo landed than the second salvo was underway.

The Naries were immediately in disarray after the fantastic losses they suffered. Like cockroaches running after a light was turned on, they bolted in every conceivable direction.

The small-arms fire continued.

The second artillery salvo landed on the dead and dying. *Adjust fire. Targets Charlie and Delta. HE and shoot.*

The group of soldiers in front of her started firing wildly as the insectoids ran through any clear ground. There were too many, and they continued into the meager lines and through. Marcie took aim with her JDS, but they passed her and kept running. The artillery started a brush fire. She shielded her eyes to see better.

"Retrograde to the camp. Fast as you can!" she shouted. "*RUN!*" The squad closest to her took off in the general direction of their northern perimeter.

All hands at the expeditionary camp, friendlies inbound. I say again, friendlies inbound. There may be Naries, but hold your fire. Repeat this message.

Marcie watched how quickly the fire spread in fascination.

Do you have anyone who knows how to fight wildfires? Marcie asked the sergeant major.

Angkmoor, the Trans-Pacific Task Force Flagship, in Orbit above Kor'nar

"Where'd they come from?" the captain wondered. He decided quickly that it didn't matter. They were inbound and probably not friendly. "Prepare to fire point defense. Recall the combat vessels."

"Sir, medevac with a Major Punyaa on board has just cleared the atmosphere. He needs immediate surgery. Bring them in?"

"Not if we want to save the ship. Tell them to hide while we wait for our escorts."

The comm officer relayed the message.

Twelve cruisers and destroyers had been on patrols to give more warning to the fleet should pirates appear, but when the pirates materialized between the fleet's warships and the transports, they defeated the Belzonian plan before firing a single shot. The captain had bet it all on the warships seeing the pirates first.

"Missiles inbound. Point defenses engaging."

The ship vibrated as the automated defense systems fired, and the captain started to lose confidence. He punched the button for the shipwide intercom. "Brace for impact!" The instant he finished the first missile rammed

419

home, blowing a chunk out of the side of the ship before the violent eruption of atmosphere and molten steel.

"Integrity breached. Damage control is on their way," the internal controls officer remarked.

"Fire at the ships!"

"They have already banked out of range for our point defense systems. We remain vulnerable."

"Helm, full speed toward the nearest cruiser." The captain transmitted the message to the other three troop transport vessels.

The ship moved agonizingly slowly as the attacking ships came again: five small ships, little more than torpedo boats, making them nearly impossible to hit for the aging and technologically challenged Belzonian fleet.

"Brace for impact," the captain told the crew a second time as a new wave of missiles raced toward the *Angkmoor*. Point defenses cycled madly to create a barrier of projectiles into which some of the missiles found their way. Others cleared the cloud and continued. The captain closed his eyes and tensed.

The ship groaned, and lights flashed with the impacts. They came back on for a moment before the darkness returned. Emergency lighting came to life after an agonizingly long time. Even the alarm klaxons didn't sound.

"Damage report."

"Engines are offline, and we're starting to drift. Power is offline. Computer systems are offline." The systems officer looked forlornly at the captain.

"Start with what's working," the captain coaxed.

"Internal communications are functioning. Automated repair systems have engaged, I think. Standby." The systems officer pressed his headset tightly against an ear while furiously jotting notes. Bulkheads at frames 120, 140, 210, and 560 have sealed to contain breaches."

"How many personnel were in those areas?" the captain asked. The systems officer studied his notes while trying to recall which sections had been penetrated. Most of the personnel worked far from the hull and exterior bulkheads, but the missiles had penetrated deep into the ship's interior.

The captain could only assume the other transports were speeding toward a quick rendezvous. The pirates could be returning to finish them off. The screens were down, along with external sensors. They were blind and dead in space.

"I'm heading out to assist with damage control. Let me know when we get the important stuff back online," the captain told the bridge crew. He left it to them to figure out what was important. At this point in time, anything they could bring to life was a victory.

If the pirates didn't kill them first.

Kor'nar, Mining Facility

"The fleet has come under attack by pirate vessels. *Angkmoor* is down. The fleet is moving to a standoff position closer to the Gate," Webster relayed.

"That means the pickup ship is coming in early," Colonel Braithwen replied. They had a ways to go to be ready, but it wasn't meant to be. *Kae, Pass the message to all hands that the pirates are early and probably inbound right now. Everyone get into position even if they're not ready.*

Kae blared the message through the suit's speakers before moving close to the landing field and repeating it.

That'll take care of it. You better get under cover. If they see you, they'll pull out, and if they bring a lot of firepower, we'll need you close.

Roger. It's a good plan, Jake. We'll execute it, if not to perfection, then well enough to accomplish the mission.

We don't have any choice since our ships won't be intercepting them now. The colonel stood in the control room and looked out the window. He wore a shirt they had found in a locker that looked like what the technicians had been wearing.

I know. I hoped they would take care of it, and then we could hand the facility over to Federation miners, but it wasn't meant to be, so here we are. Let's kick their asses and go home.

I like that plan, Kae. See you on the other side. All hands, execute Operation Sleight of Hand.

Kae blared the message before moving to the back of the building and trying to blend in with a piping system. He kept his optics online but shut down the rest of his active sensors, then settled in for a long wait, but they arrived within minutes. Once the space above the planet was clear, the pirates' time was short. This was a one-off hit. The payoff must have been huge for an operation that included a combat-capable black-market fleet.

Kae increased magnification. When he saw what they were bringing, he wanted to warn the colonel, but they were comm-silent. Any misstep could have the deadliest of consequences for the defenders.

Ambushers, Kae corrected himself.

Four aerospace fighters and a hardened cargo ship

came in; someone was getting paid well for the malageodes. Kae wondered what one looked like. He hadn't bothered to find out, but now it interested him. Why did one odd rock have value while others didn't? The rock didn't cure cancer. It was a rock.

Maybe someone would explain it to him later.

In the control room, it wasn't long before Jake saw the incoming ships. The fighters made a high-speed pass before swooping upward to bleed off speed and turning around for a second run.

The cargo vessel came in fast, hitting the brakes hard before flaring and maneuvering at slow speed as close as possible.

Inside the storage facility, a dozen soldiers waited to storm and seize the ship. The only person to be protected was the pilot because they would know the transit codes and other keys to getting inside. Jake assumed the Federation would want that information if he could get it.

The cargo doors swung wide shipping-container style, and a towing tractor drove out with a human behind the wheel. Two others jumped out a side hatch and waved. Jake smiled and waved back. He had two soldiers behind an ad hoc barricade on the floor of the control room because once the cargo ship's crew turned the corner, they would know things weren't right. That was where Jake had to convince them otherwise.

He heard them stomp up the hallway and stop when they saw the control room.

"Fucking shite!" Jake slurred. "You wunna believe what happened!" He stepped into view, waving a bottle he'd found in one of the lockers. He took a long drink of the

CRAIG MARTELLE & MICHAEL ANDERLE

water he'd put inside, shuddering afterward and shaking his head as he flopped back against a shot-up workstation. "I got another one."

Crews on ships rarely snagged a drink. Ships and alcohol didn't make for a good cocktail, so the two crewmembers' desires overcame their good sense and they sauntered up the corridor. Before they could look too closely, Jake yelled, "Fucking *blooey*! Went up like a plasma drive on o-load." He let his head weave drunkenly. Another step. Two for a bonus.

The soldiers threw themselves at the crewmen and took them down before they knew what happened, then taped their mouths shut and removed their coveralls before taping their hands behind their backs. The soldiers put on the coveralls and headed down the corridor.

Jake checked the window. Eerie silence. He couldn't hear the tractor. A door clanged, but Jake couldn't tell from where.

Two of the fighters streaked overhead and delivered a series of microrockets into the tree line on both sides of the landing field, attacking the less-than-well-concealed anti-air batteries. Only one rocket streaked skyward in response.

Gunfire erupted from the malageode storage shed, with return fire from the back of the shuttle.

At least two pirates were inside, and they were armed with cutting-edge railguns. Jake grabbed his short-barreled rifle and vaulted through the window, dropping the three meters to the ground, flexing his knees when he hit, and immediately running toward the open crew door. He bolted through it without hesitation.

He found two rough-looking men focused on shooting up the shed. He fired on full auto and took out both while the soldiers continued to fire into the shuttle.

"Cease fire!" he yelled, but a few more rounds splattered off the forward bulkhead. Jake's face was bleeding from the chips of metal ricochets. He wiped a drop of blood from his eye with the back of his arm before yanking on the access to the cockpit. The pilot and navigator had secured themselves inside.

"Open the door and give it up. No harm will come to you," Jake shouted at the doorway. The other two fighters strafed the tree line, and the shuttle started to move. "Keep this on the ground!" He ran for the open cargo door because the pilot wasn't listening.

Jake jumped out, and Kae ran past him and leaped inside. Jake hit the ground and rolled, looking at the shuttle as it quickly gained altitude. He wondered how high Kae could jump from and survive. The cargo doors sealed before the shuttle accelerated toward the upper atmosphere.

Webster, can you track where they're going? They've got Major Walton on board.

I can't go skyward with those fighters overhead. They aren't taking any prisoners, Colonel. You don't want to get abandoned on this side of the planet. It might be a while before anyone gets to you. I don't want to ping him with my sensors either because the fighters will ride that right back to me.

"Shit!" Colonel Braithwen yelled at the dot in the sky. The four fighters appeared and formed up around the cargo transport, probably not knowing it didn't have the malageodes on board.

His plan of seizing the shuttle when it prepared to leave after capturing the crew and conducting a mock load had gone to hell from the word go. The air defense team had fired one rocket that missed and paid for the shot with their lives. The rest of the infantry had been among the trees, ready to snipe security that appeared around the shuttle, but they'd been on the receiving end of one too many missiles. The two technicians had been in the tree line, too. They probably hadn't survived either.

The mini-tractor operator was on the floor of the shed, blasted by a railgun.

"Check the tree lines. Get out there and recover the wounded."

He waited behind, unwilling to reinforce his failure with images that would haunt him forever. The pirates had shown early, which had forced everyone into the trees instead of fighting holes closer to the landing field where he'd thought the shuttle would settle and the escorts would park.

Never commit all your forces to your idea of the enemy's plan, Jake thought. Hubris. He'd developed a plan that was too complex. His desire to impress General Reynolds by capturing the pirate band had failed miserably, and he'd lost Kaeden.

No, that hadn't been his fault. He would have never ordered a mech into the cargo ship.

"Where are you, Kaeden?" Jake asked the sky before switching to his internal chip. *They're gone. Bring the shuttles back to the landing field. We're going to need those body bags.*

CHAPTER THIRTY-FOUR

War Axe

As soon as the *War Axe* cleared the Gate, the systems started populating the tactical board.

"What in the hell am I looking at?" Terry asked.

"Interrogating all ships in the system for IFF transponders," Ruzfell replied. The information updated on the main screen. The Belzonian fleet had one ship remaining in orbit of Kor'nar because it was badly damaged, squawking an emergency code. Nine other ships were flitting around the system, four flying randomly and a bigger ship with four small fighters as escorts.

"Stop that ship, please," Terry said. "I'd like to talk to those people."

Ruzfell started spinning within the three-dimensional hologrid. "Requesting launch of the Black Eagles."

"You have a go," Terry replied, watching the tactical board. "They're heading for the Gate."

"Black Eagles away," Ruzfell reported.

"Block that Gate, Clifton. Can't we override the controls?" Terry wondered.

A Gate formed before the *War Axe* and the ship slid through, reappearing in front of the system Gate. Missiles jumped from their launchers and screamed across the void, and the fighters made erratic course changes while the missiles chased them. Chaff dispensers fired.

The Gate behind them came to life. "Nobody gets through," Micky ordered his crew.

Two fighters splashed, then a third. The boxy cargo ship accelerated in a dangerous game of chicken with the *War Axe*. The remaining fighter slid in behind it.

"Why does he think we won't shoot that cargo ship?" Terry asked, turning to catch the captain's eye.

Missiles raced from distant space, but the fighter didn't see them coming. It exploded spectacularly.

The Black Eagles fired a second salvo.

"Abort, abort!" Terry shouted, and Smedley relayed the command. The missiles exploded before they hit the cargo ship, but they were close. Too close. Shrapnel enveloped the ship in an expanding cloud and it started to tumble.

"Gonna hit the shield," Terry said. The hull's integrity was gone. When it impacted the gravitic shields, the ship came apart. Instantly, an emergency beacon appeared in front of the *War Axe*.

"Kaeden?"

"What the fuck did we hit?"

"You hit my ship!"

"Bring me aboard. We have to get back to the planet."

"We're right in front of you. Kind of hard to miss."

"Oh, shit! There you are. I'll be in the hangar bay as soon as my head stops ringing."

The Black Eagles raced away. Five other ships required their attention, and there was nothing Joseph and Petricia loved more than flying their space fighters. Since this was their swan song, they had no desire to return to the *War Axe* before they were bingo on fuel and weapons.

Kor'nar, Trans-Pacific Task Force Expeditionary Camp

Marcie ran out of the trees, waving her hands so she wouldn't be confused with the Naries who were interspersed with the Belzonians. When an insectoid attempted to enter the camp, they were shot. They didn't try to surrender. They didn't try to shoot back. They were terrified and would have run free within the expeditionary camp while armed. That didn't work for anyone.

Marcie cleared her space, ran through the small berm, and jumped over a foxhole to get inside. She slid to a stop in front of the sergeant major. Her eyes shot to the bandage on his leg.

Monsoon pointed behind her. "Is that yours?"

She turned and saw the angry black smoke boiling skyward.

"This stuff burns like it's made of gasoline. At least there's no wind." She looked back at the bandage. "Is that yours?"

"Just a flesh wound. I think we need to cut firebreaks around the burn."

"Do you have a dozer I don't know about?" Marcie wondered. A Narie turned away from the camp at the last minute and headed for the trees, saving himself from imminent death.

"No, but we have four companies of tanks, three of which are not far away."

"You're a genius." Marcie activated her internal comm chip. *Get the inbound tank companies to cut a firebreak around the fires. We need a shuttle in the air to direct them. Four tanks running side by side should clear enough foliage. Then they can push it away from the flames so it doesn't catch.*

Roger, ma'am. Will do.

"We could use the drones," Crantis quipped.

"Those guys have been MIA from the word go. We need better comm. We talk to the camp via our chips when we're within range, then they use their base radios to talk to the larger unit commanders on those few radios. That's how we have to contact the troops, and it's insane. Every officer and NCO needs a comm chip. Shit! We'll talk about that crap later. We have to play the hand we're dealt right now. What the hell happened with the Zirrics?"

Monsoon explained the defense and delivered his estimate of losses: a hundred killed and two hundred injured.

Marcie tried to look at it positively. "It could have been worse."

"I'd say you were trying to see a silver lining where none exists, but it does exist, and it's not silver, but gold. We were seconds from having our bright green troops overrun. They would have died by the thousands, me included, but the tanks! Kae's training with the tanks kept them cool enough to bring the firepower on target exactly when we needed it."

"I like hearing that, not because of Kae, but because of Punyaa. How is he?"

Monsoon shrugged. "His shuttle took off right when the attack started. His was the last one out of here. I haven't heard anything since then. I assume he's on the *Angkmoor* being treated by professionals. He'll be fine."

Marcie looked at the troops manning the perimeter defenses. Some of them seemed to be having too much fun. She hung her head and started to approach them, but decided to grab the responsible company commander instead.

"The Naries are terrified of the fire. Shooting them isn't sport. It's a tragedy, but we can't have them in the camp. A bottle of Scotch to the soldier who figures out how to turn them away before we have to kill them. Make a game out of keeping them alive."

The lieutenant concurred and saluted.

"No saluting in the field. My husband will be pissed if you get me killed. He'll drive his mech over you."

"Sorry, ma'am!" His hand shot to his head again before he whipped it down. "I'll pass the word to the companies on this end of the perimeter. We'll figure it out, ma'am."

"I'm counting on it." She walked away before he could demonstrate any more brain freezes.

Monsoon pointed at him. "Only front-line troops are eligible to win the prize, no matter who comes up with the idea. It's better that they think the idea is theirs, whether it is or not. Do you get me, Lieutenant?"

"I do," the young Belzonian confirmed, the light bulb coming on behind his eyes.

The two hurried to the command tent to coordinate the

firefighting efforts. Marcie was woefully out of the loop, but if she had to be everywhere at once, then she failed miserably as a commander. She didn't feel like a failure since the task force had operated without her, Kae, or Jake and done it well.

Wiriya was waiting for them.

"Are you up on everything?" she asked.

"Yes, ma'am." He held the tent flap for the colonel and the sergeant major to enter. Wiriya immediately went to the board, pulled out a notebook, and flipped to the last page that had notes jotted. The corporal reviewed them briefly before beginning to speak.

"Two platoons scoured the southern battlefield to collect weapons so the Zirrics couldn't reuse them. They've been destroyed using thermite grenades. They stopped counting and estimated at least ten thousand dead. Our dead numbered one hundred thirteen, with one hundred seventy-five injured. There are probably more injured because many didn't report to the field medics. They stayed on the line, either digging or watching for a second attack." He looked at the bandage on the sergeant major's leg before continuing.

"The drones followed the Zirric mass to a narrow chasm, where they disappeared into the darkness below. The drone is making a racetrack above it until it hits its max on-station time. You know what happened on the northern approach. The Naries have scattered and the drones have noted that there are no groups, only individuals running in every direction.

"The shuttles have mostly recovered. We lost one to a mechanical failure on its way to the Naries hive, but the crew was recovered. The three tank companies have almost made it back. They know about the diversion to attempt to cut a fire break, but I'm not sure they know what they're doing."

"Could that be because you want to be back in one?" Marcie wondered.

"Major Punyaa's tank is missing its commander."

"First, I want to tell you that this briefing answered all my questions without me having to ask or hunt down the information. Second, you can take Punyaa's tank, and I'm giving you temporary command of the firefighting tank brigade."

Wiriya smiled and turned to the radio operator who now worked out of the command tent. "Order that tank back here ASAP." Wiriya frowned. "I'll head out in a moment, but first, a couple other bits of news from above. The *Angkmoor* is considered lost, and we've not heard from the shuttle carrying Major Punyaa. Pirates returned early and attacked the fleet. The other three transports retreated to an alternate location closer to the system Gate. A ship called the *War Axe* has arrived and is now engaged with the pirate fleet, and one last thing. We've lost contact with Colonel Braithwen and his team."

Marcie's eyes started to water, so she pinched them shut before a tear could escape. Colonels didn't cry. She bit her tongue to take her mind off the tragedies of the day.

"Thanks, Acting Major Wiriya. Go catch your ride and stop that fire from spreading."

He rushed from the tent. Marcie stood and walked to the big board. The Kor'narian force dispositions were nonexistent since they had appeared en masse and disappeared just as quickly. Taskforce assets had been spread across a swath of the area but were tightening back into a cohesive unit, one that could wield overwhelming force. Splitting her unit had led to a near-tragedy.

But she'd had no choice. Mission orders directed her to stop the war. She had been played by the Zirric queen, who had given no indication that they considered the humanoids their enemy.

And the mining facility.

"Do you know anything else about Colonel Braithwen?"

Monsoon shook his head, mouth clenched tightly. He hadn't known how much he didn't know about everything else that was going on.

But that wasn't his job. He had been out there keeping people alive, just like Colonel Walton. "We can't influence those other things. We are fighting our own battle right here, still trying to carve success out of this mission."

"Trying to reshape a steaming pile into a statue in honor of the almighty malageode." Marcie shook her head. "How can we find out about the mining site?"

"Relay through ships in orbit, but there aren't any. Talk about leaving our asses swinging in the wind. It would be nice to know where the pirate ships are. If they are powerful enough to take out the *Angkmoor*, what can they do to us on the ground? And if they're in the air, we can't send a shuttle. Those things would fall out of the sky if the enemy looked at them angrily."

"It's frustrating," Marcie admitted. "So, how do we keep the Kor'narians from attacking each other?"

"They didn't do anything extreme until the queens saw an opportunity. Let's grab the fucking queens, slam their dumb asses down at a table together, and keep them there until they resolve their issues." Marcie leaned back and crossed her arms.

"How well do you think that'll work?" Monsoon asked.

"How well has anything else worked? I'm not seeing a whole lot of options."

"I get to take one of the teams in after we have the intel we need to build a plan. I recommend Kae take the other team unless he can go solo, which might work best, except we're not supposed to intimidate them with our advanced technology."

"Besides, Kae isn't here."

"Did you see a queen among the Yellows?"

"The Naries? No. Nothing that looked like a queen."

The sergeant major tipped his head down to look up at the colonel.

"Meaning she's still in the cavern while her people are scattered to kingdom come, and you've already been in there. Take as few as possible and go fast. Skim the tree-tops on your way. Do not let anyone see you."

"On my way. Looking to launch in fifteen minutes."

The comm operator held his hand in the air. Marcie looked at him. "Wiriya is in the tank and headed north."

"Thank you. Can you try to call any ship in orbit? Maybe they've returned."

"Of course." The comm operator accessed his board and started the call sequence.

"Belay that order," Marcie called before he transmitted. "We can't let the pirates know where we are. They should already suspect there's a force on the planet, but that doesn't mean we need to lead them right to us."

"Maybe the pirate ships are no longer out there?" the comm operator ventured. "Or we could launch a shuttle to call from a distance away from the camp."

"They could see the shuttle." The raid on the Naries queen was a calculated risk, but if they sent too many shuttles into the air, one of them would head the wrong way and get himself seen. Or maybe they wouldn't. They were running low on options, and with each, the risk magnified exponentially.

Marcie decided what she needed to do. "Contact me," she tapped the side of her head to indicate her comm chip, "if you hear from any of our ships or Colonel Braithwen."

She planned to stop by the drone operators, followed by the field hospital. She needed her eyes to give the camp a better warning, and then she wanted to see the carnage for herself. See how the troops were holding up under the stress of pain and violence.

The drone operators seemed to be hard at it, or five of them were. The sixth had gone forward with her, and for some reason he hadn't made it back yet, even though the shuttles had returned to the landing area of the expeditionary camp.

"Where is he?" She pointed at the empty chair. One of the operators shrugged without looking up from his screen. His vehicle was flying high over the fire, trying to keep track as it spread.

Another operator answered, "He's prepping his bird to get it back in the air. It took a few hits, traveling in a cramped shuttle."

"Thanks. How's the fire look?" The operator shifted to the side to give her a better view, and they stared at the screen together as he panned out to show the immensity of the conflagration. A dark line snaked into the bottom of the picture. Marcie pointed at it. Can you zoom in on that?"

The area expanded to show five tanks plowing through the woods and cutting a huge swath, with five more tanks behind using their treads to move trunks aside and mash the foliage into the dirt slowly but steadily. Marcie couldn't estimate the speed at which the fire moved, maybe the same speed as the deliberate movement of the tanks. She trusted Wiriya. He knew why he was out there and the cost of failure. Her job was to make sure every commander had that same level of understanding, and theirs to pass it to their leadership teams until everyone knew.

When all embraced the same goals, nothing would be impossible to achieve.

It gave her hope when her entire world was going to hell. They'd killed thousands of insectoids, both Naries and Zirrics.

Now they were going to grab the queens. *I gave you a chance to talk, and you attacked. Whether you understand it or not, whether you deserve it or not, you are Federation signatories, so fuck you. I'm taking over because we can't have our member planets acting this way.*

With the confidence of her convictions, she strode from drone operations to the field hospital where bandaged, bleeding, and broken troops filled the space outside the medical tents, spreading into the troop space surrounding.

Marcie looped around to catch those on the outside first and work her way in to those most injured.

"What was the cost?" she asked the first group of

soldiers she ran into. They were bandaged but still had color to their skin. They needed a stitch or two or maybe a cast, but they were in the right place to eventually get treatment. They looked solemn but alert.

"Ma'am?" one replied, unsure of the question.

A shuttle lifted off and flew low over the camp on its way northeast. If anyone could pull off the raid, it was the sergeant major and his chosen troops. Marcie turned back to the soldiers before her.

"The blood you shed on this mission, compared to the price the Kor'narians paid for crossing us. Our cost was high. We have a number who didn't make it, but the rest of us did. A huge number of them did not. We are still here to bring peace to this planet, and thanks to all of you, we are a lot closer. The Kor'narians know they can't match us in a battle, which leaves them with only one option: to talk. We are closer now than we were yesterday, thanks to all of you."

She had to teach them to understand. She moved up the line, sharing and thanking them for their sacrifice and their efforts to support the mission. They didn't know why this mission was deemed so important by the Federation. They deserved to know what they were buying with their blood, but she couldn't tell them.

Until she could, she could only thank them for their trust in her and the Federation.

She came across a soldier on a stretcher, a mass of bloody bandages holding his arm together. He smiled up at her. "Just need to get patched up so I can get back in the fight," he muttered.

"I don't know how much fight you left in them. They ran like rats from a cycling airlock."

"Yeah, they did. Did we do good, ma'am?"

"You did, and all the Belzonian soldiers. You've brought honor and pride to the Trans-Pac. Soon, wherever we go, they'll know not to mess with us because we'll fuck up their day."

"That's what I'm talking about." He perked up, despite being pale from loss of blood. "Maybe you can hurry this line up a bit? I need to clean my weapon before the sergeant major crawls up my ass."

A soldier next to the stretcher tapped it with his foot. He wore a bandage on his head but didn't look to be in bad shape. "You know it, Crawley. I owe the sergeant major my life. I've seen the light! Well, it looked like fireworks when I got beaned in the head. Maybe next time they'll hit me somewhere it hurts."

"Yeah, fucker. You slept through the whole damned thing."

"Unconscious after taking a bullet to the helmet isn't like sleeping," the private explained, making sure the colonel saw that he wasn't faking an injury or slacking off —at least not any longer.

"Bullshit. Look at his shirt, ma'am. That's my fucking blood because somebody had to cover his dumbass when the bugs were crawling in."

"And the sergeant major?"

Both the soldiers looked away and clenched their jaws.

"Out with it," Marcie ordered. She took a knee next to the stretcher. "Tell me."

"We were fucking off, ma'am, not taking it seriously. The sergeant major gets up close and personal with dickhead here, slamming the helmet on his melon a millisecond before the first round impacted. After that, bullets filled the air. Next time anyone says dig a hole, I'm digging a fucking cavern."

"I appreciate your candor, Private. We learn. We get better. As new soldiers join us or old soldiers who weren't in the fight are put on the front lines, someone has to teach them why we do what we do, and why we might seem fanatical about certain things. You now have insight into what discipline means and the cost of not having it."

The first injured in the day's battle nodded, winced, and stopped the movement. "You can count on us, ma'am."

"You two still look like liberty risks, so I'm not sure we'll ever let you off-base. But in case we do, understand that scars are sexy. You'll be the hit of the town—if we ever let you see it, that is. I'll let Sergeant Major Monsoon make the final decision."

"Oh, shit!" Crawley leaned back, still smiling. "He's a big pussycat. We'll have off-base privileges before you know it."

"Sure. Count on that." Marcie turned serious. "Get better first, then we'll talk about it some more. I'll hold out hope, but you know what the sergeant major says about sorry asses."

She stood and walked away.

"No! What does the sergeant major say about sorry asses?" Crawley asked.

Marcie had no idea since she had made it up. She checked the time. She'd been gone for almost an hour, and no one had contacted her. She hurried through the rest of the line without stopping, although she caught the eye of each soldier. Despite some horrific wounds, she felt far better for having invested the time in the future of the task force.

How one treated the weakest and most vulnerable was what the soldiers would remember, not how the strongest and luckiest were put on pedestals.

CHAPTER THIRTY-FIVE

War Axe, **the Hangar Bay**

Christina sucked on a tooth as Kae used his suit's jets to settle to the deck. "Whatcha doin' floating in space?"

"It's a long story. No time. We have to get back down there. They were blowing the shit out of the mining site," he replied through the mech's external speakers.

Christina lost her humor. "Tell him yourself."

Bundin and the alien squad waited nearby. Other warriors milled about, but none looked ready. Bundin and his people vibrated with anticipation.

Dad, we have to get back to the mining site right now.

We're on our way in, but we have some bad guys up here to deal with first.

Let the Belzonians handle them. We have to get back down there! Kae insisted.

The Belzonians already lost one troop transport. It's floating dead, barely high enough to keep from getting pulled into Kor'-nar's atmosphere. Their fleet set up a picket around the remaining three transports and they aren't moving.

442

Kae ground his teeth in fury. The Belzonian fleet had abandoned the ground force. He could see the rift forming between the land and space sides of the task force and closed his eyes to focus on his breathing. If they lost one transport, losing another helped the ground force even less than abandoning them.

At least the *War Axe* had made it. Kae wasn't sure who had called them in, but he'd buy them an AGB beer later.

As soon as we can, Dad. I'll be on the hangar deck ready to go. Just give the word.

Soon, Kae, and you aren't going back in alone. You'll have company if you get my drift.

A few now is better than all later, Kae pressed.

Soon as we can. Let me work on something.

Char ran to Ted's quarters to encourage him to launch *Ramses' Chariot* against the pirates so they could take the *War Axe* to the planet's surface. The Black Eagles were doing what they could, but two space fighters against five larger craft that had been built solely as weapons platforms wasn't a good match. Joseph and Petricia were fighting more of a delaying action than search and destroy.

She pounded on the door to Ted's and Felicity's quarters. "Open up. I need to talk to you!" Char pounded some more before Felicity appeared, wearing a robe that barely concealed anything and which she hadn't bothered closing.

"He's indisposed if you get what I mean," Felicity drawled.

"We need *Ramses' Chariot* to destroy the pirates so we

can take Kae back to the surface to save the other soldiers of the task force."

"Is that it?" She looked over her shoulder. "Can the Waltons take your spaceship to go teach bad men lessons in etiquette?"

Ted mumbled something from under the covers. Char didn't understand, but she didn't have to.

"Just have Plato fly the damned thing. Say yes, dear."

He mumbled something else.

"He said yes. Make sure you put gas in it before you bring it back." Felicity closed the door before Char could reply.

Char thought for a moment. Her pack was available, but if Plato was going to fly the thing, she knew a team that had already taken *Ramses' Chariot* into battle.

Bundin. Get your team on Ramses' Chariot *and take the ship out. Plato needs some hands to keep things running while he fights the evil that men do.*

Yes, ma'am! the Podder replied instantly. *We're here and will be on board in less than a minute. We'll launch when ready.*

Give Plato our best wishes for quick success. Char redirected her comm link to the bridge. *Terry, as soon as* Ramses' Chariot *has cleared the bay, take us to the Federation mining outpost. I'll meet you in the hangar.*

On my way. She could sense Terry running. He must have given Clifton the coordinates before they confirmed the plan. She took off for the stairs.

Kor'nar, Naries Hive

The sergeant major had stacked the deck. He had four

from the Lion Corps and fifteen others, many of whom had been a part of the fight on the southern perimeter. He'd seen them hold their own.

They checked weapons, magazines, and additional ammunition during the short flight, and the sergeant major briefed them on what they would see on their way into the underground, which involved going down a klick and a couple klicks of running. They had to go fast before the word could spread, although the Naries communicated through a natural method as effective as radios.

He expected they would run into little to no resistance. Monsoon wanted the hive to be empty, based on the numbers that had flooded toward the camp.

"We kill anyone who gets in our way," the sergeant major said. It sounded more ominous than he intended. "Let's make sure we get down there before any bugs can get into place to stop us. Once we have the queen, they should stay back. The queens will have just fought a group cage match, so there won't be any junior queens left. I think that means the rest of the hive won't risk her life, so getting to her is our ticket out."

The shuttle dropped into the opening in front of the hive entrance and turned the rear deck to the doorway. The soldiers ran off and arrayed themselves, ready to breach. Monsoon unleashed half a magazine on the door before he grabbed it, and with all the strength he could muster, yanked it open.

They filed in, spreading out to the sergeant major's flanks in a V formation. He started running faster than a lope but slower than a sprint. The soldiers with him were not enhanced, but they were in peak physical condition. In a two-kilometer run, most of it gently downhill, they shouldn't even get winded. He sped up.

The way had been easy when they were being escorted. Go straight to the golden doors. He didn't remember any turns off the main corridor. There were plenty of side corridors, but they looked and were dark compared to the main route.

Dark was relative. It was a crescent-moon level of lighting and wouldn't take much before it was pitch-black. The warriors had emergency lights, but those weren't meant for an extended operation. They were little more than tokens that local companies would hand out as give-aways with their logos on them.

Monsoon scowled at how far they had to go to become a professional force, then looked back at how far they'd come. It had been less than a month since the *Vengeance* had arrived on Belzimus carrying the Waltons. It seemed like that had been a lifetime ago.

"Bugs!" a soldier on the left flank reported. His light flashed to life, highlighting an alcove with three Naries standing within. They made no move to stop the Belzonian soldiers. The left flank kept their rifles trained on them as the group ran past.

"There's your answer, boys: speed and restraint. They won't know what we're doing until we've reached our objective."

The sergeant major pushed his speed further, reducing the time they'd be vulnerable, the time in the hive before they had the queen in hand.

The soldiers started breathing heavily and struggled to keep up, so Monsoon had to slow down. He pumped his fist in the air slowly, signaling to the others in the dim twilight of the hive, and took the time to let them catch their breath. They were getting close, and he needed them to be at the top of their game.

"Almost there," he told them, raising his weapon for the final approach. They rounded one final gentle bend in the tunnel to find they'd reached the end unmolested and without having fired a shot.

The guards at the door sprang into action. Monsoon stitched a series of rounds across them, firing on full automatic, then rammed into the door to stop his momentum before pulling it open. He led the way inside, using his rifle as a pointer.

The divan where the old queen had died was empty.

"We got company coming down the tunnel," the last one into the room shouted. He pulled the door closed behind him while looking for a way to bar it.

Kor'nar, Mining Facility

"Cover!" Jake shouted from the middle of the landing field. Small ships were inbound at a high rate of speed. It looked like the fighters had returned. "Get the fuck down and get under something!"

He had no hope of reaching the tree line, so he dropped where he was and tried to look like he was dead. Out of the forty-two troops who had arrived with him, twenty-eight were dead, four were injured, and Kaeden had gone into space on the pirates' cargo ship. They had no air defense missiles remaining, only small arms.

Jake cradled his rifle so the inbound wouldn't see the

weapon if the ships had that kind of optical fidelity. There was a certain peace in knowing one was screwed. His muscles didn't agree and they tensed, ready for the impact of the ships' fire. The first new intruder raced by at two times the speed of sound, judging by the double boom as it passed. Two more ships screamed by, but they were sub-mach. One flared out to the right and the other left, then soared high and banked hard to return to the landing field.

The ships weren't fighters but were much bigger, supporting crews of ten or twenty. They were weapons platforms like a gunboat or a picket ship, but they hadn't fired on their first pass. That gave Jake hope that they would land and give him and his soldiers a fighting chance.

He continued trying to become one with the ground, a dark blob in the middle of a well-groomed field. The ships slowed and hovered before accelerating away. Jake raised his head. The ships were at treetop level and heading in three different directions. Jake jumped to his feet and started running for the tree line.

A big ship appeared at twelve o'clock high. He continued running but watched as the ship grew larger and larger. It launched a series of missiles at the retreating ships, then a second salvo and a third before it arrived and descended over the landing field, taking up the space of a hundred cargo shuttles.

Jake, you down there? Kae asked.

Kaeden? Jake walked into the open and waved at the ship. The front hatch gaped open like the maw of a giant sea creature.

Kae jogged down the ramp and jumped onto the landing field, his powered combat armor unmistakable. *I'll be damned. We lost our ass down here. Ten uninjured, four injured, and the rest in body bags,* Jake stated.

We'll bring them on board. Recall the shuttles and have them land in the hangar bay. They will fit, Kae replied. A unit of mech-suited warriors jogged onto the landing field. *Point my people in the right direction. We'll carry our soldiers home.*

Angkmoor, the Trans-Pacific Task Force Flagship, in Orbit above Kor'nar

"Where's my damn power?" the captain grumbled for the nine hundredth time. The air was starting to get stale from not getting circulated, but there was plenty of oxygen remaining for the surviving crew. A troop transport ship without the troops had a massive amount of interior space.

Over time, carbon dioxide would build, so bringing the CO_2 scrubbers online remained a critical task. That meant the ship needed power.

"They're working it, Captain. There's a lot of damage to the system." The engineer flopped to the deck, exhausted and exasperated. The captain felt like he had asked the equivalent of "Are we there yet?"

"Sorry, Somchai. I'm as frustrated as you are."

"Are we going to die, Ukrit? Shouldn't someone have come to help us already?"

"You suggest everyone else is dead and can't help us. I think it has not been that long. The fact that they didn't finish us when we were most vulnerable tells me they weren't trying to kill us, only hold the fleet off so they could return to what they were doing when we arrived."

The captain slapped the metal wall. "How about this old girl holding up? She protects us while we save ourselves."

The engineer groaned as he tried to get back up. The captain lent a hand to help him stand. "Thanks, Ukrit. We will bring the ship home. Let's take another look at the cut in the primary power conduit. Instead of rerouting, maybe we build a bridge?"

"Like shoving a wrench between two live circuits? I'll do it. Just show me what I need to do."

"No, my captain. I'll take care of it. Go to environmental control and close the circuits to the system. We'll bring them back incrementally once we've confirmed the power distribution is steady. If we don't get the power back, we will have lost nothing. If it comes back with a roar and an arc, we can't risk losing our air. With air, we can survive until rescue arrives. Without it, well, we won't go without, now will we?"

"I'll take care of it, Somchai. Good luck." The captain walked away while the engineer steeled himself for the effort. The engines were running, they'd determined that, but couldn't get to them without power to open the bulkheads. They couldn't communicate with anyone remaining in the engine room since the primary and backup systems were dead.

Redundancies hadn't been a priority. It was a freighter first and foremost, without the expectation of battle damage. He hoped it could be fixed; otherwise, they would die in the dark and cold vacuum of space.

He wondered why it was so warm.

Maybe they were on fire and the oxygen wouldn't last so long. He started running.

. . .

Kor'nar, Naries Hive

"Sergeant Major!" Corporal Thanlit called. "I found a door."

"A door unlike any other door," the sergeant major started. "It's the only way out." *Unless it's a closet.* He kept his cynicism to himself. These soldiers had hope and confidence. Even if they had to leave by the main door, they would make it costly for the Naries to get in their way.

Hidden behind artwork that was easily moveable, it wasn't a closet. A search of the rest of the large chamber revealed nothing else.

They had left the main door with only the internal latch keeping it closed, and the pounding from outside became more insistent. Five of the soldiers took a knee and aimed at the main door as the rest prepared to breach the new door. A gentle turn of the latch and a push said it was locked.

"Break it down!" the sergeant major ordered in a voice that left no room for argument. Two soldiers hit it hard, which separated the lock and sent the door flying open. They fell through and rolled to the side, making way for the rest to storm through into an antechamber. The rest of the squad followed, the five rear security soldiers coming through last to secure the door and be ready in case the Naries tried to follow.

The sergeant major continued to another door. When the others were ready, he opened it with a simple push and stormed through with ten soldiers close on his heels.

Monsoon headed straight for the Kor'narian bed, where

he found the queen. She was battered and scarred. No wonder she hadn't gone with her hive.

She couldn't have.

Her attendants carried no weapons and were easily subdued. The extraction team was that much closer to accomplishing the mission. Monsoon stared down at the queen, knowing she was incapable of resisting them. He lowered his weapon.

"We are here to convince you to come to the negotiating table with the Zirric queen."

The queen struggled to raise her head, but her iridescent eyes sparked and swirled with life. "There is only one queen."

"Who better to talk to about that than the other queen?" Monsoon parried.

"My people will show you and them the way to their true queen," she claimed.

"Your people are scattered in a thousand different directions, running for their lives. They didn't even make it to our camp before artillery, small arms fire, and then a big blaze scattered them to the winds. How do you think we made it down here if your army was still intact?"

"You lie," she claimed as her head dropped back to the pillow.

"The truth doesn't care what you think. Since you don't look like you're capable of making the trip yourself, we'll carry you."

"Trip? Where? Stop them!" she commanded imperiously.

A private shoved the only Narie to move backward. "Fuck off," he told the Kor'narian.

"No! You will not take me anywhere."

"When you sent your people to attack us, we decided you weren't capable of making rational decisions, so we're going to make this one for you," Monsoon said evenly. "We're going to shepherd you through this process because your predecessor signed a treaty with the Federation, to which you are bound. We're enforcing those provisions, so you can talk to your counterpart with the Zirrics, or there are less savory alternatives we can employ. You are currently the only Narie queen. What would happen if you were to die?"

"I am not going to die," the queen raged defiantly.

"Because you're going to talk to the Zirrics and reach an understanding that ends this insane war. This is a Federation planet, and you will act like decent, law-abiding members." Monsoon pointed to the bedframe. "Pick her up, eight of you, and let's go."

"No!" she reiterated, but the queen was incapable of defying the soldiers with anything more than her hollow words.

"Rear security, you're now on point. Take us out." The five went through the door, across the antechamber, and into the queen's receiving room. The pounding continued on the outer door.

When the queen was in plain sight, Monsoon stood in front of the soldiers carrying her with the five in front of him. Two others brought up the rear.

"Open it," Monsoon ordered.

A soldier slid the latch and pulled the door inward. The Naries on the other side weren't armed, and there weren't that many. "Get out of the way," the soldier told them.

"Hear me!" Monsoon bellowed to make sure he had their attention while playing on their sensitivity to loud noises. "Your queen is under Federation protection until the negotiations are complete. No interference will be tolerated. Clear the way!"

The soldiers turned their weapons sideways and started pushing. The Naries tried to push back, but they were smaller. The soldiers found the pressure points on the insectoid bodies where they were least able to resist and created a path, spreading sideways to keep the way open. An insectoid jumped past the soldiers, a hard-shelled arm raised to slash the sergeant major.

He swung his rifle almost too fast for the eye to follow, clocking the Narie in the side of its head. It crumpled in a heap on the cave floor, and he kicked the body out of the way and continued walking, his eyes challenging anyone else to interfere.

Once clear of the cordon, the soldiers put two up front and the rest spread out, surrounding the queen. They moved as quickly as the eight soldiers were capable of going. Monsoon didn't want to push his luck. He had minimum combat power unless they wanted to drop the queen and add all fifteen rifles to his. Surrounding the queen wouldn't let them concentrate if they needed mass fire to clear a flood of Naries.

Too many thoughts held the sergeant major's mind hostage while the team trudged upward and ever forward. The artwork held no allure, but it glistened and sparkled within a texture that demanded being touched. The perfume of flowers filled the air. He wondered if that was an element of the art.

He hadn't seen any flowers and couldn't understand where the scent was coming from.

Naries lined the abutting corridors and tunnels, watching the procession heading toward the entrance. The rhythmic thump of soldiers marching in step. The fluidity of motion. The discipline of coordinated action.

Monsoon's eyes darted everywhere, expecting a trap, but there weren't any warriors in the hive. These were servants, helpers, children, and the elderly. The sergeant major watched them as they watched him. Maybe he was less alarming with his bald pate, but they couldn't see that since he had his helmet on. Or maybe he was terrifying.

That was the look he went for. Battles fought against enemies caught in the fear trap were quick. To the brave and bold went the spoils.

The queen started to pant, and the soldiers picked up the pace. Monsoon ran ahead and opened the door, looking out to make sure more Naries weren't waiting for them. The area was empty. "Clear," he told the soldiers. They would find out soon enough that the shuttle wasn't out there either.

No plan survived. He started thinking of alternatives, plans beyond plans, even if the brute force of walking twenty-one klicks back to camp was the only way.

"We will accomplish this mission," he told himself as much as the troops.

Kor'nar, Trans-Pacific Task Force Expeditionary Camp

Marcie headed through the mess tent on her way back to the command tent. Getting a freshly cooked hamburger was a healthy treatment for the dark cloud that hung over her head. Information would be the cure.

She wondered if Kaeden had encouraged them to carry his favorite food as a grab-and-go item. It suited him and made sense. Not everyone had the luxury of committing to a full meal break. That was the state of Marcie's mind. The others of her inside circle had gone on missions that mattered.

Kae and Jake committed to the mining facility because General Reynolds had called it their number one priority.

Monsoon had gone to fetch the Naries queen. She had no plan to acquire the Zirric queen, not until resources appeared that she could assign to the task. When would they be able to use the radio?

She returned to the command tent and dropped her rifle on the table before opening her burger to take a bite.

She watched the comm operator with great interest. He was taking notes from a series of messages.

"Ma'am, a ship called the *War Axe* is requesting permission to land. They need all the space we have on the landing field. They see the smoke and don't need to be vectored in."

"Pass the order to the shuttles to get into the air," she ordered, leaving her food on the table as she jumped to her feet. "Give me the *War Axe*."

She put on a headset. "*War Axe*, Colonel Marcie Walton. Who are you bringing with that executive delivery?"

"Well now, the golden child has returned," Terry quipped. "Damn good to hear your voice, Marcie. I have to say, I'm seeing a lot of devastation surrounding your camp."

"The locals took offense at our mission. And who knew! Their shit here is highly flammable."

"You've got a nice firebreak around it. You'll be fine," Terry told her. "We're bringing everyone. We've got a refugee we picked up in space—your husband."

"What was he doing in space?" Marcie asked. Terry let it go. That was a story for Kae to tell his wife.

"Your mom is with us and your stepdad. We also have this Colonel Braithwen guy. Dude needs a haircut, along with the survivors from the mining camp. We also have a Major Punyaa. He was in bad shape, but Cory has him in the Pod-doc. He should be okay."

Marcie turned away from the comm operator. "I've failed," she said.

"What kind of fucking moronic bullshit is spewing from your piehole? You've had this army for a month maybe and already survived at least one major engagement. Bah!"

Marcie laughed. If anyone ever suggested Terry Henry Walton treated his own family with kid gloves, she would have set them straight. She maintained the high standards he had instilled in all of them, seeking a perfect win every time because that was the goal to work toward.

Every time.

Even TH had lost people close to him, like Ramses and members of Char's pack, Adams and Xandrie. Two of his grandchildren had walked away, Sarah Jennifer and Sylvia. And how many people lived free because of those sacrifices? How many lived better lives?

"I wouldn't change it for anything," she said.

"Being a moron?" Terry wondered.

"No." She chuckled, heart still racing from the relief that Kaeden was okay while still buffeted by the losses at the mining facility. Shuttles started lifting off, but it would take a while to get all the pilots into their seats. "Have Kae bring you and Christina to the command tent. We have some things to talk about. This mission has mostly gone south, and then it took a wild left turn. We are now somewhere that isn't even on the map."

"You'll make the right things happen to bring it back in line. You'll find that when you turn north, everyone ends up at the same point."

A dark shadow covered the camp as the *War Axe* hovered over the landing area and half the wasteland south of the camp. The front of the ship faced the tent city, shortening the walk from the hangar ramp to the command tent. It also put the ship within spitting distance of the field hospital. Marcie had intended to wait for them but decided she could take care of her people just a little bit better now.

She told the comm operator to hold down the fort and strode out. He had no choice. He was on duty but didn't want to ruin the colonel's suggestion that he was in charge of the entire Trans-Pacific Task Force. He sat up straighter in case an important message arrived, and he needed to make a decision.

Shuttles were taking off one by one, clearing the landing area. In the distance, junior officers were chasing troops out of foxholes so they didn't get crushed under the massive supports beneath the heavy destroyer.

On the bridge of the *War Axe*, Ruzfell and Smedley made sure no one was beneath the ship. They waited patiently, providing shade for a third of the camp.

Marcie stepped into the field hospital and found the combat medic in charge. "Have your most severe cases ready to move."

"Ma'am, we can't risk moving some of these. They aren't stable."

Cory, do you have any Pod-docs available? Marcie asked.

Sweetie! Nice to hear from you. We have eight available, and five cryopods if you have someone in severe condition. We can put them in stasis until the Pod-doc comes available.

We have soldiers from today's battle who are in critical condition. The doc doesn't want to move them until they're stable.

I'll come and see what I can do. We will not further injure your people.

"We have access to the most modern medical technology the Federation has to offer to assist us, and one of the keenest minds and kindest souls is leading the way. She'll be here momentarily."

The medic looked upset until he saw the ship settling on the landing field through the open doors of the overcrowded hospital. "I appreciate any help we can get. I don't want to lose any more of these good people."

"Neither do I, Doc. That's my only concern." They shook hands quickly before Marcie headed outside to greet the party coming off the ship.

"Don't go anywhere with my suit!" Kaeden yelled over his shoulder before running down the ramp and into his wife's arms. Terry, Char, and Christina walked down the ramp. The Belzonians who watched saw the confident strides of people who had seen war and survived to tell about it.

People who won wars because no one who followed them would ever contemplate failing them.

Marcie felt that way, and her Belzonian troops were starting to feel that way about her. She didn't see it, but Terry did in the eyes of those near her. Cory ran past her parents, tapping Marcie on the shoulder on her way into the field hospital.

When Kae let his wife go, she found Paithoon standing next to her. "Where'd you come from?"

"I have to keep my eye on you so you don't greet dignitaries in your usual hillbilly human style. There are things to take into consideration. Honestly, you make my job extremely difficult." Paithoon removed his helmet and shook his head to let his hair wave and flow.

"Hey," TH said off-handedly, giving Marcie a quick hug. He thrust his hand out for Paithoon. "Terry Henry Walton."

Paithoon bowed deeply and started speaking slowly. "To the esteemed masters of this great vessel..."

"Let me stop you right there." Terry looked wide-eyed at Marcie. "What the fuck is this?"

"My protocol officer. He thinks I swear too much."

Paithoon started to sputter. Terry snorted to stifle a laugh.

"I may have carpet-bombed this army on an occasion or two," Marcie admitted.

"Fuck me! You have a swear jar guy follow you around?"

"Kind of, but not really. He helped us make inroads with the Zirrics."

Paithoon beamed.

"You mean those fuckers who attacked you? Looking at the mass of bodies out there, I'm thinking five thousand dead, maybe ten. I'm glad I don't have a swear jar guy. That fucking asswipe would be overworked and underpaid."

"Come on!" Paithoon blurted.

Marcie turned toward him, and he winced but quickly recovered. "While I have you here, we need to set up another Peace Garden, but this time, set it up inside the camp. The Kor'narians are on our turf now."

Three Trans-Pac landing shuttles maneuvered out of the hangar bay and started looking for a place to land within the camp.

Marcie stared after them. A work party appeared at the top of the *War Axe's* ramp, carrying body bags. Colonel Braithwen had one in his arms as he led the way toward them. "Secure them in a shuttle and put a twenty-four-hour guard on it until we can return them to Belzimus," Marcie called.

"May I suggest neutral ground with a view, say on top of the hill?" Paithoon pointed, but Marcie didn't look.

"Don't fuck with me, Paithoon. Put the tent right fucking here so those asshole queens have to look at our dead and injured as a reminder of the investment we've made in their peace. I know they lost people of their own, but that's their cost for making war. This is our cost for fighting for peace. Do you understand the difference?"

Paithoon looked hurt. "I do, Colonel. Please accept my apologies." He bolted as soon as he was done speaking, and Marcie watched him go.

A hand gripped her shoulder.

Christina squeezed until Marcie looked back. "This life is hard with few rewards, but those rewards are worth fighting for. You get it. We get it. Everyone out here will get it, or they'll get out. We have time to train warriors. There is no time to babysit. Now, what's your hold up in getting off this rock?"

"Getting the queens together to negotiate peace. The sergeant major went on a snatch-and-grab to get the one. We're still trying to collect intel on the other one. I haven't heard from Sergeant Major Monsoon, so we're still missing two queens."

"And one sergeant major, sounds like."

"While you're at it, Dad, why don't you give me a paper cut and pour lemon juice on it!"

Kor'nar, Naries Hive

We're out front. Where in the fuck are you? the sergeant major called using his comm chip.

We're hovering under an overhang because our asses were hanging out while we were on the ground. Be there in fifteen seconds. Cool your jets, big dog.

Monsoon's knuckles had turned white from clenching his fists too hard. The troops were angling to put the bed down.

"Hang on. Ride's almost here," he told them. They reshouldered the load and waited, breathing a collective sigh when the shuttle appeared over the trees and dropped quickly into the clearing. The rear deck popped and they hurried aboard, setting the bed down in the middle of the shuttle's deck and taking the jump seats on the sides.

"Take me back. You'll pay for this," the queen clicked and buzzed.

"You are paying for this, and the dividend will be peace on Kor'nar. That is going to be your mantra because you will not breathe another second of free air as long as your armies continue to fight. Understand our resolve. The quicker you do that, the quicker you can return to your life, and we can return to ours."

The queen stopped arguing as the deck closed and the shuttle took off.

"I don't know what's going on, but there are about thirty shuttles in the air."

"Maybe the pirate threat is gone. Call them!"

"We're still under radio silence."

"Call them," the sergeant major reiterated.

"We have air and space supremacy. We're going to have a hard time landing. There's a big ship in the way."

The sergeant major worked his way between the bodies to look out the shuttle's clear forward screens. "I'll be damned! The colonel doesn't mess around when she calls for backup. Find us a good landing spot, little dog."

"Roger that, big dog," the pilot confirmed.

CHAPTER THIRTY-SEVEN

Kor'nar, Trans-Pacific Task Force Expeditionary Camp

Marcie stopped the parade heading to the command tent when she got the call that the sergeant major was inbound with the injured queen.

"Of course, she's injured. She just won a fight to the death with the other junior queens." Marcie should have thought of that, but the mission had been done on short notice. "Can we get Cory to take a look, and you know, do the hands thing on the queen?"

"She's your sister-in-law. Why don't you ask her yourself?"

"I'll ask," Kae volunteered. He headed for the hospital tent rather than interrupt Cory's train of thought by using his comm chip to call her. Bad Company warriors were streaming from the field hospital with stretchers of patients on their way to the Pod-docs within the *War Axe*. Kae intercepted his sister and stood close to talk to her, as only siblings did.

Marcie looked for the inbound shuttle and used her

internal comm chip to contact the pilot and vector the ship close, squeezing it into a small area. They dropped the ramp on one of the hospital tent's guy lines. Monsoon stood in the back, behind a bed with a Kor'narian queen.

"Put her in the hospital," Marcie directed the eight soldiers walking into the delegation. The others filed out with the appropriate sirs and ma'ams as they passed the cordon. Monsoon strode out last.

"Secure the queen and take the unit for chow. You've earned a long sit-down meal," Monsoon told them. The eight weren't in the hospital long because Cory chased them away. The soldiers finally smiled.

One for one in missions accomplished. They walked out of sight, and a cheer went up from beyond the tent.

"Sergeant Major Monsoon, Colonel Terry Henry Walton, Colonel Lowell, and Major Char Walton."

Monsoon nodded in greeting. Someone shouted, and feet hammered the dirt. Belzonian soldiers were lining up and looking at the ramp of the *War Axe*.

"For heaven's sake, Mother!" Marcie nearly shouted.

Felicity strolled to the top of the ramp wearing a sparkling red satin dress with a matching hat that mirrored the plumage of the most robust Belzonians. It seemed incomprehensible that she could have walked across the hangar bay in the heels she was wearing, but when it came to fashion, nothing was beyond Felicity Spires. When the crowds cheered, she loved it even more.

Felicity smiled at her daughter. Marcie waved, ending by shaking a finger in her mother's direction. She dramatically threw a hand to her bosom and turned with a swirl to saunter back into the ship.

"I'd stop by before you leave or she'll be mad. Not as mad as she gets at Ted, mind you, but mad like normal mad."

Char snickered, and the women shared a knowing look.

The sergeant major raised one heavy eyebrow before looking away. "Maybe we need some more colonels?" he muttered.

"The bane of a sergeant major's existence, Monsoon. My guidance to every officer is to stay out of their senior enlisteds' way. Is Marcie treating you right?"

"Absolutely, Colonel."

"Call me, TH, Monsoon. I'm as close to being a civilian as I've ever been. Last hurrah, putting away the spurs, and all that."

"You're doing what?" Marcie demanded.

"Oh, shit! We hadn't told you. Char and I are retiring to expand the All Guns Blazing franchise. I already have my first two custom brews on tap, and there are more, so many more coming. Have you ever had a cherry-primed wheat, Monsoon? Perfection."

Christina stepped up. "Enough men-being-men talk. You have one queen, and there's another one out there somewhere. What are we doing to get her?"

Marcie nodded at the command tent, and Christina walked at her side, with Kae, Jake, and the sergeant major in tow. Terry and Char strolled to the hospital tent to watch Cory work her magic on the insectoid.

The blue glow was the first thing they saw when they walked through the doors. The queen was clicking her way through platitudes with the relief from the pains that plagued her. Her wounds were on the surface, easily managed by Cory's special nanocytes. When she finished, Terry lent a supporting arm. The medic hurried over with a chair after watching in fascination.

"How does she do that?" he asked.

Terry shrugged. "It's a gift."

"I wouldn't have known where to begin on a Kor'narian."

"At the beginning, of course," Terry quipped, helping Cory sit down.

"I thank you," the queen said. "I would like to go now."

Char leaned close. "Have you negotiated peace with the Zirrics?" she asked. The queen tried to push herself up, but Char shoved her back down.

"There can be no peace."

"There can always be peace," Char said. "At the beginning of a war, both sides dig in and refuse to budge. The cost is high, but both are sure that they're right. As a war goes on, the potential for greater catastrophe weighs heavily. That is the best time to negotiate because neither side has not yet paid the ultimate price, so they still have something left to lose. After a war goes on for too long, the sides have lost everything except the notion of winning, and the only negotiation left is when the sides are too tired to raise arms against each other. I suggest you have not yet lost it all. There is something left, and whether you lose it or not is in your hands. Hold it wisely or not at all."

The queen buzzed, but it didn't translate.

Char helped the queen stand.

"What are you doing?" Terry asked. Cory rose. The queen towered over all three of them.

"I'm helping her resume her dignity. No one likes to be carried around on a bed."

"It wasn't that bad," the queen replied, tapping Cory on the arm before trying to get outside. Terry and Char walked with her.

"I need to check on the wounded in the Pod-docs," Cory said, excusing herself and heading up the ramp into the hangar bay.

"May I see?" the queen asked.

Terry was all smiles. "Let me show the pride of the Bad Company. Welcome to the *War Axe*. We carry a few ships, but our combat capability mostly comes from our warriors and their powered combat armor." He pointed at Kae's suit, which was parked near the hatch leading to the armory. Kai was giving it a once-over. He waved at the group entering, paying scant attention to the queen.

"Inbound ships. Please clear the hangar bay. Two Black Eagles and *Ramses' Chariot* inbound," Smedley announced.

"We'll need to move to the side," Terry said, ushering the queen toward the bulkhead. Moments later, the Black Eagles smoothly maneuvered through the cavernous maw and into their tie-down spots in the aft end. *Ramses' Chariot* entered slowly and then rotated so the nose faced outward in case a rapid departure was called for.

The *Chariot* powered down, and the side hatch popped. First out was Bon Tap. He waved on his way to the ramp, looking out on a camp of people with similar yet not as exotic hair as his. "My people!" he cried and ran down the ramp. Terry and Char didn't correct him.

The others tipped Bundin up to help him fit through the doorway. The Ixtali and Yollin followed him out. B'Ichi

CRAIG MARTELLE & MICHAEL ANDERLE

and Chris Bo Runner were the last ones off. They huddled around Bundin for a cheer before breaking up.

"Report, Corporal," Terry called. Bundin hurried over, and the queen backed away. Slikira joined Bundin, sniffing the queen. The Ixtali didn't seem to care for the Kor'narian —two insect species not getting along. It wasn't the first time. It wasn't even the first time on this planet.

"Colonel Walton, sir, *Ramses' Chariot* and the Black Eagles destroyed all enemy shipping. We appreciate the assistance with the three runners who went intra-atmospheric. Did you catch them before they destroyed the facility?"

"We did. Add three more to the tally. Good work, Bundin, and with Plato doing the flying, you make a great team."

"We didn't do much. Plato splashed three by himself and the Black Eagles accounted for another four, along with the four initial fighters."

"I thought there were only five ships out there besides the fighters?"

"The others were hiding behind the moon," Bundin reported. "We took a trip to the dark side to clear the baffles, as Plato said. I don't know what those words mean, but there were no other ships in the system."

"What about the damaged transport?"

"We tried to contact them but couldn't communicate. The ship is mostly without power, but the crew is alive. We couldn't get to them, but the Belzonian fleet is on their way back. They should be rendering assistance momentarily."

"Sounds like a lot of winning," Terry said. "Meet the Naries queen." Terry turned back to the Kor'narian. "This is Corporal Bundin from Tissikinnon Four. He is what we call a Podder. He's also one of our most valued and highly decorated warriors. He saved the *War Axe* once upon a time."

"Not a humanoid," the queen clicked. She turned her head and iridescent eyes on Slicker. "Nor you."

"Neither," Terry interjected before the Ixtali embarrassed herself. He gestured with his head that they could go. "Get to the armory and clean up your gear."

Char helped move the two along.

"Then go find Bon Tap!" Terry called after them before turning his attention back to the queen. "The Bad Company does not care about race or gender or anything that doesn't directly relate to how well someone acquits themselves in battle. We are the Direct Action Branch of the Bad Company. We never start a war, but we sure as hell stop them."

The queen buzzed and clicked, but it didn't translate.

"I'm sorry, that didn't translate for me," Terry explained.

"No matter," the queen replied.

Terry shrugged. From what he had heard and seen, the pirates had been ten times more dangerous than the locals, and the pirates were no problem at all. Not to the *War Axe* or the Bad Company. Then again, he hadn't been restricted in the weaponry he could use, unlike the first time they took the *War Axe* into battle without using all the ship's capabilities. It had been a mistake that he had sworn never to make again.

Marcie had to deal with the handicap because of the limitations of the Belzonian land army and the Federation rule to not expose the Kor'narians to too much technology.

Yet here Terry stood, showing the Kor'narians some of the most advanced technology in the Federation.

The Pod-docs were working on the injured. Lights flashed as the system operated like it was designed to.

"Can I see how it works?"

"No. It doesn't show you. The nanocytes work internally, and the Pod-doc tells them what to do to make repairs at a microscopic level. The equipment gives them the guidance and power to do what they need to do. We have sufficient power to drive these at maximum, helping our injured to recover that much more quickly. Sometimes as quickly as fifteen minutes."

"I would like one of these. I'll negotiate with the other queen if I can get a Pod-doc."

"For your people?"

"No. For me. They need me to be as healthy as I can be. They will benefit from me being well, more of what I feel at this moment. The Pod-doc will help me achieve that."

"That's not how negotiations work, and you'll not get a Pod-doc just for yourself," Terry replied.

"Then there will be no negotiations," the queen stated.

"You're under the mistaken impression that you get to dictate the terms of the negotiations. You *will* negotiate with the Zirrics. You won't leave until you have, and have done it in good faith. When you two have reached an agreement that both consider minimally acceptable, Marcie will maybe consider other requests."

"That doesn't sound like a negotiation," the queen replied.

"You had other options and chose war instead. A lot of your people died because of that bad decision."

"They live to serve me."

"What you don't seem to understand is that they won't be living at all. You are killing them. When you're weak enough, the Zirrics will take over your hive, if I have all the players right. We don't want to be here any more than you want us here, but here we are nonetheless. Don't make your life more difficult than it needs to be."

Terry put a finger to the side of his head to help him use his internal comm chip. *Marcie, what am I supposed to do with this queen of yours?*

I'll send a couple of guards and Paithoon.

I'll be on the lookout for your mobile swear jar.

"Time to go," Terry told the queen.

"I'd like to see more of your ship."

"I'm sorry, maybe some other day. Right now, Marcie is sending people to collect you."

"And if I don't want to go?"

"Then we tie you to the bed and carry you. Go you will, whether you want to or not. The only question is whether you'll go with your dignity and pride intact."

"Do you treat the queens of other species so harshly?"

"We treat anyone who runs afoul of Federation law with the disdain they've earned. Respect comes on the same ship. Earn ours, and you'll have it."

She didn't attempt to argue, but let Terry guide her to the ramp to where four soldiers waited. "They'll take care of you now. You are in no danger. This is something we promise. Cory healed you for a reason, it wasn't to physically punish you in any way. They will do all they can to make you comfortable, but the one in control of returning you to your hive and your people is you. Make peace and reap the rewards."

He left her to return to the ship. He thought about joining Marcie and Christina to plan the next phase of the operation, but he had reconciled himself to moving on. He was at a point in his life where he was okay with not being in the fight.

Finally. "Char!" he called across the hangar bay. "What do you say we put on a movie and break out some popcorn?"

She smiled back, wanting to hear more. She expected he would also mention beer, but the AGB had started a line of synthetic wines. They weren't ready yet, but they were getting there. Of course, they had a couple of bottles of imported wine in their quarters to tide them over.

"Do I get to pick the movie?" she asked.

His face dropped. "I was thinking of a good war movie. Maybe *Sands of Iwo Jima* with the Duke. It's almost a love story."

"*Almost*," Char repeated. "I shall tolerate it because John Wayne, but for no other reason."

"You know you'll want my popcorn."

"Damn straight, TH. *Our* popcorn."

CHAPTER THIRTY-EIGHT

Kor'nar, Trans-Pacific Task Force Expeditionary Camp, Command Tent

Christina looked at the drone footage, pursing her lips.

"How far in are they?" she asked again. Marcie shrugged again.

"We need to go in there," Kae stated. "We'll suit up and go introduce ourselves."

"What's the easiest way to do it that's the lowest impact?" Marcie asked.

"Mechs," Christina replied. "If it's okay with you, I'll go in with them. We'll take twenty to make sure none of them escape. We grab the queen and we get out."

"That was why the Federation wanted us to operate on a level more technologically equal to the Kor'narians—so we didn't impose our will through overwhelming force, other than using an occupying land army."

"Twenty mechs could have done what your ten thousand are doing."

"But then we would be imposing our will on them."

"I hate to break it to you, but that's what you're doing anyway, at a ridiculously high risk to your troops. I think whoever prepared this mission was either an idiot or corrupt. This isn't Lance Reynolds' doing. Some diplomatic corps weenie set this up and put the cuffs on the operating force. Lance was as misled as you. I wouldn't be surprised if the bastard who championed this mission wasn't in bed with the pirates. I'll talk to my dad about it."

"The best way to prevent a war is to make it too expensive to fight. Period. Exclamation point," Marcie commented, continuing to study the images of the crevasse where the Zirrics had disappeared. "We'll figure it out when we go in there."

Marcie pursed her lips while she thought through the options. "Two groups, ten in each. Kae with one, Christina with the other. Both ends of the crevasse. I expect that there are entrances at both ends. I don't know if the cave goes down or if it goes beneath the land and back in this direction. Frankly, I don't care. Go down and root out the queen without killing any of them if you can avoid it."

"We'll do our best. They can't hurt us, unlike the Skrima. My suit should be repaired by now. I have an in with the armory."

"You're doing the bone dance with my nephew!" Kae blurted.

"Really, sweetheart?" Marcie said. "Why have you become such a Puritan?"

"Orgies?"

"It was pre-orgy," Marcie replied.

Crantis leaned close to Jake. "This is fascinating. Are all

human families like this? Video programming has a place on Belzimus if it can capture some of this."

"Nah," Jake whispered back. "No one would believe it's real."

"My nephew!"

"Is a total hunk of man-candy," Christina purred.

"Fascinating," Monsoon whispered.

Kae stroked his chin before conceding. "The queen isn't getting any closer to the table while we stand here and argue about who's plowing whom."

"This is gold," Jake whispered.

Kae finally acknowledged that Jake and Crantis were being entertained. At least they had sent the comm operator for chow. "Sorry, guys, this is going to be a suit operation only. We'll be taking expert operators to make sure this goes off without any miscues."

"We know," Jake replied. "We'll be keeping Paithoon from driving Marcie insane. This is his time to shine. This is his specialty, and while you guys get the queen, we'll get everything else ready."

Kae headed for the door. "What are we waiting for? I'm ready to get off this rock. Maybe we can liberate about twenty suits to take back to Belzimus with us."

"You're going to come back with us?" Jake asked.

Kae was taken aback. "Of course. These guys need a shitload more training, and soon they are going to be the cat's ass. They'll be what the Bad Company is not, a force able to win ground and then occupy it. The Trans-Pac will be able to do both. Kor'nar isn't the only fucked up planet out here."

"You got that right," Christina agreed. "Lead on, soon-to-be-uncle."

"Why? Why you gotta jab needles into my soul?"

"Because you love having me as a niece, my subordinate as my mother-in-law, and my new grandfather as my old boss."

"Gold, I tell you," Jake murmured to Monsoon.

"Gear up, bitches. We're going on a bug hunt," Christina said.

Angkmoor, the Trans-Pacific Task Force Flagship, in Orbit above Kor'nar

Somchai looked at the bridge he had fabricated from secondary power cabling. He had no way to shut off the flow for the few moments he needed for hookup. He fashioned small receiver cradles for the dead side of the system and cleared the ends of the torn cabling while ensuring he wasn't grounded.

The feeling of ants crawling over his body made him painfully aware of the power within that cable, but the ship needed the power. With power, it could fight the fire surging somewhere within the hull, making it warmer and stealing the oxygen.

He arranged melted insulation as a guide to align the live end with the dead end and then put in a brace to hold it in place. He angled the brace against the bulkhead and the cable. He intended to hammer the brace to straighten it, driving the cables into each other. The receiver cradles would instantly melt, and power would course back into the ship.

He wrapped tape around the largest spanner he could find in the section's toolbox and lined up to drive the brace forward. He wound up and swung, hitting the brace and breaking the end off. The two pieces fell to the deck. He didn't have anything else that would be long enough.

The pressure to save the ship weighed on him. All he had to do was shove those two cables together. One little push would do it.

The power surging into his body would make him explode. He'd seen it before. The internals instantly boiled with the application of energy. It was too much for the skin to hold.

Save the ship.

He looked into the overhead. Nothing to grab. The spanner wouldn't help. Too much power, not enough insulation.

No choice.

Save the ship.

"For the *Angkmoor*. Remember me kindly, Ukrit," Samchai the engineer said before yelling his battle cry. He jumped and kicked at the cable with both feet to drive the live ends into the receivers. With the first touch, the arcs and sparks started a glorious display of raw power unleashed.

But he was in the air, not grounded. He tried to push off, but his leg muscles wouldn't cooperate. He started to fall as the lights flashed back into existence and the emergency alarms sounded.

War Axe, the Hangar Bay

Christina ran through the systems check on her suit. She was going underground again, but this time, the enemy was ineffective against a warrior in powered combat armor, and Kaeden would be leading the mission. Too many things were bothering her.

Why am I going? she wondered. Because TH had always led the way. He made sure his people knew there was nothing he would ask of them that he wasn't willing to do himself. The Bad Company knew that about her, too. She wasn't afraid, but Kae was in charge. This was a supporting mission. She powered her suit down and climbed out the back.

She gestured to one of the backup warriors to move to the primary group, and he bolted for the armory to get his suit on.

She walked up to Kaeden. "I'm not going."

"All good," he replied easily, continuing his systems check. Now was the time for final repairs. The destruction of the shuttle had caused no structural damage to his suit, but cosmetically, it looked like he'd gotten his gear at a scratch and dent sale.

"Good luck," she told him. "I'll be coordinating anything you need from here and lining up our next gig, because no rest for the weary, right?"

"So that's it, huh? The old man and old lady are really packing it in."

"Fighting evil on a different plane of existence is how I think we'll categorize it."

"They've earned it. He's expanding the bar and restaurant chain. Pretty soon they'll dominate the galaxy."

"Free food and drink for everyone in the Bad Company forever and always!"

"Hey! Don't be drinking up my inheritance." Kae finished his systems checks and saluted Christina before running through a quick drill with his company-grade railgun.

"Minimal casualties, none if you can manage it, and bring the queen. Simple as pie. See you in a couple hours." Christina worked her way down the line of suits, giving each a quick external check before they headed out.

Kae watched her go, wondering why she'd changed her mind. He was good with her not being along because he thought she'd be wasting her time. Had he known about her adventures on Benitus Seven, he would have wondered why she had ever planned to come.

"Saddle up!" Kaeden called. "To stay together, we'll jog to the crevasse. A short fifteen klicks and we'll be there. This is also a show of force. We will run free through Zirric territory to show that it was an extremely poor decision to attack us. The Zirric queen should be expecting a response, and we'll deliver it. Then we're going to grab her." He stepped into the middle of the hangar bay. "Kimber, is your team ready?"

Her HUD showed green across the board. "Ready to run."

"Alpha Team, let's rock. I'll brief you on the way."

"Team Turok the Dragon Hunter, follow me."

Nice, sis. Really nice, Kae told Kim privately.

You took the A-Team title. What did you expect?

Nothing less, indeed. Good hunting.

And you. See you when we have the queen.

And by we, you mean Alpha dogs?

The two teams filed down the ramp. Kaeden turned left, and Kimber turned right. They worked their way through the tightly packed shuttles to get beyond the perimeter before starting to run, then urged their suits to greater speed. Fifteen kilometers over rough terrain would take them less than fifteen minutes.

That was all the time Kae needed to tell the Bad Company warriors of both teams everything he knew about the strengths and weaknesses of the Kor'narians as well as reiterating the ROE, the rules of engagement.

Minimize damage to the locals but seize the queen. He threw in a little competition, caveating that ROE was king: a bistok steak dinner to be cooked by the team that returned without the queen for the one that did.

Christina jumped on the active channel. "And I'll serve it to the winning team, but if neither team accomplishes the mission, you'll all be serving me."

"A fair trade, Colonel," Kae confirmed, breathing easily while running since his suit was doing most of the work.

It took fourteen minutes and thirty seconds for Kae and the Alpha Team to reach the trail leading into the crevasse with the cave mouth below. The drone operators had been unable to penetrate into the cave with their sensors and didn't want to risk flying a bird in there because of the tight quarters and sketchy signal from below ground.

Kae liked his line of sight and loved his suit's drones. He launched one, and it flew in front of him. He ran one of the presets to keep the drone within line of sight, no more than one hundred meters ahead of him. It transmitted its feeds to a small window on the bottom right of his HUD. If it alerted for anything, the frame would blink red. It was how he liked it and what he was used to.

That and a great deal of practice made him one of the best at maximizing the potential of powered combat armor. He took the lead heading down the wide trail to the cave mouth, a broad space that quickly narrowed but not so much that a mech couldn't fit through.

Unlike the Naries' hive, there was no door. Inside, Kae found a mob of guards, and they raised their weapons and fired. The suit barely registered the impacts. Kae strolled by, snagging the weapons he could reach and crushing them. He dropped the junk and kept moving as the Zirrics emptied their rifles. The mechs kept coming; all ten strolled by, heading downward.

Kae could have relied on the IR and active scans to show him the way, but part of their plan included intimidation. He turned on the full bank of lights on his suit, highlighting cave walls lined with Kor'narians. The Zirrics.

Tail-end Charlie, the last in line, carried a special cannon that fired comm repeaters into the rocks. His job was to make sure they could always get a signal out. It was a new procedure that Christina established following the mission against the Skrima.

"The queen is bigger and should be surrounded by guards. They will do their best to protect her because if they hid her in plain sight, we'd never find her."

"What if they do?"

"Then no steaks for us." Kae didn't need to be hardcore. Either they found her or they didn't. The Zirrics were no threat, so they could take as long as they needed to. "Spread out and get a closer look, just in case."

. . .

Kor'nar, Southeastern Approach, Zirrics' Hive

Kimber headed into the crevasse, using her jets to descend since the track was at the bottom with the cave entrance a short distance up the hillside. She couldn't see wasting the time to walk around. The mech suits provided benefits that made certain obstacles disappear.

When she hit the bottom, she took in her surroundings to make sure they weren't walking into an ambush. She was first up the incline and into the cave.

After ten meters, the opening became too small for a mech to fit through. "Well, crap."

She ducked to look through and was greeted by iridescent eyes staring back at her. She jumped back before catching herself. She stuffed a hand through to clear the opening and sent a drone in to see what the rest of the cave looked like.

From the inside, it looked like the exit had been cut through the rock. Looking the other way, the cave was large enough for Kim and her team to pass.

"We'll do this the hard way," she told her team. "Stand by."

She punched the rocks, but they didn't give like she wanted them to. She stepped back to the opening ten meters away and stitched the outline of an enlarged doorway using her railgun. Dust fountained, but she didn't wait for it to clear before accelerating, shoulder down, into the wall and crashing through. Rocks both big and small cascaded from the roof. She scampered on all fours out of the way, seeking refuge and hoping the whole wall and the hillside above didn't come down on her.

She stood and hugged the wall that paralleled the crevasse. She had assumed it provided the support for the hillside, making it more like a lean-to than a cave meandering through porous rock.

When the rocks stopped falling, she was happy to see light from the outside. "Kick those pebbles out of the way and come on in. The door is open, the welcome sign is out, and the lights are on." She activated her suit lights to find that the small contingent of Zirric guards had been crushed by the rockslide. At least she could say she didn't shoot them and kill them directly.

She fought down the urge to not go in farther. Deep down, she hoped she'd run across a chokepoint they couldn't get through, but she clenched her jaw and steeled her nerves. No one needed to know she didn't like it down here when she could spend all day within her armored suit.

There's no reason for it, she told herself.

Three strikes against her mission already. She wondered how Kae was doing.

CHAPTER THIRTY-NINE

Angkmoor, **Trans-Pacific Task Force Flagship**

"He did it!" Captain Ukrit cheered and ran for the bridge. All systems were active and engaged. Environmental controls started to pull stale air out of the system while sending freshly scrubbed and oxygenated air back in. Bulkheads opened to areas not open to space, and the automated repair bots received updated priorities.

On the bridge, the bustling crew worked to process the sudden flood of new and sometimes conflicting information. The captain turned off the alarms since everyone on the ship knew there were issues. External sensors came online to show the fleet had returned and two ships were trying to link up to the emergency airlocks. He accessed the comm.

"Emergency. *Angkmoor* reporting that power has been temporarily restored. The crew is assessing the damage, which is substantial. Crew losses are unknown at present. Can anyone read me, over?"

"This is *Gonboon*. Read you loud and clear. We are

alongside and have already dispatched our repair bots to seal the hull breaches. We're glad to know that *Angkmoor* lives."

"That makes two of us. We stand ready to receive any and all assistance." The captain changed to his internal comm system. "Engineer Chamsai, please report."

Silence greeted him, but he chalked it up to the damage near engineering. "Can anyone get eyes on the engineer for me, please? He said he would be in the forerun grid near the main power conduit."

The captain waited, and the longer the silence stretched, the more darkness invaded his mind.

Kor'nar, Southwestern Approach, Zirrics' Hive

They'd trampled a few of the more intransigent Zirrics who tried to block them, but they hadn't had to fire their weapons. The caverns were too crowded with locals for them to fire wholesale at the invaders.

Kae gave them credit. He had thought they might try a mass wave attack against the mechs, forcing the warriors to start killing them to keep them back. Maybe the insectoids knew their options were limited. There was enough resistance to convince Kae that he was going in the right direction. There were plenty of side tunnels, but they seemed insignificant by comparison.

He expected the queen's ego would put her at the end of a long approach with whatever opulence the Zirrics could scrape together decorating the tunnel and delivering unto the queen the glory of her position.

Kae talked himself into demeaning the creature. He

wanted to know why she'd sent her people after the task force and not her enemy, the Naries. He would ask before they bundled her up and lugged her out.

He wondered briefly where Kimber was.

Probably down one of the side tunnels in the limbo of the underground maze.

The launch and impact of yet another comm repeater thundered down the cavern, and Kae reported in to make sure it was working as well as to keep Christina apprised of their position. He asked for an update on Kimber since he couldn't reach her directly. *Moving slowly,* was Christina's reply.

The light at the end of the tunnel came when the Zirrics surged toward the mechs. "Looks like the bugs have decided to make their stand. Now is the time to make some noise."

Kaeden could take or leave the old Earth heavy metal that his father loved, but he knew the effect it had in combat. It boosted morale and gave any attack energy. He also expected anything loud would drive the Kor'narians out of his way. He brought up Johnny Cash's *Ring of Fire* and cranked it.

The Kor'narians recoiled from the blinding, vengeance-screaming metal monsters. Kae started running down the cave's superhighway toward a decorated grotto-looking area at the bottom where it leveled off. The Kor'narians dove out of the way of the assault on every fiber of their beings. Kae ducked under a crystal-heavy arch, scraping his metal shoulders on it as he passed through.

Inside he found the queen, obvious in her size. She had no intention of going quietly and bolted down a side tunnel far too small for a mech to go down. "Cover me!" Kae shouted at Sergeant Capples behind him. He unbuttoned and climbed out the back, then pulled his handheld slug-thrower and ran down the tunnel after the queen.

"No!" Cap shouted, but it was too late. Kae had already gone into the tunnel after the bugs, where darkness and a lack of armor were great equalizers.

Kor'nar, Southeastern Approach, Zirrics' Hive

The tunnel was sufficiently wide and high that the mechs continued unimpeded even though they were incapable of walking side by side. It was single file for as far as they could see. Kim kept her drone in front of her. Insectoids skittered here and there but stayed out of the way. She had accessed the music she had loaded into the suit and pulled up Nightwish. With one eye movement, *Planet Hell* started playing. With another simple eye movement, she boosted the volume until dust vibrated free of the walls.

"Major, are you sure you want to start a rockslide?" Private Eldis asked.

She turned it down to where it wasn't shaking the walls. "Is that better, Grandma?"

"I want to get buried down here as much as you do, Major," Eldis replied.

"I'm with you. This is kind of a tight squeeze. Auburn, make sure you get those comm repeaters spread out like pollen on a windy day. The last thing we want is to be cut off while we're in this fucking hole in the ground."

"Fucking eh," Auburn replied to his wife.

CRAIG MARTELLE & MICHAEL ANDERLE

"My wife is on the ship. If I get trapped anywhere, it better be on the *War Axe*," Eldis remarked.

"Pick up the pace, people. We're playing catch-up. The A-Team is already inside." Kimber focused on increasing her speed, ignoring the Kor'narians as she pressed farther underground, lights blazing and music blaring.

Kor'nar, Deep Inside the Zirrics' Hive

Kae steadied his breathing. It was dark in there, but not pitch-black. He could make out the faintest of outlines in order to keep moving along the tunnel. He didn't dare crack a lightstick since that would ruin his vision while not impacting the locals.

The music faded into the distance as he pressed forward, following the slight sounds of the insectoids moving in a hurry. He couldn't tell if it was the same group, a different group, a split-off group, or rats. Kae started to question his decision, wondering if he could get back to his suit. He hadn't thought the tunnel split off. It had been relatively straight with an occasional smooth corner.

Most importantly, he was walking uphill. That was the best sign of all.

Kimber? he asked, hoping the queen was headed for the other side of the hive and would run right into Kim's team. Almost like they planned it, unless this tunnel didn't lead there and he was getting himself past the point of no return.

He spent more time trying to see the tunnel than listen for movement, so he didn't notice when the sounds

490

stopped until it was too late. He ducked, dropping to the cave floor. Flashes! Shots rang out too close, passing through the space where his body had been. Kae lunged sideways into the Zirric guard, catching it around its middle section. He spun it around and pushed.

The second guard fired into the first. Kae pushed the two together, driving with his legs while stretching the barrel of his pistol around the body in front of him to hit the body behind it. Another flash and deafening report.

He let go, and both Zirrics crumpled to the cave floor. *Getting desperate*, Kae thought. The sound of insectoid skittering told him the queen had picked up her pace. He sped up too, as much as he dared.

"I'm coming for you!" he shouted to keep her moving and let him hear the way ahead. Straightaways and turns, the scene never changed: near-complete black with faint outlines. He thought he could hear something far ahead, beyond the queen.

He knew that riff. *Ghost Love Score* echoed down the tunnel. Kimber listened to Nightwish.

Kim, the queen is close and heading your way.

Kaeden! Light her up so I can see where you both are.

I'm not in my suit.

Dumbass. Leave it to his sister to state the obvious.

The queen stopped. Kae thought he could see her up ahead, outlined by random wisps of light in the distance. Kae took careful aim and fired, bouncing a round off the tunnel wall opposite her. She started to run again, heading toward the growing light at the far end. When Kae could see, he accelerated to a sprint. The queen ran faster too, faster than any human could.

She burst away from Kaeden and into a new tunnel, finding herself in the middle of a formation of mechs. Like goalies, they squatted and put out their arms to block the ball from getting past.

The queen looked in all directions but was blocked in. Nightwish continued to jam from somewhere to Kaeden's left.

"Give it up."

"Why?" the queen asked.

"We tried doing this the normal way, but you butt-fucked us, so now you're going to do this our way."

"What do you mean? I do not know what 'butt-fuck' means."

Kae closed his eyes for a moment. "It means you lied to us, and then you sent your army to attack us. That was unforgivable."

"Is that it? You stood between our enemy and us. I believe the Naries attacked you as well, did they not? That was a demonstration of our resolve to determine the fate of our people ourselves. It had nothing to do with you."

"When this planet became a Federation member, you surrendered that right of self-determination to a higher ideal. You don't get to kill each other. That's not what modern civilizations do, so we're here to stop you from fighting."

"You killed a great number of our people."

"That was a demonstration of *our* resolve. It's time to come with us." The mechs moved closer, leaving her only one viable way out. Kae saw it coming, but that didn't lessen the impact. A close combat move would have entailed grabbing the opponent to guide them into the nearby wall by redirecting their momentum, but there was nothing to get his hands around. She shoved him aside but he powered forward, wrapping his arms around her. She hammered into his back and started to carve with a hard-shelled forearm.

Kaeden screamed in agony, jumped back, and fired, blasting the queen back into the tunnel wall. She dropped to her feet, looked at the hole in her chest, and toppled. Kae rolled on the ground, his back on fire, every nerve in his body shrieking.

He got to his knees. The pain was nearly overwhelming him, and something pressed against his back. Kae couldn't lift his head to see who it was, but he knew what had to be done. "Save the queen."

"I know," Kimber agreed. "Lean back against the wall." She helped him until he could put enough pressure on it himself.

Kim looked at the queen. "Still alive, I think." She dragged her into the tunnel to where a mech-suited warrior could lift her. "Run and call in an airlift to be waiting when you exit the cave."

The warriors in the back half of the formation turned in place and pounded up the tunnel. Kim appeared in front of Kaeden. He blinked, wondering if he had passed out.

He leaned aside and heaved his last meal onto the cave floor. "This one sucks. Fucking chainsaw arms. How bad is it?"

"I'll concede that it's not good. I'm going to have to carry you face-down, and we better go, so our ride doesn't leave without us."

Kae didn't even try to stand. Kim helped him to his feet,

wrapped his arm over her shoulder, and half-carried him to the first mech in line. "Take care of him."

"Cradled like a baby," the private stated.

"I need you healthy to cook and deliver my steak."

"Who cooks who a steak?" Kae mumbled. He didn't remember anything after that.

The warrior resisted looking at the canyon the queen had carved into Kaeden's back. He focused his efforts on running up the hill to catch the other half of Team Turok.

Kim ordered the A-Team to carry Kae's suit out and recover to the *War Axe*. She didn't bother to tell them to call for a ride. She thought it was fitting for them to run back for letting Kaeden climb out of his suit and head into the tunnels alone.

CHAPTER FORTY

War Axe

The case opened, revealing the queen. Her eyes swirled as she looked around, trying to figure out what happened.

"You have been repaired," Cory stated coldly.

"It would not have been necessary if your people had not entered the hive."

The next Pod-doc over continued to work on the injured party within. Kaeden had needed major muscle and bone repair, which was taking longer.

"Come," Marcie ordered.

Slikira and K'Thrall had been detailed to secure the queen since they were both uniquely suited to deal with the insectoid. "Don't make us drag you out of there," Slicker hissed and whistled.

The queen wanted to fight, but the Ixtali warrior glared at her with murderous flashes in her arachnid eyes. K'Thrall took her by one arm and Slicker took the other to drag her out and unceremoniously stand her on the deck.

"You attacked us, and for that, you will not have our

trust. We will not turn our backs on you or your people. We will shoot first and ask questions later. Your people will suffer because of your bad leadership." Marcie walked to a table in an area by the ramp. The Naries' queen was already there, enjoying the fruit Paithoon had delivered. He had provided a separate cornucopia for each queen. His plan was that later, there would only be one with an even number of one fruit, and they'd have to share.

But that was later. For now, all they wanted was for the two queens to not kill each other. Slicker and K'Thrall were aware. The guard in combat armor standing behind the Naries queen knew that, too. Marcie had chains and manacles ready.

She'd lost over a hundred people the last time she'd tried to get them together.

The queens postured and hissed, clicking and buzzing at each other until their minders slammed them into their seats. They continued with surprising endurance, having to be restrained four times before Marcie slammed her palm on the table.

"Chain them, gag them, and make them sit there," she ordered her team. The guards rotated through as hour after hour, the two queens continued to fight their restraints.

In hour four, the Pod-doc finished cycling, and Cory helped Kaeden out. Marcie strolled to the back to talk to him. "She's not dead, is she?" Kae asked.

"No." Marcie laughed and gave her husband a hug. "She is very much alive, and unfortunately, a bit energized thanks to the nano treatments. Same with the other queen."

Terry strolled into the hangar bay with Joseph and

Petricia at his side. He casually sipped his coffee and breathed the fresh middle-of-the-night air. The vampires looked with mild interest at the negotiation table.

"How are you?" Marcie asked.

"Better than ever. Word to the wise: don't get into a bare-knuckle brawl with a Kor'narian queen."

"I'll remember that. We're in the stage of breaking them down. Not sure how long this will last, but they are going to be two miserable bitches by the time this is over."

TH joined them. "Good to see you upright," he told his son.

"I know you were worried, but I was in good hands."

"You couldn't have been in better hands than your sister's and your sister's. Ha!" Terry laughed at his own quip. "Regarding the matter at hand, Joseph has an idea."

Terry stood close to his son, wrapping an arm around him and pulling him close, revealing for an instant how much Kae's injury had worried him before he put his shields back up.

Joseph talked to Marcie. "I can plant a seed in both their minds that the Federation is the senior queen."

"Easy as that?"

"Probably not easy. I don't know how Kor'narians think. It may take a few tries."

"Then we better get started. Their hatred is visceral and I expect genetic, so your option might be the only way forward besides letting one kill the other to consolidate the hives. I'm already considering moving that to the number one option."

"I'll take a stab," Joseph said and walked to the table where the two queens were chained to the deck. "Good evening, morning, or whatever it is. My name is Joseph, and I'll be your host for today's program, which I'm calling, *Won't You Be My Neighbor?*"

The queens didn't acknowledge his existence as they continued pulling at their restraints in their desire to fight.

He didn't bother with further attempts at humor, settling in to dig into their minds, first the Narie's and then the Zirric's. The insectoid brain was wired differently, but it was susceptible from the standpoint that the main psyche resided in the id stage. The ego had been suppressed, and the superego ignored. The Kor'narians were capable of all three stages of thought to drive external action, but it appeared they simply chose not to.

Joseph suspected the insectoids produced a chemical similar to human adrenaline. Once that was spent, they would be able to think clearly at all levels and with the hypotheticals required to establish a strategic vision. Joseph planted an initial seed in both their minds based on the physical satisfaction of accomplishment, that being showing their hives fertile lands upon which to feed. A simple suggestion, but the next step would be realizing that accomplishing that goal would take not being at war.

He wiped his hands as if he'd just finished repairing a ship's engine as he strolled back to Terry and Marcie. "I want to tell you that your approach will work when given enough time, but it might not work over the long term." He explained what he had seen of their mental structure and the capacity for advanced thought they chose not to use. "Give me a few more probes into their minds, and I think I can take care of it."

"Good! I have a franchise to grow, and I can't do it from here." Terry smiled broadly.

"So, you *are* going to quit?" Kae asked, still not believing it. Terry had been a warrior for the entirety of Kae's existence.

"Retire. How long should we have to fight? I served in the Marines decades before you were born. It is time to move on, but understand that we're not gone. We'll always be here for you. Looks like Char convinced Ted to give us a personal Etheric comm device for instant communication anywhere, so we'll only be a call away. Char won't let her kids get too far from her mind."

"What about you?" Kae asked Joseph.

"Indeed, good sir, us, too."

"We're proud of all of you." Terry took a slow sip of his coffee. "Well, Joseph? Chop-chop. Git 'er done. We got shit to do."

"You, too?" Marcie asked, even though she had just heard the answer.

"We have sworn fealty to Terry Henry Walton. Where he goes, we go. Looks like we'll be back in the pub business. It has been a few centuries since I last worked as a publican. I'll have to remember how to keep customers in drink."

"Show them to the seat and then show them the menu. Everything else takes care of itself because AGB beer is fresh, brewed locally using orgasmic ingredients in the most sustainable way."

"Organic," Marcie corrected.

"What are those words? Do they mean anything?"

"That's what the publicist says we should use. I think I

might have to fire her. I prefer my version. Good food. Great beer. Right now."

"I like your version," Joseph said. "Very id. Speaking of which, I'm going in for round two. The gloves are laced, and my headgear is secure." He saluted and strolled back to the negotiating table, where the queens had visibly relaxed from their previous four hours of extreme agitation.

Joseph put his hands on the table and began without bothering to say anything. His process no longer required words.

Angkmoor, Trans-Pacific Task Force Flagship

"The last fire has been extinguished," a systems officer reported. "Hull breaches are sealed." He leaned back, relaxing his neck so he could stare at the ceiling.

"*Gonboon, Angkmoor.* Thank you for your assistance. Any engineering personnel you can provide will be critical to bring this ship back to life," the captain transmitted. He turned to his crew. "I'm heading out to tour the ship. I want her to fly again. She deserves it. You deserve it."

"We'll do what we have to to take her home under her own power," the systems officer declared.

Ukrit nodded once and headed for the ship's interior. He'd had no word about the engineer. With the fires out, he would be able to access the entirety of the ship, and he would. The engineer had saved the ship. He deserved to be found.

A few Belzonians roamed the corridors. "Keep your head up. We will pull through." He tried to be encouraging but found it difficult. He had lost at least thirty of his crew, with more than a dozen still missing. He carried the burden of command. All losses were his responsibility and his to bear. Fresh air circulated throughout the ship. Most of the lights worked, but too many relays had blown. There were few crew to replace them, and there was no engineer or engineering team to prioritize the repairs.

Gonboon had offered help. When and how many engineers would appear, they had not said. Maybe they didn't want to throw good after bad. Maybe the ship was little more than scrap. That worried him the most. He would never see another command, but he didn't care about that. He cared that the ship had become a tomb for the good people who had kept her flying.

He knew he should eat, but he didn't feel hungry. He checked a space that had been on fire. Automatic systems had removed the oxygen, choking the flames to death. They'd lost stores. Nothing critical, but the heat had warped a bulkhead, which affected the structural integrity of the section. It wouldn't be able to seal if there was a hull breach in this area.

Ukrit left the area and continued on his way to where the engineer had said he was headed, the place where the main power had been cut. Ukrit stopped at a spider-webbed observation window that looked upon the area. The shattered conduit had a replacement section jammed into place. However the engineer had managed such a feat, it had to have been superhuman.

The captain undogged the access hatch and went inside for a closer look, hoping to find the repair would last until they reached Belzimus. Inside, under the window, he found the engineer.

"Somchai!" He dropped to the deck to pull his friend's head to him, cradling it. He was still warm. Ukrit checked for a pulse—still alive. A strong heartbeat pounded beneath his fingers. "Somchai?"

"Ahh. Not dead. I had hoped," he mumbled. "I was far too uncomfortable to spend the afterlife in such a state. My legs are still tingling. Are they there?"

Ukrit examined them quickly, but there was nothing he could find. "Very much so. I don't see any problems."

He helped the engineer stand on wobbly legs.

"We are alive?"

"Very much so," the captain repeated. "And getting more alive with each passing moment. Engineers from *Gonboon* are coming aboard to assist us."

"Not those guys!" Somchai exclaimed with renewed energy. "I'll never live it down. Help me get to Engineering. I need to see the status boards."

"I thought we would go to sickbay and get you looked at."

"Too far. A huge waste of time. Work to do." Somchai tested his legs. "Getting better with each passing second," he claimed, but he held onto Ukrit's arm tightly.

"I'll take you to Engineering, but if there is an available doc, I'll send him to you."

"I find your terms acceptable, Ukrit."

"Stubborn engineers." The captain shook his head. "If it weren't for you, we'd all be dead. We'll drink to your stubbornness back on Belzimus after we've brought *Angkmoor* home."

"I will drink to that, Ukrit, but only if you help me get

back to work. You seem to be stalling. Are we dead and living in hell?"

"Your idea of hell is not being rushed back to work? I think you have your priorities backward."

"Such nonsense. I'm amazed you ever became captain. Then again, that's probably why engineers don't get to sit in the big chair. Alas, one man's hell is another's heaven. Here's to the captain who knows the difference." He executed a half-assed salute and failed at taking an unaided step. Ukrit supported most of his weight while the two left the power exchange compartment and headed for Engineering.

"I'm glad you're alive, Somchai. Now get back to work, and I won't take no for an answer."

"That's how a good captain talks," the engineer replied.

Kor'nar, Trans-Pacific Task Force Expeditionary Camp, Command Tent

Christina was casually watching the drone footage of the Bad Company's mechs cleaning up the area of the wild-fire, making sure it didn't spontaneously combust and return to raging. The werewolf pack sat around the table, eating their mess-tent takeaway burgers.

"We should be eating on the *War Axe*. The food there is, well, it's not this," Sue complained.

Christina gave her the side-eye. "No shit, but this is our way of showing sympathy for Marcie and Kaeden. We'll be back on board while they're stuck eating this swill."

"We need to get home. The shipyard needs to be cradled in the bosom of our tender embrace," Merrit said, hugging the air.

"I've seen your digs on *Sheri's Pride*. Could you make it look any more like a brothel?" Timmons chided. "I know what bosoms you're thinking about."

"Fucking no-class shitweasel!" Shonna stated. She

straightened up before continuing, "Sue, Felicity, Char, and I are starting a number of fashion stores. Between the four of us, we have the sourcing, transport, importation, presentation, and store space locked in. The only other thing we need is a massive vault to hold all our money!"

"Truth, sister," Sue agreed.

Timmons shook his head, but he had no intention of going against the will of the she-wolves. "That leaves Iracitus and me to continue exploration and cataloging of the asteroid field."

"Can't a basic program bot do the same thing?" Christina poked.

"Nice try. My goat has been got too many times for any goat to be left. No, I like it. I get to blow stuff up, and it's interesting enough. Gives me lots of time to listen to books. I feel old, but there it is." Timmons looked as young as the others, perpetually in his late twenties.

"Maybe you need a nano tune-up. When's the last time you were in a Pod-doc?"

"A long time ago. Maybe I'll grow old gracefully. I like the feeling of not being constantly on the edge. I know what you're thinking. What did you do with our Timmons? Don't tell me you fuckers don't feel it too?"

Merrit nodded slowly while the females shook their heads vigorously. Christina started to laugh.

Colonel Braithwen and Sergeant Major Monsoon showed up looking for Marcie, standing in the tent's doorway so they wouldn't interfere with close friends talking about their futures.

"You're abandoning me." Christina eyed the others closely. They stared back while taking bites of their cooling grease globules on buns ubiquitously known as mess-tent sliders. She ended with a smile. "I'm good with you guys moving on, but there are some unique missions up ahead where I know I'll need your unique skills. I heard the blood trade has started back up now that there are enough modified humans roaming free. I know Joseph and Petricia will be in since they still have scores to settle. There shouldn't be any Forsaken out here, but that doesn't mean there aren't. Otherwise, the Bad Company will continue to put out brush fires. With our expanded capabilities, thanks to the Harborian fleet, we'll need to grow our ranks rather significantly. This will be the greatest effort, but it's not what you know, it's who you know."

"Daddy! Uncle Lance!" Timmons mimicked, earning himself a fastball to the head. He tried to clean the burger bits out of his hair. Sue had to help. "Still worth it." He stuck out his tongue.

"No, thanks, I use toilet paper," Christina replied.

"Are you getting this down?" Jake whispered.

"I can hardly process what I'm hearing. I'm mesmerized. This is too much, way over the top. Our viewers will love it!"

The two clasped hands and half-hugged.

"Take care of our friends," Christina stated, staring at the two Belzonians.

"Saying 'of course' doesn't cover it. We will. They have earned our respect and the commitment of our lives to them. You don't have to worry about anything that is within our power to do for Marcie and Kae." The two held their hands over their hearts. "You have our word. By the way, do you guys orgy?"

"What in the fuck did you just ask?" Christina blurted.

"Humans! Let me explain. We are a race of hermaphrodites, and we share our DNA widely. Sex is a natural part of our existence. We have a lot of it. When we get back to the ship, it's going to be a total LAGNAF. I was being kind by offering, not insulting." Jake threw his hands up in his continued disbelief that humans knew nothing about Belzonians.

"LAGNAF?" Timmons ventured.

"Let's all get naked and fuck."

Sue choked and put her burger down. "I'm done eating."

"Kae's head didn't explode when he found out about your proclivities?" Timmons wondered.

"Like a volcano," Monsoon said. He and Jake nodded at each other.

The drone screen showed the mechs heading back to the camp. Christina pointed at the video. "Time to go back. Maybe Marcie has made progress with the queens, but probably not. They seem to be raging assholes."

Jake and Crantis stepped aside, shaking hands with each of the warriors as they passed.

Christina was last, refusing the handshake and going straight for hugs. "It's fairly universal that you might not want to ask humans if they orgy."

"Their loss," Jake replied with a shrug.

"No doubt. Gentlemen, until we meet again." She strolled away, taking in the camp and exuding confidence and strength with each step.

"I see why they follow her," Monsoon confided. "Or any of them."

Jake looked into the empty command tent. Reports

CRAIG MARTELLE & MICHAEL ANDERLE

awaited his return, paperwork to send to Belzimus and after actions for the Federation. Different formats with some duplicate information, but not enough to make it easy to fill out either.

"I'll find our radio operator so you can start finalizing information and push the patrols out to increase our stand-off distance. I don't trust that the hives won't take action while their queens are absent."

"Good call. Paperwork is an officer's domain. It is the battlefield on which we die." He bowed his head and entered.

The sergeant major saw the tanks rallying for a wash-down. He headed that way to find Punyaa standing atop his metal monster, getting sprayed from all directions. Monsoon discovered Wiriya leading the charge. He strolled into the middle of it and the streams stopped.

"Major." Monsoon dipped his chin in recognition before turning to Wiriya.

"Just a change of command, sergeant major," Wiriya explained.

Monsoon leaned close. "Are you any good with paper-work?" he whispered.

"Good enough, I guess."

"I'll take it. The colonel needs your help in the command tent."

Wiriya waved at the others and hurried away.

Punyaa pointed at his tank. "Can you believe this? Who borrows a man's pristine tank and returns it looking like this?"

Monsoon glanced at the tank and the major.

Punyaa doubled down. "It's like returning a man's clippers and leaving hair on them!"

The sergeant major removed his helmet and ran a hand over his bald head while staring at the major.

"You get me, don't you?" Punyaa waggled his eyebrows.

"I get that you have a tank to wash, just like the rest of these slackers." The sergeant major walked off after tossing the burn Punyaa's way.

War Axe, Hangar Bay

The unshackled queens ate their fruit, sharing it equally.

"You are a magician," Marcie told Joseph. Petricia snickered. "What?"

"He wants to go home," she replied.

"All of us do," Marcie agreed. "And his efforts put us weeks and maybe even months closer. How long will this last?"

"If you keep reinforcing it by being the superior queen, representing the Federation, then forever." Joseph took Petricia's hand, and they made a beeline for the hatch leading to the interior of the ship.

"Listen up," Marcie told the queens. They stopped eating and gave her their undivided attention. "Naries will take the areas to the north. Zirrics hold the areas to the south. Ten percent of the harvest will be stored for the lean times to cover the seasonal change. The remainder, when the new growing season has started, will be shared in a massive feast on this field once a year. The Federation will welcome all and hear grievances at that time, should there be any. If you do your jobs as my junior queens, I don't foresee any issues arising that you cannot handle."

"Yes, my queen," they each replied.

I kind of like that, Marcie thought, glancing around to see if anyone was watching her revel.

"What do you say we get back to it, then? You can go back to your hives and explain the rules. Meet me back here tomorrow, and then the day after. We will have our first gathering of the harvest festival in seven days' time, right here on the open field."

The queens looked at the tents and the bustle of activity.

"With your agreement, we don't need to be here. I will watch you from the sky, which is where my hive lives, and I will visit you occasionally to make sure you are following my commands. Outside of that, make sure our people live well, share much, and provide a greater life for all on Kor'-nar. We will continue to mine the malageodes on the other side of the planet, so my representatives will stop by to check on you."

"Yes, my queen."

"I could get used to that. Please." Marcie gestured for the queens to leave. The warriors guided them out before one went north and the other south. Marcie stepped to the top of the *War Axe*'s ramp and looked out upon the camp. They had deployed. They had held under a massive assault. They had started a fire and extinguished it. They had conducted a raid deep into the enemy's lair. But most of all, they had persevered despite the loss and the hardship. "Fucking eh."

Marcie headed into the camp with her helmet off and

what hair she had left flowing free. She greeted the troops with a smile and stopped a soldier on the perimeter from making his foxhole even deeper. "You've done your job. Now it is time to get ready to go home," she told him.

He threw down his camp shovel and stood up straight. With a stretch, he took his helmet off.

"Get some sun on that gorgeous hair of yours. All of you. Pass the word. Colonel Walton said to stay in your positions but be ready to go. We will leave this camp exactly how we found it. Not one piece of trash left behind. Not one hole in the ground will remain." She pointed to the foxhole, from which his head barely peeked out.

"Oh, man!" The private picked up his shovel and crawled out to start tossing the dirt back into the hole.

"Spread the word. We won. We did what we came here to do, and now we're going home."

War Axe, the Bridge

With a final wave to Marcie and Kae, Terry and Char secured the hangar bay doors to button the ship up, then strode to the bridge without talking. When they arrived, Micky nodded and Clifton lifted off, flying the ship away from the camp. He pointed the bow toward the stars, and the ship raced upward. Ted had already installed an additional power supply, bringing the *War Axe's* total to four. They gave the behemoth enough power to handle it like a sport yacht, and Clifton wasn't shy.

Micky left his chair to join Terry and Char at their usual place, standing in the middle of the bridge deck with a control panel before them and the main viewscreen to the front.

"Smedley, get me the Belzonian flagship," Micky requested.

Gonboon replied. "Acting Flag *Gonboon.* Welcome to space, *War Axe.*"

"It's good to be back. Puts us one step closer to home. Do you or any other members of the Belzonian fleet require further assistance?"

"We are good. *Angkmoor* will be ready to fly when we leave. She won't be carrying any troops, but she will carry a bit of cargo to make space on the other transports. We will all go home when the task force completes their retrograde. Thank you for the assist. May the stars continue to guide your journey. *Gonboon* out."

"Smedley, can you get Timmons on the hook for me?"

"Iracitus here. Timmons and Sue are busy at the moment. How can I be of assistance?"

"What do you mean, they're busy? They were going out to confirm the site survey and forward that information to the Federation so their repair team could bring the right stuff."

"They are inside the facility, and they're *busy.*"

"Leave us in a high orbit," Micky ordered the pilot.

"Three orbits, and if you're not in the air to join us, they can walk home." Terry looked pleased with his order.

"I don't see how that is possible, Colonel Walton," Iracitus replied. "They will need to get to space to get home."

"Tell them to get their bare asses up here. They're messing with my retirement. Walton out."

"Chow hall!" he declared and walked away. Char

watched him go. "Come on, boy. Let's see if we can find you some sausage."

Ooh. Sausage. Dokken was instantly a captive audience. The two walked side by side, Terry with his hand on Dokken's hairy neck.

"Have you been traded in for a hairier model?" Micky joked.

"Members of our family move in and out, and then they move back in. It's the cycle of life in the Walton household. I better join them so Dokken doesn't make himself sick. Or my husband."

"I'm sure Jenelope will keep an eye on them."

"She is powerless to resist his charms," Char replied.

"Aren't we all?" Micky chuckled to himself and returned to the captain's chair. "Be ready to spin us a Gate to Keeg Station. Once *Iracitus* is on board, best possible speed home, Mister Clifton."

"Aye, aye, sir. Stars are aligned and power to the sails." Clifton tapped his screens. He was always ready to Gate to their home station. He had a girlfriend back there he couldn't wait to see.

"Come on, Iracitus, stop fucking around." Micky smiled at the screen. He thought it was time to get another cat. Dokken was going with Terry and Char, leaving the ship without a mascot. He spoke softly so the others wouldn't hear. "Smedley, search the cat rescue places and see if you can find us an ornery beast to bring on board. The *War Axe* needs more personality than we can give it."

"I shall find you three," Smedley confirmed in a hushed voice.

CHAPTER FORTY-TWO

THE FINAL CHAPTER

Kor'nar, Trans-Pacific Task Force Expeditionary Camp

The heavy equipment had been moved to the orbiting transports. Many of the support and logistics troops were already gone. The body bags had been stored in an unheated section of *Angkmoor*. One hundred fifty-seven dead, another three hundred injured. Add that to the forty-three lost on *Angkmoor*, and it had been an expensive operation.

The only forces remaining on Kor'nar were the front-line infantry, the first soldiers on the planet. Their claim to fame would be first on, last off. They were already shouting their motto.

Marcie, Kae, Jake, and Monsoon toured the long perimeter of where the camp had been. The troops had filled in the foxholes, policed the brass, and removed any other trash that had fallen out of someone's pockets. It was clear that an army had made camp there, though; they couldn't change that.

The wildfire had left the worst damage, but that too would grow back after the additional terraforming the Federation committed to.

The Federation's mining contingent was on the other side of the planet, working hard to fix the damage to the facility while the automated processes continued to churn out malageodes to fund the cure for cancer.

Marcie tried not to think about the machinations too hard. She was a sometime diplomat, a sometime therapist, a teacher, and a taskmaster. In simpler words, she was a soldier. She accomplished her mission so others could take care of theirs.

Kae stopped to look down at the camp from the western hill. The field was barren land but wouldn't always be. "Sometimes commanders don't get to choose the terrain for the coming battle, and other times, they do."

Jake waved it away. "We fight where the fight finds us. How many battles were fought here? How many lessons learned?"

"All of them," Marcie replied. "Until next time, when we learn more. I need to speak to General Reynolds and make sure we've validated the concept of overwhelming force without being overwhelming, but we need better weapons. Once we're confirmed as funded, I'll start pushing for modernization. We shouldn't be handicapped when far better stuff is available. It's like we're using antiques to fight."

Monsoon kept his hands clasped behind his back. "They

are not antiques to us."

"Perspective and perception. That's why we keep you around. And you should keep yourself in shape, so if we resort to cannibalism, you won't have all that annoying fat sizzling on the grill."

Jake and Monsoon looked at each other, making more mental notes.

"I don't know what you two are plotting, but keep us out of it," Kae said, putting Marcie between him and the Belzonians.

"He's hiding behind his wife because of the scary herms... More gold. We're going to be rich," Jake ejaculated.

"I said, we don't want to know!" Kae reiterated.

Marcie pointed toward the north. "The Naries are coming. I don't see any weapons. It's looking good so far."

She turned to the south. The Zirrics' hive was on its way, too. "We better be there to greet them after making sure the troops are geared up for war. They have not forgotten the earlier deceit."

"Nor I," Monsoon said. The nanocytes in his blood had healed his leg wound, and not even a scar remained. "We move on, nonetheless."

The four walked quickly down the hill. They had set up two long rows of tables that faced north-south. The hives would intermingle as they passed through. Marcie had high hopes that the queens had inculcated their new roles where they weren't looking to fight. She wondered if the workers harbored the same animosities within their ids that the queens did.

They would see. She had two thousand troops in full

combat gear and extra magazines standing by to deal with any outbreaks.

From the middle of the field, the Trans-Pacific's leadership received the queens from both hives. They approached without giving recognition to each other, deferring to the senior queen. "My queen." They dipped their bodies slightly.

"Welcome to the first Harvest Festival. The Federation is providing all that we have for *our* people to enjoy."

"You are too kind to us," the Zirric queen clicked.

"Far too kind," the Naries queen added.

"Good work lies ahead. I hear the Federation terraforming is growing well. There is enough for both hives to feast for a full year, and then there will be more, and we can expand the hives! But that's for later. Now is the time to celebrate and feast."

"Thank you," the queens deferred.

"Bring your people through," Marcie directed.

Both queens stood before their people, clicking and buzzing the instructions. The mobs moved in en masse, intermingling and jostling. Marcie, Kae, Jake, and Crantis stood back to back to back to hold their ground, but the Kor'narians bore no malicious intent. They were doing as they did.

"You can change what they do," Jake offered, "but you can't change how they do it. One massive cultural change at a time."

"I'm going to take the win for what it is." The Kor'narians swarmed over the tops of the tables in a massive food scrum.

"To the victor go the spoils," Kae suggested. The mobs

turned and flowed away toward the north and the south, taking their queens with them.

Many tables were overturned, but not a scrap remained —not a stem or a seed or a tray, as it turned out.

Paithoon came running toward Marcie. The sergeant major snorted before excusing himself and heading the other way, shouting orders to pack the tables into the waiting shuttles. Two thousand troops hopped to his commands, flying through the tasks as the last before dust off.

"Colonel Walton, I must protest!" Paithoon started.

"I would think you've been kidnapped if you didn't. Please. That was a huge success. Accept it while earning my personal accolades for pulling it off. The Trans-Pac pulled it off. Mission accomplished. Time to go."

"But look what they did!" Paithoon couldn't make his point since the troops had already removed half the tables. There was no greater motivator than a trip home.

"They enjoyed a meal with their fellows. Victory, Paithoon. It smells like victory!"

"I must protest. We need standards of conduct to raise them to our level of civilization."

"Nah. They are happy as they are, and for one day, they didn't have to send out the hordes to carry food back to the hive. Tomorrow, they'll be foraging anew, but for today, protocol was served and victory declared. Get yourself on a shuttle, Paithoon. We're out of here." Marcie raised her hand and twirled a finger. Jake and Monsoon left for *Praithwait* and *Thilamoot*. Marcie and Kae were on their way to *Angkmoor* to ride it home. They would be the only troops aboard. The others would be on *Gonboon*.

Marcie refused to transfer the flag. She intended to bring her flagship home, even though she'd had nothing to do with the fight that had kept *Angkmoor* alive. However, she could show respect to those who had fought that battle.

Where are you, Webster? It's time to go! she called.

On my way, Colonel. Clearing the riffraff out of the way. Shuttles drifted sideways as one came from above, dropping straight down on their position. Kae guided it in.

The other shuttles filled and lifted off, pointing their noses skyward and accelerating toward space. When the only shuttle remaining was lucky Number One, she walked around it to make sure nothing remained. She reached down and picked up a small rock, spitting on it and rubbing a thumb across its surface to appreciate the look of the planet captured in a single rock. She put it in her pocket and climbed the ramp.

"Take us on a fly-by of the facility on the other side of the planet, Webster," she shouted over the passenger din.

"I love fly-bys. Mach five coming up."

Marcie didn't correct him. They both knew the Mach 5 was a car.

Webster made quick work of the trip, soaring to near orbit before descending at a fantastic speed. He leveled out and slowed. "Park it, ma'am?"

"No need. Drop the ramp so I can wave at them from here."

Webster complied. The control room's glass window had not yet been replaced, but the workers inside took a moment to appreciate the shuttle hovering in front of the building. They had their own ship parked on the landing field, so they could leave if they wanted. The Federation vowed not to leave it unattended ever again.

"Take us home, Webster."

He had the decency to close the ramp before firewalling the throttle and racing for the transport.

They met it in orbit and landed as it started to accelerate toward the system Gate. Marcie and Kae hurried to the bridge, passing areas heavily damaged during the pirate attack. Some bulkheads were blocked open and others had been cut through for access, but they were able to reach the bridge without making a detour.

"Good to see you, Captain," Marcie said, reaching for the captain's hand to shake it heartily.

"It is good to have the mission accomplished," he said. "But I fear it was the last for *Angkmoor*."

Marcie turned away from the main screen to stand in front of the ship's captain. "I think this is only the beginning for *Angkmoor*. You see, I have an aunt and uncle who run the biggest military shipyard in the Federation. My stepdad can provide us with a Gate drive, gravitic shields, and ice cream. Give it some time, and *Angkmoor* will be the envy of the Belzonian Fleet, as well as the flagship of the Federation's Trans-Pacific Task Force for some time to come."

She leaned into Kaeden, and together they watched the rest of the fleet form up on *Angkmoor*, the lead ship taking them home.

Keeg Station, The Bad Company's Direct Action Branch Headquarters

Terry guided the two crates of their stuff onto the dropship.

How did you end up with so much shit on board? Dokken asked.

"We lived here. Come on, it's not that much," he pleaded, pointing to the crates that nearly filled the Pod.

Char watched with amusement. She was sorry to go, but not sorry. It was time to move on. She had a shoe and handbag empire to build, and she was determined to make it the greatest the galaxy had ever seen. She knew she'd have the support of the Queen. She needed a ship to check out sourcing planets, those who could make shoes to specifications as well as create new styles. "An infinite number" was the answer to the question of how many different shoes could exist.

"That's it. Time to go." They had already said their goodbyes to the crew. *Iracitus* had swept Timmons to the asteroid field, and Merrit had caught a shuttle to the shipyard. Sue and Shonna had left on *Ramses' Chariot* with Felicity and Ted.

"Wait for us!" Joseph called from across the hangar bay, trotting over with Petricia at his side. "We had to pack."

"Are you sending your stuff over later?" Terry wondered.

Joseph held out his backpack. "This is our stuff."

I told you, Dokken said.

Christina and Kai appeared in the door to the armory. Kimber and Auburn stood by them.

Kai waved and beamed a smile from his ridiculously young face. "Bye, Grandma. Bye, Grandpa!"

Christina shook her head.

"Don't worry. I'll make an honest woman of her, maybe in a hundred years or so!" He pinched her butt and ducked.

Terry shook a finger at Kimber. "You raised him wrong!"

"Maybe. The jury is still out. I'll see you later at AGB. I'm not missing out on my free meal. Three squares and a cot. It's not a rose garden, but it's what we got," she said in her best Terry Henry voice. "See you all there. Big party coming."

Cory walked past her parents to give Dokken a big hug.

She knows the important one.

"My dog can be kind of mouthy," Terry said, needling Dokken right back.

Clearly, I need to spend more time training him. Alas, such is a dog's life.

THE END

If you like this book, please leave a review. Reviews buoy my spirits and stoke the fires of creativity.

Don't stop now! Keep turning the pages as Craig & Michael talk about their thoughts on this book and the overall project called the Age of Expansion (and if you haven't read the eleven-book prequel, the *Terry Henry Walton Chronicles*, now is a great time to take a look).

Terry, Char, and the rest of the Bad Company's Direct Action Branch will continue to make cameo appearances in *The Kurtherian Endgame* as well as in our favorite space lawyer series, *Judge, Jury, & Executioner*.

THE LINE UNBROKEN

Missing TH? Catch up with his granddaughter in *The Line Unbroken*. Earth has been plunged into Madness, but Sarah Jennifer will stand for everyone. Living by the Walton code, honor, courage, and commitment remains her greatest weapon in the fight to unify the UnknownWorld and end the Madness.

Available now at Amazon and through Kindle Unlimited.

AUTHOR NOTES - CRAIG MARTELLE
WRITTEN MAY 31ST, 2020

I can't thank you enough for reading this series to the very end! Terry Henry Walton and the fine characters who surround him have become a part of my world. I hope they've become a part of yours as well. Honor. Courage. Commitment. Something we can all live for and be proud of.

Thanks to Michael Anderle for asking me to write this character back in September of 2016. Terry has taken on a complete life from his time as a secondary thread in TKG12 and TKG13, but he was a compelling character with unlimited potential. A million and a half words later, I agree. He did have unlimited potential. Thanks, Michael, for letting me take this journey with you.

Why, oh, why are you ending this series? It is my favorite!

That it is. It is one of my favorites, too, but you've followed other series that went well past their prime, where the authors seemed to be writing them just to earn money and not to keep their fans entertained. If you're going to give your money to me for these stories, I need to tell each new one better than the last. Over the years, we've lost a large number of readers, and a new Terry and Char volume hardly makes enough money to keep the lights on. I figure that although there are many who still love the characters, I have grown stale as the author of this series. I tried to recapture the magic with this final volume while giving you a lot extra —about an entire book's worth of extra words.

That's how I want Terry and Char to go out...with a fantastic story, reigniting what made them great in the past as part of their swan song. I finished this series out of respect for you, the readers, because you deserve better than what I will be able to give you if I tried to continue the series. Terry and Char are not done. You'll see cameo appearances in a lot of books to come. Rivka is going strong, and I'll continue writing that series for quite a while. I have a great number of main plots to explore.

Because the law is cool when you get to define it and interpret it and then kick the asses of those who are wantonly violating it. That is what Rivka brings.

I hope you enjoyed the last *Bad Company* and that you are willing to leave a review for me to tell me that my efforts in writing this series over the past three and a half years have been worthwhile and entertained you in a good way.

In the fourteen months that have passed since the last *Bad Company* (*Discovery—Bad Company* 6), there have been a large number of changes in my life. I finally convinced the doc that there was something wrong with my heart, and the cardiologist took a better look and found it was a lot screwed up. I finally had heart surgery in January, but that was three days after our dog passed away. The heart surgery went okay, but I still have problems that we're trying to get under control with medication instead of digging in again. And this month, a friend of mine right here in Fairbanks was killed in a plane crash. I went back and rewrote the landing scene to make Webster the pilot in Jim's honor. I flew with Jim, and he was a great pilot. He was one of the most Alaskan men of any I have known. I already miss him.

For this story, I leaned heavily on my insider team of Jim Caplan, Micky Cocker, Kelly O'Donnell, and John Ashmore to make sure I addressed open storylines from previous volumes as well as maintained a smooth flow in this story that was rather complex. You've read it. You already figured it out. It's two stories in one, with multiple tendrils for each of the twin plot lines. That being said, this was fun to write. I returned to the old Terry and Char and added a new Marcie and Kae to show how they are expanding Terry's influence galaxy-wide and beyond in support of the Queen, Bethany Anne.

Overall, I think I accomplished what I wanted with this book and tied up the Terry and Char main stories while leaving plenty of room for you to use your imagination to fill in the blanks. You cannot be wrong because the continuing story can be written in your mind.

Terry, Char, and all they've influenced will never stop having adventures. Just which ones make it into print is the limitation. They will always be on our minds and forever a part of our souls.

Thank you for joining them for a short while on a long, long journey.

Peace, fellow humans.

———

Please join my Newsletter (craigmartelle.com—please, please, please sign up!), or you can follow me on Facebook since you'll get the same opportunity to pick up some of the books at fan pricing (only 99 cents) on that first day they are published.

If you liked this story, you might like some of my other books. You can join my mailing list by dropping by my website **craigmartelle.com** or if you have any comments, shoot me a note at craig@craigmartelle.com. I am always happy to hear from people who've read my work. I try to answer every email I receive.

If you liked the story, please write a short review for me on Amazon. I greatly appreciate any kind words; even one or two sentences go a long way. The number of reviews an ebook receives greatly improves how well it does on Amazon.

Amazon—www.amazon.com/author/craigmartelle

Facebook—www.facebook.com/authorcraigmartelle

BookBub - https://www.bookbub.com/authors/craig-martelle

My web page—www.craigmartelle.com

Thank you for joining me on this incredible journey.

Holy CRACKERS a million and a half words?

I don't think I'll ask a favor from Craig for a few years...Well, months. Weeks?

Maybe.

When I originally asked Craig to help out with the Terry Henry Walton Chronicles, which became the Bad Company (yes, I was listening to the awesome song on a train going UNDER the water at the time), I felt the fans would want to know more.

The only problem? Craig wanted to move on to another set of characters.

There is a saying my wife is fond of (I should know, I hear it enough), which is, "What's the worse they can say? No?" Emboldened by that thought, I reached out to Craig and asked him.

Would he be willing to do this? Write more in the Terry Henry Walton part of the Kurtherian Gambit Universe?

Surprisingly (and humbling) for me, he said yes!

Now, we are coming to the conclusion of Bad

Company, and I have already told Craig there was no way I was asking any favors whatsoever.

But I have one for you, the faithful readers.

Craig is writing a new set of stories, thrillers this time, set not in a far off universe, but right here in our timeline with no science involved. Normally, this isn't my gig, but I've read the first part of the story.

And I'm hooked.

Craig has managed to take a type of character, and without giving away too much, made me care about the character with minor surprises and "Oh, no!" right there in the first couple of thousand words.

So, my favor is, be on the lookout for his new series. Maybe sign up for his email (link is at the bottom of his author notes) and give it a try when it comes out.

I know I'll be on the front lines, buying the book as soon as it is available. Now, I might ask him to not put me in the book as an annoying mayor with disreputable vices (which isn't just for this series, but he has done that to me before, so I feel it is warranted to ask this of him.)

Either way, you haven't heard the last from the blue-collar author. He's just getting started.

Whether the characters are out in the deep dark of space drinking beer or here on Earth, taking care of people in an oh-so-violent way, Craig has a way of creating characters you want to hang around.

And he has done it again!

Diary Entry Saturday, June 6, 2020 to Friday, June 12, 2020

Las Vegas is slowly opening from the Covid shutdown.

It is interesting what is going on here in Las Vegas as the city slowly opens back up (I live on the Strip, so I don't know what is going on downtown.) I have been to the Venetian / Palazzo Hotels/Casinos on Thursday night and to Gold Coast on Friday night.

Specifically, I wanted the chicken wrap with spicy sauce in the Grand Lux and Chinese food at Ping Pang Pong in Gold Coast.

It was *delicious*.

While I did gamble on Thursday night, it just wasn't the same as I remember back before the Pandemic shut all doors. Back then, everything was either a party, the late-night party, or the people leaving the party and more flying in to start that next night's party.

Now, I'm waiting to see if the folks from California drive here or what happens if they don't. Only a few hotels are open at the moment, and even the restaurants inside the open hotels are occasionally not open for business (or if open, they don't have the same operating hours as before.)

It's really weird.

But I'm thankful it IS happening.

I was talking w/ fellow author Craig Martelle driving to breakfast Wednesday, and I happened to be driving next to the airport and saw one jet land while another was taking off. I then looked around the runways and noticed about five jets lining up, waiting to take off.

My jaw almost dropped.

I hadn't seen jets (more than one) on the tarmac in over two months. The airport had become almost like a ghost town. I remember one night last year counting seven jets lining up, their landing lights trailing off into the sky to land, and recently I couldn't see seven jets at all unless you count a few parked somewhere.

Covid-19 has hurt the planet in so many ways. From the obvious of lives taken early to families' savings wiped out, to pesticides and machinery not able to get to locations for the swarm of billions of locusts rampaging across east Africa and India.

If I had put all of this into a story, I think more than one reader might have told me I had placed too many challenges in the mix, and they thought 'C'mon! Epidemics, swarms, floods, *and* famine? Get real, Michael!'

Real life has hit us all.

And yet, humans fight back. We fight back for all of the right reasons. Sometimes it's amongst ourselves, sometimes against the insect population and sometimes against contagions.

I know that a couple of planes crossing a lonely tarmac in Las Vegas isn't the same kind of sign as a beautiful flower amongst a destroyed landscape, but for me personally, it was a small sign that we as a world are getting back on our feet.

May you find your own flower as we rise up out of a completely horrible first half of 2020.

Ad Aeternitatem,

Michael Anderle

 # - available in audio, too

Terry Henry Walton Chronicles (# co-written with Michael Anderle)—a post-apocalyptic paranormal adventure

Gateway to the Universe (# co-written with Justin Sloan & Michael Anderle)—this book transitions the characters from the Terry Henry Walton Chronicles to The Bad Company

The Bad Company (# co-written with Michael Anderle)—a military science fiction space opera

End Times Alaska (#)—a Permuted Press publication—a post-apocalyptic survivalist adventure

The Free Trader (#)—a Young Adult Science Fiction Action Adventure

Cygnus Space Opera (#)—A Young Adult Space Opera (set in the Free Trader universe)

Darklanding (#) (co-written with Scott Moon)—a Space Western

Judge, Jury, & Executioner—a space opera adventure legal thriller

Rick Banik (#)—Spy & Terrorism Action Adventure

Become a Successful Indie Author (#)—a non-fiction work

Metamorphosis Alpha—stories from the world's first science fiction RPG with James M. Ward

The Expanding Universe—science fiction anthologies

Shadow Vanguard—a Tom Dublin series

Enemy of my Enemy (co-written with Tim Marquitz) —A galactic alien military space opera

Superdreadnought (# co-written with Tim Marquitz) —an AI military space opera

Metal Legion (# co-written with Caleb Wachter)—a galactic military sci-fi with mechs

End Days (# co-written with E.E. Isherwood)—a post-apocalyptic adventure

Mystically Engineered (co-written with Valerie Emerson)—dragons in space (coming Jan 2019)

Monster Case Files (co-written with Kathryn Hearst)— a ghost-hunting adventure mystery series